It's Just photo

A Larry Stylinson Fanfiction

Prologue:

Harry and Louis were inseparable for most of their childhood, constantly playing and joking with each other. The boys spent most of their time at Louis' house, which caused Louis's mom Jay to unofficially adopt Harry.

Harry has always had a special way with kids; maybe it was the amount of time he spent with Jay, or perhaps it was the fact that Harry was the most loving and affectionate person on the planet. Whatever it was it made it so that every Friday night for the past four years, Harry has babysat Phoebe and Daisy, the youngest of the Tomlinson family, and let's face it, they were practically his kids! The girls loved how Harry would dress them up as princesses and take photographs of them and turn them into real princesses with a castle and all.

That was another thing Harry was great at. Photography. While he started taking photos to escape from the world; it just so happened he was so good people started paying him, so he decided to start a small business. Harry often found himself taking photos for kids' parties or dance photos for teenagers since he never went to those events himself.

Louis became the classic high school hotshot, athletic, intelligent, funny. He was the whole package. Of course, he had just about every single human with eyes swooning after him; I mean, who wouldn't with those bright blue eyes and sharp cheekbones. However, one lucky girl held or instead stole the key to his heart. Louis and Veronica, or Ronni as she preferred, had been dating since December of freshman year and are the definition of a power couple. Everywhere they go, people stop and stare, practically gawking at how much beauty ended up in one relationship.

The looks seem to block most people from how controlling Ronni was over people, especially when it came to Louis. Sometimes he feels like he is suffocating in his own life because it's not his anymore; it's Ronni's.

Chapter One:

5:00 pm on a Friday and Harry's standing at the same place he has been every Friday at 5:00 pm for the last three years. A doormat that says " Always. Forever. Family" lays in front of the Tomlinson's front door. After standing in this spot so often, Harry always found comfort in those three words because he knew that he always had a family on the other side of the door.

Before he heard the sound of the front door unlocking, Harry could hear the twins running around upstairs and laughing along with a voice yelling at them to go away. Louis, he thought. For being an older brother, he was never really good with kids but also, what did Harry know about having younger siblings? After all, he was the baby of his family.

Soon enough, the door opened, showing phoebe dressed up as a princess and Daisy as the prince. As soon as one foot entered the house, both girls jumped into Harry's arms. "HARRY" they yelled. Phoebe and Daisy genuinely loved him, so much so they said they would both marry him. They said it was only fitting to share him since they share everything else. "MY GIRLS," Harry replied, holding the twins as they hung from his neck in a sweet hug.

Little did Harry know Jay always watched these interactions, Harry with the twins, it was the relationship she dreamed of Louis and them having, but unfortunately have never had. It was okay though, as she loved Harry as her son anyway. He might as well be her best friend too, even if that sounds lame; Harry thought the same.

"It's always so good to see you, Harry!" Jay entered the front room where the three children stood and attempted to hug what was left of the boy since the girls still clung to him.

"Now you girls know the rules no yelling, no fighting, no sugar after 8:00, and please don't kill Harry."

The youngsters laughed, knowing that they always had pillow fights and sang at the top of their lungs doing karaoke every Friday night with Harry. Not to mention if Harry were in a good mood, he would bake some delicious treats for the girls, even if it was after 8:00 pm!

"Okay, and Harry, I'll be gone until tomorrow morning, but Louis is upstairs. He's going over to Ronni's soon, but he should be back by midnight; as soon as he's back, you're free to leave!"

Now her with full attention on Harry Jay eyed up the stairs and let out a soft sigh.

"And if he's not home by then, you have every right to call him until he's back home or call me, and I'll handle it."

The energy in the room went cold, with both of them knowing Louis was most likely not going to come home on time. That was alright with Harry because this house was just as much his own home as the tiny house he really does live at.

The three-wave goodbye to Jay as she walked into the car and headed off to her destination; as soon as the car was out of sight, the door slammed shut, and the girls shouted, "dance party" and ran straight into the massive living room. Harry chuckled and followed the girls. He knew he was in for a busy night.

Harry connected his phone to the Bluetooth speakers placed all over the first floor of the house, all

5,000 square feet of it. Oh yeah, did we forget to mention Louis lives in a mansion? Harry chose a clean throwback station to play, and soon enough, Phoebe, Daisy, and Harry were all dancing around the room, jumping from couch to couch, sliding across the floor, and singing at the top of their lungs.

The golden Hugh bursting through the windows began to show the time was getting later. Harry knew the girls hadn't eaten yet and hungry himself; he declared it dinner time.

"So, my ladies enchanted, what do you think about a decadent pizza for dinner?" He did a curtsy and bowed in front of the girls, who giggled in response.

"Why that does sound lovely, Prince Harry."

"Pizza should be our kingdom's official food!"

With a dimpled smile, Harry pulled out his phone and ordered a large cheese pizza. Somehow, he had miraculously gotten the girls to change out of their princess dresses and into some pajamas. Afterall, what princess wants to get pizza sauce all over their beautiful gown? Certainly, not Phoebe and Daisy!

It had been about thirty minutes, and the pizza tracker showed that the delivery guy was almost to the residence. Harry prepared drinks for the girls and started walking his way back through the maze of the downstairs hallways and to the door in an attempt not to keep the poor delivery guy waiting outside all alone.

Just as Harry made it back into the entryway, the doorbell rang, in an odd fashion though he could hear the faint cheers of three people, not just the twins. Upstairs, Louis had called from his room saying.

"I'll be there in a second!"

In an unusually happy tone, Louis came running down the stairs less than ten seconds later dressed in a pair of skinny jeans and a vans t-shirt with the sleeves rolled up on his biceps. Over the top, a distressed denim jacket laid over his tiny but muscular frame. The sight caught Harry off guard and ultimately took his breath away. It was just something that Louis could do, no matter how he dressed. He just always captivated Harry.

"I-I think it's just our Pizza Louis."

Harry opened the door to reveal a young teenager, probably around their age, dressed in black pants and a red shirt with a bite of pizza embroidered in the corner holding a large bag in one and a pizza box in the other.

"Pizza for Harry?"

"Yep, that's me. Here you go." Harry handed him the cash, enough to cover the pizza and the tip, and in return, the guy gave him the pizza box. Harry took it and closed the door. He could hear the growing sound of little footsteps running towards him. When He turned around, he just about ran into Louis, who was standing way too close for comfort.

"oh! Sorry!" Louis gave him a glare of annoyance and didn't say a word; Harry just moved around his ex-best friend, where the twins were waiting for him.

"Hey! I thought I told you to stay in the kitchen!"

Harry laughed as the girls fell into step right beside him, together they all made their way back into the gorgeous kitchen, which in reality could very well be fit for a queen. Harry got out the plates and gave each of the girls a slice of pizza and took two for himself. Don't tell Jay but Harry always allowed the girls to sit on the counter when they ate while he stood. It was just something they seemed to love, he figured it was just them getting to see the world from a different point of view.

Like always, dinner was filled with jokes between each mouthful of food consumed, each person took turns telling knock-knock jokes. By the time dinner was just about done, everybody's stomach was full and also sore from the amount of laughter.

Nobody heard the doorbell ring again, which is why when suddenly Louis appeared in the kitchen with Ronni hanging off of him, all three of them almost jumped at their presence.

"Don't mind me. I'm just grabbing some water for us, and then we are out of here."

You see, Ronni has never gotten along with the Tomlinson's, of course, besides Louis, but for everyone else she was always just a rude, problematic person they had to put up with to keep Louis happy. Whenever scenarios like this happened, Harry always tried to make sure that whatever Ronni said, that she never hurt the twins or talked bad about Louis or Jay around them. Even if that meant he had to wear all the bullets from her words.

Although Harry was technically a guest in this house, he still the host offering the duo some pizza since there were leftovers. At first, it seemed to be okay as Louis went over to the box and picked up a slice and put it on a napkin.

"Thanks!"

However, Ronni had different plans. Let's be honest, everybody knew that Ronni would never eat pizza a day in her life, but not even her boyfriend expected the reaction she gave him. All she had to do was give her Satan stare, that's what everyone secretly called it when her eyes narrowed, her jaw set, and the furrow of her perfectly maintained eyebrows curled up onto her otherwise flawless face. You could see the anger travel off her face and into the atmosphere; that's how strong it was. In an instant, he set the pizza down, and picked up the water bottles he had sat down and walked back to Ronni.

Phoebe, Daisy, and Harry gave each other knowing looks as they watched the couple walk out the kitchen and into the garage. The faint voice of Ronnie bounced off the walls, and it was safe to say that she was pissed.

"Why the hell would you even think about eating pizza? You know I won't kiss you if you have oily, greasy, and gross lips! Do you really want me to have to kiss Jeremy tonight? That's what I thought."

Harry's heart hurt hearing the way Ronni talked to Louis, and it broke a little more when he realized that was how 99% of their conversations went. Only a second later, the house rattled with the slam of the garage door. Harry flinched only to remember that two little girls had to witness the same thing he did, and worse, it had been their brother in the middle of it, not a long-lost friend.

Harry felt guilty for not distracting the girls and for the fact that the girls had to pull him out of his trance by asking for ice cream. Harry quickly agreed grabbing all of the toppings to make his famous nothing but the kitchen sink sundae. He scooped some ice cream into three bowls and due to guilt, he allowed the girls to put as many toppings as they desired.

The trio had transferred into the movie theatre and turned-on SpongeBob. If we are completely honest Harry wasn't watching the cartoon but replaying the argument he just heard. He hadn't noticed that the girls were talking or rather what they were talking about until he heard her name and snapped back into reality.

"What are you two talking about?"

"Oh, just that maybe Ronni needs to eat one of your magical sundaes!"

"Yeah! I mean, how could you not become sweet after eating it!"

"Wow, I am flattered! But I think maybe she'll come around soon, or maybe it was just a bad day today."

The two girls looked at each other, talk about the twin telepathy between them. It certainly was a real thing. They knew just as well as Harry, even with being thirteen years younger, that some people are just born bad people, and they won't ever change, and Ronni was just one of those people. But Harry always insisted on treating every single person with kindness because you never know just how one simple smile could change their day.

"Alright, princesses, it's time to brush those pearly whites of yours and climb into bed."

"But Harry," they both said in unison, trying to persuade him into letting them watch another episode of the cartoon.

"Nope, you already got guilt ice cream out of me tonight. Besides, it clearly states in our kingdom's law that all princesses must be asleep peacefully by 10:30 pm, which is only twenty minutes away!"

"Okay, you win this time."

Harry turned off the giant television, and the three of them headed up the large, spiral staircase that led to everyone's room.

Chapter Two:

Harry got both girls to sleep with very little fuss. He roamed the empty halls that held magnificent echoes with each footstep. If it were any other residence beside the Tomlinson's, Harry would feel incredibly guilty about snooping around, but he knew his limits on where exactly he could go.

The artwork that hung delicately on the cream-colored walls never seemed to bore Harry; he was one of those kids that could look at Victorian paintings all day and genuinely love it. His brain could bring the photographs to life in his head. Each brush stroke faded into a picture of reality, giving him the image that the original artist saw before their own eyes. Harry loved to recreate the paintings, in a photo form, of course. If Harry ever attempted to paint, you would never be able to tell what the end product was supposed to be. His talent was solely behind the camera lens.

Jay had already let Harry recreate the pictures that used to be the twin's room. It was his birthday present for the girls last year. He got them dresses almost identical to the ones the real princesses were wearing in their portraits; he also built a throne out of some scrap wood. One day Harry woke the girls early and brought over his best friend Cassie to do their hair and makeup. Then he drove them to the edge of the forest where he had already placed the throne and added decorations such as artificial flowers and butterflies to add to the already beautiful scenery.

He will never forget the way the girl's face's lit up when they finally pulled up to the location. They spent nearly the entire day taking photos before going home for their birthday dinner. It may have been the twin's special day but being a part of it made Harry feel special as well. A week later, he surprised the girls and Jay by hanging up the photos in place of the paintings while they were away shopping. Since then, Harry knew that he was meant to have a camera in his hand for the rest of his life.

He continued to walk the halls passing every single room, one after another. Every time without fail, he stopped at the same door, Louis's. He always left his door unlocked and opened when he wasn't home. Nobody ever really knew why but Harry was thankful for the decision. He never actually walked into the room, instead always just leaning against the door frame and looking inwards.

There wasn't much he could see as the room was so big that most things faded into a blur because they were so far away from the entrance, but the one thing that always caught Harry's attention was the trophies and plaques. Neatly organized on an entire wall of shelves was every trophy, medal, plaque, and certificate Louis had ever received, all placed in chronological order. You could see the slow progression from the school awards and ribbons change into youth football trophies and finally into national level trophies and medals. That section still held some academic awards but nothing like what Louis used to accomplish in school, but can you blame him? The kid seemed to juggle just about everything under the sun and still be an okay human being. The keyword being OK.

Harry sighed at the memories that flooded his brain. The two had been exceptionally close throughout primary and secondary school, but it all changed when Louis was offered a spot on the varsity football team in year nine. At first, the two still hung out, but after nearly two months, Louis had changed into the popular boy every girl had a crush on, and Harry was well... he was Harry. Dorky, talented, caring, lovely Harry, and the two just didn't seem to fit into the same story. At least at school anyways.

They still talked like normal when Harry first came over to babysit; at that point, the twins were only three, and Jay had to drive Louis to the moon and back for practices and club meetings and tutoring sessions. She asked Harry if he would be interested in watching them since he's known them since they were born and already had knowledge of the house rules and layout. It was just easier than hiring an actual babysitter, plus Jay knew the boy's relationship had begun to falter, but she had always liked Harry. She didn't want to see him disappear from the family altogether. She couldn't handle another loss, especially one that could be avoided.

Harry remembered the day that everything officially changed. It was the same day he met Cassie and bless her soul because if she hadn't sat with Harry that day at lunch, he had no idea what would have happened to him. There were only three days left until school let out for winter break; he was sitting in the courtyard eating his lunch at an empty table. He never really minded eating alone as it gave him time to prepare for the rest of the day and just sit and observe people. He would never admit it, but Harry was a high-class eavesdropper and always kept up to date with the latest drama.

Call it a gut instinct or a side effect of his habit but he knew precisely who people needed to stay away from, and at the top of his list was popular Girl Veronica 'Ronnie' Cade. He had always thought that the movies were being dramatic when they portrayed the popular girl as being cruel, ruthless, and beautiful, but somehow Ronnie matched all three of those categories, and honestly, it scared him.

At first, he thought nothing of Ronnie standing unusually close to Louis; she seemed to be that way with every decently attractive boy in a ten-mile radius. He hadn't meant to be listening in on their conversation so intently, but something just pulled him in. Moments later, his jaw was wide open, hanging in the air and eyes wide, staring directly at Louis and Ronnie, who were now holding hands. The thing is, he had actually laughed just a second earlier when Ronnie had asked Louis to be her boyfriend. The thought of Louis ever hanging out with somebody like her seemed absolutely impossible. Harry didn't realize he was no longer alone until a voice as smooth as honey asked him if he was okay; it was Cassie. Since then, she had been his right-hand man- or rather women.

Harry shook his head away from the memories and came back into the present day, where all that was indeed left of him and Louis were the few photos Jay kept up of the two of them. The memories were bittersweet, always leaving Harry wondering what would have happened if Louis didn't make varsity that year or if Harry had followed in his footsteps. But that would always be a what if.

Nobody knew why Harry always lurked around Louis's room; well, in reality, nobody even knew that he lurked there, to begin with, but if they did, they would never find out. Nobody knew that Harry had fallen in love with Louis. Not a single soul. And truth be told, maybe that is why he reacted the way he did when his old friend did when he started dating Ronnie or why he seemed to be the only one hurt by their fallout, but he knew that it would only ever exist up in his head.

Harry made his way back to the staircase and back onto the main floor; once back down, he pulled out his phone to check the time. 11:45 pm. Had he been daydreaming for over an hour? He shook off the concern because he had nothing else to do; he knew Louis wouldn't be home until at least 1:00 am, so it really didn't matter. It's not liked a ghost would have caught him. The only damage was to Harry's emotions, but he always puts those through the wringer, so he didn't care much about that.

Harry made his way to the living room, it housed a TV, much smaller than the one in the theatre, but it was still huge and worked well enough for Harry to watch a movie and curl up on the couch. He grabbed the throw blanket that occupied the end of the sofa while turning on the television. He decided to watch Dirty Dancing since it had just started, so it should end around the same time he would get to go home.

The movie ended, and Harry was seriously trying not to fall asleep; it was just past one in the morning, and he was exhausted. However, he knew this was never a good sign. The whole reason Harry never put up a fight about Louis staying out until one when his curfew was midnight is that he knew that Louis wanted to feel like a rule breaker, and if breaking curfew by an hour fulfilled that and kept him out of further trouble; Harry could deal with it. But he usually was always walking through the front door by 1:10 with a feeling of guilt and accomplishment plastered across his face, but if it was ever any later, even by just ten minutes, Louis walked through the door absolutely hammered.

Harry groaned, realizing it was going to be a rough night, and unfortunately, a rough morning not only for Louis but the twins as well. Sometimes he wished that Louis would take some responsibility with them and act like the brother he knew he could be, the one he was when they were first born, but he was lost when Ronnie came into his life. While he was never genuinely mean to them, he sorts of just started ignoring them unless the entire family was together.

Harry knew that Louis wouldn't be up the next day until well after the twins woke up, and unfortunately, it wasn't one of those nights Harry could sleepover to watch them while Louis slept as he had an early morning photo appointment to do in now, less than eight hours. However, that didn't mean he could make them breakfast and set up some games to keep them busy until Jay got home, or Louis woke up.

Harry got two bowls, filled them with yogurt, and wrapped the top with plastic wrap to keep it fresh, then he cut some fruits and placed them in little baggies in the fridge. He got down the granola and honey and put them on the counter next to the refrigerator so the girls could have a parfait for breakfast. He wrote a little note and stuck it on the fridge, saying that he had prepared breakfast for them. In the last-minute decision, he got out a third bowl and put some yogurt in it for Louis just in case he woke up at a decent time.

Harry wrote out two other little notes, ran them upstairs to the girl's bedroom, and placed them on their nightstands to know the situation. Of course, not the part about Louis being drunk or hungover but that he would probably be vary sleepy and to try not to disturb him if they could. And of course, that he had set up breakfast and a few board games for them to play downstairs until their mom got home because he had to work.

By the time Harry was back downstairs and finished setting up the few games he picked, he heard the garage door open and the soft humming coming from a very, clearly wasted Louis. Harry quickly got up and helped the boy to a chair before he could fall onto the ground.

"Wow, Styles, I can walk on my own but thanks." A drunk smile was spread from ear to ear, and as much as Harry wanted to be mad at Louis, which he still was, he couldn't help but think that even in such an intoxicated state, he still looked perfect.

"How much did you drink?"

"Louis!"

"Yup, that's meeee."

"How much did you drink!" Harry's voice was firm, but he kept it quiet. Sound traveled far in this house, so he had to be careful."

"Hmm, uh-not, not THAT much." Louis looked genuinely confused, as if he couldn't remember anything from the party he just came from. Harry had to be careful here, he knew Louis was an emotional drunk, and he didn't need to be babysitting his seventeen, nearly eighteen-year-old ex-best friend right now.

"Did you by chance eat anything?"

The loud grumble that followed answered the question for Harry before it even registered in Louis's brain. Great, he thought, probably already enough alcohol for two people, and now it was on an empty stomach.

"Okay, you need to eat something to absorb all that liquor. I'm going to get you some of the leftover pizza."

"Oh my god, pizza, that sounds like heaven."

Louis was practically drooling already as Harry headed to the fridge. He didn't bother grabbing a plate but instead just laid the box in front of Louis and let him dig in. It didn't surprise Harry when he had eaten all of the halves of the leftover pizza within ten minutes. The man could eat, always could. It was probably a side effect of working out so much.

"Good. Are you still hungry?"

" Yeah, I could still eat a horse right now."

"Okay, I'll make you a sandwich, but you have to drink a glass of water while I make it."

"Deal."

Harry went and got two glasses of water, one for him and one for Louis. While pouring the water, he heard the loud scooting of a chair, and something fall and hit the ground.

"Louis wh-"

"Since when do we keep warm blankets in the kitchen."

Harry picked up the glasses and walked back over to the table.

"Since irresponsible big brothers get wasted at a high school party leaving a tired teenager watching a movie waiting for said big brother to get home after watching his two amazing little sisters and making sure that they have breakfast in the morning and things to do when they woke up."

Harry knew he was being a little harsh, but then again, he really wasn't, and he didn't say it in a rude tone, so he thought nothing of it. It's not like Louis would remember this conversation anyway. He went into the pantry and fridge and got out the ingredients to make a sandwich. Once he was done, he brought it back and handed it to Louis, who scarfed it down in four bites.

"Okay, let's get you to bed so I can go home, please."

Harry got up, put the dishes in the dishwasher, and grabbed a plastic grocery bag to hand to Louis if he needed it during the night. Louis had already stood up and wrapped himself in the blanket while walking to the stairs. Harry followed, and their footsteps fell in sync.

"Here, take this; you might need it."

"Thanks."

Louis grabbed the bag and retreated his hands back underneath the blanket. He took a deep breath.

"Hmm, this blanket smells soooo good."

Harry just laughed at the comment and continued walking shortly after arriving in the entryway with the staircase just behind them.

"Are you sure you can make it upstairs without making a ruckus?"

"Yes. I'll be fine, don't worry."

"Okay"

And with that, Harry made his way to the door, opening it and turning around and started closing it when he heard his name being called. He looked up to see

Louis standing at the top of the stairs leaning against the railing.

"Thanks for the food, Styles."

"You're welcome, Tomlinson; now go get some sleep."

Louis turned around and disappeared into the shadows. Harry shut the door and locked it, placing the key in the flowerpot next to the door. He went and climbed in his car, sitting there until he saw the light in Louis's room turn on, then back off again a few minutes later, signaling that he got in bed safely, then drove off. He looked at the time on his dash, nearly two am. He was surely going to regret this in five and a half hours, but for now, he just drove down the long, winding driveway and through the gate of the Tomlinson residence and back into his own reality.

Chapter three:

Harry's alarm was blaring, the sound of cowbells flooding his eardrums. He slapped the top of his clock, allowing silence to return into the room. Every bone in his body was begging to stay in bed and just fall back asleep. He hadn't gotten home until a little past two am, and it was now just before seven. The four and half hours of sleep did little to rest his body. Eventually, he groaned, pushed his covers off him, and headed into the bathroom to brush his teeth. When he saw the dark bags that circled underneath his eyes, he cursed himself for being out so late. He should have just let Louis deal with the monster hangover by himself; indeed, that would teach him a lesson. But no, he cared too much about him to willingly let him suffer like that.

Thankfully, Harry's shoot today was just photographing two little newborn babies, so he didn't have to dress professionally since he was more than likely to be puked on in the next four hours. He threw on some light-washed jeans, a white t-shirt, and a blue flannel. He completed the outfit with some black high-top converse. Walking into his kitchen and grabbed a banana for breakfast since there wasn't enough time for a proper meal. Sitting in his car, he thanked himself for already having all of his equipment packed away and ready to go from the previous night. He typed in the address he was given into his GPS and was on his way.

The house was about twenty-five minutes away from his own, leaving him just enough time to call Cassie for their annual Friday night recap. He dialed her number through his car, and the call rang through the speakers.

Cassie never answered until the last ring, so Harry just waited patiently until her voice appeared.

"Hazzy Harry! What's up."

"What did I tell you about calling me that! Nobody gets to call me Hazzie!"

"Fine, Hazza."

"Not that either!"

"Okay, whatever you say Haz."

"NO! none of that either, just Harry!"

Laughter filled the car; this was their unofficial way of greeting each other. Harry has always hated nicknames; the only thing he allowed was Styles because, after all, it was his name. It just happened to be his last one.

"So, what events filled your mysterious Friday night that somehow hasn't ended up all over your social media by now."

"Harry!"

"what! You know it's true!"

"Well, at least you have to ask me. I already know what you did."

"Well played, Cas, well played. But really, what did you do?"

"Not much. We went to the movies with that Niall guy. It was surprisingly good; he was super sweet."

"Aww, did you see the sparks flying!"

"Life isn't a romcom, Harry!"

"I'm just saying. But did you?"

"Maybe there was the start of some..."

"CASSIE AHH"

"Shut up!"

"Oh, come on though, the two of you are so cute together!"

"We can talk about this later; wanna meet up at Groundz?"

"Sure, but it will have to be later. I have a shoot until twelve this afternoon."

"Okay, see you soon, Styles."

"Bye Cas."

By the time the call ended, Harry was driving through a neighborhood and began looking for the house number. 4575. 4575. 4575, finally Harry spotted the house. It was average size, perfect for a little family. The exterior panels were painted a deep shade of navy blue, accented with a white framework and a bright yellow door. Harry grabbed his bag from the passenger seat and got out of his car, walking up to the door. He softly knocked on door so that if the babies were still sleeping, it wouldn't wake them up but made sure it was loud enough that the parents would hear. The shuffling of footsteps came closer to the door before opening.

"Hi, you must be Harry. Come on inside. I am terribly sorry for the mess. We're sort of new to this whole parenting thing."

"Don't worry, I know it's not an easy job."

Harry smiled adoringly at the young couple, maybe in their late twenties. Each one held an adorable baby boy. Twins. For some reason, it never registered that when the order was placed for two children, it might be twins. He was always good at handling babies, but with all the practice of looking after Phoebe and Daisy when they were little, he was a master when it came to dealing with twins.

"And these must be Nick and Noah" he put his bag down and smiled at the two little boys that now both sat in the arms of their father.

"You are correct there, young sir. Hi, I am Jack."

"Nice to meet all four of you all. So, before we get started, are there any pictures in particular that you would like today."

"We really just want some of them together but also some by themselves."

"Okay, great! I typically like to work around the children. This allows their true emotions to come across better in the photos; it also makes them more unique. Since they seem to have a lot of energy right now, we can start with the photos of them together, get them all happy while we can."

"Yeah, that sounds like a good idea. We can start in their playroom; it's just upstairs."

"Perfect."

Harry had already been snapping some shots while the parents were busy handling the kids. He always liked to get the parents in with these photos as well. It also allowed him to see how the features of the kids showed up on camera so he could get the best angels for later in the shoot.

Time always flew by when Harry took photos, especially when photographing young children due to him climbing all over the floor just like the kids and trying to keep them happy with silly faces and unique games. It really was a miracle that Harry could take photos while doing all of it, let alone good ones.

Before he even knew it, he was helping put Noah back in his crib for a nap as the photoshoot came to an end. He looked between the two cribs again and snapped a photo, his favorite kind of photo, especially for twins—a birds-eye view of them sleeping in separate cribs. In every picture he took like this, the twins always somehow reached for each other while in their sleep. He loved capturing that connection. The only reason he could even take this type of photo is thanks to his immaculate six-foot frame. Once walking back down the stairs with Jack and Oliva, the parents, they all let out a sigh of relief. It was always work for everyone when working with babies, and he could tell the parents were in need of a nap themselves.

"I'm quite surprised I have never met a teenager that is so good with babies, let alone twins, and you were amazing."

"Thank you. I've had my fair share of twins. I have babysat my friend's little twin sisters for the past four almost five years. Thankfully, they have prepared me well."

"Well, they really did. Thank you so much for everything. I know it was quite early for a Saturday."

"No worries, I know how hard it is to work around a baby's schedule. I'll just upload the photos to my laptop and organize them for you, and you should get an email with three album attachments within a few days where you can select the ones you like, and then I can send them off to editing for you.

"Thank you so much. "

"Of course, you two have a nice day now!"

"You are too."

Harry was back in his car now; he turned on his playlist and put the car in drive. He started driving to Groundz, the rustic coffee shop that he and Cassie had been going to every week since the middle of freshman year. Within ten minutes, he pulled into a parking spot. He grabbed his camera, laptop, and wallet then headed into the shop.

It didn't take long to spot Cassie. The strawberry blonde hair was glistening in the light of their unofficial, official table. She already had a cup of coffee and a book in front of her, classic Cassie. Harry walked up and sat his things down before pulling out his own chair and sitting down.

"Took you long enough."

"I did tell you I was working, right?"

Harry gave her a knowing look right as a waitress came and took his order. He ordered his usual winter meal, a bowl of potatoes and leek soup, a large coffee with extra cream and sugar, and a piece of spice cake. Harry then turned and pulled out his laptop and camera, connecting the two and allowing the photos to upload.

"So, who did you photograph today? Thor? Cinderella? Oh, I know Queen Elizabeth!"

"Oh, so close, two little twin boys named Nick and Noah, quite adorable actually."

"I still don't know why you love twins so much."

"Oh, come on, wouldn't it be amazing to have a living, breathing replica of you that is destined to your best friend."

"No, sounds annoying. that's why I have you."

"I just don't understand you sometimes."

Little did Cassie know that Harry was fully aware of why he loved twins so much, and it wasn't because of having a person that could always read you like a book. It was because it was a set of twins that allowed him to stay close. Close to a real family, close to the person he used to be friends with, close to the person unknowingly stole his heart.

Louis wasn't the only reason why he loved the Tomlinson's, but rather that they always had family nights, and sometimes they would even invite Harry, especially after he and the twins grew super close. You see, at home, it was just Harry and his mom. It wasn't bad. He had a lovely home and always had food on his plate. It was just that for him to have those things, his mom worked two jobs, rarely giving the two time together. That's also the reason why Harry decided to turn his gift into a job, so he wouldn't have to ask his mom for money to do things.

The one thing that he shared with the entire family was the absence of their fathers. Harry never met his dad; he left his mother before he was ever born. He's seen photos of him, but frankly, he had never wanted to meet him. Why waste his time on a man who didn't even bother to once send him a birthday card or at least just email him a simple 'Hi." The first time he felt true heartbreak was the day that Richard or Mr. Tomlinson passed away. It was three months before the twins were born. That day still haunts everybody.

It was a drunk driver when Mr. Tomlinson didn't come home from work. Jay called Harry, no one knew what had happened yet, but they knew it wasn't good. Harry was there when the cops knocked on the steel-carved front door. He still remembers the way his heart sank when the police took off their hats; only an instant later, he heard the tears escaping Jay's crystal blue eyes. He wanted to hug her, but at the time, Louis needed him so much more. After all, they were only thirteen. They were still friends, basically attached at the hip, and at that moment, he saw his best friend's life fall apart in an instant. Louis never knew why his mom called Harry or even how he got there that day because he couldn't drive. To this day, it's still a mystery to him. But Harry knew why Jay called him. Richard was like the dad he never had. It was just as devastating to him as it was for Jay and Louis.

"Hello! Earth to Harry!"

Harry's head snapped up from his computer, and his eyes met Cassie's swirl of hazel ones.

"Did you hear a word I just said?"

"what, sorry."

A shameful blush crossed Harry's cheeks as he realized it had been nearly ten minutes since he last spoke and had absolutely no clue what in the world Cassie was talking about. She rolled her eyes and got up from her chair and moved to the one next to Harry and pulled his computer in front of her.

"These kids better be the cutest dang things on earth for you to not pay attention to me."

"Hey, give it back. I haven't backed them up on the hard drive yet!"

"Calm down. I just want to see them."

Harry gave up and just let her look through the photos. In almost perfect timing, the waiter came and dropped off Harry's food. Instantly the starved boy reached for the ginormous cup of coffee and placed the cup to his lips allowing the warm and sweet beverage to cascade down his throat. He desperately needed the caffeine at the moment.

"Wow there, are you trying to drown yourself in that coffee?"

Quickly he put the cup down and wiped the corner of his mouth with his shirtsleeve.

"Sorry, I didn't get much sleep last night."

"I figured, aren't you supposed to leave at midnight, though?"

"Yeah, I am, but-"

"But, let me guess, Mr. Hotshot stayed out past curfew again, and perfect Harry here stayed up until who knows when waiting up for him because he didn't want to call him or his mom. Am I wrong?"

Harry just took back his computer and pulled out his spoon, dipping it in his soup all while giving her a side-eye. She wasn't wrong, but he didn't want to admit it out loud.

"Dude, didn't you guys used to be inseparable."

"yeah."

"So why don't you just talk to him about his whole partying fiasco when you're the one who has to watch his little sisters? It's not like it's coming out of nowhere. It's not like a stranger would be telling him what to do."

"It's, it's just different now. He wouldn't listen even if I screamed at him with a megaphone. I think the only person that can talk to him and actually make him change would be Ronnie, and you and I both know the world would end before she told Louis to actually take care of his family and not be at a party twenty-four-seven."

The pair let out comical laughs at even the thought of Ronnie being a nice human being. They were aware they weren't much better by laughing at her, but at the moment, they didn't care.

"They are pretty cute. I mean the twins, not Louis and Ronnie, although they are too."

"Gee thanks, does that mean I am forgiven?"

"Yeah, you're forgiven. But you do have to let me talk about Niall for the next hour while you go through those photos, and you have to listen as well."

"Fair enough. So, start from the beginning."

Harry went through all of the photos, placing them into three separate folders, one for each child's individual photos then one for the group ones. He could hear the excitement of Cassie's voice ringing in his ear as she rambled about how lovely Niall was and that he was a complete gentleman but also how he could eat like a horse. He smiled at the comment remembering just how much food Louis had eaten the night before. He thought he could imagine Niall with the memory, just you know, make him blonde, taller, and well not wasted.

The two sat in the coffee shop for nearly four hours before deciding to go home. Harry packed up his things before getting up to hold the door for Cassie; after all, his mother did raise a gentleman.

"Between you and Niall, I'll never have to open my own door again!"

"Oh, don't you get too comfortable there, your Highness one day, I might drop dead right in front of the door, and you'll have to open it all by yourself."

"Oh, shut up, Harold."

"What did I tell you about nicknames!"

"Might I add that you started it!"

"Fine, do you need a ride home?"

"Thanks, but no, Niall is working just down the street, so I'm just going to pop in and say hello."

"Okay, suit yourself. You are missing out on riding in an old beauty."

"I think I'll have plenty more opportunities."

Harry opened his car door and put his belongings in; he sat in the car, rolled down his window, and shouted to Cassie.

"Have fun with your boyfriend, Cassie!"

He laughed as she turned around bright red from embarrassment and flipped him off in the distance. He rolled the window back up and started the drive back to his house.

Chapter Four:

The week had been dragging on as if it was never going to end. It was only Wednesday yet Harry felt like he had lived through nearly a month's worth of studies and weeks' worth of editing on his photos. He desperately needed a night off, but he still needed to somehow complete his homework for the night. When he got home from school, he threw his bag onto the couch and went to the kitchen to grab a snack. The house was sitting in its usual silence, Harry thought he would enjoy the quietness after having to deal with the craziness of school, but instead, he realized he needed to be around people. It just had to be people he liked. Immediately he called Cassie to ask if she wanted to come over to study. She agreed but only with the terms that she could bring Niall with her so the two could officially meet.

Harry sat down on the couch and pulled out his laptop. He had about thirty minutes before Niall and Cassie were set to show up, so he decided to finish sorting through the photos of his last job. It didn't take that long to complete his task, and he soon sent out an email to the client with the photo files of the twin boys. Just as he sent the email, he heard the ring of his doorbell. He got up and went to open the door. Standing in front of him was his best friend, who was wrapped around a blonde boy. He had bright blue eyes, full cheeks, and a thin nose. Overall, he looked like a perfectly nice guy. Cassie dropped her arms from Niall and went into hug Harry while whispering in his ear.

"I swear if you scare him away, I will forever only call you by a nickname."

All Harry did was roll his eyes; what could he possibly do to scare away this kid. Besides, if he could scare him away, how could he deal with Cassie? Harry stepped back into the house and invited Niall inside.

"You must be the Niall that Cassie keeps chattering my ear off about."

"I hope it has been good."

Niall let out a roaring laugh along with Harry while Cassie sat on the edge of the couch, covering her face with her hands as she blushed, embarrassed by Harry outing her to Niall.

"It's nice to finally meet you; come on inside."

"Same to you, thanks."

The two boys went inside and joined Cassie on the couch, Niall sitting closer to her while Harry went to the other end of the sofa where his computer was still propped open. As he sat down, he pulled his bookbag up onto his lap and started pulling out his textbooks.

"So, what have you been doing for the last half hour? Just sitting and contemplating life?" The amount of sass that laced her voice made it clear she was trying to get back at Harry for ratting her out just moments before. Quickly, he responded with just as much sass.

"Well, if you must know, I was finishing up the photos for the twins I took photos of on Saturday and finally got them sent out."

"Oh really, finally, now you've got one less thing to worry about now."

"Geez, thanks, Cassie, for all of the support there."

"You know what I mean."

"So, you take photos?"

Harry was honestly shocked that Niall sounded genuinely intrigued and interested in what was going on in his life. Maybe this guy is better than he initially thought.

"Yeah, whenever I can, I use it as a way to make money. I usually do things like school dances and photos with little kids."

"That's so cool. You must be outstanding for people to pay you for it."

"I suppose. I mean, I hope they like the photos."

"Oh my god, quit underestimating yourself."

Cassie had basically shouted at Harry before turning to talk to Niall.

"He doesn't want to accept the fact he's basically a photography prodigy. His photos are always spectacular, and he somehow can always make the kids act like little angels. Last year he even had me turn two little girls into princesses so that he could recreate the photos in their bedroom. I had to spend the entire day in the forest watching a real-life fairytale. "

"Wow, that's impressive. Not to mention how in the world did you get Cassie to deal with anything princess-related."

" I still don't know how I did it, but she still uses it as leverage on me."

Shortly after, all three began to work on their homework. Everyone was working on the semester's end science project; it was easily the most demanding project the students would have this year. It was also the last large project all three would have during high school, seeing as it was their senior year, and the next semester of courses would be filled with electives such as music, drama, and art classes. This was the only fact that kept them going.

The time flew by, and soon all three students were starting to get hungry, so they decided to order some pizza. Initially, Harry was just going to order only one pizza for all of them; however, Cassie urged him to order two while on the phone. Harry had no idea how three people could eat two large pizzas, but he took Cassie's advice anyway and ordered two. Within only fifteen minutes, a knock on the door echoed through the house. Harry got up and went to the door to grab the pizza. Niall came up behind him and paid for half the pizza before each boy took a box and headed back into the kitchen.

Soon it was clear to Harry why Cassie had urged him to order an extra pizza. Before he could even get the plates out of the cupboard, Niall had already eaten a slice and a half of pizza. Cassie wasn't lying on Saturday when she said that Niall could eat.

"Hey, man, would you like a plate or just keep the box?" Harry couldn't help but laugh through his words.

"Ahh, I think I'll stick with the box; it's fewer dishes for you."

"Thanks for looking out for me, mate."

"Sure thing."

Shortly after finishing their food, Niall and Cassie decided it was getting late and started to pack up their belongings to head home. Harry walked them out to the door. He gave Cassie a hug and Niall the class bro handshake. He stayed put in the doorway as he watched the two walk to Niall's car. He smiled when Niall opened the car door for Cassie before walking to the driver's side to get in himself. He had to admit he quite liked the guy, and he seemed to be a total gentleman, just like how Cassie described him.

Harry went back inside and cleaned up the downstairs before heading upstairs to his bedroom. He stripped out of his regular clothes and slipped into a pair of sweats and a jacket and a pair of socks. He never loved the reality of winter thanks to its harsh winter; he really only loved it for the aesthetic. He cuddled up in his bed, pulling his comforter high and tight against his body, trying to keep warmth within his body. He turned over to reach his lamp and cut the lights out. Out of the corner of his eye sat a picture that he had never taken down. The first photo of him and Louis when they were still little boys, just four years old. He sighed, remembering that the boy in that photo was no longer the boy he saw walking the halls, nor was he the boy walking the halls, the real Louis he loved.

Before he could let his mind go too far down the dark path of reminiscing, he turned off his lamp and shut his eyes, finally allowing for his body to rest

Chapter Five:

The bell rang through the speakers, finally signaling the end of the week. Students rushed from their desks and out into the hallways and parking lot as they discussed their weekend plans. Harry rushed past everyone, desperate to make it to his car before being pulled into unwanted plans. When he got to his car, he was met with the sight of Cassie and Niall sitting on the back of the vehicle.

“I'm going to guess you want a ride?"

"See, I told you Haz you're a mind reader at heart."

Niall's eyebrows furrowed at his girlfriend's choice of words. Oh yeah, it's officially official now. After leaving Harry's house, Niall drove Cassie to an outlook under the stars and popped the question, which clearly had a good reaction.

"Call me that one more time, and we'll see who's laughing."

Harry unlocked his car and got in the driver's seat while the others climbed into the back seat together. He rolled his eyes and laughed.

"Thanks for leaving me all alone up here!"

"You are most certainly welcome."

Harry gave her the look, you know, the don't push my buttons look that also says, don't worry, I'm just messing with you. He finally got the chance to pull out his phone; when he looked at the screen, a flood of messages from Jay were projected.

"Hi Harry, I know you're in school right now, but I was hoping that you would be able to watch the girls for longer than usual today. I just got pulled into a meeting out in Birmingham."

"I don't know all the details yet but just as soon as possible, could you head over? You can bring a friend or two over if you would like."

"I'm sorry for doing this so last minute."

As Harry read the messages, he could sense the urgency in Jay's tone; she never liked having to leave her kids so unexpectedly. She also never wanted to drive long distances after losing Richard. In all honesty, though, he couldn't think of a better idea than spending almost an entire Friday night at the Tomlinson's.

"Is everything okay?"

"Do the two of you have plans tonight?"

The couple looked at each other, confusion glimmering in their eyes.

"Uhm, nothing set in stone."

"How does hanging out at the Tomlinson's sound."

It was more a statement than a question, and Harry knew that he left it as a question Cassie would be more likely to refuse. As for Niall, well, he hoped it didn't sound like pressure."

"Wait, like *the* Tomlinson's as in Louis the football team captain Tomlinson's house?"

Harry laughed at the excitement Niall clearly did not bother to try and hide. He took the sign as a yes and responded to Jay.

"Of course, don't worry about it. I'm heading over now. I have Cassie and her boyfriend with me. I've already explained the rules to them!"

"Thank you so much, Harry I seriously don't know what I would do without you! I also haven't gotten a response from Louis, so if you see him, which you better, can you inform him on the matter?"

"Sure, I'll make sure he knows."

With everything set, Harry started driving his typical Friday route, leaving the parking lot and heading onto the freeway. He decided he better answer Niall's question, so he doesn't think he's getting kidnapped.

"Yes, I mean that Louis Tomlinson."

He still couldn't hold back his laughter at the blonde boy's excitement. He's never seen anyone so thrilled when the Louis' name was mentioned. Still, maybe that's because he's used to being surrounded by people who, just like him, live a completely different life than the school's most popular jock—preferring to stay in the shadows rather than being the center of attention.

"How in the world are *you* able to get us into *his* house?"

"Believe it or not, Harry and him used to be best friends when they were little."

"You're kidding!"

"She's not."

"wow!"

Harry could see his blue eyes go wide in astonishment. No one would have ever guessed the friendship that was once so strong ever existed at all since all traces of it were now wiped clean from 99% of the world.

"Better yet, they used to be inseparable, can you believe it!"

"There is no way!"

"I know I didn't believe at first either until the first time he brought me over."

" So why are we going over?"

"Well-"

"Cass, let me explain my life, please."

"Okay, go ahead."

"Well, as you just figured out, we were best friends when we were little. I used to go over all the time. A few years ago, his mom had a set of twin girls, Phoebe and Daisy. I treated them like my own siblings because I don't have any of my own. As they grew older, they really started to trust me, and Jay, their mom, needed some help watching them on the weekends so she could help Louis with football and everything. Ever since I have been watching them at least once a week, and today it will be all three of us watching them. But don't worry, they are nearly five now and total sweethearts."

"Wow, you could write a book about that."

"Tell me about it."

Soon everybody settled down in the car, and Harry turned on the radio allowing the faint beats of guitars and drums to bounce around in the confined space. It wasn't a long drive to reach the front gate, only fifteen minutes, but it was still long enough for Harry to forget about his backseat passengers until he heard Niall's jaw drop as he parked his car.

"Okay, so I probably should have explained earlier, but there are a few rules. One, especially for you, Niall, since it's your first time here, never go anywhere alone. It's super easy to get lost in there. Two food is only allowed in the kitchen, backyard, and sometimes the theater room, but you can bring water just about anywhere. Three, if a door is closed, don't go inside; if it's open, it's typically fine.

Oh, except for Louis's room, he always leaves his door open when he's not home, but if he finds out somebody was in there, he'll lose his shit. And finally, since we, well I'm, watching little kids, please no profanity or arguing once we go inside. Got it?"

"Yeah."

"Got it!"

"Okay then, let the party begin."

All three got out of the car, the couple following behind Harry. If they didn't know any better, they would have assumed that it was his house with how comfortable he was, not to mention the fact that he had a key to the place.

Harry unlocked the door and held it open for his friends. He could hear the sounds of Phoebe and Daisy running around in the distance. It always surprised him how the two of them could be left alone and they would still somehow never notice it because they had each other. He called out to the girls as they stood in the doorway. Harry held a big smile on his lips when he heard the footsteps turn into the sounds of a stampede, traveling closer to him. Just like always, the twins jumped up into his arms, and he twirled them around before finally setting them down. He secretly loved this ritual with all his heart. He would gladly do it every time he greets the girls, even when they eventually grow up and think the whole thing is stupid.

The girls hadn't noticed the extra guest until they saw Harry looking at them. They noticed Cassie and went to hug her before stopping in front of Niall. Harry walked up closer to them.

"Girls, this Niall, Cassie's boyfriend."

The girls looked at each other excitedly before giggling and looking between the two guests standing before them.

"Niall, this is Phoebe, and this is Daisy, and yes, you will get them confused, but I'm sure by the end of the night, you'll be able to differentiate the two."

"Hi, girls!"

"Hi!" both girls responded in unison; everybody chuckled.

"So, I guess the whole twin telepathy thing is real then."

The girls looked confused at the words. They heard them all the time but never knew what they met; what kind of four-year-old does? Harry and Cassie, however, knew the answer all too well.

"Oh, it really is, and it can be astounding. Also, a little terrifying"

After the exchange, all five headed deeper inside the house, making their way into the kitchen, which opened up into the enormous living room. The whole space was easily three times bigger than the entirety of three friends' houses combined.

"Have you two eaten yet? Do you want a snack?

“Oh! Can you make your fairy wands?"

"Absolutely, you two really seem to love those things."

Harry chuckled before asking the other guests in the house if they wanted some as well. Everyone agreed, so Harry went into the refrigerator, grabbed the fruit basket, and brought them to the counter where a cutting board, knife, and cookie cutters were laid out. He rinsed the fruit and began making kabobs, or wands as the girls called them. Harry cut the fruit turning them into stars, tiaras, and castles. In the back of his mind, He knew that the only reason the girls actually liked these so much is that he always made them with princess shapes.

Harry noticed that all four of the others in the house traveled to the large dining table. He could hear Phoebe and Daisy telling Cassie and Niall all about princesses; he couldn't help but laugh at how much Cassie was probably hating it but put up with the torture just for him. Harry walked into the room with a large platter filled with his delicious creations and sat it down in the middle of the table, allowing everyone to grab a kabob.

"Which princess story are you enlightening these two with?"

"Just the one about the one who turns into a fairy."

"Oh, one of my personal favorites."

"I never would have guessed that there were so many different types of princesses."

Niall seemed to be genuinely intrigued by the girls' topic of conversation; Harry seemed to like Niall more and more every day with every growing day. He clearly made Cassie extremely happy, and he has been nothing but pleasant to Harry. He also kind of reminded him of a large child, but either way, he still liked the guy.

The girls began telling the stories of princesses again as all of them continued eating their snacks. It had been around twenty minutes before Harry heard the garage door opening; knowing Jay wasn't going to come home tonight, he figured it had to be Louis. The giant footsteps started to hush the voices sitting at the table. When his statue stood at the edge of the table, everybody froze.

"Are we having a party here?"

"NO, and don't get any ideas of one. Your mom just had an emergency meeting down in Birmingham and asked if I could watch the girls until she got back; she said I could bring Cassie and her boyfriend since it was so last minute."

"Yeah, she texted me the whole story."

"Did you respond?"

"Nah, I figured she already called you."

"Just text her saying you saw the text."

"Whatever, Ronnie will be over soon, and then we're heading out."

Without another word, Louis left the room and headed down the hallway and up the spiral staircase, ultimately landing in his room. Back downstairs, the mood was definitely tampered. Phoebe and Daisy seemed utterly unphased by being completely brushed off by their brother; sadly, they had become used to it. While Harry was also used to it, he still just couldn't understand why someone would choose to ignore their siblings, especially when they were as amazing as his. He had to give Cassie *the look* again in order for her to keep her cool and not follow Louis upstairs and rip his head off, on the other hand Nialls jaw was basically on the floor as he was left in utter shock at what he just witnessed.

Before anybody had even noticed the girls had left the table, they came back with monopoly. Harry was a little grateful for the distraction but upset; he left it up to the girls. He set up the game while Cassie and Niall took the dishes back into the kitchen, and the twins went upstairs to get a few CDs. When everybody returned to the table, the game was set up, and Harry was one of the CDs in the player, which was conveniently built into the table. Soon enough, Bruce Springsteen was filling the air along with the laughter of all of the friends.

Nobody noticed when Louis entered the kitchen until they heard the rustling of silverware. The twins looked up almost in surprise of seeing their brother but also held glimmers of hope.

"Louis, do you want to play monopoly with us!"

"I'll watch for a little bit. How's that?"

"Okay!"

Louis walked over and stood just over Phoebe and Daisy. It was a sight that Harry loved to see, Louis acting a little like his old self, the one before his father died before he started dating Ronnie, but he could tell it was just on borrowed time.

Less than ten minutes later, the doorbell rang, and Louis left once again. While the twins didn't seem to mind Harry was hurt enough for them, he kept his eyes on Louis as he walked away to answer the door. When Louis felt Harry's gaze burning in the back of his head, he turned to meet his eyes, telling him to fuck off with just a look. Harry didn't let it phase him and instead just raised his eyebrow before returning to the game.

All five people sitting at the table could hear Ronnie's presence, not just her voice but also her iconic white high heels hitting the marble floors. Harry noticed the slight change in the twin's demeanor when Ronnie entered the house, and frankly, he changed with them.

"Let's be real-life princesses!"

Suddenly Daisy got up from her chair, dragging Phoebe, who, along with her now, also had a bright smile hanging from her lips. The three older friends were still confused, making the girls stop and explain their idea in further detail.

"Let's get dressed fancy, well Daisy and me, and let's throw a ball in the dance hall. Besides, we all have princes to dance with, so come on!"

Harry and Niall both agreed easily to the idea. Still, it took a few minutes to convince Cassie to join, but eventually, after the four promised not to tell anybody, she agreed. The twins each grabbed one of Cassie's hands, and the three ran upstairs. Harry knew this was his fault that they dragged Cassie into it as he introduced them to her and also used her in last year's princess photoshoot.

The boys stayed downstairs and went into the dance hall while Cassie was turning the twins into princesses. Harry always loved how the Tomlinson's kept a real vintage record player in the dance hall along with records of classical music, which quite frankly was perfect for hosting a princess ball.

Niall and Harry had been talking about how Niall actually met Cassie when all of a sudden, he stopped talking, his eyes slowly went wide, and a soft smile glowed on his face. Harry turned around and saw the reason why. Standing at the room entrance, Cassie stood in the middle with her hair and makeup done, most likely because the twins forced her to get dolled up, and Phoebe and Daisy each in a dress with their one hair and makeup done standing on each side of her.

Harry started the record player and made his way to the girls with his hands held out.

"May I have this dance, your highnesses?"

All three of the girls giggled, including Cassie, which was surprising. She let go of their hands as they walked gracefully to meet Harry. He took each girl in his

hands and began twirling them around. Niall then took Cassie into his own hands.
The night had genuinely turned into a magical evening, and nobody would have ever guessed that two little girls who dreamed of being princesses would allow three teenagers to escape from their own responsibilities and live in a dream world as well.
After a while, the twins asked if they could switch Harry out for Niall, an excellent sign that they probably like him. While Niall frolicked with Phoebe and Daisy, Harry took his turn dancing with Cassie. The boys took a break to get some water leaving the girls dancing along to the music.

"I hope you're enjoying seeing Cassie dolled up and dancing because, let me tell you, it may never happen again."

Harry laughed while Niall continued enjoying his gaze on Cassie, unable to tear his eyes away from the girl that held his heart.

"I'll enjoy Cassie anyway I can get her."

"Great answer. To be honest, I never thought I would like one of her boyfriends, but luckily for you, you have passed not only my approval but the princess's approval as well."

"Thanks, man, it means a lot. Just don't try stealing her, and we're good!"
Niall let out his signature laugh, which caught the girls' attention, who started walking over to join them. As if almost perfect timing Phoebe came running up to Harry, jumping in his arms.

"When are you going to bring a princess around here? Cassie brought her prince?"

"Well, I won't be bringing a princess, but as soon as I find a prince, I'll bring him over."

"Okay!"

She jumped down from his arms and danced her way over to Phoebe. Niall seemed to get what Harry had just told Daisy and gave him an accepting smile.

"LOUIS, ARE YOU READY!"

Ronnie's screeched like nails on a chalkboard as all five of the kids looked at each other in a confused manner, not knowing how she could have lost her own boyfriend.

Chapter Six:

Louis was standing at the edge of the entrance of the dance hall. He heard the commotion of laughter and giggles coming from his sister's room and became intrigued. Typically, when Harry is over, they stay downstairs. Being up in their room was unusual unless he was putting them to bed. It wasn't long after that he heard a voice that he knew wasn't Harry's, but instead Cassie's.

He was tempted to go and see what they were doing. Louis missed seeing his sisters laugh. He never really got to see, especially nowadays since he's always so busy. As Louis got up to check the laughter from across the hall, he was shocked to hear his girlfriend's voice. He had forgotten she was over, well not really; he knew he had let her in the house and took her to his room, but he was so fixated on what was happening across the hall.

"Oh, thank god, I was getting tired of hearing that mess."

"Huh?"

"You are closing the door, right? I mean, how in the world can two people have a conversation with such a loud and rude disruption? Did your sister never learn how to respect a guest?"

Louis wasn't shocked at Ronnie's choice of words, they weren't any harsher than just about every other time she spoke, but he was surprised that she used them to describe two four-year-old. Sure, Cassie was with them, but she probably didn't know that. Instead of picking a right with Ronnie, Louis just obeyed her request. However, when he went to shut the door, he was met with the sight of his sisters in their favorite princess dresses. It was the ones Harry gave them for their last birthday. He smiled at the memory of how happy they were when they came home that day.

Louis traveled deeper into the hall, watching as his sisters clung to Cassie's arms until they finally disappeared down the staircase.

"Louis! How long does it take to close a door?" Quickly he dashed back into his room and shut his door, snapping back into the Louis he created years ago.

"Sorry, I just went and asked them to keep it down. We should be good now."

Louis sat at the edge of his bed while Ronnie was sitting on the edge of the bay window with a bag of makeup sprawled out all over the navy-blue pillows that lined the area. She held a mirror that lit up around its edges in one hand while having a beauty blender in the other as she redid the day's makeup, turning it into a gamified night look. Ronnie didn't seem to notice when her boyfriend came back into the room, simply ignoring him.

"Why do you have to do your makeup there? There is plenty of space in the bathroom."
Ronnie stopped her motions and set down the mirror and lifted her face to look at Louis. A deep breath was let out, signaling her annoyance at what Louis had just said.

"Louis. Why would I do my makeup in a dingy bathroom that is filled with disgusting artificial light? Do you really want everybody at the party to make fun of my makeup just because you made me do it in a bathroom? Besides, the view is better sitting here."

"Just please don't get any of that on the pillows. They aren't easy to clean."

Louis was already giving up on the argument; he knew there was no chance of him winning. He also just didn't have the energy to deal with an upset Ronnie all night. All he wanted to do was just go to the party and drink a beer. Drink a beer and escape reality. Ronnie resumed her routine picking up her mirror, which had left a slight outline of powder. Louis noticed and let out a soft sigh earning him another glare from his girlfriend. He already needed a break from her. Louis stood back up and walked out of his room.

"Louis! Where are you going!"

"I'm just grabbing some water. I'll be back."

Louis left his room and leaned up against the wall and let out a deep breath. Louis walked down the staircase to head to the kitchen. When finally arriving at the fridge Louis was shocked not to see any of the others that were also occupying the residence. Nevertheless, he goes and grabs two water bottles.

Louis started to make his way back up the stairs before changing his course, instead allowing himself to drift throughout the halls of his house. He figured Ronnie wouldn't notice his missing presence, so he took his time. Louis's footsteps created a soothing rhythm as his shoes connected with the floor while walking down the familiar empty halls. He keeps his eyes fixated on the paintings hung along the walls. Louis always wished he was good at something like art. He loved football with all his heart, but it also broke him to know that one day he would have to give it up, give up the thing he did with his father for thirteen years because his body just wouldn't be able to handle the stress of the activity anymore.

He remembered his father hanging up some of these paintings, and he is the reason they have so many to begin with. You see, Mr. Tomlinson's family had owned an art gallery and museum for over a century, and sometimes, when he truly loved a painting in one of the exhibits, he would save up enough to purchase the artwork for his personal use. Every room in the house had at least one painting; it was a way of keeping his memory alive.

Louis stopped at a painting, an oil painting by Leonid Abramov titled Vertical Rain's Rustle. Two people were walking down a dimly lit park street as rain drizzled down around them as the umbrella sitting between them kept them sheltered. It was the last painting to be brought back before he passed away. Two weeks before the crash, Louis, Jay, and Harry had watched Richard hang the picture on the wall.

At the time, Louis never really appreciated the painting for what it was worth. To him, it just kind of looked like little blobs of colors on a canvas, but he never voiced his opinion because he saw how happy the rest of his family was, even Harry. Louis knew that Harry was close with his dad; quite frankly, they used to joke that Richard was Harry's honorary father.

Their relationship was different than Louis, and he had. Louis brought out the athletic, high-spirited, rambunctious, and go with the flow side of his father, while Harry brought out the calm, charming, and secretly nerdy side of him. He knew that they always bonded over the antique and artistic ways of life, which at the time was perfectly fine with Louis since he really didn't care for it himself. He was just glad that his father always got to express that side of himself, even if it was with Harry and not himself.

The sound of classical ballroom music caught Louis's attention causing him to take his eyes off the painting and instead land on the door at the end of the hallway. Confused, he wearily walked forward. The noise was clearly coming from the dance hall, but why? He has never heard of the dance hall being in use in the last four years, not for a meeting, not for a party, not anything after his father's visual. Louis honestly thought that the room might have been locked shut.

Quickly Louis stopped in his tracks as he appeared at the entrance of the room. The large French doors opened all the way, and the antique record player was spinning. He pressed his body against the doorframe, trying to keep out of sight. At first, he saw nothing but only heard the shuffling of feet and the wave of laughter filling the room. Soon enough, he saw the source; Harry waltzed into his point of view with Phoebe and Daisy linked onto his hands as he twirled them around to the beat of the music. Niall and Cassie then came up, following behind Harry and the twins dancing much more realistically.

Louis's lips curled into a smile as he watched his baby sisters dancing with the biggest smiles he has ever seen. He pulled out his phone and snapped a few pictures of the moment. Louis was tempted to walk right in and join in on the dancing. He saw himself going in and sweeping one of his sisters swiftly from Harry's grip and taking over the dance moves but instead, his phone rings. Startled by the sudden bringing, Louis jumped back, hitting his back against the edge of one of the French doors causing it to swing slightly before reaching out to steady it. Louis felt the painful imprint of the door on his back; there was undoubtedly going to be a bruise. He slid his finger across the glass screen in his hand before bringing it to his ear.

"How long does it take you to grab some water? It's been almost a half-hour; I am almost ready! "

"I'm sorry, Ronnie, I just got distracted."

"Of course, you did. Just come back up here. We need to get you ready for the party as well."

"Okay, I'll be right there."

"k"

And with the brief exchange of words, Louis turned to start making his way back to his room. As he walked away from the impromptu gala, he turned his head around one last time, looking at how happy everybody was. What stood out to him was that it was not fake happiness where people pretend to be okay because they didn't want people to know they were sad but genuinely happy. Happy enough that he knew everybody in the room would forever hold a memory of the night.

Two minutes later, Louis was back in his room. The wall of windows where Ronnie resided not too long ago allowed the golden light to flow through the room, signaling the day was fading into night. As soon as Louis placed the water bottles on his dresser, Ronnie pulled him into his closet and began pulling down shirts and hovering them in front of her boyfriend. She was always determined to be the best-looking person at a party, and Louis always had to match.

Louis stood silently while Ronnie talked to herself as she picked out his outfit, a muted yellow button-up and a pair of cream-colored shorts, it clashed horribly with Louis's skin, completely washing him out, but that didn't matter. His ensemble matched to near reflection with the yellow dress Ronnie had already changed into; it implemented her tan skin beautifully and brought out the gold flakes in her honey pool eyes. While she looked stunning, Louis was going to look like he belonged in a dumpster.

Louis went into his bathroom to change, closing the door before Ronnie decided to join in. The last thing he needed was her critiquing him even more or worse, trying to start a makeout session. Technically he knew she wouldn't even dare to mess up her makeup before she even left the house, but since she still had all her products sprawled out on the bay window, nothing was stopping her.

Looking in the mirror, Louis cringed. Literally any other outfit known to humanity would be better than the monstrosity on his body. He just didn't get why he couldn't wear what he had worn to school earlier that day as he knew the rest of his friends would be; their girlfriends didn't care if they matched or not. With a spray of his signature cologne and a quick brush of his teeth, Louis let out an exasperated sigh before unlocking the bathroom door and walking back into his room.

To no surprise, Ronnie had already picked out a pair of shoes, gray Sperry's, and placed them on the floor near her gray heels. He walked over and picked up the shoes before sitting down on the bed to put them on. Ronnie put down her phone and slipped on her shoes as well. Louis never knew how she managed to walk in heels; they looked like a death contraption. He was also thankful that Ronnie was super short, so much so that

even wearing the four-inch stilettos, a₩ she was still a good three inches shorter than Louis.
Louis stood up and offered his hand to help Ronnie up as well.

"Well, once again, you look stunning."

"Well, I would hope so. I didn't put in all this work for me to just look pretty."

Ronnie took Louis's hand and walked slightly closer to him. Standing nearly on top of Louis's feet, she began to ruffle with his hair changing its direction back and forth with an extremely focused look placed on her face.

"Ugh, I should have called you earlier, so I had time to do your hair. It's a mess."

"It's my signature look; no one is going to notice, let alone care about it."

"Well, I notice and care about it."

Louis rolled his eyes, making sure he masked his annoyance with a hint of playfulness so Ronnie wouldn't make a fuss."

"Come on, let's get going, or else we are going to be more than just *fashionably late*."

"Oh, you're right. It's already almost seven!"
Ronnie placed a sloppy kiss on Louis's cheek; as he wiped away the gesture, Ronnie ran across the room to grab her clutch and a jean jacket. It was nearly the dead of winter in London, and the only warmth she had to rely on was a flimsy denim jacket, damn she really only cared about how good she looked. Who cares about getting hypothermia when you have every guy in a ten-mile radius drooling over you?

Louis grabbed his jacket; a fleeced laced denim one that, of course, matched Ronnie's, but it surprisingly helped offer some protection from the cold weather. The pair left Louis's room and walked through the house, which still seemed eerily empty unless paying enough attention to pick up on the soft beat bouncing through the walls.

Louis picked up his keys from the key hook by the garage and helped lead Ronnie to his car, a black model three Tesla, and open the door other allowing her to get in the passenger seat quickly. Louis walked around and got in the car himself. He opened the garage door and started backing out before coming to a sudden halt.

"LOUIS!"

"I'm sorry. Just hold on a sec Ronns. I forgot to tell Harry and the girls I was leaving I'll be right back." Louis dashed out of his car, running back into the house. Due to the still, otherwise emptiness of the house, he made his way back to the dance hall. His steps started to slow from a jog to a dash walk to just an average pace, the house was too big to run from one end to the other without working up a sweat, and if Louis returned to his car with even a trace of sweat, he knew Ronnie would flip a switch.

When the doors of the dance hall came into view, he could hear the light mummers of two boys' voices. Knowing Harry had an extra guest over, he thought nothing of it. When he saw Daisy jump into Harry's arms, he stopped walking and decided to listen in on the conversation. It would be rude to interrupt the middle of a conversation.

Still hiding out of sight, similarly as he had done just an hour earlier, he began eavesdropping.

"When will you bring a princess around here? Cassie brought her prince?"

"Well, I won't be bringing a princess over, but as soon as I find a prince, I'll bring him over."
Louis was confused; what had Harry met by that? He let the words replay in his head until the realization hit him. Not a princess but a prince, not a girl but a guy. Harry was looking for a guy, he had just told his four-year-old sister he was gay, and Louis was shocked. He had absolutely no idea.

Louis took a moment to process the information; even being friends with Harry for almost fourteen solid years, Louis had no idea that he was gay. After allowing his brain to calm down, he knocked on the door, gaining the attention of the five people occupying the room.

"Hey, um, I just wanted to let you know I 'm-uh we are heading out."

Nobody seemed shocked by the lad's words; who would be when this had been the routine for the last four years? Cassie and Niall simply ignored his presence, which didn't shock him. He knew Cassie never liked him and probably rubbed her feelings onto Niall. Harry, however, had the same look held on his face every time he told him he was leaving rather than staying home, a mix of empathy and disappointment.

"Alright, just remember curfew."

"I know, I know."

Phoebe and Daisy came running up behind Harry, hiding behind him and his unnaturally long legs.

"Bye Louis!" They said in unison.

"Bye girls, you behave like a nice princess, alright."

"Okay!"

Just like that, they ran back deeper into the room to find Cassie and Niall so they could begin dancing again. Harry and Louis were left there standing in silence before Harry gave Louis a half-smile and turned around, jogging forward to catch up with the rest of his party. Louis state put for a second before turning around himself and heading back to his car.

When he returned to the driver's seat, he saw Ronnie scrolling on her phone, obviously upset by the delay he just made.

"I'm sorry, Ronnie, you know I have too or else my mom would kill me."

"Just drive already, please."

He put the key card in its place, and the car revved back to life. Louis put the vehicle in reverse, this time successfully leaving the garage and beginning to drive down the long and twisted driveway carrying them away from the palace estate.

Chapter Seven:

Soon the sun fell deep into the sky, and it was time for Harry, Cassie, Niall, Phoebe, and Daisy to grab some dinner. Unlike the last week of getting pizza Harry decided he would instead just make a large pot of spaghetti and meatballs for everyone.

Everyone was back in the kitchen; Phoebe and Daisy had changed out of their dresses and into some pajamas and were sitting on the kitchen island in the middle of everyone. Cassie and Niall had pulled out bowls for each member of the dinner party and brought them near the stove. Harry pulled the tomato sauce from the pantry with the noodles already boiling and the meatballs in the oven and got out the colander.

Fifteen minutes later, the water had been drained, and the noodles tossed back into the pot along with the freshly cooked meatballs. Harry poured the container of sauce over the food and stirred the concoction. Harry laid out the five bowls near him then divided the food among them. He carried three bowls, one for Phoebe, Daisy, and himself, to the dining table which they had occupied earlier.

The girls already sat in their chairs, each with a glass of water, silverware, and a napkin in front of them, leaving enough room for the bowls to be placed in front. Harry sat down the bowls, then put his own bowl down on the table and pulled out his chair and sat down.

Cassie came strutting in the kitchen with Niall close on her tail with a bowl in each of his hands.

"I'm so sad to see we are not high enough on your royalty list not to have our food brought to us."

"Oh, don't worry, Cas, you have your own prince now. No need for me anymore."

She turned around with a smile on her face as she saw Niall setting down two bowls of spaghetti on the table. She blushed at the gesture before sitting down. Cassie grabbed Niall's hands, and she whispered a thank you.

With all five people enjoying their dinner, they began to talk in between bites—everything from the retelling of Disney princess stories to stories of each of the elder's childhood memories. Memories of everyone's first day of school was the main topic of conversation. The images of a little Harry, Cassie, and Niall infiltrated Phoebe and Daisy's head as they could only imagine the three being as little as they are.

Pretty soon, the moon hung high in the sky, and the bowls of food now sat empty in front of the chattering group. Both Cassie and Niall both had to be home soon, and since Harry had driven them here, it was his responsibility to get them home too. Harry knew that he couldn't just leave the girls here by themselves; well, he could. They would honestly be fine without feeling incredibly guilty. It was in times like these that he was thankful to be driving his old 1996 Toyota Corolla, it may not be the prettiest, but it had just enough room to fit everybody in.

It took a little bit of thinking, but eventually, seat assignments were settled, Harry as the driver, Niall riding shotgun, Cassie riding backseat behind Harry, and the twins sitting next to her in their car seats. With everyone cramped in the car, Harry began driving. Niall began to give him directions to his house, which was surprisingly only about ten minutes away.

The drive, although short, was anything but quiet. Once again, Bruce Springsteen was playing through the car's speakers. Harry and Niall had a conversation going on in the front seats while the girls held a discussion all their own in the back.

Pulling into a lit driveway, Harry put the car in the park, allowing Niall to unbuckle his seatbelt and begin gathering his things. Harry bid him farewell as Niall got out of the vehicle; then, instead of walking towards his front door, he walked across the front of the car and to the window where Cassie sat. He quietly knocked on the window, and Cassie rolled it down to remove the space between them. Niall kept his voice quiet so as not to expose his words to the others of the car.

"Thank you for tonight. I've never had so much fun before."

"Yeah, I had fun too. I didn't know you could dance like that."

"Maybe sometime soon you'll get to see those moves again!"

"As long as I don't have to get all fancy again."

"I can take that."

Niall bent down to kiss her cheek before wishing her goodnight. He also waved goodbye to the little girls sitting next to Cassie before walking back up to his house and disappearing behind the door.

Harry once again began driving, this time on his way to drop off Cassie. Phoebe and Daisy started to talk to themselves swiftly among themselves, not allowing the other two in the car to hear what they were saying. Harry and Cassie had their own conversation about the events that had taken place throughout the week. They treated this time as if it was their time at Groundz because they both knew that it would be for a short time if they did meet the next day.

Fifteen minutes later, they arrived at Cassie's house. Just as she was opening the door, Phoebe lightly pulled on her arm, and Cassie bent back down to see what she wanted. Phoebe signaled for Cassie to lean farther down so she could whisper in her ear.

"How long do you think until Harry finds a prince?" Cassie let out a soft laugh before responding in a whisper as well.

"Until he finds a prince that he wants to treat like a king and when that prince treats him like a king too."

And with that, Phoebe turned back the other sister, and the two began smiling and giggling, Cassie for once, didn't mind all of the princess talk. After all, she had a pretty fantastic night, thanks to the two girls. She smiled as she finally made her way out of the car and said goodbye to Harry.

"Are you ready to head home, girls?"
Harry's words pulled the girls out of their conversation as they nodded. Once getting out of the neighborhood, Harry turned up the music, and pretty soon, the three were jamming out to She's the One like no one was watching.

Time had passed effortlessly as they sang their hearts out, and they pulled back into the gated estate, pulling up and parking near the entrance of the house. Harry got out and proceeded to help the girls out of their car seats before heading back into the warmth of the home.

With it already being almost ten-o-clock Harry knew he had to start getting the girls ready for bed. Thankfully, the girls didn't put up a fight and listened to Harry without complaint.

Upstairs, Harry helped the girls brush their teeth and tucked them into bed after reading them a bedtime story. Phoebe fell asleep quickly, leaving only Daisy and Harry still awake when the story ended.

"Harry?'

"Yeah, Dais?"

"Are you going to a sleepover tonight?"

"I was planning on it tonight."

"Okay, thank you!"

"Good night, Daisy."

"Good night Harry, see you in the morning."

Harry gave each girl a kiss on the forehead before heading out of their room, leaving the door open just a crack. He couldn't help but think about why Daisy had wanted to make sure why he slept over. Harry knew that she knew that he would never leave them home in the house by themselves, especially at night. No matter how late it was, Harry always waited for Jay or Louis to return home, and in the case where it began to get too late, he always spent the night. He wondered if the girls didn't want to wake up to a house that just occupied them and Louis since they knew Jay wouldn't be home until the afternoon.

Harry made this way back to the all too familiar open door that led to Louis's room. He leaned his tall stature up against the solid wood frame and exhaled his thoughts. He wished Louis was just home more, not so he could see him more but for the rest of his family's sake. All Harry really wanted was for Phoebe and Daisy to know the Louis that Harry once knew, the one that seemed to parish the year they were born, the one that Harry would still see when he looked at the articles that lined the wall he starred at.

He allowed his head to create false memories. However, they weren't so much false memories rather than combining bits and pieces of specific memories. He imagined that some nights when he was watching the girls when they would play games, have dance parties, do midnight baking, and have massive hide and seek games that it was Louis he was doing it with and not his little sisters. Harry would never trade his time with the girls, but if it meant that they could have those memories with their brother, he would do it.

Harry also couldn't help but wonder how Louis found them earlier in the dance hall so easily. There was no calling out trying to find them. It's not like they were in an obvious place, it was a rare occurrence for anybody to be in the dance hall, and there were so many more places that they could have been that it should have taken Louis ages to find them. And Judging by the fact that Louis hadn't looked annoyed or in a rush, he figured that he probably hadn't searched for very long.

Little did Harry know that Phoebe had been watching him for quite some time. At first, she thought Harry was just admiring the art hung on the walls, and that's why he was moving so slow, but when she saw the way Harry longed to go deeper into her brother's room, she realized there was more to the story than what she was seeing. It's safe to say they Phoebe could read Harry reasonably well, and she knew that the look in his eyes and the tilt of his head that Harry was doing much more than admiring the space in front of him, leaving her to remember the words Cassie had told her just an hour before.

"Harry?"

"Phebs? What are you doing up? Is everything okay?"

"Can you make us a warm cup of milk?"

"Yeah, sure. You go climb back in bed. I'll be back in a few minutes, okay."

"Okay, thank you."

"Anytime."

Harry went downstairs and got two cups and filled them a little more than halfway with milk before placing them in the microwave to warm up. Thirty seconds later, a beep signaling that the cups were ready, Harry picked up the two warm cups of milk and headed back upstairs. When he went back into the twin's room, he found both girls quietly talking to each other. As soon as the door began to creep open, they stopped talking, and the girls just gave each other one of their twins looks, Harry had no idea what that look meant, but he knew it was some form of communication between the two.

Harry handed one cup to each of the girls, who happily took their cups and drank the liquid. Harry waited until they were done and took the cups back so he could put them in the dishwasher downstairs.

"Already for bed now?"

"Yeah, all ready."

Daisy spoke before Phoebe.

"Can we do something fun tomorrow?"

"What do you have in mind?"

"What about ice skating at the mall?"

"I am pretty sure we can make time for that."

"Yay!"

"Now it's time to go to bed, Goodnight girls."

"Goodnight!"

They squeaked excitedly in unison as Harry left the room, they knew full well what they were doing, but Harry was utterly clueless to what the girls had planned.

Even though Harry was spending the night at the Tomlinson's and he could technically go to sleep at any time he cared for, he still tried to stay up until Louis got home. Harry was able to keep himself busy for nearly two hours just by setting up the guest room the way he liked it and by searching up the ice-skating rink at the mall. Because he knew that Louis wouldn't wander his way to the guest room when he got home, Harry decided to go back into the living room so he could hear when the garage opened.

It was a little past midnight, and Harry fully expected to have to sit on the couch for over an hour waiting but after only twenty-five minutes, at 12:35 am, he heard the rumble of the garage door along with the suffering of feet and car keys. Harry grabbed a blanket and wrapped it around him and walked over to make sure it was indeed Louis or some bizarre robber.

Sure enough, it was Louis. He looked slightly disheveled and like he was absolutely exhausted. An odd sight to see when Louis was just coming back from a party, drunk or sober, he seemed happy.

"You're back early?"

"Wasn't really feeling the party scene tonight."

Louis walked into the kitchen and grabbed a glass of water, quickly downing the whole glass before continuing to speak.

"Hey, I know I shouldn't be using you as my personal slave, but do you think you can watch the girls for a few hours tomorrow? I'm supposed to go out with Ronnie at eleven."

"Don't worry. I already promised the girls we'd do something tomorrow anyway, plus I'm spending the night, so you are off the hook."

A look of sad realization was painted across Louis's face, hearing that his sisters had asked Harry to do something rather than him, but could he blame them? Not really, it was more his fault. He was the one that always leaves them with Harry.

"Oh, okay. Well, I'm just going to go print something in the office, then head to bed."

"Okay, I guess I'll see you in the morning."

Harry then made the small trek to the guest room while replaying the conversation. It was still incredibly awkward to talk to Louis. He never really knew why Louis changed the way he did, he knew it probably had something to do with his father's death, but he just couldn't connect why that would make Louis turn into the person he now was. Harry hoped that one day he would be able to talk to him about everything, go back to the way things were before everything, and just leave the awkwardness behind.

Harry knew that it would take a long time to get to that place, so many things needed to happen. Louis would have to want to talk, Harry would've to leave his feelings in the past, and that the two would have to rebuild their trust with one another. The stars would have to be perfectly aligned for that to happen.

Instead of thinking of what he could only dream about, he decided to let his eyes close and get some rest for the day that was ahead of him.

Chapter Eight:

Harry rose early in the morning. He always slept quite finely while at the Tomlinson's, which usually allowed him to wake early while still feeling promptly rested. When he checked his phone, he saw that the time was 7:45 am, seven hours of sleep, not too bad. Harry also sent a text to his mother saying that he would be out for most of the day with the twins but would be back in time for dinner.

Harry quickly got out of bed and went to the kitchen as he felt his stomach begin to grumble. Harry always adored being in the house this early in the morning, the way the light filtered through the curtains and added a golden glow to the accessories of the house. The frames of the paintings shimmered, almost making it look like the paintings were floating; it was an absolutely fantastic sight. This was the sort of thing that made Harry wish that he brought his camera so he could capture the moment. Even though this typically wasn't the type of thing he photographed, Harry still recognized its beauty and wanted to be able to share it with everyone; it was the type of scenery that a 17th-century artist would paint, a painting he knew Mr. Tomlinson would have fallen in love with and brought back home like so many others.

Once finally arriving in the kitchen, Harry grabbed the tea kettle, filled it with water, and placed it on the stove. While the water was heating up, he grabbed a mug and a teabag, as well as the container of milk from the fridge. In perfect timing, whistling rang through the air, and he picked up the kettle pouring the steaming water in his mug with the teabag. Harry allowed the tea too steep for a couple of minutes before removing it and pouring in the milk. Harry threw out his tea bag and put the milk back into the refrigerator before picking his mug back up and walking to the kitchen's bay window. Harry was thankful that he had his tea to keep him warm as the window was not doing much to keep out the cold wind blowing outside. The window's view was of a dainty garden that fell just in front of a small pond. Littered among the trees was a treehouse that used to be a part of his daily life. It was one place where Harry and Louis would go after school to relax.

They always kept games like checkers, playing cards, and Jenga along with an endless supply of comic books and journals. It was also the best place to hide during a full house game of hide and seek. The fond memories were replaying in his head of the reason that Harry stayed sitting by the window. They were worth the cold biting on the tips of his nose and ears.

When Harry finished his tea, he decided to start making breakfast; he had already pushed it off long enough. Harry wasn't the best cook in the world, but he definitely wasn't the worst. He could easily follow directions on the back of a box or successfully recreate a dish with a recipe, so in reality, there was no reason to be uncomfortable cooking, but he still was.

While roaming the pantry, he came across a box of pancake mix and decided that pancakes did sound like a good breakfast on a cold winter morning. Even with the box sitting on the highest shelf, Harry easily grabbed it and brought it to the counter.

Harry also grabbed a mixing bowl, pan, spatula, and the rest of the ingredients he needed to make the batter. Halfway through, Harry decided to mix in some sprinkles to create a confetti effect in the pancakes. What's so wrong with making pancakes more fun anyway?

Harry already had the pan heating up on the stove, so by the time the batter was completely ready, he didn't have to wait to begin cooking. Spraying the pan with oil, harry proceeded to pour the batter in, somehow creating perfectly circular pancakes. Within ten minutes, Harry had nearly twenty pancakes made, and the batter was all used up. He portioned out the pancakes onto four plates, he didn't know if Louis would be up for breakfast, but it was worth saving him some just in case.

Looking at the time, it was nearly nine now, and with breakfast already finished, he decided to go and wake up the girls. Harry made his way up the spiral staircase and to the bedroom. He lightly knocked on the door before entering to see Phoebe and Daisy already awake and dressed in day clothes.

"I see you are very excited to go ice skating today."

The girls began dancing around doing arabesques and turns, pretending to already be skating on the rink.

"Who wouldn't be!"

"Only a crazy person! But before we go, there is breakfast downstairs."

"what is it"

"Pancakes!"

"Oh!"

Both girls ran right past him and down the stairs leaving Harry by himself upstairs. Harry started making his way to the stairs when he walked past Louis's room like always; the door was open. Harry debated whether or not to go into the room and tell him about breakfast. Instead, Harry settled on knocking on the door and calling out to him.

"Hey, Louis um-there is breakfast downstairs if you want some. Its pancakes. I know you're not much of a morning person, so uh- if you don't come down, I'll just cover them and put it in the fridge for later."

Harry heard the ruffling of sheets but no footsteps, so he just decided to go and enjoy breakfast himself. Harry entered the kitchen to see Phoebe and Daisy touring syrup and whipped cream on their pancakes. He knew he shouldn't have left them alone in such a situation with so much sugar. Harry could already see them bouncing off the walls later on.

Harry sat down himself and added his own sugar spell on top of his pancakes before digging in. While enjoying breakfast, Harry allowed the girls to talk excessively while eating since they clearly had no shortage of topics of conversation, everything from the dancing they had done the night before to talk about their favorite princesses and princes.

About halfway through his stack of pancakes, Harry heard footsteps coming from down the large hallway, shortly after seeing the reason why and his breath hitched in his throat.

Walking up, entering the kitchen was Louis but not just any Louis, a sleepy and incredibly adorable-looking Louis. Harry couldn't help but stare at the stray hairs that fell away from Louis's face, which was glowing from the morning light. His eyes glimmering a crystal shade of blue had encapsulated Harry's thoughts. It wasn't just the soft features of Louis's face that made him look like an angel but also the way he looked so effortlessly comfortable in just grey sweatpants, a white t-shirt, and a black jacket hanging closely off him. The fluffy socks that occupied his tiny feet also added to his adorableness.

Harry finally snapped out of his daze when the sound of a kitchen drawer, Louis had grabbed his plate of pancakes off of the counter and grabbed a fork and was now on his way to the table. Harry's tranced state, however, didn't go noticed, but Phoebe and Daisy were now giggling into each other.

With Harry sitting across from the girls, who sat opposite of him, Louis chose the seat next to him so he could view his happy sisters. Due to Louis sitting so close to him, Harry couldn't help but smell the natural aroma of Louis, which smelled of a mix of firewood and cinnamon, an odd combination, but it was suddenly Harry's favorite scent.

Harry sat back and allowed the siblings to enjoy their breakfast together, knowing that it wasn't something that happened very often, usually only on holidays and other special occasions. Louis clearly had one of his sister's obsessions with princesses and had asked them to tell him their favorite stories. Pretty soon, laughter filled the air as Louis did his best prince impersonation, completely letting his hardcore reputation, which he held at school, go out the window.

Harry had never seen anything so precious, so adorable, and so family-like in his life. Because the three siblings were so invested in each other, Harry was able to snap a few photos of them without anyone noticing. Ten minutes later, with everyone having finished their food and calmness finally falling back upon the family, the realization of time had snuck up. Looking at the time,

it was 10:30. Harry had reserved his, Phoebe, and Daisy's spot at the ice rink for eleven.
“I truly do hate to ruin, this moment but girls we got to get going if we want to make it to the mall in time."
"Oh yay!",
The girls swiftly got up and out of their chairs to go put on their shoes while Harry and Louis took the plates to the kitchen sink.
"So, you're going to go to the mall still dressed in your pajamas?"
Louis said it jokingly, but Harry hadn't realized that he was, in fact, still in red flannel pants and a grey long sleeve shirt.
"Well. At least it's festive?"
"Well, that is Styles."
Harry smiled at the angelic laughter that left Louis's lips and turned away before he began to blush as well. Harry decided to switch the topic of conversation before he lost himself in a trance again.
"So, what are you doing with Ronnie today?"
A look of shock and horror flushed the color out of Louis's already pale face. He frantically turned to look at the oven clock, and his eyes grew wide.
"Oh shit, I forgot I have to go get ready!"
Louis began running to the stairs in a frantic hurry.
"Oh, and thanks for looking after the girls today!"
Louis's voice bounced along the halls as Harry hurried to put on his own shoes. He laughed as this was a total Louis situation, forgetting he had plans with someone. Harry didn't have time to reply as he was busy running up to the front of the house with Phoebe and Daisy by his side as they rushed to get into the car.

Thankfully, there was very little traffic on the road, which was usually packed with it being two weeks away from Christmas. Harry fully expected everyone to be out and about shopping. In twenty minutes, he pulled into the parking lot. Once safely parked, Harry got the girls out of the car, and they headed into the mall.

It didn't take long for the three of them to find the giant ice-skating rink that laid in the center of the mall. Easy to distinguish with the massive twenty-foot Christmas tree in the center of it all. With Phoebe in one hand and Daisy in the other, Harry headed to the line of people who were already waiting in line to get skates. Thankfully because Harry had already reserved everyone's skates, they didn't have to be put on a waiting list and instead immediately got their skates. Harry helped the twins put their skates on before putting them on his own. And with everyone ready, they three made their way to the ice.

As soon as their skates hit the ice, Phoebe and Daisy disappeared around the rink skating as if it was second nature to them. Harry was stunned. Harry himself made his way onto the ice but had less of a fantastic experience gripping onto the railing for dear life. Harry had barely made it thirty feet when he saw the twins pass him again with giant smiles plastered on their faces. Suddenly his struggling and embarrassment were highly worth it.

It took forever for Harry to finally make it one full lap around the rink; he was working so hard to stay on his feet that he was already ready for a quick break. Harry stepped off the ice and stood by the side entrance, keeping an eye on the twins who somehow managed to skate in circles and take turns skating on one leg. Harry started to believe they might be prodigies; he didn't see other four-year-old's looking like they had been skating for years. When the twins spotted Harry standing off to the side, they quickly made their way back to him.

"Why aren't you skating? It's so much fun!"

"Oh, don't worry, I'm just taking a quick break. When I get back out there, you two are going to have to teach me how to skate!"

"Can we do that now?"

"Oh, what am I getting myself into..."

"Yayy!"

Both girls jumped slightly up and down, as much they could while skating, and each grabbed one of Harry's hands and led him back onto the ice. Immediately they pulled him right into the center of the ice, away from any form of support other than the hands of Phoebe and Daisy.

"Girls, I don't think this was the greatest idea!" Harry could barely keep his feet from slipping out from under him, tightly gripping the little hands in his. The girls, however, couldn't stop giggling at the sight of seeing Harry looking like a baby giraffe.

"Just trust yourself!"

"As long as you're not afraid, you'll be okay!" Harry took the girl's advice, and soon enough, he was almost steady on his feet. He certainly was still struggling to keep his balance, but he no longer needs to strangle the railing to be okay. Harry has still, however, kept holding on to the twin's hands. After all, they did kind of drag him into it.

Suddenly, while rounding the corner of the ice-clad arena, Phoebe and Daisy suddenly let go of Harry's hands, leading him to slide on the ice all by himself, and soon the panic set in.

"Phoebe! Daisy! What are you doing? Come back!"

Harry tried to hide the fear overtaking his body; he also didn't want to attract the attention of the fellow skaters around him. Harry's arms began flailing arms to help his large body stay upright. After nearly thirty seconds, Harry began to regain his balance and replaced his uncertainty and fear with an accomplished smile. Pretty soon, Harry was able to glide pretty comfortably. Eventually, the twins came back to harry and skated along with him. After nearly an hour of practice, it began to look like Harry and the girls were dancing again, but this time instead of Prince Harry leading Princess Daisy and Princess Phoebe lead Harry in tiny twirls on the ice. Harry decided that after quite a while of skating, it was time for some hot chocolate. Harry was able to get the twins off the ice and back into their regular shoes so they could head to the vendor. Harry returned the three pairs of skates then joined the line at the hot chocolate vendor with the girls by his side.

Christmas lights, wreaths, and fake snow littered the ground around them while little matching red chairs and tables laid out near the open area around them. When they finally got to the front of the line, Harry ordered three hot chocolates and three candy canes which had been displayed on the front counter.

Harry followed Phoebe and Daisy to an open set of seats with a drink carrier in his hands and a small bag containing the peppermint sticks. Once sitting down, Harry handed out the candy and drinks as everyone wanted the warmth offered by them after being on the ice for over an hour.

While enjoying their snacks, everyone began talking about the fun they had while skating, having no mercy at the early memories of the day, especially when it came to harry. Laughter was definitely on no shortage as they three enjoyed their break, so anybody passing by it would have looked like sibling goals.

Harry couldn't help but take a few photos of Daisy and Phoebe as they laughed and played with each other, the Christmas themes background made for the perfect backdrop. He made a mental note to get them printed for Jay as a little Christmas gift since she always loved to have new photos of her kids.

After sitting for quite a while, all the hot chocolate was drunk, and all that remained of the candy canes was the plastic that once wrapped around them. Harry had gotten up to go throw the trash away. He returned to see the girls had left the table they had been sitting at. Harry felt as if he was having a heart attack while looking for the twins. His eyes scanned the entire area quickly.
He soon found the matching brown hair standing near a table at the edge of the seating area. Quickly he ran up to them.

"Phoebe, Daisy! You can't just get up and go anywhere; we aren't at the house anymore."

Harry changed his view from the girls up to the people who occupied the chairs of the table. His eyes went wide when he saw Louis and Ronnie sitting in the bright red chairs, each with a cup in their hands. At first, Harry was quite relieved, Louis seemed quite happy, even smiling and picking up Daisy and putting her on his knee, but when he turned to look at Ronnie, well, she was a different story.

Red tints laced Ronnie's cheeks, and her eyes held a dark glare mounting genuine fear among Harry's body once again. Instead of continuing to stay haunted by the devil who decided to embody Ronnie, he turned his attention back to Louis, who had now also propped Phoebe on his knee. Instantly overwhelmed at the affection he saw between the siblings, he once again pulled out his phone, snapping yet again another photo. While it may not have been as good as his professional photos, he still knew that it held great importance. Ronnie cleared her throat, bringing Harry and Louis both back into reality.

"Um- sorry for crashing your date. I didn't realize you'd be here."

"Oh, don't worry about it. It's always fun to have some extra people around."

It was evident that Louis was trying to calm down a very tense Harry, but it really wasn't working as he could feel Ronnie's eyes burning the back of his head. It wasn't surprising that Ronnie would be upset by having Louis's attention being taken off of her, but it was undoubtedly weird that she could be so jealous of him talking to his little sisters for all of two minutes.

"Well, uh, we'll get going and allow you two to get back to uh whatever you're doing."

Harry motioned for the twins to come back to them, which they happily complied, hopping off of Louis's knee and hugging him before walking back up beside Harry. Just as Harry was starting to walk away with the girls grabbing his hands, Phoebe stopped and turned to face Ronnie.

"If you wanna come over later we can be princesses and dance in the dance hall!"

"Oh, how cute! But honey, let me tell you something. I don't play princess anymore, I my dear, am a queen."

Phoebe simply turned back around, grabbing Harry's hand, and all three began walking again. However, this time it was Harry's turn to look back and burn his gaze in Ronnie's head.

Chapter Nine:

Louis watched as his sisters walked away, leaving him alone with Ronnie. Just a week ago, Louis would have brushed off the words Ronnie just spit out at his sisters but now, after spending just a few hours with them, he was livid.

"That was pretty rude, Ronns. They are just little girls."

"Just because they're little doesn't mean I need to take insults from them!"

"Ronnie, they're four!"

"Maybe now they'll know how to talk to someone with higher authority."

"Are you being serious right now?"

"Would you stop making this such a big deal? It's not like I told them to go sweep the floors or something. They probably won't remember a word I said to them anyway."

Louis closed his eyes and drew in a sharp breath to help contain his anger. His finger tapped rapidly on the table, only adding to the visible amount of rage that was coursing throughout his veins.

"What is up to you lately? You're just off and it's not making us look good."

"And that's what you care about right now, us looking good, not me or what I'm feeling?"

"Louis-"

"No, just forget about it."

Louis picked up his drink and just turned his head the other way. Ronnie didn't put up a fight and did just as

Louis said and forgot about the situation as she went back to scrolling through her Instagram.

The couple sat in their places for an hour, not saying a single word to each other. Louis had only started to grow angrier as he replayed the situation in his head. Based on the fact That he really didn't want to deal with Ronnie at the moment and knew he had to be home by three-o-clock, Louis decided it would just be best to head home now.

Louis pulled out his phone to read the time, 1:47 and deemed he could probably blame the early departure, in fact, on Harry having to go home soon. Instead of telling Ronnie the three-o-clock time he knew was true, he would change it to two-thirty. A half-hour isn't that big of a lie.

Scooting back the chair, Louis stood up and grabbed his now empty cup. He hit his hand on the table lightly to gain Ronnie's attention, which ultimately failed. Louis threw his cup away and came back to see Ronnie hadn't even moved; she hadn't even noticed that Louis had left. It would have been so easy for Louis to just leave that very moment and not drive Ronnie back to her house and leave her to find an alternative way home. As appealing as that whole situation sounded, Louis knew that that would only make the entire situation worse. Knowing that Ronnie and her crew would blow up in his face and that his mom would probably take away his car privileges if she ever found out.

"Ronnie, get up. We have to get going."

"What, I haven't gotten to finish my shopping!"

"You're more than welcome to stay here and finish your shopping, but I have to leave, so you'll have to figure out a different way home."

Ronnie rolled her eyes in disgust as she remembered that she and Louis had driven to the mall together. She thought about calling one of her friends to pick her up, and they could shop together but soon realized she would probably have to tell them that she and Louis had gotten into a fight, and no one, not even Ronnie's closest friends, could know that there was trouble in her paradise."

"Fine. I'm coming."

Ronnie went up and swung her purse over her shoulder before walking up to Louis, who was already making his way to the parking garage. The walk was silent, the tension was still rising between the two, and it was noticeable to every person who walked past them. After a short walk, Louis and Ronnie finally arrived at the doors to Louis's car. Louis unlocked it and got in himself, not bothering to be the gentleman he was raised to be and opened Ronnie's door. After all, she could handle pressing a button to have the door open itself.

As soon as she sat down, she got back onto her phone; What a surprise. She made no movements to put on her seatbelt, and it was a clear act to try and annoy Louis even further. She knew that he wouldn't start driving until every person was buckled safely in the car.

"Buckle up."

Louis had stopped trying to hide his anger and annoyance, allowing his voice to come out in its harsh manner.

"Nah, I'm fine."

"I said buckle your seatbelt."

"I said I'm fine."

"Then get out of my car and find another way home."

"God, fine, I'm putting on my seatbelt."

Once Louis heard the click of the belt buckle, he put the car in drive and left the parking garage. In an attempt to drown out the click of Ronnie's nails on her phone Louis turned on the radio. When exiting the highway and finally pulling onto a residential road that led to Ronnie's house, suddenly the music shut off.

"Why did we have to leave anyway?"

"My mom is out of town until later tonight, and Harry has to go home at two-thirty, and I'm not going to leave Phoebe and Daisy by themselves."

"of course."

"Excuse me?"

"Nothing."

Louis was nearly at his breaking point with Ronnie. The sight of the smoothly paved road that led to Ronnie's house had never brought so much relief to Louis before, but at the moment, it felt like heaven. Louis quickly pulled up the driveway and drove as close to the front door as he could, immediately he unlocked the car, and Ronnie unbuckled and got out of the vehicle.

"I'll call you later, Louis."

"Bye"

Louis drove off, leaving a stunned face, Ronnie standing at her front door. Louis didn't care though he knew that whenever she called him later, he would get an earful about his behavior, and he knew he wouldn't really listen but end up apologizing anyway and that the next day things would go back to normal at least for Ronnie. Louis drove around a while to help clear his mind and dump the negative tension out the window. Eventually, he made his way back to his own palace of living. He saw Harry's car in the front of the house parked on the driveway, exposed to the cold temperatures and rain that has turned into sleet in the cold of the season.

Louis pulled around to the back of the house and entered the large-scale garage, which mainly sat empty. The Tomlinson's had never been a family to collect cars, so the large space seemed rather useless, only ever having two cars parked inside, even when the house would be flourishing with people.

Walking into the house, Louis could hear the TV playing in the living room. Rudolf, the Red-Nosed Reindeer, was playing through the surround-sound speakers. Fully walking into the room, Louis wasn't with the sight of Phoebe and Daisy laying on their stomach on the floor watching the movie while Harry sat on the couch with his book bag also watching the movie.
When Harry Spotted Louis standing in the doorway, he began to stand up, grabbing the bag that sat next to him. The girls hadn't noticed still being entranced by the Christmas magic playing in front of their eyes. Harry pauses the movie, which caused both girls to look back at him.

"It's my time to go, girls."
Harry nodded his head to where Louis was standing, showing the girls that their brother had come home. Phoebe and Daisy both smiled and got up, running to give Harry a hug. No hug there was ever complete without Harry extending his hand to Phoebe and Daisy as they curtsied like princes.

"Your mom will be back soon. Until then, please don't trouble Louis too much!"

Harry laughed letting Louis know it was only a joke, but there was still some truth behind it. He knew that if the girls acted like they did with him, even though they were never bad, it would be way too much for Louis to handle, especially with the look that covered his face. The girls giggled and went back in front of the TV. Harry pressed play and walked out towards the front door to make his way home.

Halfway to his car Harry heard the front door open and the patter of footsteps. Turning around to make sure it wasn't one of the girls running out for some reason, he was relieved but also shocked to see Louis jogging up towards him.

"Hey, Styles, hold up!"

"Um yeah?"

"Why do you park out here? The weather is pretty harsh, and I'm sure it's not good for a car."

"Says the guy who's wearing jeans and a t-shirt when it's starting to snow."

"I was in a rush, but really why? There is plenty of room in the garage, you know. It's only me and mom's car. Yours can easily fit."

"I don't know. I guess I just always parked here; nothing bad has happened yet."

"Well, uh, you're more than welcome to start parking in the garage, especially when the weather is bad like this, here."

Louis handed Harry an extra garage door opener and waited for a response.

"uh- well, thank you. I'll keep it in mind."

The boys stood in uncomfortable silence. It strange for Louis to really interact with Harry by himself. It really hasn't happened in nearly a year. Every other time besides today, Louis only acknowledged Harry's presence when he was drunk or during times, he was over with the entirety of his family. Neither of the boys knew what to do. It should have been easy, two best friends talking to each other again, but no one knew who exactly the other person has turned into over the last few years.

"So... I better get going because my mom is home waiting for me."

"Yeah, o-of course, say hi to her for me?"

"I will."

Both Harry and Louis held a soft smile on the corners of their lips as Harry climbed into his car and hung the new garage door opener on the passenger's side visor. Pulling around the house, he saw the small figure of Louis making his way back to the house. He stayed standing at the door with it open until he couldn't see Harry anymore.

As Harry drove home, he tried to make sense of the situation. He didn't know what to think. Of course, he would love to mend his broken friendship with Louis, maybe even help bring back the Louis that he once knew, but he also didn't know if he could hang out with him and strictly stay just friends.

The teen pushed all his thoughts out of his head while he pulled into his own driveway. He smiled happily when he saw his mother's car in the driveway as well. He was excited to finally have some family time of his own, especially with Christmas being so soon.

Chapter Ten:

A week has passed, and that meant that it was now winter break and Christmas was only five days away. With it being Friday, Harry would usually be headed over to the Tomlinson's to watch the girls, but instead, he was headed over to drop off his gifts for them. With Jay being home, Harry didn't see the need to park in the garage, as he didn't plan on staying too long, and instead parked in his standard space in front of the home. Once parked, Harry went to the trunk of his car and grabbed the two large bags that contained gifts for Jay, Phoebe, Daisy, and yes, Louis.

For Jay, Harry had printed out almost all of the photos he had taken of the twins and Louis and created a year of memories scrapbook. This gift has become a tradition since the twins' first Christmas, and every year, it was one of Jay's favorites gifts. Harry had gotten Phoebe and Daisy Louis each a new princess dress with matching tiaras. Cassie also threw in a set of play makeup and hair clips. Now the tricky thing for Harry was getting a gift for Louis. He knew he would have to; it would be a way to get something from everyone else but him, the problem is he really didn't know what to get him.

Harry could have easily gotten Louis One of those premade gift boxes you could buy at any department store, you know the ones with a set of pajamas, socks, and cologne. Still, it seemed way too impersonal since, in reality, Harry knew Louis way to well not to put in some thought. However, Harry also didn't want his gift to seem

like he had been stalking Louis, which he wasn't, but he was very observant of everything Louis did.
The idea came to Harry just two days ago as he was cleaning out his garage. While organizing, he came across a football that had LT and RT written on the side of it. At first confused by why he had one of Louis's footballs, his head quickly recalled a memory.

It happened ten or eleven years ago. Richard had just begun teaching Louis how to play football. It was back when Harry was still open to the idea of playing sports, and since his best friend had been talking non-stop about how much fun it was, he decided to give it a try. One day Louis came over to his house with his dad, Richard, and began trying to teach the game to Harry. The day actually hadn't gone too bad, but it was clear after that day to Harry that Football was definitely not his thing, but he was too nice to tell Louis and Richard that he really didn't want to play. This caused them to leave the football with Harry so he could practice. Harry never did, and subsequently, he forgot about the ball in its entirety.

When Harry saw the ball, he instantly knew that Louis would appreciate it, the next day he went out to the store and bought a clear plastic case and mount to store the ball.

Snow had started sprinkling from the sky as Harry made his way to the front door. Since everyone was already home, he didn't want to use his key and just walk in, plus he probably couldn't even reach his keys with his hands being so full. Instead, he settled on ringing the majestic doorbell.

Jay came and opened the door, immediately smiling as she recognized the boy standing outside her door.

"Harry!"

"I come bearing gifts!"

"Come inside, let's get you out of that freezing weather! You know you don't have to give anything to anyone here. Having you is a gift enough."

"Always leave it to Momma Jay to make you feel loved! You know I absolutely love spoiling people though, besides it's really no big deal."

"You are too pure for this world, Harry, please don't ever change."

Jay went in and gave Harry a hug.

"Don't worry, I don't plan on it!"

Harry giggled as he pulled away; this allowed Jay to see the two bags he carried, and the realization crossed over that Harry probably wants to put them down.

"Oh, let's get those to the tree. Here hand me one; I'm sure your hands are getting tired."

Harry didn't protest and gave her the lighter of the two, before they both started walking through the house and towards the Christmas tree. It was clear that the family had spent the last week decorating the residence as lights, garland, and small winter-themed statues now dangled around the house. It was indeed a sight to be seen, especially as the snow now poured in a blizzard state.

Once arriving at the tree Harry was truly stunned. Every year the tree had a new theme. This year the theme was black and white. A tall twenty-foot white Christmas tree was covered in beautiful glittery and matte black ornaments and garland. The light reflecting off the decorations created a disco-like effect in the rest of the room.

Harry started taking out all of the wrapped gifts he had brought and laid them orderly under the tree. Once finished, he slowly stood up, observing the tree a little closer. While doing so, he noticed something incredibly beautiful, something he wished he could have come up with.

Intertwined with the black ornaments of the tree sat clear, small picture frames filled with black and white photos of the family, Jay, Louis, Phoebe, Daisy, their grandparents, and most heartwarming, photos of Richard as well.

Jay walked up behind Harry as he was entranced looking at a photo of Richard holding up two little onesies. He remembered the image as it was only two weeks before he passed away. Jay leaned her head on Harry's shoulder and took in the photo as well.

"You really outdid yourself this year, its-it's absolutely stunning."

Emotion was pulling heavily on Harry's voice as the words poured out of him; he then leaned his head on the top of Jays, trying to find comfort in her presence.

"Thank you, but it wasn't just my idea. The photos were Louis's touch."

"Really?"

"Yeah, for whatever reason, when I got back on Saturday, he was super engaged with all of us. You know he hasn't helped decorate the house since Richard passed?"

"He changed after that, but I think that he's maybe coming back around."

"Me too. it's nice."
Harry and Jay stay in the room looking at all the pictures hung on the tree, pictures ranging from little Phoebe and Daisy, Louis ranging from a newborn to present day, Jay and Richard and kids and photos from their dates and wedding all hung telling the story of their family. Periodically pictures containing Harry were also hung in the tree. After all, he indeed was an honorary Tomlinson. Soon enough, a clatter of footsteps flooded into Harry's ears, short after Daisy's voice came bouncing down the hall as she entered the room with Phoebe just on her tail.

"Mommy, it's snowing! Can we go make snow angels?"

As soon as the girls fully entered and saw Harry standing beside their mother looking at the Christmas tree, a whole new wave of excitement covered their petite bodies.

"Harry!"
Both girls ran up to Harry and jumped into his arms, giving him a hug once perched in his arms. With the girls in his arms, Harry turned back to the tree. Initially he was just going to point out some photos of them, but before he could speak, Phoebe stole the show.

"Wait, that one!" she exclaimed excitedly. Harry stopped and followed the trail of her finger. Harry's heart melted as he saw the photo, a picture of Mr. Tomlinson sitting by a window with a mug in his hand and a huge smile plastered across his face.

"That's our favorite photo of daddy!"
Harry smiled to push back the glimmer of tears that arose in his eyes. The girls didn't know that the photo they were looking at was the moment Jay had told

Richard she was pregnant again; the broad smile on his lips was because of them.

"That is a beautiful photo."

Harry and the girls took another moment to look at the photo before Harry's phone emitted a roaring noise prompting him to set down the girls and pulled out his phone to see the reason behind the horrible noise.
A blizzard warning illuminated on his screen. Road closures and stay inside orders read beneath them for the next few hours.

"I'm sorry, girls but I don't think you'll get to make snow angels tonight. We're under a blizzard warning, no going outside."

"A blizzard?"

"Yeah, it just means that it's a really, really big snowstorm."

"Does that mean that there will still be snow tomorrow?"

" It's highly likely. I would say you could probably make snow angels then. Until then it's time to stay warm."

"Oh, like hot chocolate and cookies?"

"We might be able to make that happen?"
The girls then ran out of the room to go look out the large window in the kitchen to see the swirling of snow outside. Jay and Harry smiled while following them, and boy when they saw the white haze outside that they truly understood the precaution placed around the storm.

"Hey girls, what do you think of some soup for dinner!"

"Tomato soup and grilled cheese?"

"If that's what you want."

"Thank you!"

Jay smiled and went to the pantry to grab the necessities for the meal. Harry joined her in the kitchen, leaning on the island talking to her as she did so. Harry gawked at the massive container of tomato soup that Jay had begun pouring into a massive pot on the stove.

"Wow, are you feeding an army tonight?" Harry laughed.

" Do you think six people qualify as an army?" Harry's face morphed into a confused look, trying to figure out who the sixth person was, even with him now staying for dinner that only made five. Realizing that Harry was clearly missing some information, she cleared up his confusion.

"Ronnie is over as well. I think this is actually the first time she's having dinner with us after what, four years now?"

"Oh. Has she never had dinner here before?"

"Nope, not once, normally Louis picks her up for things, or when she is over, she's never downstairs with everyone, even if Louis is."

"Wow. Do you by chance have a salad in your fridge?"

"I'm sure I do. Why?"

"Well, I'm not too sure on Ronnie's dinner habits, but I have never seen her eat anything besides a salad, even for breakfast, so I would say it's a safe bet to make one just in case delicious food isn't her thing."

"Oh, I suppose there is no harm in adding a salad to the mix."

"Here, I'll make it while you stick to the yummy food."

"Harry, you are the guest here!"

"A guest who loves to be helpful!"

Jay just smiled and got back to preparing the cheese sandwiches, knowing that she wouldn't be able to stop Harry from helping her. Pretty soon, the soup had begun to simmer, and five grilled cheeses had been made, Harry told Jay not to make the sixth until she got confirmation from Ronnie that she would actually eat it, and Jay had the twins go upstairs and grab Louis and Ronnie for dinner.

Harry brought down the soup bowls that were sitting high in the kitchen cupboard and brought them to the dining table once Jay had ladled some soup into them. Each bowl sat on top of a white plate underneath to catch any spills that might occur; it also served as a place to put the sandwiches which had been cut in half diagonally. In perfect timing, all the kids walked into the kitchen, Phoebe and Daisy first followed by Louis and Ronnie. Harry immediately knew that something was wrong with Ronnie; she emitted an eviler feeling than usual, and it scared him. Jay sensed it as well and proceeded to ask Ronnie with great caution.

"So, Ronnie, there is tomato soup and grilled cheeses if you want some, but we also have a salad if you prefer that instead."

Without looking up from her phone and an emotionless look glazed over her face, all responded with "I'll take the salad." and sat down at the only chair without a soup bowl.

Jay and Harry exchanged concerned and confused looks; Louis added into the silent conversation with a look of apology in his eyes. Everybody except Ronnie washed their hands; she didn't get the memo apparently and went back to the table. Louis carried the already prepared bowl of salad and placed it in front of Ronnie.

Louis decided it would be in Everyone's best intention to try and start the conversation since Ronnie was the apparent reason for the tension congestion in the room.

"So uh, I didn't know you were coming over today, Harry."

"Yeah, I just came by to drop some things off, and then the whole blizzard thing happened, and now I'm here."

"Yeah, that blizzard really came out of nowhere."
"It really did."

"Harry said that he might be able to make snow angels tomorrow!"

"I bet you will be able to. You might even be able to build a snowman at the rate it's snowing out there."

"Just like Elsa!"

"exactly, just like Elsa."

Suddenly Ronnie dropped her phone on the table, causing ripples to move through everybody's soup, and her hand gripped her temple, and her entire face began to cover in a light red color.

"Ronnie, are you okay."

You would have thought that something serious was wrong at the sudden change like a sudden strike of pain in her head or wave of nausea had passed through her. She inhaled deeply before responding to Louis as everyone else held their breath.

"The photographer I hired to take our pictures for the dance tomorrow just canceled. She is in France and can't get a flight back in time because of the stupid snow."

Nobody really knew what to do; they were thankful that it hadn't turned about to be a dire situation, but they didn't want to try and make the situation light again in fear of Ronnie freaking out on them.

"What about Harry?"

Ronnie's face turned from pure anger to evident confusion; the only thing she knew about Harry was that he watched the girls while she was out with Louis.

"What about Harry."

"Well, um, Harry here is an excellent photographer, especially with people. I'm sure he could take your photos, of course, if he isn't already completely booked."

"Yeah, no, I'm sure I could fit you in tomorrow. We just might have to meet at a location."

"If you want, we can show you some of his work, he did some amazing photos of the girl's last march."

"Yeah, babe, Harry would be a great option."

"I'll look at the photos, I'm trying to get in contact with my backup photographer, but she might be all booked up."

"Okay, once we finish dinner, we'll head upstairs."

The rest of dinner passed with everyone on edge except for the twins, who each brought laughter and topics of conversation among the group. Louis, Harry, and Jay all carried the empty dishes back into the kitchen before heading up the stairs with the rest of the girls. Everyone made their way into Phoebe and Daisy's light pink princess oasis of a room decorated with fairy lights and lace streamers outlining it. Hung on the main wall were the portraits of the girls as princesses. The girls went and stood under their respective photos and took the poses they held in the images.

Harry always forgot how much he loved the photos; they might be the favorite photos he has ever taken. Louis had never actually fully seen these photos; he saw the digital version but seeing them on a large canvas, he was truly in awe.

"So, you took these?"

"Yeah, a few months ago."

Ronnie examined the photos as silence fell upon the rest of the room. She also checked the status of her backup photographer, who indeed was all booked for the next day—taking one last glance at the photos, she made up her mind.

"You better make sure I'm a queen."

And with those words, she walked out of the room and down the stairs. Harry took that as a sign that he indeed would be adding Louis and Ronnie to his schedule for the next day.

Chapter Eleven:

Harry decided on just spending the night at the Tomlinson's even though the blizzard warning ended at midnight and the roads opened back up since his car was under about a foot of snow. Harry allowed himself to sleep late into the morning as he knew he had an extremely busy afternoon. Starting at 3:00 pm Harry was booked back-to-back for four hours taking Everyone's Winter Wonderland dance photos, he was kind of hoping since the blizzard happened last night that some people would cancel and just stay safe at home but that did not happen.

At eleven Harry rolled out of bed and headed to the kitchen to make some tea before heading back to his house to prepared for the day. With a cup of warm tea in his hands, he resumed his normal seat at the bay window. Far out in the backyard, he saw two shadows running around, after a minute of concentration he realized it was just Daisy and Phoebe playing in the snow, he smiled knowing that he would get to hear all about their adventures later on.

With one cup of tea down Harry poured himself another, this time being in a travel mug, and headed towards the door. Harry needed to get home in time to ensure he could go over all of the details of the afternoon, booking times, locations, and any needed props that he would have to bring along with him. Walking out to the car Harry sighed, his car was covered in snow and ice. There was no way he was going to be able to break his car free of the frozen icicles covering the windows and doors. He really should have just parked in the garage.

Harry walked back inside to grab an ice scraper and some hot water to free his car. Standing on the stairs was Louis all tousled with bed head eyes still hanging droopily from his slumber.

"Already back styles?"

"Is that a problem? I just came back to get some warm water and ice scraper. My car is currently an ice block."

"I did give you a garage opener, right?"

"Yeah, you did. Don't worry you're not losing your mind."

"So why didn't you park in there?"

"Well, I'm not sure if you remember but I was only supposed to be here for ten minutes but then a blizzard decided to come and my plans kind of changed."

"Oh right, that whole thing."

Harry laughed and went into the kitchen and put some water on the stove to heat before heading to the garage and looking through the copious amounts of drawers that were installed on the back wall. It wasn't until his elbow made contact with a pair of ribs that he realized Louis had followed him in.

"Oh god, I'm sorry I didn't know you were here."

"Don't worry it's my fault, but hey the ice scraper is in the winter things, not the potting soil."

"I guess that would make sense. Thanks."

Harry walked to the other end of the echoing garage while Louis stayed in his place with a half-smile and his hand placed on his ribs. Louis was surprised by the amount of force Harry had hit him with when it was just simply his arm moving back normally, it's not like he purposely tried to shove his elbow between his tiny ribs. He figured it was probably thanks to Harry's much larger stature, a good five inches taller than himself and well he did notice the sharp definition of muscles that now lined most of his body.

It was only a small ache but the small circles he was rubbing into the bone felt oddly soothing, almost as if someone else was taking care of him. Soon enough Harry found the ice scraper and headed back inside, he held the door calling to Louis to come back into the house.

This time Harry followed Louis to the kitchen until his long steps surpassed the much smaller ones Louis was taking now once again allowing Louis to follow Harry. Harry turned his attention to the pot on the stove which just began to simmer, he turned off the stove and put on some oven it's and laid out cork pot mats on the kitchen island.

"Dear God, you're like a cat."
The sight of Louis sitting on the counter kris crossed caught Harry off guard. Either Harry was completely deaf, or Louis literally had the ability to move without making a single sound.

"Okay?"

"You do realize you turn eighteen in three days and you are sitting the exact same way your sisters sit on the counter, right?"

"And what's so wrong with that!"

Harry just let out a low, deep chuckle before turning back around and grabbing the pot and placing it on the mats which sat next to Louis.

“How do you remember my birthday?"

"We were friends for like ten years you know."

"I know, I just didn't expect you to remember."
"Why?"

"I don't know I guess I kind of figured you wouldn't try to remember after we stopped hanging, besides, it seems like your life has been busy the last few years."
"Well yeah, but I also still come here at least once a week, it would be hard to forget."

Silence fluttered into the room, it was the comfortable kind that you crave, the kind that told you everything was okay. Harry began rummaging through the large utensil drawer before pulling out a turkey baster. He returned to the counter and grabbed the pot and made his way back to the front door, Louis still following his trail.

"If you're going to continue following me you better help me free my car."

"That was my plan."

Harry gave a side-eye look of speculation, as they entered the frigid outdoors. Louis walked closer to Harry who was still holding the pot of water which was giving a heat source. Sensing how cold he was himself Harry brought down the water closer to Louis because of him for some reason he thought it was a good idea to go outside in a t-shirt.

Once at the car Harry placed the pot on the ground and filled the turkey baster with hot water.

"Okay I know I'm not the smartest person on the planet but why the hell do you need a turkey baster?"

"Well unless I want to throw an entire pot of water on one little spot of Betsy and scorch her and leave the rest of her frozen, I use the turkey baster to drizzle the water one the ice that needs melting like the windows and door handles."

"Betsy. You named your car Betsy?"

"What? Does your car not have a name?"

"Why would I name my car?"

"Doesn't everybody name their car?"

"No, not everybody names their car."

"Just grab the ice scraper and push the snow off will ya?"

"Okay okay, I'm doing it!"

As Louis shoveled the snow off the hood and windshield of Harry's Car Harry was strategically dripping hot water on the door handles and doors of the car. Harry felt bad for sort of making Louis help him but then again, he did just follow him, so it wasn't like he was doing forced labor. Both boys were sneaking glances at each other, it was weird for them to be acting so friendly that it almost felt like they were back in the eighth grade. "Hey, thank you for taking such good care of Phoebe and Daisy, they really do love you."

"It's nothing, they're really great, it makes my job a lot easier. Besides in a way I guess I treat them like my own sisters."

"Well, you're definitely a better brother than me." Harry immediately stopped what he was doing and stood up to see Louis still pushing snow off his car across from him. Harry wouldn't call Louis the best brother in the world, but he saw the way he was with the girls when no one was looking when he wasn't with Ronnie. Harry knew that Louis was a good brother, it might be hidden from the majority of the world's population, but he saw it, he saw with his own eyes, he saw it in the way the girl's eyes would light up when they saw Louis or when they talked about him.

"Don't sell yourself short, you are still a good brother."

It came out a little defensively than Harry meant but he hated when people put themselves down and it really wasn't a lie. In all reality, Louis could have been a lot worse after everything he has been through, Harry has seen it with other people.

"Yeah, because a good brother's sisters will always talk about the guy that they spend every Friday with and not him."

"If you must know half of the time, they won't stop asking about you and they always tell me about you. They are very observant when it comes to you."

The silence that was once comforting was known as chilling as the wind blowing around them. Both boys went back to work, Harry now working much after then he had before suddenly just wanting to get out of the situation. He soon realized that he would be freeing his car for at least the next ten to fifteen minutes.

Because Harry really didn't like uncomfortable silences, he started thinking about all of the topics of conversation that would be easy enough to not cause another wave of silence. Soon it came to him.

"So, are you excited for the dance tonight?"

"Yeah, I guess so."

"You guess so?"

"Why do you sound so surprised? It's going to be the same dance as it was last year, and the year before, and the year before that, hell it might be the same as the first dance ever put on."

Louis chuckled, he really didn't see the big deal about dances like this, the only reason he has even ever attended one is that Ronnie always insisted they go because she wanted to. At first, it wasn't too hard but then again, he was just almost fifteen and nothing was really expected of him except to just show up and have his mom drive the two of them to the school. The pictures were just taken on a cellphone and details like Louis's tie didn't have to accent the proper shade of Ronnie's dress, a simple black and white tux worked just fine, but now anymore.

Every year it got worse; it began to be really taxing. Ronnie wanted Louis to get specific haircuts for the dance, so it looked pristine in pictures, the pictures now had to be professionally done as well as her hair and makeup. She would drag Louis along when she went dress shopping for hours upon hours and invited herself to his tux firing, this year completely changing it because it was too simple. They spent the next six hours afterward driving to three different malls just to find a tie that was the same color as her dress, it also had to be a complementary material and the pattern had to be plain but also exciting. Not to mention she now was so obsessed with the entire school knowing she was going with the most popular guy, the school's living legend himself Louis Tomlinson. Ronnie would stalk social media and come up with the most extreme and extravagant ways for Louis to ask her to the winter dance, but it was always worse for the spring formal. This year, for example, she ordered herself four hundred roses for the four years they had been together and created a whole scavenger hunt with a little clue card that was printed on photos for her with Louis and set it up during lunch hour so everyone could see. Don't get it wrong it was probably the cutest thing you have ever seen but Louis had no idea what was going on so when he walked into the cafeteria with everyone looking at him, he had no idea what was going on.

It wasn't until halfway through when he saw Ronnie walking towards him with a bin of roses that he realized what was happening. Louis was so thankful that he had a good poker face to hide his surprise. He wondered why Ronnie always had to have validation from everyone else, from people who didn't even know her or Louis. Wasn't it enough to just have him? Who cared who knew about it if they had each other, it really shouldn't, he should be enough? Right?

" I'm sure that not every dance is the exact same. Besides, don't you like spending time with Ronnie?"

"Have you ever been to one of the school dances?"

"No, they're not really my forte."

"So, what do you do then, just sit at home while everyone is out?"

"Didn't you just say that you don't like the dances either?"

The awkward silence had left once again, Louis was now completely relaxed and laughing at everything, Harry, however, was trying to figure out why Louis seemed so nonchalant about the dance, he always thought that he loved them.

"Besides it's one of the busiest nights for work so Cassie usually comes over and we watch movies while I edit the dance photos."

"So, you spend the entire night looking at everyone else's dance memories while binge-watching unrealistic events unfold on a tv screen with your best friend?"

"Well when you put it that way it sounds kinda lame, but I promise you it's a lot more fun. It's also a way to celebrate our friendiversary, besides, it's usually filled with snarky comments from Cassie, which always makes it interesting."

"Did you just say friendiversary?"

" Don't sound so weirded out, it's the anniversary of us becoming friends. always something to celebrate."

"Okay. I wouldn't doubt she makes some interesting remarks on the photos, she is a character. How long have you two been friends?"

"Just over four years now. She's great, but this year it's just me since Niall somehow managed to convince her to go to the dance with him. But that just means I get to make fun of her photos forever now!"

"I see someone is totally not salty about that..."

"Hey! I am not salty about it, I'm happy for her. She's finally found a nice guy and she deserves to have a fun night out."

"Okay then. Just promise me you won't be making fun of me in my photos while watching some ancient movie and I'll stop."

"I am not promising anything."

Harry raised his eyebrows and gave Louis a challenging look before bursting out into laughter. Louis couldn't help himself and fell victim to Harry's contagious laugh. Due to the cold air gripping tightly to the boy's lungs they soon fell silent again trying to allow a good breath to flow back into them.

"So have you seen Ronnie in her dress yet?"

Immediately tension rose from the melting ice frozen beneath their feet and Louis's face became glazed over with almost no emotion. His features became stiff and the light in his eyes faded away into greatness. Harry had never seen something so weird, clearly, he hit a nerve of some kind but all he asked was a simple question.

"Oh- no, I haven't the only thing I know is the color of the dress. As Ronnie would say, it's champagne pink."

"So, you have never even seen a picture of the dress?"

"No. Why?"

"It makes my job a little easier tonight."
Louis just looked at him in a suspicious gaze while Harry was pulling at the driver's side door handle, finally freeing it from the ice it had been frozen in. With Harry now being able to get into his car, he unlocked it before returning the turkey baster to the almost empty pot of water at his feet.

"Here I can take everything back inside. I know you need to get going."

"Are you sure?"

"Yeah, go ahead. Besides, I need to start getting ready anyway."

"Okay, uh thanks. I'll see you later. Six-o-clock downtown in case Ronnie hasn't reminded you already."
Harry laughed even though he knew he really shouldn't have but his shoulders relaxed when he saw Louis's lips curl slightly at the corner of his tiny mouth.

"Yeah, I bet when I go inside, I'll have forty missed calls and probably one hundred texts from her."

"Oh, and next time styles park in the garage even if it's just for five minutes.",

Louis turned around and hit the hood of Harry's car while carrying the pot and ice scraper in one hand and a chuckle still coursing through his body. Harry just shook his head with a tight smile on his own lips as he began to leave. Harry's hectic afternoon was only a few hours away.

Chapter Twelve:

To say that Harry was beginning to feel overwhelmed was an understatement. He hasn't sat down for more than five minutes in almost three hours. He knew that today was going to be the busiest day he has worked ever but he seriously underestimated.

Harry had booked photo shoots twenty minutes apart and only allowed them in three locations which were all within five minutes of each other in downtown London so he could have a breaker between clients and clear his mind so he could focus. Unfortunately, as soon as he would arrive at another appointment every person that was there immediately began wanting to take photos even though the session hadn't started yet. Not wanting to cause excess drama and stress everyone else's around him out, especially the girls he just went along with it.
It was now 5:58 and Harry was sitting in his car before walking over to the fountain at Buckingham Palace to meet Louis, Ronnie, and their families. Harry knew he only had to make it through this one last photo shoot before he could go home and it should be the easiest,

unlike the other photos he already knew exactly how to pose Louis and Ronnie, he knew which angles would look good with their features since he already knew them very well.

While pulling into the parking spot Harry already saw Ronnie standing with a lady who he assumed was her mother and a man that looked like her father, although he saw no signs of Louis anywhere. Harry hates to think about it but he was sort of relieved because that meant that he could sit in his car for another minute before getting out.

Harry shot a quick text to Louis and Jay in a group chat asking them to call him when they got here and not to immediately walk up and stay in their car and wait for him. Once the text was sent Harry got out of the car and walked up to Ronnie and her family. He introduced himself to the parents and took in the extravagance of Ronnie's dress, it was absolutely stunning, one of the most beautiful dresses Harry has ever seen. But he wouldn't have expected anything less from Veronica Cade.

The dress was certainly champagne pink, Louis certainly hadn't lied about that but the way it complimented her skin tone was perfection. The dress was all the same color but starting from the waist and working upward a floral pattern was embroidered delicately and rose up the two thin straps that hung off the edge of her shoulders. Simple pearls were seen in all the right places, the pearls on her dress matched the jewelry she wore. A necklace sat just under her collar bone while earrings dangled from her ears and rings sparkled on her fingers.

The neckline of the dress fell into a deep V-shape, a piece of skin-colored mesh had been sewed along the lower portion to keep it in the dress code. The skirt of the dress was the same color as the top, but the material was similar to silk, glitter sprinkled throughout the fabric allowed a small shiny aura to surround Ronnie. Her shoes were small silver stilettos, a simple strappy design covered her feet in fairy like fashion.

"You my dear are going to make my job so much easier. You look absolutely stunning; you truly look like a queen."

"Why thank you, I'm glad my work paid off."

Ronnie spoke in a surprisingly happy tone, there was no sign of her regular temper in her voice. If she always acted like this then maybe she wouldn't be so bad, Harry didn't know why she was nice. He thought maybe it was because her parents were here or maybe it was because she was being treated like royalty and not a normal human being. But whatever it was Harry was thankful. If he had to treat her like this for the next thirty minutes, he would happily hold back his sarcasm if it kept her this happy.

Harry could tell by the way Ronnie was looking at her phone every few seconds that she was starting to get upset about Louis's late arrival, he took this time to interject himself and explain the first photos so it would buy Louis some time and hopefully keep Ronnie happy.

"Hey, so I wanted to explain the first set of photos I'm going to take since Louis hasn't seen you in all of your majestic queenly beauty. I want to do a first look. For this, I want to keep you here standing on the last step at the base of the fountain and then bring in Louis while you close your eyes. Then once you hear his footsteps you can open your eyes again and it will be your reaction as well. These always turn out beautiful and I expect that you will have the best reaction coming from Louis."

" I actually like that idea. I think it's cute, but I've already seen Louis in his suit. I picked it out."

"Don't worry, remember he is all dolled up for you tonight. He will look even better than normal."

"You're right, okay. I'm sorry for Louis being late. I called him like every ten minutes to make sure he was getting ready on time, but he never picked up my calls."
It was perfect timing, as soon as Ronnie stopped talking Harry's phone began ringing with Louis's name appearing on the caller ID. He quickly answered it, telling them to stay in that and that he would be right there.

"Well, no need for anymore apologies Louis is here so I'm going to set you up then go and grab him, come with me."
Harry grabbed his camera from the bench he placed it on and gestured for Ronnie to follow him. He stood at the base of the stairs and held out his hand to help Ronnie up the small step. He turned her around a few times to find the best lighting and took a few reference photos. Once he found the perfect spot, he told her to close her eyes and stay still. He then jogged his way over to the parked car of Louis.

Once arriving he saw the whole family sitting in the car. Jay in the driver's seat, Louis in the passenger seat, and Phoebe and Daisy in the back seat. Jay had her window rolled down and Harry told everyone they could now get out of the car and began explaining his plan for the first look photo. He was loud enough for everyone to hear and Harry guided them to a spot opposite the fountain. When he turned around to see that indeed everyone had followed him, he lost his entire train of thought.

Louis was standing right beside him in an off-white suite that held a rosy undertone with a champagne pink tie hanging in between the two panels of his jacket. The golden hours glow fit his features in an ungodly way. The definition of his cheekbones created a perfectly symmetric face that could have belonged to a movie star. Louis's chestnut hair now glowed with golden and red hues as the sunlight filtered through each strand. And his eyes. His eyes illuminated like the ocean on a summer day and Harry was growing in the waves.

Harry snapped back into reality and immediately he felt his cheeks burn with embarrassment as the beat color rushed to the surface of his skin. He looked down at his camera to bring himself back to reality and focus on the task at hand. Capturing the adoring look that would be on Louis's face in just a few minutes as he looked at his beautiful girlfriend of four years.

Harry had enlisted the help of the twins to bring Louis to the location of the photoshoot. Harry sent Jay ahead of them to be with Ronnie's parents so they would see the arrival. Harry ran ahead of Louis and the twins standing in the middle of where the two would eventually meet.

As Louis came into view with a sister at each of his sides Harry began snapping pictures, they weren't so much for Ronnie or the Cades but for all the Tomlinson's. He could envision the picture blown up and hanging in one of the hallways or even maybe in the living room. When Louis had come into the proper position Harry moved back behind Ronnie, so she was in the corner of the frame and Louis was in the opposite corner.

Harry counted to three and told Louis to open his eyes. He saw Louis's eyes focus on Ronnie For a few moments before finally going wide. Harry began snapping photos and halfway through he started to see Louis's facial features begin to change but not in the way he normally saw. His features didn't soften adoringly then raise back up with excitement like every other guy he had taken these photos with, instead his features moved in sharp motion, almost as if they were calculated. Louis still looked happy and in awe to the naked eye but even through a lens, Harry could tell that something was not right with Louis.

When Louis got near the beginning of the steps, he told him to stop and told Ronnie to open her eyes. Her face did the exact same thing as Louis's face did, moved in calculated movements. None the less he took photos, adjusting the angles to add a little photographic magic. Harry captured the movements of Ronnie as she ran her hands down the front of Louis' suit jacket, smoothing out the material before looking up at Louis. Harry moved closer up and took a close up of the interaction.

"Okay absolutely lovely, now Louis tilt your head down just a smidge and lean it slightly on the top of Ronnie's forehead."

"Perfect."

Harry continued directing the two and taking photos. They did the classic dance pictures where Louis stood behind Ronnie and wrapped his arms around her waist but also played around with the scenery of the fountain by sitting on its edge and positioning the camera to make it look like they were under streams of water being emitted from the fountain.

Thirty minutes, hundreds of photos, and almost a full sunset later the photoshoot was officially done. Harry stood in the middle of all seven other people and did a short replay of the photos he had taken. He gave his normal speech for the twelfth time about how they should get an email with all of the photos and a form to fill out about the exact ones they wanted.

While Mr. and Mrs. Cade hugged their daughter goodbye away from the rest of the group Louis stayed with the rest of his family and Harry.

"So, I guess you're going to have a busy night Styles with all the photo stuff."

"Yeah, just me going through about three thousand photos while a Michael J. Fox movie marathon plays. But hey I wouldn't change, it's very relaxing."

"Sounds like a joy, I still think it would be funny to hear Cassie's comments on the photos."

"Oh, don't worry I'll probably drag her back after the dance, maybe Niall too and it will be a whole party."

"That might be a better afterparty than wherever I'm headed afterward."

"It's my favorite day of the year."

Everyone laughed as Ronnie came back to the group. She immediately went up and grabbed Louis's waist signaling she wanted to go. Everyone got the signal and wrapped up their conversations.

"Ronnie you truly look like a queen and Louis as always you clean up very nicely. I am extremely excited to look back over your photos so I'm going to go and finish my night's work. Don't boogie too hard at the dance."

Harry nodded towards the couple and then bent down to Phoebe and Daisy to give them a bear hug before giving a softer one to Jay. Soon everyone dispersed into three separate groups, the twins and Jay heading towards the line of taxis while Ronnie and Louis headed towards Louis tesla and Harry made his way back to his own car.

Harry put his camera in the passenger seat and tried to shake the image of Louis that has been inked into his memory since he saw him forty-five minutes ago. He knew that whenever he would close his eyes, he would see that face and create a portrait that would accent his face to perfection.

Harry droves home in complete silence, attempting to shake away the memories of Louis but it was utterly useless. When he got home, He turned on the tv and put in *For Love or Money* and sat down on the gigantic leather chair with a bag of chips, his computer, and his camera. Harry pressed play and for the movie and started downloading the photos to his computer.

The night was just beginning.

Chapter Thirteen:

It was now almost midnight and Harry were lost in the storyline of yet another movie, Doc Holliday. There was a bowl of popcorn with caramel drizzled on top along with m&m's sprinkled on top was sitting on the arm of his chair. After the first movie Harry changed into some pajamas, a pair of sweatpants and a hoodie with fuzzy socks covering his feet and grabbed a fluffy heated blanket to keep him warm and headed back to his chair. Harry has gone through almost all of his photos and organized them into files and are just about ready to send. He only had one more set of photos to go through, the one set that he wanted to go through the most but also the one set he knew would be the hardest to get through. Harry decided to take a break before starting the daunting tasks and set his computer to the side and curled up into the chair like a puppy.

As the movie illuminated the small living room Harry began drifting off into a formidable daze as he pulled at the edges of the blanket that he was encased in. Harry was thankful to be sheltered inside away from the chaos of the outside world. The wind was roaring like race cars outside causing the windows to emit a shaking rattle throughout the house. Posted all over social media were videos and photos of everyone at the dance, eventually, Harry just tossed his phone to the other side of the room. If he had to see another group of random teenagers dancing to some cheesy pop song, he was going to lose his mind.

Just as the credits began to roll up on the screen Harry saw the handle of his front door begin to twist back and forth causing Harry to jump up from his position on the chair and grab the metal bowl next to him. Harry kept the heated blanket over him, covering him from his shoulders down.

Standing on the very tip of his toes Harry moved stealthily forward with one hand clenched around the bowl and the other around the edges of his blanket. Harry shoved himself up against the wall of the hallway that connected to the living room so whoever was trying to break in wouldn't be able to see him in the windows that sat adjacent to the front door.

Harry had gotten nearly all the way to the front door, his body beginning to tremble with fear causing the leftover m&m's to rattle slightly against the metallic sides of the bowl. Trying to keep quiet he moved the bowl up against his stomach to try and keep it steady, just as he did the door handle stopped moving. It should have been a good thing; it should have been comforting. But it wasn't

Maybe they heard the rattling, maybe they are going to break through the window because they couldn't unlock the door. What if they heard the rattling and are now thinking of a way to kill Harry once they finally break-in? All of these thoughts caused Harry's breaths to grow rapidly and short causing his whole body to move with each exhale.

With his eyes still fixated on the door handle, Harry's heart dropped when the handle began shaking again. Harry took one more step towards the door now entering the line of fire for the intruder to see him. Harry raised the bowl bringing it to his chest just as the door handle moved all the way around and the door creaked open.

A foot appeared and stepped onto the wooden floors, immediately Harry threw the bowl and its contents at the person with an ear-piercing shriek of terror. Before the bowl had even hit the floor Harry was running back deeper into his house trying to find anything else to throw at whoever just entered his home. To his luck a cast-iron skillet had been left on the stove, Harry picked it up and reluctantly jogged back towards the front door.

The only thing keeping Harry moving and not turning into a statue of fear was the adrenaline that was coursing through his body. His brain no longer had control over his actions, all he could do was hope that his body knew what to do.

Harry raised the heavy pan up over his shoulder as he turned the corner. Suddenly he stopped like a deer caught in headlights. Standing in the middle of the entryway stood Cassie and Niall laughing surrounded by a mess of half-melted m&m's. After a few moments, the two noticed Harry's frozen presence and only began laughing even more.

A mixture of horror and relief was etched along every feature of Harry's face from the set of his jaw to the glaze covering his fairy green eyes. His chest rising and falling deeply trying to gather as much oxygen as he could, little droplets of sweat had appeared on his hairline as his body tried to come down from the adrenalin rush.

"Ha-Harry! I-I'm, I'm sorry."

Cassie could barely even speak through the fit of laughter that had taken over her.

"I tex-texted you."

"I- I haven't been on my phone."

Slowly Harry brought the pan down from over his shoulder and held it with two hands as he slowly was able to reestablish a sense of reality. Cassie had fallen into Niall's grip as they started to calm down and catch a breath of their own. With a blast of frozen air blowing down the hallway the three suddenly remembered that the door was still wide open. Niall was able to move his foot and shut the door.

Both Cassie and Niall shifted themselves towards Harry and looked down at the mess they were standing in. They then walked towards Harry who had turned to lean against the wall. Once they had caught up with him Harry pushed himself back up and they all began walking towards the living room.

"So out of everything you choose to throw twenty m&m's and an empty bowl at us thinking' we were intruders?"

"Okay, I still have a pan in my hand, so I suggest you quit laughing. Besides it all I had!"

"are you sure you don't want to throw some more m&m's instead?"

Niall and Cassie then took off running behind one of the couches for cover. They couldn't contain other laughter once again as Harry jumped on top of the couch and pretended to hit them with the pan hulk style. A minute later he helped them up and moved them this time, so they were actually sitting on the couch normally. Harry threw the bag of leftover m&m's at Niall who immediately opened the bag and poured some in his mouth.

"See if I threw m&m's at Niall and he was trying to rob me I would have totally stopped him!"

"But I would never rob a house, especially yours." Harry rolled his eyes and took a handful of the candy and plopped the pieces in his mouth before finally retaking his position back on the sizable chair.

"So how was the dance? Was it a winter wonderland?"

"Oh, quit being so sarcastic, would you! it was fine, a typical high school dance."

"Oh, like you know what a *typical high school* dance is like."

"Oh, but Niall sure does."

Niall's head shot up and the comment before a hefty smile appeared once he comprehended Cassie's words.

"It was just like every other dance, a bunch of people dancing to cheesy music just waiting for the actual thing to be over so they could go get hammered at an afterparty. That's what dances are really about, the afterparty. Nobody really cares about the actual thing. Well, maybe girls like Ronnie but they are the minority in that situation."

"Oh, trust me even with not going I still saw way too many people doing the macarena."

"Is that why your phone is stuck between these cushions?"

"Yep, that would be the reason why. It was either that or boil my eyes, but I quite like those so phones in the cushion it was."

"Oh, and you say I'm the dramatic one!"

"Well, I'm just glad I didn't miss much. But if everyone only goes to those things for the afterparties, why are you two sitting here on my couch?"

"Cassie told me about your guy's movie marathon tradition and about how she always impersonated the photos you had to sort through and there was no way I was missing out on more of that."

"Plus, I don't think that at any other afterparty we would have had m&m's thrown at us and created a fake robbery. So, I would say this is the best afterparty ever."

"Oh god, I'm never going to live that down, am I?"

"Nope, every year I'm now going to give you one hundred pounds of m&m's."

"Don't worry man I'll taste test them and make sure she didn't poison them."

"I'm going to have to buy you a grocery store aren't I Niall?"

"I wouldn't be opposed to that idea!"

"Can the two of you get any cuter!"

The words caused a matching blush to float over both Niall's and Cassie's cheeks. Harry knew that he had just saved himself about a half-hour of couple banter between the two, as much as he adored them, he knew his mind would begin to wander to a person he really didn't want to think about.

"So, are you done with the photos already?"

"Oh, ah just have one more set to go through actually but I think I was just going to do it tomorrow. They were a last-minute client so I told them it might take later to get them their photos."

"No way Harold we are going to go through them together! It's my favorite part, plus are you really going to deny Niall of my amazing commentary?"

"One day I'm just going to get a stay bottle and spray you like a cat anytime you use a nickname, maybe that will teach you!"

Harry thought for a second on just refusing to go through the photos and taking the idiotic comment she knew he would receive. But then he remembered that Cassie knew the password to his computer and if she really wanted to go through the photos, he knew she wouldn't hesitate to log in herself and if she did, he knew he wouldn't question why he put up a fight of not going through the photos of Ronnie and Louis. and Harry couldn't lie, at least not like that, he couldn't lie to Cassie and he couldn't lie about his emotions. So, Harry went with what he deemed the smarter decision and caved, cleaning over the chair and grabbing his computer before moving to the middle of the couch in between Cassie and Niall so they could see.

"Okay before I pull these up, I know I usually give you free rein on whatever you say because I won't ever tell anyone but please just don't go overboard with these ones please."

Immediately Harry knew he already almost gave himself away, he felt his cheeks warm up as the light from his computer acted like a spotlight on his face. Harry just hoped that Niall and Cassie wouldn't read into his words so much.

"Uhm, okay that's fair, I guess. So, who is it?"

"It's Ronnie and Louis."

"OMG, you're kidding! Why did you not tell me you had to photograph the devil tonight, I would have brought you some holy water."

Cassie was laughing, normally Harry would be laughing too but now he felt guilty. It wasn't because Ronnie was secretly a nice person but because Louis was with her and he wanted to pretend that Louis was with someone who deserved him, someone who could bring out the happy and easygoing Louis, and Ronnie just wasn't that.

"Cassie"

"Gez I'm sorry, I promise no more remarks like that."

"Thank you."

Harry finally pulled up the file that contained the last of his photos and put them on full screen.

"Don't mind these ones, they were just for references for a first look."

"They did a first look?"

"Yeah, Louis hadn't even seen her dress before."

"I would have bet that Ronnie would have brought Louis along on her dress shopping extravaganza but hey it's nice to have surprises."

Harry continued to use the little arrow keys at the bottom of the keyboard to move through all the prep photos he had done. He considered skipping the ones with the twins, but he determined that they were just way too cute to pass up so when he got to those, he stopped for a few seconds on each photo instead of skipping over them at lighting speed.

"Awe, those are cute. I didn't think the twins would have been there."

"Yeah, I really wasn't either, but it was kind of like they were there either, they started off with Jay for the majority of the time."

"Makes sense though, you were working though."

"Yeah"

Niall had begun to notice that the rosy tint on Harry's cheeks hadn't faded away but instead grew into a deeper shade. He also noticed how Louis wasn't taking his eyes off of the computer to look at either of them. Niall noticed the soft crinkling between Harry's eyes as he looked at each photo. Niall knew in the pit of his gut that something was up.

When Harry got to the first look photos of Louis he slowed down even more, once again his heart began to beat faster and his breath ever so slightly picked up.

Harry tried with every ounce of him to control his body, to keep covering cool. As soon as Harry realized he had started staring he immediately went to the next photos. Harry rushed through the photos that were only Louis so he wouldn't get lost in them. Once he finally reached the photos of Ronnie, he let out a sigh of relief which he didn't know he was holding in. When Harry went to look at the photo won't he came to a trailing halt, he realized that he had taken over 150 photos of just Louis. it was worse than he thought.

Once the photos of Ronnie came on the screen, he could see Cassie get up from her spot on the couch and move the center of the room. He knew what was coming, Cassie was going to recreate the photo. It was never really to make fun of the original but rather to mock Harry for always having to recreate old paintings.

"Harry aren't I the perfect person to recreate it. I'm just radiating beauty!"

"I wouldn't have any other person recreate it Cas!"

Cassie came back over and sat on the couch. Niall was still studying Harry trying to get complete confirmation of his theory."

"Oh, Niall recreate this one with me!"

Both figures got up off the couch and went to the center of the room. It was the most basic photo that they were repeating, you know the one with the guy's hands around the girl's waist from behind. Everyone's parents had taken photos like that back in the '80s and '90s and now it was just used kind of as a joke.

"See we are so much better than them!"

"I agree but I wouldn't mess with a class like that. Which reminds me. Why did you let me take your guy's photos?"

"Hey! Niall and I are much better than whatever Ronnie and Louis have, much better than that *classic* shot! Besides having two photos of me in a dress is enough, the last thing I need is an entire photo album."

"What if Niall wanted a photo album to commemorate tonight?"

"Hey, you leave me out of this, I got her to go to the dance. I'm perfectly happy if he doesn't want a photoshoot!"

"OMG do you two have too literally be perfect for each other?"

"Yeah, that's how it works!"

Harry shook his head and returned his eyes to the photo displayed on his computer screen. As he stared at the photo Cassie's words just kept replaying in his head *Niall and I are much better than whatever Ronnie and Louis have.* Looking at the way Louis looked to have a thing glaze plastered through his eye and how Ronnie's eyes had been searching for something, he knew that she was right. Whatever they had was real compared to whatever he was looking at.

The thought made Harry's heart break into little shards causing splintering pain in his chest. Louis deserved better. He deserved better than someone who was chasing perfection, he deserved someone real whoever that maybe. Harry really didn't want to continue looking through the photos, he was scared that if he did, he might say or do something he'll regret later.

"Are you good with your little game now."
Harry put a laugh after the words to help them sound less harsh, he hadn't meant to seem agitated but there was no way he could hide all of it."

"Awe so soon?"

"I just don't really have the energy to properly go through them right now, how about a movie instead?"

"Okay, that'll work. I'm just going to go upstairs and change really quick."

Cassie always kept a spare pair of pajamas at Harry's because she never one when they would have an impromptu sleepover and she much prefers to sleep in her own clothes then borrowing Harry's.

"Cool, thanks, and BTW it's a Michael J Fox night so think of what you want to watch!"

With Cassie having fully disappeared up the staircase Niall Came and sat down next to Harry on the couch.

"Hey, I know it's not really my place, but you seemed pretty intrigued with those photos in the beginning."

"They were good photos."

"They were good. But you think that part of the reason that they were so good was that the subject was easy on your eyes?"

"Well, all photos are better when the subject looks good."

"Harry."

"Niall."

The two now had their eyes locked tightly on each other. Niall knew that if he won, he had his answer, and it didn't take long for him to receive it. In less than ten seconds Harry looked away with his cheeks burning so hot that even Niall could feel the warmth.

"I knew it!"

"You can' tell anyone, not even Cassie. I'll be dead if you do. Then I'll come back and haunt you for the rest of your life."

"Don't worry I won't. Now I know why you always watch the twins."

"Louis is just a benefit of watching them."

"Yeah sure."

"OMG, what did I get myself into."

Chapter Fourteen:

Three days have passed since the dance meaning it was now December 24th, to many people it was just Christmas eve but to Tomlinson's and the Styles they also knew it as Louis's birthday.

Harry woke up wrapped in his pile of blankets, a comfortable warmth of the holiday season spreading throughout his body. The sunlight filtered through the curtains allowing a steady stream of light to infiltrate the room. The heat of the light contradicted the frozen snowflakes sitting on the window beside Harry's bed. Harry rolled over in his cocoon of blankets now facing the light, small particles of dust floating in the air played out like a snow globe.

A gentle knock bounced off the wooden door leading into Harry's room followed by small footsteps. Soon Harry saw the figure of his mother, Anne, standing by his nightstand with a ug in her hands.

"Good morning Harry, you're sleeping late today."

"m-good morning mom. What time is it?"

"It's just past eleven."

"Oh wow."

Harry sat up a little bit more now leaning on his elbows while looking around his room trying to wake up. It wasn't long until he realized that his mom was dressed in her scrubs and his face began to falter.

"I thought you had today off?"

Anne made her way to sit on the edge of Harry's bed while setting the mug full of tea down on his nightstand. She took one of her hands and began to smooth out the ruffled curls that ran wilds on top of her son's hands.

"I know baby I was supposed too but-"

"But."

Anne let out a melancholy sigh that matched her heartbroken tone, she hated having to always leave Harry by himself so often, especially on holidays.

"But the hospital got thirty patient transfers last night and they need the extra staff. I'm sorry baby."

Harry's body deflated deeper into his sheets and allowed the small circles on top of his head to help bring calmness back into his body. He never wanted to act in a way that made his mom worry about him or feel bad about working so much, he knew she didn't really have another choice and he was grateful that she did so much for him. It also made Harry feel better that he knew his mom was helping so many other people, he knew about the people's lives she helped save and the families she helped take care of. Harry one that by not being with him today that she was helping save so many other families from a terrible holiday.

"I made you some tea if you want it."

"Thanks"

Harry gave an amiable smile with the corner of his lips and sat up all the way now leaning against the wood of his headboard. While reaching for the mug she set down a few minutes before Anne noticed the manila folder sitting next to the lamp on Harry's nightstand.

"What's in here?"

"Oh, those are just some photos I took Saturday."

"Can I look at them?"

"Yeah, go ahead."

Harry was still in his morning fog and hadn't remembered whose photos were in the folder and if he did, he certainly wouldn't have allowed his mom to look inside. What made the situation even worse was the fact that Harry has never once printed the photos he has taken, he has always sent them digitally. The worst part is Harry had no idea why he decided to print out the 500 photos he had taken of Louis and Ronnie, well to be fair the ones he printed were mainly of Louis which only made the situation worse.

"Oh, these are of Louis!"

"Awe, the girls are so big now!"

"Wow, he looks really good in these."

"Hey, isn't it his birthday today?"

Harry had turned his body slightly away from his mother and glued his eyes on the foot of his bed while taking sips of his tea in hopes of the mug concealing the war of emotions fighting over his face. Fondness, embarrassment, and fear all traded places on Harry's features as his mom turned back to him. It finally registered to him that his mom had asked him a question.

"Hm?"

"Isn't it Louis's birthday today?"

"Oh, yeah it is."

"Wow that crazy to think that he's eighteen now I remember when y'all were just little three-year-old!" The mood in the room was extremely uncomfortable. Anne and Harry had never really talked about the falling out of his and Louis's friendship. Anne knew that losing Richard was hard enough for Harry and she didn't want to pressure him about why she stopped hearing about Louis, she figured that because Harry still went over and watched Phoebe and Daisy that he was okay.

"Maybe you could head over there today, I'm sure everyone would be happy to see you. You could also bring them the photos."

"Yeah, maybe."

"Well, these are amazing, I still can't believe how talented you are."

Anne closed the folder and placed back onto the nightstand and turned back to Harry and gave him a kiss on the forehead before standing up. She checked her watch and let out another sigh, her eyes matching the sad tone in her voice.

"I hate to do this, but I have to go."

"Go save some lives."

Harry gave her a soft smile that helped Anne feel better about leaving Harry alone. As she walked out the door, she noticed Harry's Eyes had become locked on the folder she just set down, her mother's instincts began to flutter but she thought that he was contemplating whether or not he was just going to stay home or go to the Tomlinson's.

Now left alone in his room once again Harry flopped back down in his bed continuing to look out the window. For a long time, Harry just let his brain wander away from the world and didn't think much of anything. Harry was really trying to soak up every moment of relaxation of his winter break as he could and to him, that meant not clouding his brain with the thoughts of Louis. At some point, Harry had drifted back to sleep. Finally, his body just couldn't sleep for any longer and woke up to the soft splatter of raindrops colliding with his window. It took quite a long time for Harry to finally get up and out from under his covers when he walked across his room to go to his closet his eyes caught the corner of the folder once again. Even while changing into a pair of jeans and a sweater his eyes never left the yellow tint. Harry went over to the nightstand and grabbed his phone, before checking it he ran his soft fingertips over the smooth folder contemplating whether or not to just open it and look at the photos, he wanted too so bad. He wanted to see Louis' crystal eyes and caramel hair glowing in the light of a sunset and his angelic cheekbones, but his brain knew better. Reluctantly Harry pulled his hand off of the folder, grabbed his phone, and walked out to the kitchen.

Sitting on the couch with yet another cup of tea the television was playing in front of his eyes.

The sound effects of *A Christmas Story* helped ease the emptiness of the house, but soon the story began to remind Harry of the very thing he was trying to forget, a family filled holiday and unfortunately Louis. The entity of the character Ralphie completely reminded him of Louis, while his eyes weren't as blue as Louis's, and his hair was blonder than Louis's has ever been even when he was little his actions followed Louis to a t.

The mischievousness of Ralphie matched perfectly with Louis, well not so much anymore but rather when he and Harry had still been friends. They wore the same smirk across their faces. Suddenly Harry's head began to fill with almost every memory he had of Louis, a majority of them being the small little pranks Louis would pull on people. They were always kind of small and ended up being more annoying than anything because even with as funny as real pranks sounded to him Louis could never think of possibly hurting or scaring somebody with a prank.

Harry remembered the time the both of them sprayed Richard and Jay with silly string when they came inside the house from the backyard and the time when Louis started randomly dropping water balloons outside the window of his dad's home office, even the time when he added hot sauce to Jay's biscuits when she wasn't looking. Harry could see the wide smile and shining eyes that used to be so common of Louis's face, he never realized how much he had taken that look of pure happiness on Louis's face for granted.

Before he knew what he was doing Harry had already sent a text to Jay asking if he could come over. When his phone emitted a soft ding Harry's entire body stiffened, with the words, *of course, you know you are welcome over anytime you want!* glowing on his screen he slowly stood up and grabbed his tea mug before heading over to the kitchen.

"Oh God, what have I done?"

Harry was expecting to have a Louis detox over the next two weeks before going back to his regular schedule of seeing him in the halls and the ten minutes he did every Friday afterward, he needed it. If he didn't see Louis, then maybe his brain would quite imagine him at every waking second of the day.

Harry knew he was definitely going to have to go over to the Tomlinson's now, if he made up some excuse not to like being sick, he would have a knock on the front door in thirty minutes. He sent off one last text saying he'll be over soon before heading back up to his room. The first thing Harry did was grab some thick knitted socks and a pair of winter boots as well as his jacket. Once Harry had his shoes on, he walked over to his desk and grabbed the folder of photos with one hand and his jacket in the other. If he was going over to the Tomlinson's, he might as well bring the photos anyway. It took aloof about five minutes and Harry was back downstairs with his car keys jumbled in his hands.

Even just walking out into the small garage his body filled with chilled goosebumps, he realized it was probably a better idea to just set his things down on a counter and put his jacket on inside rather than waiting to do it in here. Quickly he unlocked his car and dropped the folder and his keys onto the driver's seat and put on his fleece-lined jacket. The denim that laid on top added a certain flair to the otherwise soft outfit he had on underneath. Harry took a second to appreciate the newfound warmth the jacket brought him. He moved the teams from the driver's seat and tossed them to the passenger seat since no one would be sitting there. Just after leaving his neighborhood Harry's stomach let out a low grumble similar to the sound of gears turning and he realized he hadn't eaten anything yet today, all that was sitting in his stomach, or rather swimming was four cups of herbal tea. Harry checked the time, 4:37, he did a double take as he didn't realize it was already so late in the day. A McDonalds came into view as he turned off of the street he was driving on and in a desperate hurray he pulled into the drive-through and ordered himself some food.

Harry decided to eat his cheeseburger and French fries in his car while parked in the parking lot, one because it was safer than driving and eating, and two because he didn't want to bring it into the Tomlinson's house. In seven minutes, all of the food was gone, Harry's stomach was happily full, and he was more awake now that his body had a source of energy rather than just caffeine. He turned on the radio and officially began the drive.

After pulling through the gate Harry started to have the mental debate of whether or not to park in the garage, it just still didn't feel right but after remembering the fiasco of his car becoming an ice block the other day and seeing that the clouds above looked like they were around to start dropping snow any minute he decided it was best to just park in the garage. Harry felt the need to text someone, either Jay or Louis, that he was going to park in the garage so they wouldn't freak out, but he also knew that they always got an alert when someone pulled through the gate and since they already knew Harry was coming over, he thought he should be okay.

It felt weird, almost like he was breaking some unforeseen rule. Harry sat in front of the massive white metal door situated at the back of the house still unsure about his decision, not once had he even driven back here, he had been in the garage multiple times and knew the layout like the back of his hand but actually having the ability to open it and drive his car inside just felt off. He had to keep reminding himself that Louis had given him permission to use the garage and actually encouraged him to use it.

As if it was an act of bravery Harry pushed the button on the garage opener having onto the visor of his passenger seat and pulled into the large open garage. Harry parked his car in between Louis and Jay's car. Not wanting to back out of his actions Harry immediately grabbed the folder of photos, turned off his car and got out. Once arriving at the door that led to the actual entrance into the main part of the house Harry stopped and contemplated whether or not he should knock on the door or not before walking in but when he remembers that he never knocked when he entered, he decided to just walk inside.

Walking through the long hallway that led to the kitchen the worry and fear that he felt all morning began to wash away, as silly as it was this house almost felt more like home than his actual one. Harry could smell the cinnamon of apple pie and the herbs that were seasoning the turkey that was in the oven. The smell of fresh pine swirled into the mixture as well allowing Harry to finally melt into the feeling of Christmas.

Jay was the only one in the kitchen leaving her to be the first one to see Harry. She stopped her cooking and wiped her hands on her sparkly red apron before waddling her way up to Harry and giving him a hug.

"Ah, you made it! I was begging to think you9 got stuck in the snow."

"No, although that would have made for a great story! I stopped to get some food on my way over."

"I hope you didn't spoil your appetite for my Christmas dinner!"

"I could never miss out on such an amazing meal, even if it meant my stomach would burst, I would eat all of it!"

"Have I told you how much I love you?"

"Many times!"

Both Jay and Harry were laughing, they walked back into the kitchen Harry cleaning against one of the many counters, and Jay resumed her place at the stove stirring a pot of homemade cranberry sauce.

"So how does it feel to be the mother of an adult now?"

"I don't even want to think of my Louis as an adult, he will forever be my baby boy. Although judging by the amount of food he ate this morning he kind of counteracts that."

"Did you make your famous birthday buffet?"

"You bet, I had the works french toast, pancakes, hash browns, fruit, sausages. Oh, you should've been there, it was so good!"

"Just the thought of all of that makes me feel hungry and I just ate!"

"Get this Louis ate over half of it just by himself! I knew he had an appetite during football season, but I guess being eighteen made him eat like he's bigfoot!"

"He may be small, but he definitely doesn't act like it!"

Jay was trying to keep a straight face, but she knew that Harry was right and soon enough he burst into laughter right alongside him. With the commotion, they were causing they hadn't heard the back door open followed by multiple sets of footsteps. It wasn't until Phoebe, Daisy, and Louis were standing beside them.

“Did Harry finally make a good knock-knock joke?"

Sarcasm was radiating from every inch of Louis, from the squint in his eyes, the slight life of only one corner of his mount, the pitch of his voice, and Harry knew it.

"Oh, don't be jealous that you missed it!"

Harry hadn't even realized that he had picked up the girls until he felt the iciness that had appeared on his cheeks.

"Wow, you two are freezing, what are you doing?"

"We were building snowmen!"

"How did I not know that! How many did you make?"

"We made six!"

"Six! wow, that's impressive!"

"There's one for me, Daisy, Louis, Mummy, and Daddy, and you!"

"That's incredible!"

"We even took a photo of all of them, Louis can you show him?"

Louis walked over with his phone in hand and had to lean slightly into Harry's chest to show him the photos since both his sides were being occupied by his sisters, but he wasn't complaining the warmth that was radiating off of Harry was comforting.

"I think you may have two sculptors on your hands here Jay!"

"Well, technically they are on your hands right now!"

Everyone laughed and Louis began to slowly move away from Harry, he suddenly missed the proactive presence that Harry had. Harry hadn't realized how much he loved having Louis be so close to him, it wasn't until he wasn't there anymore that he loved the way Louis was able to stand so close to him that he could've rested his chin on top of his head or listened to the steadiness of his heartbeat. The thought caused Harry's cheeks to fade into a light shade of pink and when the twins saw they gave each other a high-five and giggled.

"And what are you two so happy about?"

"Nothing!"

The unison in their words altered Harry that they definitely were up to something, but that something he just didn't know.

"Hey, why don't you all go change into some warm clothes before you get sick then all of you can play games or watch a movie until dinner is ready."

The girls began to squirm, signaling to Harry they happily complied with their mother's statement so these them backed down and as soon as their feet hit the tiles they began running to the stairs. Louis was a bit slower, as he turned around to exit, he grabbed onto the counter when his hand brushed the unfamiliar texture.

"Hey what's this?"

Harry's panic alarm was ringing high in his ears, without even looking he knew what Louis was referring to, it was the photos. Jay put down her spoon and turned around looking at the folder with a confused look as well.

"Oh, those are some of your photos, they are all the ones of just you along with the ones with Phoebe and Daisy. You can look at them."

Jay walked right up behind Louis as he opened the folder to reveal the glossy photos that lay inside. They each began to grab photos and show each other, their smiles continued to grow with each new one they saw. This was a moment that Harry hardly got to see, people's reactions to his work. He always got an email stating how much they loved the photos, but he never got to see the first reactions and to him it was priceless.

"These are amazing Harry!"

"Well, you made my job easy, you came prepared." Harry added laughter at the end to try and hide the embarrassment of what he just said, thankfully though Louis had been too busy still sifting through the photos to comprehend his comment. All of a sudden, a sizzling noise price through the kitchen and everyone's eyes travel to the stove at lightning speed to see the cranberry sauce boiling over the edge of the pot.

"Oh, the cranberry sauce!"

Jay ran over to the stove and turned down the heat while stirring the mixture to help reduce the number of bubbles. Harry and Louis just looked at each other and laughed quietly.

"So is your mom working today?"

"Yeah, she got called in this morning, the hospital had a lot of transfers overnight and needed the extra staff."

"I'm sorry."

"Eh it's okay, she's making sure nobody has to lose anyone today. It's good work."

"You are right. Hey, why don't you spend Christmas here? When your mom gets off of work, she comes over too."

"Oh, I don't know I don't want to intrude on your holidays."

"Oh, Harry please you're not intruding, you know that. Come on it can be like old times?"

Harry heard the uncertainty in Louis's voice, it wasn't the kind that was like he was afraid of Harry staying but rather the kind that told him that Louis was nervous about asking because after all, he knew that he was the reason the tradition stopped in the first place and Harry had every right to deny the request.

Harry began to weigh his options, but he didn't get very far before Jay came running over with a big holiday smile across her face.

"Awe it can be like one last Christmas as kids before you two go off to college!"

Harry's eyes shot back and forth between Jay and Louis trying to make his decision, the thought of spending Christmas with them and the twins really was appealing but it also made him feel scared. If he became even closer with them then they had the opportunity to leave again, not so many Jay, Phoebe, and Daisy but Louis. But Harry knew that the holidays were about spending time with the people you love and that made the decision clear.

"Yeah okay, I'll text my mom."

Jay pulled the three of them into a group hug and started singing let it snow before dancing her way back to the stove to make sure nothing else was going to boil over. Louis gave Harry a smile of relief.

"It's going to be fun to do this again."

"Yeah, it will. Thank you."

"Of course, you are just as much a part of the family as I am. Uh-um I'm going to go change and check on the girls. You better not change your mind when I get back!"

“I won't. oh, and Tomlinson. Happy birthday."
Louis turned around and his entire demeanor softened at the words, Harry was the first person outside of his biological family to wish him a happy birthday, none of his friends had texted or called, Ronnie hadn't been in touch with him since the dance on Saturday and just hearing those two words made a whole lot better.

"Thanks, Styles."

Chapter Fifteen:

While Louis, Daisy, and Phoebe were upstairs changing, Harry went back into the kitchen to continue talking with Jay. He began to feel the heat that was being emanated from the kitchen appliances and had small pellets of sweat begin to form on the surface of his skin. No longer needing the warm fleece covering his upper body Harry pulled off the jacket and hung it up in the coat closet that was located in the hallway leading to the garage.

Harry had turned on the Christmas radio on his phone allowing the sound of winter bells and piano notes to surround the room. Outside the windows, white flurries started dancing around seemingly in beat with the music inside. Harry began to dance softly around the kitchen grabbing some mugs, milk, and hot cocoa powder. Grabbing another pot from one of the many kitchen drawers, Harry headed over to the second stovetop located at the backend of the kitchen. Harry poured half of the gallon of milk into the pot and turned on the heat. With a few more twists and turns of his body matching the rhythm of the jingle bells, a soft simmer began to form where the milk met the stainless steel of the pot. Almost as if on cue little footsteps came rushing near him.

"What are you making?"

"A Christmas classic, hot chocolate!"

"Can we help!"

"Sure, you can each add in a scoop of the mix."

"Yay!"

Harry quickly got a measuring cup out of the cabinet in front of him before taking the lid off the container of the sugary, sweet-smelling, chocolate powder. Harry then picked up Daisy in one arm and Phoebe in the other.

"Okay, so each of you can pour one scoop in, just dip it in the container until this is full. Then gently and I mean gently pour it into the pot."

Both girls nodded, Daisy took the measuring cup out of Harry's hand and did as she was told, and Phoebe followed suit. Just as Harry set the girls down and began reaching for a spoon to stir the mixture another set of footsteps grew, this time being heavier than the last. Harry turned his head only to see the ocean waves of Louis's eyes.

Harry kept the contact for a fraction of a second, there was just something hidden beneath the surface of Louis's eyes that had a hook-on Harry though he couldn't quite figure out what it was. The instant returned his eyes back to the stove in front of him he wished he hadn't.

"Whatcha making over here? It smells good!"

"Why thank you, it's hot chocolate!"

"Oh, I can help!"

"You're just like your sisters Tomlinson!"

Harry gave a quick side-eye complemented by a soft laugh and the tiny back and forth movements of his head.

"You can pour another scoop of the mix in; both the girls already did one though so it might be kind of strong."

"What's so wrong a little extra sugar? It's Christmas!"

"And your birthday!" the twins chimed in.

"Well then, be my guest birthday boy!"

Harry moved aside to give Louis enough room to reach the hot chocolate mix and gave him the same measuring cup Phoebe and Daisy had just used. Louis took it with a smirk and dipped it into the chocolate powder.

"Wait! He has to do it like how we did!"

"What?"

"Yeah, just because you're a big fancy adult now Louis doesn't mean that you are too big to do it as we did!"

"And how did you two do this?"

"Well, Harry picked us up and held us as we poured our scoops!"

Both Louis and Harry looked at each other with a mix of confusion and laughter. Neither of them knew where the suggestion was coming from. Even Jay turned around and let out a laugh at the girl's request.

"Well unlike the two of you little princess, Louis here is somehow tall enough to reach the pot by himself safely."

Harry made sure to add in joking wink at Louis when the time was right. The girls in perfect unison let out little pouts on their lips and put on their best pair of puppy dog eyes.

"Just this one time, please!"

"It's not like it's a big deal, come on please!"

Harry was now shifting his gaze between the girls standing in front of him to Louis at his side and Jay still standing by the stove. Harry was still trying to come up with any sort of response that would get him out of this situation. While the thought of having Louis be that close to him was certainly not a bad thing, it was the thought of having everyone else around seeing it. It was the thought that if he held Louis in his arms, he might never want to let go, or that if he held Louis in his arms, it would make everything weird.

Harry didn't want to screw up his relationship with Louis, after four years of barely speaking all of a sudden, he was coming back into his life. The last thing Harry wanted was to scare Louis with his emotions. Louis was just starting to come back around to his usual self.
It was Louis's voice that broke the still silence of the room.

"The two of you really want this don't you?"

The girls turned away from Harry and now fully faced Louis only to enhance the desperate look on their faces. Louis took one last glanced at their eyes before turning all the way towards Harry with a smirk traced on his lips.

"You are lucky I love you."

A second later Louis jumped into Harry's arms with the measuring cup in hand. Harry let out a grunt at the newfound weight added onto his body. Phoebe and Daisy squealed in excitement right in tune with Jay's shriek of laughter.

Harry had to adjust the positioning of Louis on his body, he might be lite but if the extra weight kept hanging off of his neck Harry was sure his neck would snap. Harry placed his hands on Louis's waist and lifted him to the side of his body, so he was now resting on his hip.

Louis let out a roar of laughter at the feeling of Harry's cold fingers placed firmly on his stomach. Little dots of iciness that somehow manage to wrap around almost his entire torose. From the base of his hip bones to the middle of his ribcage Louis was squirming underneath the firm grip.

"I see you are still very ticklish."

"Qui-quit moving! I-I'm trying to get th-the scoop!"

Harry stopped his movements and allowed Louis to catch his breath after laughing so much but that didn't last too long. The second Louis took a deep breath in and everybody else started laughing. Jay had to steady herself by leaning on the counter while the twins succumbed to the excited laughter and fell to the floor holding each other as they watched their brother in Harry's arms. Harry allowed himself to let out a soft laugh to enjoy the situation and abide by Louis's *quit moving* request.

"Wait hold on I need a photo of this!"

Jay pulled out her phone and snapped a picture before whipping the laughter filled tears from her eyes.

"Okay, you may proceed now."

She could barely get the words out in a steady voice. Phoebe and Daisy were now huddled together shifting their gaze from each other to the pile of boy standing in front of them. Harry had to bend down just a smidge so Louis could fill the metal scoop with the hot chocolate powder. Once Louis was ready Harry stood back up all the way.

"I hope you're enjoying what it's like to be tall, I may never happen again!"

Louis glared his eyes right into Harry's green ones, this time Harry couldn't help but let out a monstrous laugh, his entire body began to shake up and down with the sharp exhale of breaths. The movements caused Louis's body to come to erupt with the tickling sensation once again. Louis was trying to keep a stern face and tell Harry to stop but he took another glance into his eyes and decided against it.

The forestry green in Harry's eyes were shimmering, intertwined with sparkles of happiness, hope, and love. The sight melted Louis's heart, there was no way he was going to ruin this moment for Harry, he already had to be alone for most of Christmas eve the least he could do was allow one short joke. But that would be it, the next time Harry was going to get it! Louis dumped the entire of his scoop into the still-simmering mix that was in the pot, but because he was a little higher than he probably should have been some of the hot chocolate mix puffed up and came right back at him and Harry.

"Oh my god, you're worse than the girls!"

Harry was still laughing; he was actually laughing even harder now, and he really didn't know why. Maybe it was the adrenaline rush or the weird combination of hormones he was probably experiencing but laughing felt nice, so he just continued.

Louis gave Harry's arm a slight slap with the tips of his fingers for the comment before tossing the measuring scoop onto the side of the counter. The ricocheting echo of the metal hitting the granite counter helped pull Harry back into reality. Harry took a deep breath not only calming himself but Louis as well, the man he had some type of power.

Harry decided not to warn Louis about putting him down, he wanted to experience another wave of laughter. The instant Harry wrapped his colossal hands back around Louis's petit torso he felt his muscles stiffen as his breath shortened before escaping in a little burst of laughter as if he was trying to hold it in.

Once back on the ground Louis grabbed onto the edge of the counter to steady himself and slowly bring himself out of the tickling sensation that even with Harry's hands gone still lingered against his skin. Harry had to bend down on the counter placing his forearms on the counter and placing his head down in between to keep himself steady. A few seconds later his large body came back to its standing position and he used his thumb and pointer finger to pull off the small watermarks under his eyes that leaked out while laughing.

"That was way too easy Tomlinson!" A slight giggle was still detectable in his voice.

"Oh, I'll get you back, Styles, just you wait!"

Louis turned his body and looked down at his sites who were still happily on the floor looking up in lighter.

"I hope you enjoyed that!"

" Very much so!"

"Best Christmas ever!"

The girls got up from the floor and took a step closer to the small stove before looking up at Harry.

"Oh, right I better mix that."

Harry quickly grabbed the spoon he had earlier and took the pot off of the burner and placed it onto a cork hot mat mixing the powder as he did so. Soon the smell of hot chocolate began to grow thick in the kitchen, you could problem absorb the amount of sugar through your skin it was so strong. Knowing that the third scoop definitely tipped it over the edge Harry smirked over at Louis as if to say *this is all your fault.* He thought he was being sneaky about it, but Phoebe and Daisy saw the look, all they did was turn towards each other and nodded in agreement. They were certainly happy.

Once completely made Harry poured the hot liquid into five Christmas themed mugs. He handed each mug out to the proper person. The original plan was to drink the hot chocolate while watching a movie while waiting for dinner to finish up but with the little fiasco that had happened so much time was added that there was less than an hour now. So instead, everybody stayed in the kitchen and its connected dining room dancing along to Christmas music.

Harry helped Louis set the table, he really couldn't go one day at the Tomlinson house without helping and bring the serving plates of food to the table. Turkey, roasted potatoes, stuffing, Yorkshire pudding, mince pies, and of course gravy and cranberry sauce. As soon as the last plate was placed on the table, hands were flying everywhere reaching for food to put on their plates. Within two minutes five plates were stacked with food and everyone was sitting back down in their chair. Jay suddenly began laughing once again.

"Oh my, we really are some hungry animals!" Everybody followed suit in the laughter before diving into their dinner. Harry checked his phone and saw a reply from his mom, she was still working but would call before she left to come over. Louis noticed the slight fall on Harry's Face and nudged his shoulder.

"Everything okay?"

"Yeah, just my mom. She's still working."

"I'm sorry."

Both boys gave each other a smirk, however, they weren't the same. Louis wanted him to comfort Harry to truly express his remorse while Harry was trying not only to convince Louis but himself that everything really was okay. Deciding to enjoy the time he had in front of him Harry put on another big smile on his face and joined in on the conversation around him.

An hour later dinner was finished, minus the dessert because everyone was so stuffed at the moment, they decided to postpone that until later.

"Mommy, please! Just one!"

"Just one please mommy!"

The twins were begging Jay to let them open a gift early, but the little kid never begged for that. Jay had done pretty well at saying no when there was food in front of everyone to diverge the conversation away but now, she was struggling to say no to her two little girls. It didn't help that Louis was encouraging it by giving them thumbs up every time they asked.

"If they really want, they can open their present from me. you all can."

Jay gave Harry a thankful glance before nodding her head.

"You two better than Harry!"

The girls jumped from their seats and ran into Harry's lap since he was still sitting down.

"Thank you, thank you, thank you!" They kept repeating with smiles on their little faces.

"You're welcome. But first, help your mom clean up, then you can open them."

Almost immediately the girls got up and started gathering the dirty dishes and empty plates and Harry just laughed.

"How do you get them to do that?"

"They always need an incentive, even if it's just a piece of candy"

"Maybe I need to start keeping jolly ranchers on me at all times."

Harry laughed at Louis's comment before standing up and picking up the large serving plates that still had food and carrying them to the kitchen. Louis filled him and pulled out some storage containers and helped Harry transfer the food. Surprisingly both boys were civil, and no food fights broke out, but hey it's not like that would have been the worst thing. right?

Pretty soon the kitchen and dining room was spotless, and Phoebe and Daisy were bouncing up and down. During the cleaning process, Harry threw some water in the kettle to get some tea ready. The cups were full one for him, Jay, and Louis. With mugs in hand, the three followed in the path of the twins who had already run the little room containing the Christmas tree. It was the second time Harry had seen the tree, but it still took his breath away, it truly was an amazing concept pulled off to the best extent it could have. Remembering what Jay had told him he turned to face Louis.

"I love what you did with the tree."

Louis raised his mug to his face in an attempt to cover the slight pink tint that rose to his cheeks. Hearing that he did something good that was artistic meant so much to him, more than anybody could ever know.

"Thank you."

Harry took a seat in one of the large recliners in the room as did Jay. Phoebe, Daisy, and Louis all sat down on the floor after each grabbing their gift. It was a tradition for the people opening presents to sit on the floor, no matter how old they were so even eighteen-year-old Louis sat crisscrossed on the carpet.

"Whenever you're ready."

And with those words, the sound of paper ripping filled the room. Phoebe and Daisy went first letting out excited squeals at the sight over their new dresses, immediately they held it up to their bodies and curtsied as if they already changed into them. Their happiness was contagious as everyone's cheeks grew fuller, some smiling.

"There is one more thing in there for you, it's from Cassie."

With the dresses still in hand, their hands dug back into the brown cardboard box and each pulled out a princess play makeup set. More squeals entered the air as they ran up to Harry to give him another hug along with another round of thank yous.

"Can you tell Cassie we said thank you too please!"

"Of course, I'm glad you like it!"

Phoebe and Daisy twirled back to their spot on the floor. Once they sat back down Louis started pulling at the wrapping at his gift. At first, a puzzled look glazed his eyes but as soon as he realized what he was holding he stopped tearing the paper off and just admired what he was holding. A small layer of tears began to cover his baby blue eyes. Still, in awe he spoke to Harry.

"H-how did you find this?"

Harry's heart melted into a river when he saw the look held in Louis's eyes. He could see Louis's tough exterior fall to the ground.

"I found it in my garage a little while ago and thought you might want it back."

"Thank you."

Nothing so sincere had come out of Louis's mouth in so long that everyone went quiet. Harry kept his eyes tightly on Louis taking in the softness on his features, his slow and deep breaths, and the way his hand cradled the clear box in his hand as if it was an angel. The sight made fiery tears pickle in Harry's eyes.

"What's that?"

"This Phebs is the first football I ever had."

"Wow, so it's old!"

"It is. Wait did you just call me old?"

"Well, you are an adult and adults are old!"

Louis ruffled Phoebe's hair before she walked back over to Daisy and sat back down. Jay squeezed Harry's arm before mouthing a thank you to him. She knew just how important it was for Louis to see that ball again and she thought it was lost forever, but it was just buried under the craziness of life.

"Alright, I think it's time to bake some cookies for Santa and watch a movie before bed!"

"Cookies!"

"yay!"

Jay got up and the twins followed suit still holding their dresses in hand. Louis slowly stood up and Harry waited for him. Once Louis caught up, he gave a hug to Harry simply melting into him.

"Seriously thank you."

" It's no problem. Are you ready for some cookies?"

"Yeah. I'm just going to go put this upstairs first. don't let them wait up on me okay."

"Okay."

Harry and Louis walk out of the Christmas room, Harry turns right to make his way to the kitchen while Louis turns left towards the staircase. Both boys gave each other one last glance before disappearing from sight.

Chapter Sixteen:

A 1930's classic, Miracle on 34th Street was being projected onto the back wall of the dining room so Phoebe, Daisy, Jay, and Harry could watch while making Santa's cookies. Based on a group's decision it was decided that sugar cookies with royal frosting would be made. While pulling out the cookie pans and mixing bowls Harry kept his eye on the entrance of the kitchen waiting for Louis to walk through, but he never did.

Harry picked up both Phoebe and Daisy and placed them on the counter so they could reach the two stand mixers they planned on using to mix the dough together. Both Jay and Harry measured out the flour, sugar, butter, milk, eggs, vanilla, and baking powder before handing it to the girls who added the ingredients into the separate mixers.

The buzzing sound of the mixers filled the room as the comments started to form a thick beige dough. Soon enough the dough was ready to be rolled out and cut into shapes. Harry took the liberty of smoothing the dough with the large granite rolling pin as he had the muscles to do so. While handing a box of cookie cutters to the twin's Jay noticed that Louis still hadn't come back.

"Harry, do you know where Louis went?"

"He said he was going to go put the ball away in a safe place."

"Do you mind going on checking on him? It's been a while."

"Sure."

Harry went to the sink and washed the flour and sugar remanence from his hands before heading out of the kitchen. Walking up the large spiral staircase the sounds of giggles and music slowly morphed into stilled silence only the sound of Harry's footsteps could be heard. That was until he came upon a closed-door belonging to Louis's room.

Coming to a halt outside the door Harry heard the faint voice of Louis. Harry placed his ear close up to the door to try and listen to what was being said but Louis was too far into his room only allowing a faint echo to travel into Harry's ear.

Harry only made out a few words like Christmas, I hope you like it, forever, among other seemingly random words. To Harry it sounded as if Louis was on a phone call, perhaps with Ronnie wishing her a Merry Christmas or maybe she had called to wish him a happy birthday so instead of interrupting Harry just turned back around and went back downstairs figuring that once he was done with the call he would come down.

"Is he coming down?"

"He was on a phone call so I'm sure he'll be down soon."

Harry passed after the words left his mouth, now that he was thinking about it, it seemed kind of strange. Louis had been like his old goofy self just an hour earlier, he seemed happy to be with his family but now he just disappeared from everything, not to mention that his door was closed when the only time that Louis's ever closed his room was when he was sleeping when Ronnie complained about the noise level. So why was his door closed when he was clearly still awake?

"Harry!"

"Hm- what?"

"How long do we bake these for!"

"Oh! uh start with twelve minutes then we can check them."

"Gotcha. I thought you turned into a ghost for a second there."

The three girls laughed as Harry's cheeks began to take on a hint of color from the mix of embarrassment of his knowledge of Louis's life and the thought that he might have just lied to Jay. He also had a burning feeling of guilt from not really checking up on Louis.

Since the cookies had already been in the oven for nearly seven minutes Harry decided to start making the frosting while Phoebe and Daisy still sat on the counter with their eyes glued to the black and white outline of little Natalie Wood who was moving across their dining room wall.

Just as Harry poured the water into the bowl of powdered sugar the timer went off so before he turned on the mixer, he put on some oven mitts and opened the oven. A puff of warm vanilla sugar scented air escaped from the oven and floated within the air capturing the attention of everyone who now took in the sweet smell while their eyes followed the tray in Harry's hands. Quickly he removed the cookies from the blazing pan and placed them on a cooling rack so the second and final batch of cookies could begin baking.

Back at the stand mixer, Harry began to turn the mixer speed up slowly until the mixture in the bowl became a pearly liquid. Pulling out smaller bowls Harry poured the icing into each keenly so they could be colored. Harry placed a box of food coloring in the middle of the girls so they could choose which colors they wanted.

While Phoebe and Daisy were mixing red, green, blue, pink, black, and yellow into the icing that sat in front of them, leaving one with the white pearly color. Jay was busy getting the second batch of cookies out of the ovens, and Harry was digging through the pantry to find the containers of sprinkles.

Everyone finished their tasks at the same time, three sprinkle containers, a plate of cooled cookies, and seven bowls of royal frosting came together to make the perfect cookie station. Cookies were cut into snowflakes, angels, trees, stars, presents, snowmen, and even into the shape of Mr. and Mrs. Clause.

Everyone was dipping cookies into the icing bowls and spooning the colors onto them as well. While some of the cookies were left perfect with just the added colored sugar some were given an extra sparkle with the sprinkles.

Mountains of cookies began to stack up on the multiple plates laid in front of them. A special white plate with a gold rim was dedicated to the best of the best cookies which would be left for Santa Claus himself. By the time all the cookies had been decorated droplets of frosting covered the counter and small piles of colored sugar dusted the floor. Harry grabbed Phoebe while Jay grabbed Daisy and lifted them off of the counter and placed them back onto the floor. Jay handed her girls the plate of cookies they determined worthy for Santa while Harry got out some milk and poured a glass for the girls to set aside the plate.

While Harry covered the remaining plates with plastic wrap to keep them fresh Jay walked Daisy and Phoebe to the Christmas room where they placed the plate of cookies and glass of milk on a little glass table that laid directly in front of the black and white Christmas tree.

When the three returned to the kitchen they were met with two glasses of warm milk prepared for Phoebe and Daisy. Harry had already started to wipe up the dried frosting, but Jay had pulled the washcloth out of his hand. "No. No more cleaning for you Harry, it's Christmas and you're seventeen not third seven. You leave this to me." Harry released the cloth in defeat, he knew there was no way he would win the fight no matter how much he wanted to help. Harry pulled out three kitchen stools and sat down with the twins while Jay finished cleaning up the counters. The ending credits of A Miracle on 34th Street began to appear against the wall. Jay walked over and switched off the projector.

"Okay girls', that means it's time for bed."

Surprisingly, the twins did not put up much of a fight as they were so excited for Santa to come once they fell asleep. Both girls jumped out of their chairs and finished their glasses of milk before placing them into the sink. The girls then began to skip off into the hallway.

"Why don't you take a plate of cookies up to your brother!"

Phoebe and Daisy had indeed heard her mother's request. At first, they did stop and contemplate whether or not to indeed go back and grab the plate of cookies up to Louis but soon whispers were exchanged between them they simply continued to skip up the stairs and up to their room.

"Here I'll take them up."

"Harry..."

"No, it's literally not a problem it's just a plate of cookies or... I could help you finish cleaning up down here."

"Fine, take the cookies."

Harry gave a cheeky smile and picked up one of the many plates that sat on the counter. Harry was able to balance the glass plate steadily on his large hand with perfect balance on his trip back up to Louis's room. Once back up on the second story of the house a sudden wave of memories was the events that took place an hour earlier began to tug at Harry's heart and brain. Harry had hoped that when his footsteps landed in front of Louis's room, he would come to see the familiar sight of the door left open as the words he had heard Louis speaking earlier replayed in his head hoping that he really was just on a phone call. But then again, he really didn't want that to be true because that would mean that Louis abandoned his family on the final hours of his birthday and in the middle of the holiday celebrations.

Just like last time Harry softened his footsteps as he came up to the wooden entrance. Instantly Harry's heart felt as if it had been assaulted with a heavy force. The engraved wooden door was still shut. Harry slowly lifted one of his hands while pressing his ear to the door, this time he began to worry as he couldn't hear any words, only slight whimpering sounds. The blood flows in Harry's veins began to quicken along with his breath, was Louis crying? The thought truly pained Harry so much that he had to close his eyes to regain his composure before knocking the door with the back of his pointer finger.

"Louis?"

Harry heard a quick shuffling of movements but no response.

"Hey, I brought cookies."

There was still no response. The silence that left no echoes in the large house Harry was beginning to worry more than he had been earlier, his foot began tapping aimlessly on the floor waiting just to hear a response from the other side of the door.

After a few more minutes of defining silence Harry's hand reached for the doorknob. His fingertips rested on the cold metal as he wondered if he was doing the right thing, but before Harry could have a full-on debate inside his head his hand began twisting only to find that the door was left unlocked.

The door creaked as it slowly opened, the soft glow of the moon and stars shining through the large window was the only light inside the large room. Harry passed the small hallways decorated with awards and trophies with small and tentative steps. Curled up in his comforter Louis was pressed up against the window holding a picture frame.

Chapter Seventeen:

Harry's footsteps came to a stop as his eyes adjusted to the darkened room. Harry's eyes scanned the room like laser beams from one side to the other. As Harry's eyes landed on the bundle on the bundle of blankets laying on the bay window, he felt a weird mixture of relief and concern. With the plate of cookies still in his hands, Harry took a few tiny steps heading straight for the window that laid across the room.

"Louis? Are you awake?"

Suddenly Harry saw a small little hand emerge from the bundle and reach upwards. Louis sat up fast and his head snapped up following the path of Harry's voice. His shoulders feel relaxed again realizing it was indeed just Harry. Seeing that Harry was continuing to walk towards him Louis quickly dropped his head and raised a portion of the blanket wrapped around him to wipe the tear stains away from his cheeks and cleared his throat.

"Yeah, I'm awake."

Harry quickened his pace only having to take four steps to reach the bay window. When Harry sat down Louis was back to facing the scenic view out of his window. Unwrapping the plastic covering on the plate Harry brought the plate forward closer to Louis offering him one, but he didn't take one he didn't even move at the offering.

"Okay then."

Harry's torso twisted tightly as he turned around and placed the plate of cookies on the edge of the small table. Harry sat back against the rough textured wall that framed the seating area to just observe.

Harry observed every small detail of Louis. The way his hair had become ruffled, and the edges curled up slightly at the base of his neck as Louis's hair had grown to the longest length it has ever been, and it looked good. Perhaps a little too good. The corners of Louis's eyes dropped down as his eyelashes fluttered upwards through the moonlight that was glistening outside. Harry noticed that the tip of Louis's rounded nose was slightly swollen and held the shadow of a rosy hue.

Harry's eyes continued to move downward and saw the little hairs that collected above Louis's upper lip when he didn't shave for a couple of days. A shadow was held above his lips allowing Harry to see every little crevice. Harry could see that the normally thin straight lips now held a slightly swollen shape and combined with the small little indents and breaks in the skin Harry knew that Louis had been biting them. It was only then that he noticed that his heart began to splinter, Louis's lips held a faint quiver.

He took in every inch of Louis once again, this time with searching for any other details that he had missed when he was entranced by his early presence, and sure enough, he did. Louis's knuckles were white, and his cuticles had been picked at, his hands still clenched the blanket around him. Louis's chin had been tilted down making him appear smaller than he already was. A sure-fire sign something was wrong.

One last good look at Louis's eyes solidified Harry's splintering heart. Microscopic lines of bright green stripes appeared in the normally crystal-clear ocean that occupied Louis's face, something that only ever happened when he cried. Harry could still see the watery layer that was covering Louis's eyes and it hurt. It hurt so bad.

"Louis?"

"Yeah?"

"Are you okay?"

A long silence fluttered between the small space between Harry and Louis. Only Louis's eyes moved, they shifted from the bottom of the window up and outward towards the fountain that laid outside. Louis's room overlooked the backyard, meaning that the view truly was something that had the ability to take your breath away, but that wasn't the reason why Louis was still silent.

"Louis."

Harry leaned in slightly and reached out to tap Louis on the shoulder, or what he was fairly sure was his shoulder since he was still wrapped in his comforter which seemed to only be growing in fluffiness.

"I'm good."

Harry rolled his eyes and a deep sigh escaped from his lips; he knew that wasn't the proper answer. Even if he hadn't noticed all the little signs Harry was still able to detect the minor waves that broke in Louis's voice when he spoke. Louis really never did a good job at hiding his emotions and with Harry always being so observant there was no way for him to get around it.

"Louis..."

"I'm fine, don't worry."

Harry's second-hand grabbed Louis's other shoulder pulling the pint-sized boy fully off of the window. Louis made no attempt to hold himself up but rather just allowed Harry's strength to keep him proper up, Harry's own shoulders fell when he realized that even with his hands wrapped around Louis there was no laughter. This had to be bad for Louis to not to fall into a fit of laughter when he was so ticklish.

"Louis."

Harshness was not a common tone to Harry's voice but when it laced his words it was commanding. Louis's head made a slow turn, his eyes fell behind still staying locked on the late night on the other side of the glass.

"Louis!"

Finally, the words made their way into Louis's head and his eyes left the window and made their way to Harry. The eyes that only two hours earlier held so much joy and happiness looked ice-cold, frozen yet growing in pain. The bags underneath was weighing him down filled with sorrow, his eyes stayed drooped, eyelashes were dripping with emotion. The muscles on his face made no movement, there was no sign of anything. Louis was blank.

Suddenly Harry's hands dropped from Louis's shoulders and pulled him into his chest, wrapping his arms tightly around him. Louis's head was placed directly on Harry's heart, he was hoping to find a steady beat but instead all he heard was a fast and irregular pattern. A single tear fell. Then another, and another, and another. Louis fully collapsed into Harry as the tears continued to stream down his face. Harry stroked his fingers through the overgrown edges of Louis's hair. Harry tightened his grip as he placed his head gently on top Louis's. Quickly Harry's shirt became soaked with salted tears as Louis's body shook against his chest. Louis had finally let go of the heavy comforter he had been wrapped in and instead gripped the side of Harry's t-shirt. Each time Louis's fingers moved slightly against him goosebumps ran down every inch of Harry.

Now that Harry had time to process the gut-wrenching events taking place his system began to calm down allowing his heartbeat to steady back into a normal rhythm. The soft rhythm echoed into Louis's ear and slowly calmed his shaky breaths. The once heavy whimpers were gone, the silence brought a small sense of relief upon Harry, but now he just had to figure out why Louis had fallen apart in his arms.

Harry felt a slight pressure on his chest in the form of two small hands, Louis had lifted himself up off of Harry's chest. Harry lifted his head allowing Louis to properly sit up. Louis kept his gaze over Harry's sculpted shoulder instead of looking into his forest green eyes.

"I'm sorry."

Harry's hand retook their place on Louis's petit shoulders as his broken voice shattered the silence. Harry bent down one shoulder to bring his face to the same level as Louis's and turned to force eye contact.

"Louis, hey look at me."

"Look. at. me"

"Thank you. There is no reason for you to apologize, especially not to me."

Louis's eyes softened ever so slightly at Harry's words. He didn't feel judged or pitied or embarrassed by his breakdown and the only reason for that was because he was with Harry, a person who had known him for practically his entire life. He wasn't scared of showing Harry the real him because well, he already knew the real him. Not the Louis that Louis created when his father died, that was the Louis that pretty much everyone at school knew, his friends, his teachers, his teammates, Ronnie. None of them knew the story that was held inside his eyes.

"I-if you don't mind can I ask what's going on?"

Louis's head moved only mere centimeters as a nod signaling, he would indeed give an explanation. Louis moved off of Harry's lap and moved in between him and the window against the wall. It was a tight squeeze causing one of Louis's shoulders to press deep into Harry's arm while the other was squashed up against the freezing cold window, but nobody moved.

Both boys learned their hands back against the wall that the rest of their bodies already used for support. Four eyes stared straight in front landing upon the opposite end of the bay window which looked exactly the same as the side they were sitting on, an empty wall with a small table on the side, except there was a minuscule difference, an engraved silver photo frame stood all alone.

Harry felt Louis's body turn back towards the window as he leaned more and more on Harry's arm. A deep, hot breath left Louis's lips and fogged up the window, lifting his arm up to wipe off the conversation Louis began to speak.

"It's, well it's a lot of things really. I guess I just never expected for everything to suddenly hit me all at once, especially not now."

Harry's eyes drifted from the photo frame to the reflection of Louis in the window. Out of everything he expected to hear Harry certainly wasn't expecting to hear what Louis was saying, because he had no idea of what could possibly follow what he had already said. A mystery.

Harry kept his eyes on the reflection in the window, a crease formed in the narrow space between his eyes as he saw Louis reach for the base of the windowsill that was covered in the comforter, he was wrapping him and uncovered the clear box with his football inside. If Harry thought that he felt pain in his chest before, then he was wrong. This was an unworldly amount of pain.

"Please don't tell me I'm responsible for this?"

"No. This isn't your fault, well maybe you triggered it but this. this mess you are not responsible for, I brought this upon myself."

Harry had now turned to look down at the tiny human sitting beside him, however, the action caused Louis to fall in between Harry's chest and arm. Once again nobody moved, Louis still held his gaze out at the dozens of stars outside.

"When my dad passed, I... I stopped trying new things. I didn't want to do anything that he wouldn't be able to see. I didn't want my life to turn into something he wouldn't be proud of. I didn't want anything to change. But soon everything did, and I just didn't know what to do. You see when I made varsity freshman year, I felt close to him again, it felt like he was with me at every training session. Sometimes when I'm playing super hard, I can still hear his voice whispering in my ear cheering me on. It's the one thing that I still have left of him, of us, of being father and son."

Harry stayed still in shock as he tried to process everything as Louis moved his hand up to wipe a stray tear that had fallen down onto his cheek.

"When I started dating Ronnie, I had no idea what I was doing, hell I never kissed anyone before her, but I was tired of having every single girl throw herself at me and I thought that if I went out with her that maybe some of it would die down. Selfish I know but I didn't know what else to do, I didn't want to talk to mom about it since she was so stressed preparing for the girls by herself and now, I couldn't talk to my dad anymore and well we... I kinda just left you by yourself without a reason and when I saw you with Cassie, I figured you were fine without me and I didn't want to barge back into your life as if I owned it. So... I just went along with it. After a while, it was a good distraction from everything, being the person, I was with Ronnie. When I was with her and the rest of the Populares I wasn't some poor lad who lost his dad and had no idea what to do, I was simply just one of them."

Louis had now picked up the encased football and set it on his lap with his wrist crossed over top of them. Harry had moved his gaze to the window just like Louis but unlike him, he wasn't staring at the sky or the pond or the snow, he was starting at Louis's reflection.

"When the twins were born, I hated it, I hated that they changed my life so dramatically. I hated that I couldn't control it. I know, hand me the world's worst brother right now, it only gets worse. It was then that I started hanging out more and more with Ronnie. At first, it wasn't so much to see her but rather get away from what was happening here and pretty soon I just associated being with Ronnie as sort of being like I had my own life back even though it's crazy because she was never in my life when Dad was around and if I'm being completely honest, she isn't the kind of girl he would like anyway but soon I was stuck. Stuck living in a false reality.

I began to view my life from a third-person point of view. And the longer I lived like that the more I began to hate it. I knew you were there when Phoebe and Daisy took their first steps and spoke their first words. and i-i missed all of it. I missed my sisters growing up because I was too afraid of change. I saw how when you came over the girls suddenly were brought to life, how they always ran into your arms, how every moment of every day they talk about you. How they don't do the same to me, how they don't really know me, how I know I'm not a part of their early memories because I wasn't bloody there."

"Louis-"

"No, let me finish."

"When I saw this, the ball again, it made me realize that I had something that they... they never had. I had him. I had a dad for almost fourteen years. I have memories of him, of his eyes, of his smile, of his laugh. I have memories of family dinners and picnics in the park. I remember how he would come home and hang a new painting in the hall every month. I remember the day he first taught me how to kick this thing. I remember him because I had him. But they, all they have are his photos, his story, they never got him."

Tears had begun to pour rapidly like Niagara falling down Louis's cheeks and his voice was hoarse and breaking on every other word, but he didn't stop, he kept talking as he fell deeper into Harry's grasp.

"They have grown up their entire lives without him, I was lucky enough to have him and i-i should have been there for them. I could have given them a sense of him, I could have made sure that even though he isn't physically here that he still got to meet his daughters and I ruined it. When Phoebe didn't know that Dad was the one who taught me how to play football, I- I realized everything. I realized who wrong I have been for so long, I realized that I wasn't the same person I was when he passed and not in the, oh it's been four years, of course, you going to change way, but I had become the very person I never wanted to be. I became a person that if my dad walked through that door right now, he would be ashamed of me. I-I just don't know what to do anymore.

I just wish I could talk to him, apologies for everything. I just want to tell him how sorry I am for losing myself, for not being there for mom or Phoebe or Daisy when they needed me. I wish he could tell me what to do. I wish he could tell me how to fix all of this. Most of all I wish I got the chance to tell him how much I love him and how much I miss him every day. I wish I got to say goodbye to him."

Louis was in full-on sobs once again and Harry was left in disbelief. Harry just held Louis tightly against him, he didn't know what else to do. There was so much he could say but Harry just couldn't bring himself to talk but Louis didn't mind. He didn't want to hear any words, he just wanted to be heard to know that for once somebody was listening to him and by the way Harry had moved him around his back and through his waist to pull him closer, he knew that finally, someone cared.

Chapter Eighteen:

The moonlight poured onto Louis as he stayed curled up in Harry's embrace, his head completely buried in Harry's chest as he cried. Harry rocked gently from to side to side in an attempt to help Louis calm down, it broke him to Louis so broken.

Louis kept ingesting the scent of Harry as he laid broken and lifeless on top of him, the smell of burnt firewood and cinnamon was the only reason Louis's chest was still rising and falling with a purpose. The heat radiating from Harry's mass of muscles warmed the cold and shaking Louis but still left him cold, Harry pulled the large comforter around not only Louis but himself as well.

The whimpers and shaking slowly stopped but the silent leaking of tears from Louis's eyes still remained. It was only when Harry felt the steady heartbeat in Louis's chest that signaled, he had finally fallen asleep that he allowed himself to cry.

It was harsh and heavy like how Louis had been crying but the silent tears that burned his cheeks as if they were fire. Harry didn't move, with his breath still yet his head was screaming. Harry's tears were left unwiped and began to gather and cling to the edge of his jaw, every so often a droplet would have enough weight and did one last free fall before ending up in Louis's hair. Harry looked down at Louis in his arms and saw the exhaustion that overtook the small boy and it acted as an anchor, pulling him back down to earth. Deep creases lined Louis's eyes and his lips were still swollen bringing back the harsh reality of the words he had told Harry. Even their beds talking about what might be under the Christmas tree. The girls were riddled with excitement, they only had a few more minutes until they could go and wake everyone up. The rule was that they couldn't wake up anybody before six am to go and open Christmas gifts, they also couldn't leave their room unless it was an emergency before then either just in case, they ended up shopping around the tree.

The girls watched the clock and heard every little tik too the second hand made in the quietness of the room. Only one more minute. As soon it struck six the girls shoved their comforters off of them, put on their matching pink slippers, and ran out their room down the hall in their mother's room. The barges through the door filled with excitement as they ran up to the partially sleeping mother and shook her awake.

"Mommy it's Christmas wake up!"

The girls were jumping up and down not knowing how much longer they could go before running down the staircase by themselves.

"Is it six?"

"YES! It's 6:03!"

"Okay, go get your brother up, I think Harry's in there too. I'll wake up Mrs. Styles, but you kids need to wait at the top of the stairs until I tell you to come down okay."

"Okay!"

And with the instructions given they girls ran back down the hallway their brother's room.

"Wait, did mommy say that Harry was in here too?"

"I think she did why- OH do you think they had a slumber party?"

"Of course, they did! Why else would Harry sleep in Louis's room?"

The girls giggled as Daisy mentally opened the door leading to their brother's room. Louis didn't have a big chandelier light in his room as the girls did, rather just settling for two lamps and the natural light of the sun. This meant that as Phoebe and Daisy walked in, they were almost in pitch-black darkness except for the tiny amount of light that crept in from the hallway along with the moonlight peeking through the clouds.

The hadn't risen yet causing the girls to only see the faint outline of Harry and Louis on the bay window. A knowing smile crossed their lips as they made sure to keep their footsteps as light as feathers as to not wake the boys, a track contrast to what they originally set out to do.

Phoebe and Daisy held onto each other's arms tightly as they finally got close enough to see what was really going on. Each girl took their free hand and covered their mouths as they squealed in excitement. Had their small efforts begun to work?

Phoebe spotted Harry's cell phone sitting on the table next to them, she couldn't resist picking it up and opening the camera app. Even being four years old Phoebe was smart enough to make sure the phone was one silent, so it made no noise. She took two photos of her brother curled up in Harry's chest before setting the phone back down carefully. With a simple nod of the head both girls retreated out of the room. Once back in the hall the girls gave each other a high five.

"It won't be long now!"

"Are You ready?"

"Yup, let's go wake them up!"

This time the girls barged through the door just like they had when they woke their mom up, loud and full of energy. The small footsteps shook the floor so much that both Harry and Louis already began to squirm lightly.

"It's Christmas!"

"Wake up, wake up, wake up!"

"We have to see if Santa came!"

"Also, Harry your mom is here! Let's go see her!"

Phoebe and Daisy had climbed on top of the bay window cushions and were jumping. Phoebe pulled at the hands of Louis while Daisy pulled at the hands of Louis, at first both boys gave quite the fight of letting go of their surprisingly strong grip on each other but once fully awake it took no force at all to pull them apart.

Louis came flying off of Harry along with the warmth of the comforter which instantly awoke Harry as he became freezing without Louis's body and the blanket to give him warmth.

"Okay, okay I'm up. Did you already wake mom?"

"Yeah, she said to get you two up while she gets Harry's mom up and to wait at the staircase."

"The top of the staircase."

"Right."

"Wait my mom got here?"

"I'm pretty sure, mom said she was here."

"Come one the quicker you get up the faster we can see them!"

Louis was now standing up with his feet on the floor as he tried to shake freeform Daisy, but she was relentless. Harry didn't need another incentive to get up, seeing his mom was enough. Unlike Harry, Louis remembered virtually all of last night the moment his eyes opened. The only problem with this is he had absolutely no idea what it meant, everything. The words or how Harry held him or how he cried into his chest for hours. Taking a glance at Harry to see if he remembered he saw the large stain of salted water laying on the side of Harry's torso, reminiscence of where his head had rested. He couldn't allow Harry to walk out to his mom with a stain on his shirt that he might have not known how he got it. Worse, he does remember, what would Harry say? Would he tell the truth, or would he act oblivious? Louis didn't want to find out.

"Hey Harry change into this, you left it a while back and it made its way to my laundry."

"Oh, thanks."

Harry didn't think twice as he quickly took off his current shirt revealing the very toned abs and pecks that normally stayed hidden underneath fabrics. Louis's eyes lingered a little too long at the sight, there was a reason why he was comfortable sleeping last night. Just as the shirt covered the rigid muscles Louis began to walk forward finally giving in to the pulling Daisy was still doing, as he moved away his body no longer blocked the small table behind him. That's when Harry saw it.

The picture frames. Suddenly in a tunnel vision of memories, Harry saw the events of last night play out right in front of his eyes all over again. Everything from the tears to the words spoken to the way Louis fell into him, the way he cried once Louis fell asleep. He looked down at the shirt he just took off and saw the salted residue.

Just as Phoebe was pulling his hand Harry began to follow, however, he kept his head turned and eyes focused on the silver picture frame. Even with the light still, dim he could now make it out. It wasn't a very old photo, no not at all, very recent actually and good Louis wasn't in it. Harry stood in the middle and dressed in princess dresses with their hair curled, Phoebe and Daisy were holding his hands. It was the night that Harry had Cassie and Niall over, the night that they had the extravagant ballroom dance, the night that Harry had told the girls he would never bring over a princess. But how had Louis gotten the photo?

"Harry come on!"

"I'm coming don't worry!"

Harry jogged his way with Phoebe to the edge of the staircase where Louis and Daisy were already waiting. As soon as he arrived Harry noticed the stiffening of Louis's shoulders, it wasn't something that didn't expect to happen given the heavyweight of what happened last night, but Harry could only hope that it was because he finally said those words out loud not the fact that it had been to Harry or the fact that he fell asleep on his chest. Harry vowed to keep a close eye on Louis for the rest of the time he was over and to come up with a plan to help Louis.

"Okay, you can come down now!"

The twins bolted down the stairs while the boys simply walked. Both Jay and Ann were standing at the bottom, as soon as his feet left the last step Harry made his way to his mom and engulfed her in a bear hug.

"Merry Christmas mom!"

"Merry Christmas baby."

Louis was leaning on the railing watching the interaction, even still confused on what was going on in his head Louis held a slight happiness arising in his heart seeing Harry finally be able to spend some time with his mom. He walked his way over to his own mom and gave her a kiss on the cheek.

"Merry Christmas mom, and thank you for such an amazing birthday. You really outdid yourself!"

"Oh, don't make me cry Lou. Merry Christmas my newly young man!"

The four elders laughed as Louis rolled his eyes. They all began walking towards the Christmas room as the very impatient twins stood quietly waiting like the good girls Jay had raised. As the sounds of Ann and Jay talking along with the bubbly excitement from Phoebe and Daisy crashed loudly against the openness of the house Harry was able to look over Louis and felt another ping of sadness hit his heart, it must have hurt him to see Harry reunite with his mom.

Walking into the room there were four cups of tea and two glasses of milk sitting on the table between the reclining chairs, one mug for each of the six people. Because there were only two chairs' Louis and Harry each grabbed a mug of tea and sat on the floor alongside Phoebe and Daisy.

To Harry's surprise his mom had brought over all the presents from their own house and laid them under the Tomlinson's tree. The twins began to act like little elves and separated all the gifts and placed them in front of the proper person. With the pile of gifts now organized everyone began to rip the wrapping paper and open the boxes to reveal the treasures inside.

An hour later everything had been opened, everything except for one. Everyone knew what was left, Jay held a midsized box that was decorated with golden reindeer with pearly flakes of snow against the dark green background in her hand. It was the classic photobook Harry made her every year. A beautiful smile appeared as Jay focused on the family picture on the cover of the album. Soon everyone crowded around her, Louis sat on the arm of Jay's chair with Phoebe perched on his lap as Daisy crawled on the other side of the chair and leaned up against their mom.

As the Tomlinson's looked through their year of memories captured in the photos Harry went and shared a spot in his mom's chair. Even being as tall as he was the mother and son duo fit quite nicely. Harry was so happy to see that everyone, including Louis, smiling full of love looking down at the book. It made Harry so happy to see how close of a family they really were, he hoped

Louis would treasure this moment and remember this moment he next time he felt sad. Ann noticed Harry's focused gaze on the Tomlinson's and gave him a tight squeeze as she whispered in his ear.

"You've done some amazing things Harry, bring them all back together by these photo albums is one of them. You have your talent and heart for a reason. I'm so proud you are using them properly."

"Thanks mom."

Harry extends his arms forward until his hand rests on his mother's shoulders. They watched the smiles continue to grow. Harry knew that in a sense that the photo albums reminded Jay and Louis of Richard, the artistic side of him, he knew that by the way their faces looked the same as when they looked at the paintings Richard had hung on the walls.

Harry was in a cheerful daze as he sat there embraced in his mother's loving hug, he longer focused heavily on the reaction of his gift but rather on the light snowfall he could see on the window. For the first time in a while Harry was happy, content, and felt at peace with everything. Nothing in the moment had to be done, there was no responsibility to uphold Harry could just sit and relax.

A strong force was gnawing at Harry pulling his attention back to the real world. Looking around the room he saw Louis giving him a soft smile as his sisters were talking to their mom. Harry had to shift his gaze slightly to see which photo was on display. A smile appeared softly on his lips as he took the photo, it was from the mall only a week ago when he and the twins had accidentally crashed Louis and Ronnie's date and the girls sat on each of Louis's knees.

When Harry had chosen to put that specific photo in the album for Jay, for her to have some photos of all of her kids together, he never knew that the Photo would also be important for Louis, but he was glad it was. Harry looked back up to Louis and gave him a real smile. Louis had wrapped his arms tightly around Phoebe to keep from falling off of the chair, he liked how he was beginning to feel close to his sisters, in response to the smile he just received the mouths thank you paired with soft eyes to Harry before turning his focus back to the photo album.

The rest of the day went by relaxingly, everyone huddled in the living room watching movies while they ate Christmas candy and leftovers from the dinner before. Soon the sun began to sink back down from its highest point in the sky. Harry knew that his mom had to work a night shift later on and needed to get homeland change into a new pair of scrubs before she went back to the hospital.

Not wanting to make his mother feel bad about leaving Harry suggested that the two of them catch an early dinner, just the two of them, so she didn't have to head back home alone. Harry had gathered all of his gifts and placed them in a bag and his mom did the same. Since Ann had taken a cab back to the Tomlinson's since she likes to drive after midnight, she began to take the gifts out to Harry's car.

Harry remembered that he still had a shirt up in Louis's room, but seeing that Louis had fallen fast asleep on the couch Harry just went up to his room by himself to grab the shirt, it's not like Louis would mind anyway. Once back in his room Harry picked up his wrinkled and stained shirt from the floor. A pad of sticky notes and a jar of pens sat on Louis's desk and Harry felt compelled to write something as he took another glance at the silver picture frame.

You are a better brother than you think, don't be so hard on yourself! :)

Harry stuck the note on the small table and left the room. Finally, back downstairs Harry had joined his mother in saying goodbye to Jay and the twins. Harry told Jay not to wake up Louis and just let him sleep as he knew that he would see him soon and if anybody needed anything he had his number. As Harry and Ann made their way down the hall to the garage Jay called out to Harry.

"Harry don't forget your jacket! I hung it up in the coat closet!"

"Thank you, I'll get it!"

Quickly Harry grabbed the denim jacket off of the hanger and tossed it over his shoulder not knowing that there had been two of the dame jackets. Harry joined his mom in his car, and they were on their way home.

Chapter Nineteen:

Days have passed leaving it to be New Year's Eve. Harry was laying on the couch just dazing at the tv, a marathon of Criminal Minds had been playing for the past ten hours. Every now and then Harry would log into his phone and check his social media, it wasn't long until all of his feed was filled with alerts of a party.

An Instagram post with an address, time, and other details had been retweeted, reposted, and sent in almost every group chat that involved people from school. It wasn't long until Harry got a text from Cassie.

"Get ready to party!"

"Cassie, I'm not going to do that thing!"

"We'll be over in an hour."

"Cassie, NO"

"Be ready!"

"I'm not doing this."

Harry threw his phone down beside him and just pulled his blanket up to his face, he had no intentions of going out tonight. As Harry laid comfortably on the couch the moon began to replace the shining sun. Just as the ending credits came on the tv Harry heard knocking at the door. Grudgingly he got up still wrapped in the warm blanket and walked towards the door. Harry knew who exactly was standing on the other side of the door and was ready to put up a fight to stay home.

Cassie and Niall stood outside the door. Cassie was wearing a silver metallic dress that hit at her middle of her thigh along with a pair of silver flats and a black coat hanging over her shoulders. Niall wore a pair of lavender pants paired with a black shirt and brown shoes.

"You guys look amazing!"

"Why thank you-"

"But I'm not going."

"Harry!"

"What! you know I don't like parties."

"You are not spending tonight alone, and we are going out, so you are coming with us."

"Cas this isn't up for discussion, I'm not going!"

"Both me and Niall will be there, you will be fine!"

The three had moved into the house and stood by the stairs. Harry tried to make his way back to the living room, but the couple had blocked his way.

"Cas please."

"Nope, up the stairs you go!"

"Niall a little help here!"

"Sorry mate, I'm with Cassie on this one, no one spends new year's alone!"

Cassie pulled Harry's forward by grabbing the blanket wrapped around him and began walking him up the stairs while Niall jogged up behind them. At the top of the stairs Harry immediately tried to turn around but was met with Niall's hands turning him back around and guided him into his bedroom.

Once inside Cassie immediately headed straight to Harry's closet as both Niall and Harry sat down on the unmade bed.

"What's gotten into you Cas, why do you want me to go out so bad?"

"Harry, I don't want you to be alone. I want you to have other people to hang out with besides me. As much as I know you love spending your Friday nights watching Phoebe and Daisy you need to be with people our age Harry. Besides, it's our senior year and we need to live a little."

Cassie patted Harry's head before turning back around shuffling clothes around on the hanger. Harry began fiddling with his hands. He knew that whatever he said he would still end up at the party, and truthfully it wasn't that the idea of the party complete revolted him it was knowing that everyone that would be there was going to be a couple, every senior and possibly junior couple would be there and well Harry was going as a third wheel.

While hard at work in Harry's closet Niall began to talk to Harry sensing that he was hesitant.

"So how was your Christmas?"

"Oh, it was good I had a movie marathon, made hot chocolate, went to the Tomlinson's house, had dinner with my mom. what about you? How was your Christmas?"

"Fun! My older brother came home from college so it- wait did you say you went over to Louis's house!"

"Shhh. Quiet! What did I tell you!"

Harry shoved his hand over Niall's voice to keep him quiet as his heart raced in his chest and his eyes widened as he turned to make sure Cassie hadn't heard anything. Niall was beaming, a huge goofy smile and playful look had appeared on his eyes and he was basically bouncing in excitement.

"Stop it, calm down!"

Harry was screaming through a whisper and it worked. Niall calmed down, as he stopped moving, he removed Harry's hand from his mouth and pulled him close to whisper in his ear.

"How was it, did anything happen?"

"Oh my god will you shut up! "

"What in the world are you two whispering about!"

Cassie turned around with a pair of acid-washed jeans, a white t-shirt, and a red flannel in her arms. Her eyes shifted between the boys looking for an answer, but they didn't talk. Niall giggled while looking between Harry and his girlfriend while Harry just looked at the edge of the floor.

Harry was caught between two worlds, he felt like absolute rubbish for lying to his best friends but on the other hand, he wasn't ready to tell her, he just couldn't possibly explain everything. He didn't even know everything.

"Nothing."

"Hm- yeah okay. Anyway, put these on. I'll go downstairs to pick out some shoes so you can change."

Harry now had a pile of clothes in his lap and Cassie walked out of his room closing the door behind her. Harry's head dropped back as he let out a groan before standing up.

"Okay did anything happen?"

"No, maybe, I don't know. It's literally nothing."

"Don't bullshit me, what happened."

"It's literally nothing Niall, we made hot chocolate with his sisters, opened presents, celebrated Louis's birthday, and well we just talked. Besides he's not into guys so don't let your mind wonder."

As Harry pulled on his new white shirt over his chest Niall had rolled onto his stomach leaning on his elbows with his hands propping his head fully hooked on the story.

"You never Styles, people change their minds you know! And what did you talk about? Christmas? School? Old memories? Life? Love?"

Harry's cheeks burned ablaze and became flustered as he remembered the late-night conversation he and Louis had not too long ago. Niall sat and watched as Harry's eyes became glazed over and frozen. Niall let out a large laugh and threw Harry his flannel that still laid on the bed.

"Earth to Harry! Harry!"

Harry snapped out of his trance just in time to flail his arms in order to catch the mustard flannel flying through the air. Niall just gave him a knowing glare as he continued to laugh.

"Yeah, you certainly talked about nothing!"

Harry fled onto one of the sleeves of his shirt and flung the rest of the shirt at Niall hitting him over the head with the fabric.

"SHUT YOUR MOUTH!"

"Sure, thing lovebird!"

Harry just bit his tongue and finally put on his flannel. A knock on the door indicated that Cassie was back with a pair of shoes.

"You can come in."

Cassie walked through the door holding Harry's black high-top converse in her hands. She handed the shoes to Harry along with a pair of socks she got from the laundry room. Without even exchanging words Harry had already begun to put on the shoes. Once they were laced up, he cuffed the bottom of his jeans to reveal the shoes.

Because Cassie was now in the room Niall had, to Harry's relief, let go of the conversation revolving around Louis. Conversation flew naturally as the three talked about their winter break, future plans for the rest of the school year, and eventually the party they were headed to.

Harry did his hair while everyone was talking. The sides of his hair were gelled slightly to keep them in place while the curls that sat on top of his head remained untouched with the sticky product and instead, he just fluffed his hair with his fingers.

"Okay, are you ready!"

"I guess, I just need to grab my jacket."

The bag of gifts that contained everything, including his jacket, that he brought back from Tomlinson's house sat in between Harry's bed and his desk. He lifted the bag to the bed and shuffled through until he saw the inner fleece of his jacket. He pulled it out but didn't put it on instead just folding it over his forearm before he, Niall, and Cassie left the room.

Harry grabbed his keys off of the counter as he offered himself to be the designated driver for the night and they all headed over the garage and hopped in his car. Harry tossed his jacket onto the center console of his car before the hot air came flowing through the air vents.

"I can't believe you dragged me into this." Harry backed out of the garage and started driving to the party's address.

The doorbell kept ringing relentlessly, but Louis wasn't supposed to have anyone over, and his mom and sisters went to the store for a special grocery run, none of their friends would show up without them here. Beginning to get aggravated with whoever was at the door Louis paused his show playing on the tv and began walking towards the door. While walking Louis checked the security app on his phone to see if the cameras had captured whoever was at the door, but no luck at all he saw was the notification saying the gate had been open by someone entering the code.

The doorbell kept ringing, this time it was nonstop, so Louis started to jog to the door. Annoyed Louis opened the door only to be confused. Instantly Ronnie gave a relieved sigh and walked inside.

"Finally, I was begging to think that you were ignoring me. Anyway, have you heard that Ashley and Jeremy broke up? Only three days ago. It's such a shame really just before new year's, guess they won't be getting a kiss tonight. Wait? Why aren't you ready?"

Louis was still sold holding the door open wrapped not only in a blanket but a wave of confusion and shock. What was Ronnie doing here? What party?

"What-what do you mean?"

"The party. Please tell me you didn't forget babe. Sierra and Luke are having their annual New Year's party, everybody is going to be there!"

"Did you tell me about this?"

"Babe we go every year, why wouldn't we go this year?"

"I just hadn't realized you wanted to go since we haven't talked since break."

"Are you sassing me right now? Louis, I was in Italy for Christ's sake I can't just call or text you whenever I was busy."

Louis just stood there, almost in shock. Had Ronnie not realized that she hadn't spoken to Louis in nearly fifteen days? Not to wish him a Merry Christmas, not a happy birthday, not anything. Why in the world would Louis believe she wanted to suddenly go out whenever she got back?

"Sorry, Ronnie but I have other plans tonight."

"Oh really? What plans are more important than being with me at Sierra's party?"

"I'm supposed to then go out with my sisters and my mom."

"Louis you can do whatever boring things with your family any other time, but only tonight can we go out and have the party of our life with all of our friends! Why would you want to stay here where you can't drink anything?"

"Ronnie, they are my family. I'm eighteen and I may not be back here next year for the holidays and I want to spend time with my sisters."

"Louis, come on you'll be back tonight, besides are your sisters even capable of staying up until midnight?"

"Ronnie that's not the point, I want to spend time with them."

Footsteps came up behind, it was Jay. She and the girls had come back from the store and when driving up the driveway she saw the door was open and decided to check it out once she got inside.

"Oh, hi Ronnie, what's going on here? Are you just going to invite penguins into our house Lou?"

"Oh sorry, mom!"

Louis gave an odd chuckle and rushed to shut the door while moving Ronnie began talking to his mother.

"I just came over to grab Louis so we could head over to a friend's house for a new year's party."

Suddenly Ronnie had turned into a sweet teenage girl. Her voice was light and soft, not a single ounce of anger, annoyance, or rudeness could be traced from her words. All visible tension on her eyes and muscles had disappeared completely.

"Well, I hope you aren't going dressed like that baby. You better go get changed."

Jay had turned around to go back to the girls and Ronnie just gave Louis a smile before she began to walk up the staircase. Reluctantly Louis followed his girlfriend up the stairs and into his room.

As soon as he walked in his room Ronnie was already in his closet comparing his shirts to the color of her dress, a bright lime green. Louis knew he had to be careful because he could already feel his annoyance leaking out of him. Louis plopped himself down on his bed and pulled his blanket over his body. He really did not want to go to this party.

A small thump fell by Louis's rib cage causing him to prop himself up and see what was lying next to him, it was awful. A neon green polo was folded next to a pair of gray pants.

"I'm not wearing that."

"Of course, you are, we need to match."

"No. if I'm going to go to this party, I'm not wearing that."

"Ugh fine. but please be presentable."

Louis rolled his eyes and got up off the bed pushing himself past a very clearly upset Ronnie. Walking into his close Louis grabbed a pair of black skinny jeans and a black fitted t-shirt. A pair of white slip-on vans made their way to his feet before he made his way over to his bathroom, pulling out his favorite hair gel before styling his long hair.

Deciding to put it into a light quiff the edges of his hair fell onto his angular right cheekbone while the back hairs gracefully curled upwards from against his neck. The ruggedness of his messy hair paired with the sharp angles of his face mixing with the ocean blue of his eyes created a bad boy illusion.

Ronnie was sitting on Louis's bed on her phone going through her social media as Louis walked back in his room. Walking over to his nightstand to grab his wallet and watch, while sliding the cold silver over his small wrist all of a sudden Ronnie looked up and her eyes widened, but not in the way you would think. Her jaw dropped open and her eyebrows furrowed downward as she scanned Louis up and down. Louis rolled his eyes before turning around to grab his keys which laid on his small table near his bay window. A soft smile crossed his thin cherry lips as he saw the photo of his sisters with Harry.

It wasn't until Louis heard Ronnie's voice that a wave of guilt washed over him. Here he was trying to be a better brother, the brother he wanted to be, but he was too afraid to say no to Ronnie that he was leaving them once again.

"Please tell me you will put on a nice blazer or something or change your shoes?"

"If you want me to go to this stupid party then I'm wearing this, Ronnie. Deal with it."

"God Louis why are you so pissy today?"

"Let's just go already."

Louis shoved himself past Ronnie and made him out of his room and down the stairs. Ronnie had quickly followed right behind her boyfriend in an attempt to talk some sense into him before they got to his family but that wouldn't happen.

When Louis finally came to a stop, he was standing by the kitchen table where his mom and his sisters were now eating dinner. Both Louis and Ronnie were able to put on a good act and acted civil to each other while in front of the family.

Louis gave his mom, Daisy, and Phoebe a kiss on the cheek before telling them that he was off.

"Lou honey, make sure you grab your jacket, it's hanging in the coat closet!"

"Of course! Thank you, mom,"

Louis opened the closet door and began scanning for the denim washed jacket. Finally, his eyes landed on his cream-colored fleece lined jacket. Quickly tugging it down off of the hanger Louis shoved the jacket under his arm as he walked out into the garage with Ronnie now staying close to his side.

Once he unlocked his car Louis pulled out his jacket and slid his arm into the warm sleeves. Weirdly the sleeves fell an extra three inches past his hands and the bottom hem now fell just under his but instead of sitting loosely on his hips. Beginning to observe the jacket it looked exactly the same to him, the same denim wash, the same-colored fleece, the same stitching patterns, the same buttons on the sleeves. Everything was the exact same except now he was swimming in the jacket.

Knowing he couldn't stand there forever and continue to think about his unusual jacket Louis opened his car door and slid into the driver seat of his self-driving Tesla. Now trapped into a small, confined space something husky begins to fill the car grabbing Louis's attention. It smelled like perfection.

Chapter Twenty:

After a fifteen-minute drive Niall, Cassie, and Harry finally arrived at the site of the party. The sun had already sunk behind the horizon leaving the only light to be that of the streetlights and light coming through the windows of the nearby homes. The street was packed with cars along with teenagers walking towards a large mansion style house.

"Are we really doing this?"

Harry immediately felt his stomach drop at the sight of so many people. All he could think about was that he could be cuddled up on his couch with a cup of tea watching a movie. Harry really did not like being in a crowd.

"Yup, we are going to have some fun tonight!"

Cassie patted Harry's shoulder before opening the door and getting out.

"Come on dude, just try to enjoy it."

Niall and Harry gathered their things before Harry turned off his car as they both got out of the car joining Cassie who was leaning on the car. Niall walked around the car causing Cassie to join him before wrapping her arms around his waist before they began walking towards the party.

"How much farther is this damn party?"

"It's not too much farther."

"Ugh, thank god."

"Well if somebody had been ready when we got to his house, we would have gotten a better parking spot."

"Yeah yeah, whatever."

The concrete sidewalk in which the trio along with many other high schoolers began to buzz with small vibrations of the loud music playing through dozens of speakers signaling the party of close, and sure enough only minutes later Harry's sight was filled with dancing teenagers all with a red solo cup in their hands.

Cassie and Niall both grabbed a cup of what they assumed to be beer before heading around the house into its backyard where a band was playing. It had already been decided that Harry would be the designated driver since A, it was his car they drove, and B, he was underage anyway so he couldn't drink. It's not like that stopped a lot of people, especially on New Year's but breaking the law was out of the question for Harry.

By the time Harry had followed his friends, they were already on the dance floor along with upwards of another one hundred people.

"Oh god, why did I agree to this..."

Harry's Adam's apple bobbed slowly as he tried to swallow away his fear. He began to try and walk around the dancing bodies politely but when you are walking through dozens of already half-drunk teenagers that aren't paying attention that doesn't really work, so Harry's attempt at being polite ended up failing as he was pushed up against random bodies as he made his way through the crowd.

"I'm sorry. Sorry, Excuse me, Oh I'm sorry."

It felt like an eternity before Harry finally caught a glimpse of Cassie's autumn hair as it swirled from side to side matching the beat of the music and her free hand was intertwined with Nialls. Harry decided it was best to try and match the smiles that they both wore on their lips, the least he could do was pretend to be happy for them.

The couple finished their drinks in a large gulp before placing their empty cups into one of the many garbage bags laid on the floor. Soon both Niall and Cassie each grabbed one of Harry's hands on their own, pulling him into a tight circle.

The band continued to blare their music through the heavy-duty speakers so loud that even being less than a foot apart from each other they three friends couldn't hear each other unless they screamed their words. Covers of songs like Teenage Dirtbag, She's Out of Her Mind, Mr. Brightside, and Jasey Ray made the dance floor turn into a time machine allowing many people, Harry included, to forget about the current problems in their lives.

Tired of dancing and beginning to feel his stomach grumble Harry decided to pull away and head inside.

"I'm gonna go get some food!"

"WHAT?"

"I'M GOING TO GET SOME FOOD!"

"OKAY!"

"HAVE YOU AND NIALL EATEN ANYTHING?"

"OF COURSE, MATE! DO YOU THINK I WOULD NEVER NOT EAT?!"

Harry just laughed as he walked away, at least he knew that at least a little of the alcohol they had been consuming was going to be absorbed by some food. Harry made his way over to the opened sliding glass door that led into the kitchen area of whoever's house this was. Harry thought it was insane that somebody would feel okay having a bunch of strangers over to their house, but hey Harry didn't judge too much as he knew that he himself would never do anything to concern the owner.

As Harry's feet went from the outside grass to the cold tile floor, he noticed the shift in the atmosphere. Instead of a cover band playing with people dancing there was Ariana Grande, Shawn Mendes, Justin Bieber, and Khalid blared through the surround sound speakers with people sitting along the couches and stray chairs just doing shots.

Anybody could tell you that it was a clear divide of the poplars and the regulars. A comical laugh escaped from Harry as he walked straight into the kitchen trying to avoid the drunk teens on the other side of the wall. Harry was thankful that unlike Louis's house the kitchen was completely cut off from the rest of the house, only a faint beat of the music could be heard.

Harry quickly realized that all of the alcohol and major party food weren't in the kitchen, and suddenly it made perfect sense now that the kitchen itself wasn't packed to the brim like the rest of the house. Harry saw a loaf of bread sitting on the counter and took note as he walked to the open pantry. Sitting on the edge of a shelf was a jar of peanut butter and Harry had never been so happy. Harry's large hand grasped jar and pulled it out before walking over to the counter and setting it down. Trying to keep things clean Harry laid down a small paper towel sheet before opening the bread loaf and taking out two pieces and setting them down on top. Harry unscrewed the lid of the peanut butter jar before realizing that he didn't have a knife. Quickly and quietly, Harry began to open the kitchen drawers looking for something to spread the food.

With his back turned away from the kitchen entrance Harry was still rummaging through the kitchen when he heard the door open. Harry immediately stopped and his head snapped upwards.

"Wow there Haz it's just me, no need to become a deer in headlights!"

Louis's voice registered in Harry's head before the sight of him registered in his eyes. Harry's shoulders dropped with relief knowing that it was just Louis.

"Sorry, just wasn't expecting anybody."

"Oh, you weren't expecting anyone to come into a kitchen at a New Year's Eve party?"

"Shut up!"

The boys let out a laugh as Louis walked deeper into the kitchen while Harry stood up.

"What are you looking for?"

"Just a knife."

"in the drawer to your left. Wait, you aren't going to stab me, right?"

"If you keep interrogating me maybe!"

Now with a butter knife in his hand, Harry jokingly turned around pointing the dull knife at Louis.

"I'm just trying to make a sandwich."

Harry now walked over to where he had already begun to make his sandwich.

"You know there's food outside, right?"

"How much of that food is laced with some form of drugs or alcohol?"

"Good point."

As Harry dipped the knife down into the tan, creamy peanut butter Louis appeared right at his side brushing up against his bicep. Damn, he smelt good. Harry hadn't meant to but with Louis pressed so close to him his actions slowed dramatically almost going in slow motion. Just as Harry started to spread the mixture onto the small pieces of bread Louis jumped up and off his arm.

"You know what would make this sandwich so much better?"

"What..."

Louis tried to hold back a mysterious smirk but failed as his lips slowly curled into a smile. As fast as a cheetah Louis jumped up onto the kitchen counter opening a high up cabinet. He began to shuffle through seasonings and spices before turning around triumphantly.

"Honey!"

"Oh my god, Louis!"

Louis jumped right off of the counter and ran to where Harry was standing basically shoving him out of the way as he uncapped the bottle of honey before squeezing the sweet gold liquid on top of the peanut butter.

"Louis you're gonna drown the sandwich!"

Because Harry was so much taller than Louis, he was able to grab the bottle from his hand before too much honey left the bottle, however, some of the honey dripped into Louis's hair.

"Styles!"

"Hey, you're the one ruining my dinner!"

"you got my hair sticky!"

"Oh boo-hoo, I think you'll service Lou!"

Harry was full-on laughing as he tried to finish making his sandwich as Louis tried to rub his fingers through his hair attempting to get the honey out. With the slices of bread now sitting on top of each other Harry decided to cut the sandwich diagonally, handing one half to Louis.

"Thanks."

"Of course."

"How did you remember peanut butter and honey?"

"How could I not remember the one piece of food we ate every day after school for nearly a year. It's probably the only thing I can make!"

"I don't know how I'm not sick of these by now, I'm sure we've eaten at least five hundred of these each!"

"You're telling me I think I ate two of these a day after my dad passed! He loved them."

"Wasn't he the one who first made us one?"

"Yeah, mom was away on business and it's all he knew how to make, the two of us ate them for breakfast, lunch, and dinner for a whole week!"

"Are you sure you're not made of peanut butter and honey?"

"Maybe."

Both boys held a smile as they finished their food. Louis had once again needed up on the counter, this time sitting on top while Harry stayed standing. Harry began to clean up his mess, tying the bag of bread shut and putting the jar back on the jar of peanut butter before taking it back to the pantry. Remembering where Louis had gotten the honey Harry put the bottle back where it belonged.

"How in the hell can you reach that!"

"Not all of us are short like you Louis."

"How tall are you?"

"Around 6ft I think."

"Geeze."

"How short are you?"

"Hey, give me a break, I'm tall!"

Harry shot daggers at Louis as if to say, 'yeah right'.

"How tall?"

"5'9"

Harry burst into laughter before trying to cover his mouth with his hand.

"You're not 5'9, Niall is 5'9 and you're at least an inch shorter than him."

"Shut up, I am in fact 5'9 you can call my doctor if you want!"

"Yeah, sure okay Mr. 5'9."

"Stop laughing!"

"I-I'm sorry!"

Louis had picked up a washcloth and ran it under water wetting the material so he could attempt to get the rest of the honey out of his hair.

"Here let me help."

Louis happily gave Harry the washcloth since he couldn't reach the back of his own head where a glob of honey still laid in his hair. It wasn't until Harry stood right behind him with one hand holding the side of his head and the other rubbing his hair against the wet towel that he noticed something strange.

Louis's chest began to feel tight, and he could feel his heartbeat quicken. All of his muscles began to go stiff as he continued to feel Harry's presence strong behind him. What was happening?

Meanwhile, Harry had tried to keep himself calm. He focused heavily on keeping his breaths slow and steady while having to remind himself to not rub his free fingers along Louis's soft feathery hair. They were friends and nothing more. They could never be anything more so why would Harry allow himself to get carried away at the moment. Harry just made sure to take in every moment, he knew there would never be another opportunity like this.

"Okay, you're all good."

"Thanks."

Instantly Louis jumped off of the counter, his small feet colliding loudly with the floor before he quickly made his way towards the kitchen door. The last thing Harry saw was a half-smile of Louis as the door started to separate the two.

Harry stood there confused for a minute before walking over and washing out the washcloth in the sink before folding it neatly over the edge of the sink. Making sure the kitchen was indeed clean Harry himself walked out the kitchen slowly, still trying to commit the events that just happened to his memory. Finally looking at his phone Harry saw the time, 11:45 pm.

"Huh, at least the time passed."

As Harry stood between the barrier of the preppy popular that stood insides listening to the pop radio icons and the average people just like him who danced like nobody cared he only remained of the difference between him and Louis. Harry felt a sharp sting in his chest and heaviness deep in his gut.

Stepping back out onto the grass Harry caught one last glance at Louis. He was sitting on the edge of a white leather couch with Ronnie sitting on his lap talking happily while he was staring blankly at a painting hanging on the wall.

Not having a clue where Cassie and Niall were and not coming here with a date Harry decided it was best to just sit on a barstool that was next to a table high top. And for the next fifteen minutes, that's where he stayed, just sitting and observing his fellow classmates, many of them looking like they had met their soulmates under the December stars.

When Louis finally returned to his group, he could tell that Ronnie was absolutely pissed, but of course, needing to play the perfect couple Ronnie didn't say anything instead just climbing on top of Louis's lap. Louis had absolutely no idea what his friends were talking about, but he felt a sharp tugging on his wrist.

"Come on Lou only one minute until midnight!" Louis tried to contain his eye roll by deciding to put on his jacket. Something begins instantly pulling his attention. Louis popped up the collar of his jacket and a vaguely familiar scent entered his nostrils intoxicating his body.

Louis was still trying to figure out why this random scent of firewood and cinnamon felt so close to him when he felt Ronnie slip her hand around his waist pulling him down slightly before she pressed her lips to his.

It wasn't until Louis opened his eyes and looked out the window that he figured out what the scent was. It was Harry.

Chapter Twenty-one:

Louis's eyes flickered open in a rush of fear, panic, and confusion. Ronnie had begun to kiss his neck and his cheek messily as the intoxicating alcohol was coursing through her veins. With his head tilted to the side he caught a glimpse of the curly hair he knew all too well. Harry was sitting at a table with his phone in his hand, all alone. The sight pained Louis, out of all the people at this party Harry was the last person who deserved to be sitting alone as the clock struck midnight. Louis hadn't realized he had been staring until Ronnie's lips had stopped moving and her own eyes began to pierce through Louis's now hot and flustered skin.

"Louis what's wrong babyyyyyyy"

Her words where so slurred Louis almost didn't know what Ronnie was saying. While Louis shifted his head back towards his girlfriend his eyes stayed locked on best friend. Ex-best friend? Friend? Oh god, Louis didn't even know what they were anymore.

"Louisssss who are you looking at?"

"N-"

"AH, are they prettier than me?"

Just then Harry got up out of his chair and started walking towards the crowded dance floor, and sure enough, Louis's eyes followed him until he could no longer track the curly head. Little did Louis know that Ronnie was trying to follow his own eyes to see who he was staring at. Much to Louis's relief, she was so drunk, and her vision was so blurry she couldn't tell anybody apart.

Something was pulling deep into Louis's gut, he needed to get out of here. Louis needed to think he needed to figure out whatever was going on with him. As if God had heard Louis's silent prayers his phone started bringing.

"Sorry, I have to take this."

Louis stood up leaving Ronnie looking like a lost puppy sitting on the couch. Louis went behind a pillar and accepted the call. Holding the phone to his ear Louis expected to hear a voice, he didn't expect to hear anybody he knew as the number was unknown and every person, he has ever known was either at this party with him or safe at home. But no voice came through.

Confused Louis kept moving the phone away from his ear so he could see the caller ID. After nearly a minute of silence Louis decided it was probably a misdial and he hung up the phone, however, Louis made no moves to go back to his group of friends.

Instead, Louis just stood there listening to all of the slurred words and blaring music mixing with the sounds of bottles and cups being tossed on the floor. It was a sad realization for Louis, he didn't want to be here, not at all. The worst part is he didn't know how everything had gotten so out of hand. Louis knew he couldn't stay much longer at the party if he did, he might lose it on someone and he knew that that was not going to be good.

Being a clever little lad, he was Louis knew that he could easily get out of this situation with only a little white lie. Quickly Louis walked back over to the couch where Ronnie softly tapped her shoulder.

"Hey, can I need to speak to you."

"what's up?"

Ronnie wobbly stood up leaning heavily on Louis for support. Louis tried his best to not get annoyed at Ronnie's current state and just complete his plan, but damn was that hard. Louis hated it with a burning passion when people of drunk off the feet because he knew they made stupid decisions, deadly decisions.

"Look so that was my mom calling, apparently the twins are very sick, and she doesn't know what to do and she needs my help, so I need to go home. I know I drove here so I can give you a ride home right now if you want because you are certainly not driving, or I can give you money for a cab.

"Did they drink too much alcohol? Oh, they'll regret that in the morning!"

Ronnie was full-on laughing while she brought a cup of coke and bourbon to her lips before swelling the intoxicating liquid. It took absolutely everything Louis had to remain calm, his fingertips were shaking, and he could feel his temperature rising. Louis took a deep breath and bit his bottom lip until the taste of blood hit his tongue.

"Ronnie, I have to go do you want a ride home or are you going to take a cab?"

"I'm not leaving when this party is still amazing, I'll figure it out. I'll probably just sleepover with Ashley, after all, it is her house!

"Okay, but here's a twenty in case you change your mind. Whatever you do, do not drive or allow anyone else to drive either you take a cab, or you stay here. you got that?"

"Yeah yeah, whatever don't drive I got it. Bye!" Ronnie took the twenty-dollar bill and shoved it into her small purse which hung over her shoulder before walking back into the massive living room. All Louis could do was shake his head as he turned around and started walking towards the back yard.

The crowd outside was starting to fizzle out and Louis could see everyone looking for the friends and asking for people who hadn't drunk to give them a ride home. There were garbage bags full of red solo cups and food wrappers littered everywhere, in the poorly lit dark night Louis had to keep a close eye where he stepped in order to not trip over the bags.

Louis weaved his small frame through the groups of his schoolmates with his hands buried in his, well potentially Harry's jacket and eventually made his way out onto the street.

Cabs could be seen entering and leaving the street, the sight helped calm Louis down a little bit. With the streets now buzzing with traffic Louis and the other teenagers were all forced to walk on the sidewalks. Thankfully though the sidewalks were extremely wide allowing for nearly seven people to fit from side to side with room to spare between them.

Louis could tell that the people who had been outside dancing during the party were definitely less wasted than the people who decided to party inside the mini mansion just by the way they were walking. well, most of them except for a group of three people who caught his eye.

One guy stood in between a girl in a lavender dress and a blonde boy who wore a pair of matching pants where stumbling so much it looked like their legs were made of jelly. He could tell the man in the middle was struggling to keep his friends up as he could see the man's hands shifting every few seconds trying to keep ahold of their bodies.

Because the group was only a couple feet ahead of him Louis decided to speed up his pace to meet the group and help get the people their car or offer them a cab ride if needed. The closer Louis got the more intense a certain scent got, with every step the smell of burnt firewood to stronger. Louis sniffed the collar of his jacket and of course, it was the same exact scent. Harry.

"Here let me help you."

Louis grabbed the hands of the blonde boy shifting the boys' bodyweight entirely onto him.

"Thanks."

Louis was lucky that the group had stopped walking because he froze at the voice. Louis looked up to see the familiar red flannel and the mop of curls turned away from him almost picking up the girl who he now recognized to be Cassie which meant he had Niall practically wrapped around his own body.

"Are you staring at my girlfriend?"

Nialls slurred yet still chirpy voice brought Louis back to reality realizing they still were standing in the middle of the sidewalk surrounded by other people. Oh shit, had anyone else seen him staring?

"Ugh--ugh no don't worry Niall she's all yours."

"OH MY GOD, you know my name?!"

"I do Niall." Louis left out a soft chuckle as the blonde boy was just so happy.

"wow, I must be pretty cool if YOU know my name."

"You are one of the coolest guys I know."

"That must be how I got Cassie; I mean look at her!"

Niall stood up a little bit and turned his head to sneak another glance at his equally drunk girlfriend. His blue eyes grew bigger, filling with love and admiration for the strawberry blonde girl. It was clear to Louis that Niall loved Cassie with all of his heart, it should be clear to anybody who saw the way he looked at her or how even when he was piss drunk, he only thought of Cassie. Louis realized that it was that type of relationship he craved so badly, not the one he currently had.

"She is a beautiful one Niall, but I think she lo- likes her because you're a good guy, not because I think you are cool."

"Hey! that's my girl, go get your own lover!"

"Alright alright. But don't worry I don't think she'll leave you."

"Oh, why is she looking at me?"

Louis just couldn't help it. He found Niall absolutely hilarious at the moment that he was laughing every time he spoke.

"She is."

"Wait do I look good?"

Niall frantically started messing with his hair and rubbing his hands around his face trying to clean himself up.

"Yes, Niall you look great."

"Good because she looks amazing!"

Only a few steps later Louis spotted Harry's car and the four of them started to cross the street.

"Hey, Harry do you want Niall in the back or the front?"

"Oh, he goes in the back, he gets very touchy when he's drunk."

"Okay then."

Louis let out another chuckle as the two pairs finally reached the door handles. Harry reached into his pocket and pulled out his keys to unlock the car.

"I'll put Cassie in on this side if you'll put Niall in on the other."

"Yeah, no problem."

Louis moved himself and Niall around the trunk of the car while Harry already had his side door open and was trying to get Cassie into the car. Louis reached for the door handle of the car pulling it to open it. Niall seemed confused about getting into the car almost refusing to get in the car voluntarily.

"What's wrong Niall?"

"I'm not being kidnapped right?"

"No, you are not being kidnapped, Niall. You remember Harry, right?"

"Of course, he's Cassy's best friend."

"Well, he is going to drive you and Cassie home to make sure you stay safe."

"Ahh, he's a good friend."

"He is, isn't he."

Louis suddenly got really quiet, he knew how good of a person Harry was, he had been his best friend, but he let him go. It was painful to see exactly what he lost, he wished more than anything he could turn back time and make sure he never lost his friendship with Harry.

Niall could tell the sudden change in Louis's demeanor even being as drunk as he was. While Louis helped a now compliment Niall into the car and buckled his seatbelt for him, he was now completely quiet almost as if he was now placed behind a wall.

There were small little details that Niall picked up on such as the way Louis's eyes would flicker towards

Harry with a sad look in his eye or the deep breaths, he was now taking that something was up. Something was going on between Louis and Harry, Niall just didn't know what that something was.

Once Niall was safely buckled in the car Louis shut the car door now encasing Niall and Cassie inside. Quickly Niall rolled down the window and his eyes followed Louis.

"Do you need something Niall? Are you going to be sick?"

Louis was now back at the window leaning down onto the car frame.

"No. just thinking."

"Okay. Maybe keep this window down just in case you get sick, okay?"

"Okay. you're a good friend you know that?"

A soft smile appeared on Louis's cherry thin lips. Those seven words meant so much to him, especially coming from somebody who he knew was such a good person.

"Thank you, Niall. That means a lot."

Harry had now gotten into the driver's seat but had all his attention on Cassie who was dancing in her seat. Louis's eyes were now stuck on the sight happening in front of him. Louis knew that none of his friends, teammates, or even his girlfriend would act this way, so helpful, so caring. All they would do it video him puking his guts out on the side of the road.

For the second time in just a few minutes, Harry felt another ping of guilt, sadness, and regret pass through him.

"Why are you staring at Harry?"

Shit.

"Do me a favor Niall?"

"Okay."

"Don't ever let go of people like Harry. You will always need a person like him in your life and if you let them go it will hurt. It will hurt a lot. So please, do not take him for granted."

Louis hadn't meant to give Niall such a deep piece of information, but it was too late to go back now. All that Niall responded with was a simple head nod. Louis slowly stood back up, tapping his hand twice on the car before he finally was able to make his way back into the street and to his own car.

"Louis!"

Or maybe not. Harry's window was rolled down and his body was turned to face the open street. Louis couldn't be mad though, after all, it was Harry.

"Hey."

"Thank you for helping me with Cas and Niall, I know it was a handful."

"Don't worry, it's nothing. You are getting them home safe, it's the least I could do."

The world around them seemed to go silent. It felt as if it was just the two of them standing in the middle of nowhere. It was a serene feeling.

"Um well I'll let you get going, I know you have a lot on your plate."

Just as Louis was starting to back up, he caught a glimpse of a familiar-looking fabric. Sitting on the passenger seat was another identical jacket to his. It looked small like it would fit him. Louis started to pull at the end of the sleeves of the jacket he was wearing seeing just how big it really was on him.

"Yeah okay, thanks again for your help."

"Of course. Get home safe styles."

"You to Tomlinson."

Harry rolled up his window and watched as Louis walked back across the street and onto the opposite sidewalk. When his feet finally hit the busy pavement, Harry pulled out of his parking spot and began to drive his drunk friends back to his house.

Chapter Twenty-two:

The radio was turned down low in the car so Harry could keep an eye on his two passengers. Harry always hated driving on holidays where people drank, New Years, St. Patrick's Day, World Cup finals, even though he only has driven during one of those, and surprisingly Halloween. Harry knew the dangers all too well, which is why he's always the designated driver, but he still held onto that little ounce of fear that someone else may not be doing the right thing and that he'll have to pay the price. Just like Richard Tomlinson.

Thankfully Cassie and Niall were keeping themselves busy by heavily flirting with each other, apparently, they really didn't know they were already dating. At least it was a cute sight to see.

Harry always droves on the backroads on nights like these when he knew for a fact there were drunk drivers because let's be honest, they weren't aware enough to think about taking them. Harry turned off of the busy neighborhood street and onto an unlit street turning on his bright headlights to be able to see. It was then that Niall stopped talking, at least to Cassie.

"I knew it! I am being kidnapped!"

"Relax Ni, I'm not-"

"No, I know Louis put you up to this didn't he!"

"No. what? Where did you get that from?"

"I knew Louis was behind this!"

"Niall, Louis isn't behind anything because no one is being kidnapped!"

"Cassie we are so being kidnapped!"

"I repeat no one is getting kidnapped! I am just taking the back roads because it's safer!"

"Harold are we being kidnapped?"

"I might just kidnap you if you use a nickname again."

"CASSIE! Don't use a nickname!"

"Wait-"

"Niall are you oka-"

"Where is Louis? Where is he hiding?"

"Louis isn't here!"

"Is he in the trunk?"

"What? No! Niall listen to me very quickly. Louis. Is. Not. In. The. Car."

"So, you're not helping him kidnap us?"

"No. I am taking all of us back to my house so we can sleep."

"He's not at the house, right?"

"No. Why would he be at the house?"

"Why wouldn't your boyfriend be at your house?"

"Niall! HE IS NOT MY BOYFRIEND!"

It wasn't until Harry flicked his eyes back into the rearview mirror and saw Cassie's jaw practically hitting the floor that he remembered she was in the car. This wasn't good.

"Hold up you're dating Louis?"

"Cas-"

"Of course, not baby, he's just secretly in love with him."

"NIALL!"

"What! it's not like I'm wrong!"

"I am not in love with him!"

"You totally are!"

Harry rolled his eyes, there was no use in trying to deal with Niall at this point he clearly is too drunk to change his mind. Harry's mind instantly went to Cassie, she's going to be so pissed.

"Wait- when did Harry fall in love?"

"I don't know at least two weeks ago but probably longer."

"And he loves Louis, as in Louis Tomlinson. The Louis?"

"Yes, the Louis."

"Will you quit speaking about me as if I'm not sitting right in front of you!"

"Fine. When did you fall in love with Louis?"

"I didn't fall in love with Louis."

The tension in the car was enough to fuel a rocket to Mars. Harry felt as if he could cry; he was so overwhelmed with guilt. Cassie was filled to the brim with shock. Even with the dead silence of the car, Cassie was struggling to comprehend the situation. Maybe it was the alcohol. Maybe it was the shock. Maybe it was the feeling of betrayal. Maybe it was because she was piecing the puzzle together. Maybe it was all of it.

Everyone in the car stayed silent for the remainder of the ride home. Niall sat in the middle of his seat clearly uncomfortable with the situation building between Harry and Cassie. But he could deal with that since, in a way, it was his fault that this was happening right then and there.

Cassie had shifted over to the edge of her seat leaning against the window, her eyes locked on the empty abyss outside. Harry had somehow managed to continue driving safely. However, both of his hands gripped the steering wheel so tight his knuckles looked like they belonged to a ghost.

Because Harry took the backroads home instead of the highway the ride was extended to a thirty-minute drive but finally, he turned onto his quiet little neighborhood street that was illuminated by glowing streetlights and pulled into his garage. Harry knew his mom wasn't home, the hospital was crazy during the new year. Alcohol paired with a lack of common sense meant a lot of weird hospital visits.

"Cassie-"

As soon as Harry had put the car in park Cassie had unlocked her door and ran into the house. This really isn't going to end well. Harry fell limp in his seat as he let out an exaggerated breath of defeat. Knowing Cassie as well as he did Harry knew that she needed some time to process all of this information, she needed to understand what was happening first before he could explain himself to her. But that didn't make waiting any easier.

"Harry, I'm really sorry I didn't mean for Cassie to find out."

Deafening silence hung in the air that was trapped inside the car. Niall's voice was shaky, he clearly felt awful about ruining Harry's secret.

"Don't be. It's not your fault Niall. I shouldn't have ever kept a secret from her in the first place. If anything, you helped me from this being any worse in the future." Harry gave Niall a weak smile over his shoulder before he turned back around and started to pull his keys out of the ignition when Niall spoke again.

"Louis was right."

The words were only supposed to be for himself but since everything else was still. Harry heard the three words that barely escaped from Niall's lips causing him to stop in his tracks.

"What did you say?"

Niall's eyes went wide with panic, he didn't know whether or not it would be a good thing to tell Harry the things Louis had said. Was it his place to tell Harry? Probably not but at this point, he's already ruined one secret why not just add another?

"U-uh that L-Louis was uh-right."

"Uh-huh and ah what exactly did Louis say?"

Harry was now unbuckled and completely turned around in his seat practically sitting backward on his center console to look Niall directly in the eye. It was pressure. It was scary. It was nerve-racking. Did He really want to know what Louis said? What if it's bad? Worse. What if it's something good and all it does is complicate things?

Niall could sense the timidness that poked and prodded at Harry's already timid voice. He didn't want to say too much but if he said too little what was the point of Cassie finding out about Harry and Louis through himself instead of Harry?

"Uh-he s-said that you where-are an amazing person and friend and to never lose you because it will hurt. A lot."

Harry slumped backwards in shock as he tried to process the words he just heard. So many thoughts were flying through his brain Harry felt as if he was spinning out of control. However, one sentence kept replaying in his head.

"When I saw you with Cassie, I figured you were fine without me."

All this time Harry thought that Louis had just kicked him to the curb when he got popular, but after Louis broke down the thought lingered in his head that maybe he left Louis just as much as he left him. Now. Now though Harry can't help but wonder if the only reason that Louis officially left the friendship was that he felt as if he was being a burden on Harry's life.

"He said that?"

"He did."

Niall could tell that Harry had traveled to another dimension and knew that if they didn't get inside now, they never would.

"Come on, let's go inside. I'm sure Cas will be calm enough soon."

Harry did a slow nod as he reached for his jacket that still laid into the passengers' seat. He couldn't help but wonder how he made the whole night without needing it, or how he forgot it in the car in the first place. Nonetheless Harry eventually got out of his car and locked it before leading Niall into the house.

Walking inside the body could hear the upstairs shower running signaling that Cassie was still wrapping her head around the situation. Niall went towards the front door and picked up a navy-blue duffle bag that he brought over that held a change of clothes, a toothbrush, and a phone charger. Needless to say, he came prepared for a sort of impromptu sleepover.

Harry stood at the base of his narrow and creaky staircase looking up as fear crept into his normally peaceful gaze. Harry didn't know what to expect once he was actually up there, he has never been in this position before. In their four years of friendship neither of them has lied to each other, about anything, and there Harry was. Faced with the burden of a lie, well more like delaying of truth but it was still a lie.

Niall walked out of the guest bathroom now dressed in a pair of basketball shorts and a t-shirt still holding his duffle bag.

"I'll be on the couch if you need me. I know how she can get too. I trust you with her, I know it's between the two of you, so I'll give you space to figure it out together."

"Thanks, man."

Both boys gave each other a weak side smile before Niall's footsteps filled the empty air. Harry stood in the same place for another ten minutes looking up the stairs and back down at his feet over and over again. The shower had stopped running what seems like ages ago and Harry had heard Cassie's light footsteps walk across the hall into his room. He knew where to find her if he would just walk up the stairs.

It took all of the courage Harry had to move his feet up each and every stair, he felt as if he was walking a never-ending marathon not sixteen wooden stairs. Once he finally made it to the second floor Harry froze once again. Clutching his jacket in one hand and his keys in the other he dragged his body to his door. Harry's large and sturdy knuckles tapped lightly against his wooden door, even with it being his house, his room Harry knew he needed to knock.

When he got no response, he placed his palm on the door handle and slowly pressed it down before opening the door ever so slightly. With one little tap from his pointer finger, the door continued to open at a snail's pace until the opening was large enough to get through. Harry took a hesitant step inside. He expected to find Cassie either laying or sitting on his bed but instead it was empty. Walking deeper inside Harry's heart rate felt heavier every time his foot hit the carpet. It was only made worse when he spotted Cassie sitting underneath his desk wrapped in a blanket starring out his only bedroom window.

Harry threw his keys on his bed and walked over crouching down and crawling on the floor to meet Cassie. Cassie was small enough to be able to sit normally and still not have to worry about hitting her head on the wood above her while Harry had to lean forward as his back leaned against the wall behind him just so he could even fit.

Nobody said anything. For nearly thirty minutes Cassie and Harry just sat side by side, Harry stared forward, and Cassie still kept her head sideways to look into the night sky. No one wanted to speak first, both were walking on uncharted territory, both felt lost.

"Cas-"

"Har-"

Chapter Twenty-three:

Cassie and Harry quickly snapped their heads back towards each other. For the first time in nearly two hours, they saw each other like they really saw each other. The fear, the regret, the pain, and every emotion in between was easily etched into every crease of their tired faces.

They kept their eyes locked on each other's while they kept their mouths shut. Cassie now shifted her body backwards to lean back on the wall uncomfortably just as Harry was sitting. She removed her eyes from Harry's and let them linger to the wall across from her.

"Why didn't you tell me?"

Cassie tried her best not to let the tears slip out from her eyes as she spoke softly. Her lips were quivering, and she dropped her head down on top of her bent knees to hide her face from Harry.

"I-I didn't think there was anything to tell."

It was now Harry's turn as he felt the steaming burn of a single tear roll down his cheek as he spoke. Once the silence had hung the air long enough Harry turned slightly to get a better look at Cassie.

"Cas."

"Will you please look at me?"

It was a desperate plea; Harry was exhausted, and he felt as if his heart was being ripped right out of his chest. He knew that Cassie must have only felt worse which is why he was being so patient with her.

Slowly Cassie turned her head over so she could now see Harry. When she saw the dark tear stain on his cheek, she knew she was in for a tough conversation. Cassie knew that Harry was hurting because she knew with all her heart that the last thing, he ever wanted was to hurt anyone.

Knowing she wouldn't be alone she let a tear of her own fall down her freshly washed face. She couldn't handle it anymore even as much as she hated Harry at the moment, she needed him. Cassie collapsed onto Harry's broad shoulder and let her tears fall like raindrops down her freckled cheeks.

Harry dropped his jacket in his lap and moved his far hand across his body pulling Cassie closer to him. Harry didn't say anything to her, he just let her cry. As he felt Cassie's uneven breaths, he couldn't help but think back to when Louis was the one in his arms crying. It's kind of funny really, how the whole reason Harry and Cassie ended up here crying on each other shoulders were because of the one person that also cried on Harry's shoulder.

"I'm so sorry Cas, I didn't mean to keep this from you."

Harry's voice was breaking with every word. His mop of curls fell heavily on top of Cassie's' wavy locks. Cassie sunk deeper into the crook of Harry's shoulder.

"How did Niall know? Did you tell him?"

"N-no I didn't tell him. I mean I told him I was gay when we were at Louis's house dancing, but I never told him I liked him."

"Then how does he know?"

Even as hurt as she was Cassie, was happy to know that Harry felt comfortable enough with Niall that he came out to him as early as he did.

"Well remember after the dance when you came over and I was finishing editing the photos I took of people?"

"Of course, it's a tradition for me to be there and I still made it somehow."

"Yeah, you did."

Both Harry and Cassie let out a small bit of laughter as they remembered the four-year-old tradition. Quickly after the silence came creeping back in between the two. Cassie began to try and recall all of the events of that night trying to figure things out.

"Do you remember how I didn't want to go through them once you and Niall came over?"

"Yeah..."

"I didn't want to go through them because of who was in them."

"They were Louis and Ronnie."

words were being spoken in a poetic softness and gentleness as the two were finally able to be calm with each other. The tears that had fled from the two pairs of eyes only dripped out sporadically.

Cassie began to move her head out away from under Harry's as she turned the rest of her body towards him slowly. For once her memory was being a blessing and allowed her to recall one very specific moment from that night.

"You told me to not be too mean because it was Louis. You didn't want to go through them with us there because it was Louis."

"I didn't want to feel bad for Louis about going to the dance with Ronnie."

"Oh, Harry. Come here."

Cassie wrapped her arms tightly around Harry and pulled him into a deep hug. Cassie began to rub small little circles up and down Harry's back when she noticed his breathing had shifted to the sharp inhales and exhales of crying.

Harry's arms were stuck in between him and Cassie, slightly squished by the sudden intrusion Cassie had made but one thing still laid in his arms. His Jacket. Harry hadn't realized he had begun crying until his cheek felt the cooled wet spot one Cassie's shoulder. Harry pulled back out of Cassie's' comforting embrace and whipped his tears with the back of his hand before he returned his fleece jacket.

"How long have you liked him?"

"I don't know honestly. I have always liked him. For the longest time, he and his family were everything I had. He has always been important to me."

"Do you remember when you started looking at him differently or when you stopped telling people all of your thoughts about Louis? Like your mom, his mom, the twins?"

"I guess the first time was when his dad passed away. I don't-didn't think that what I was feeling was anything out of the ordinary. Wh-when my mom told me that there had been an accident and we needed to go to Louis's house my first thought was Louis. Was he okay, is he is in pain, please just let Louis be, okay? I didn't think of Richard or Jay. It was just Louis you know. After all, he was my best friend, I spent my days mainly with him. I thought it was normal.

When I walked into the house and saw that Louis was indeed okay, I felt a wave of relief, he was okay. I breathed easier until I noticed that his eyes were red and puffy. He looked like he hadn't slept in days. He looked broken. All I wanted to do was go run to him and give him a hug. I wanted to do anything to take away the pain he was going through. But I-I couldn't and that hurt me. I wanted him to be okay even if I wasn't."

Harry had kept his head bent down as he looked down at his hands which laid on top of his lap while his fingers fiddled with the cuffs of his jacket sleeves. One single tear dropped from his left eye straight down into the fleece.

Cassie's heart broke into a million pieces as she saw her best friend in so much pain, so much pain that she had missed for so long.

"Harry, i-i'm so so sorry."

"W-what are you sorry for?"

"For not noticing it earlier."

"Cas it's not your fault, i-i didn't want anyone to know."

"I still should have noticed something was up, even Niall did."

"There is no reason for you to feel bad. I am the one that should have told you, you shouldn't have had to figure it out for yourself."

Cassie gave Harry a half-smile, she knew that she couldn't change Harry's mind. Cassie never knew why Harry always refused to see that a problem was never just his fault, but she learned to just go along with it. What Cassie did know was that Harry needed another hug.

Harry finally dropped the jacket from his hands and let it fall open across his knee.

"I just have one question."

"Yeah?"

"How the hell did you make it through photographing Louis without losing it?"

It made Harry chuckle, he sniffled his nose and playfully punched Cassie's shoulder.

"I'm glad to see you have so much faith in me Cas!"

"Hey! It's a real question!"

"Of course, it is."

If he wasn't careful Harry's eyes might have just rolled out of his head if he rolled them any harder. Harry started to lay down on his carpeted floor so he could comfortably extend his body, Cassie followed suit until they were both laying their stomachs still underneath Harry's desk.

Harry began to tell Cassie the entire story of the day of the dance, starting from the very beginning when Louis had to help him unfreeze his car in his driveway.

"Wait, how often do you sleep over there?"

"Um, I don't know maybe an average of like twice a month or so."

"Oh my god, you are so lucky! Do you know how many people would kill to sleepover at their lover's house!"

"He is not my lover! Oh my God, you are just as bad as Niall."

"Well, maybe you aren't lovers... yet!"

"Cassie!"

"Okay fine, get back to the story. I'm officially intrigued!"

Harry went on to talk about how busy the entire day was and how he began to regret adding Louis and Ronnie's photoshoot last minute, but he did it anyway.

"Okay, can you please get to the good parts?"

"Calm down I'm getting there don't worry!"

"Fine."

"So, since Louis hadn't seen Ronnie in her dress, yet I wanted to do a first look because well, you know those are always cheesy and romantic. It was also good because when I walked up to the location, guess what?"

"What?"

"Louis wasn't there! Like at all!"

"You're kidding!"

"Oh, honey I wish! Anyways so I used this time to take Ronnie up that fountain, you know the one with the giant staircase? Right so, of course, I told her the plan and gave her the whole *You are absolutely stunning* speech, but let's be honest she was stunning anyways. Thank the gods above because just as Ronnie was entering her annoyed state Louis called me saying he had finally arrived. So, then I ran over to where he said the car was and the whole family was there."

"Even the twins?"

"Even the twins. Which... just made everything worse because God Cassie you should have seen him, he looked so... ugh, it should be a crime for anyone to look so good! I kid you know his eyes looked like paradise, I have never seen anything so blue, they looked like crystals! And his hair, I swear the sun was pushing me because with every light beam, he would get these strands of hair that looked like they had been dipped in gold. His cheekbones though! I swear they could have cut off my heart in half right then and there! Oh, have I mentioned his eyes? Nothing will ever beat his eyes. I don't know what it is, but they are just something! Cas it was horrible I must have been so red, I stood there for like ever just staring at him! I couldn't even look at him the rest of the night unless it was through my camera and even then, I would stutter. I don't understand how one person can be so photogenic! Like how, just how is it possible? It was sad though because that only made it worse."

"Wait made what worse?"

"Oh, I forgot, the first look."

"Was it bad?"

"Oh, it was horrific! Louis had been so happy before we actually took the photos. He was happy to be with his mom and sisters. I thought for a second that might smile to death but when I turned him around to see Ronnie... Nothing happened!"

"Nothing?"

"Nothing! His face just went all plain. All he had was a tiny little smirk on his lips but his eyes, his eye just didn't look right. He didn't look happy or in love or anything! Ronnie did the same thing! At first, her face was stern almost as if she was looking for something to be wrong with Louis then all of a sudden, she plastered on his big fake smile. Honestly from my point of view, it was obnoxious, no one ever really smiles that big! They just didn't look in love."

"wh-"

"But it doesn't stop there! When Ronnie went to say goodbye to her parents, or rather case them off it was just me, Jay, the twins, and Louis and we were standing in a little circle and Jay started to ask me about what my plans where for the rest of the night and I told her that you were going to the dance with Niall, so it was just going to be me editing all of the photos and watching movies. I told her that I was kinda sad you weren't going to be there with me but that I was happy for you because really, I am so happy that you have Niall and he got you to go to a high school dance. But then! But then Louis said that he wished he could come over after the dance because it sounded like a really cool afterparty!"

"Oh my god..."

"I know right!"

"You are so in love with him!"

"What? I told you I am not in love with him!"

"If you aren't in love with him then why did you just tell me that entire story with the biggest smile on your face while you twiddled your hands in HIS jacket, not yours?"

"Well, it's so nice to finally tell you about him and wait what? This is my jacket, what do you mean?"

"Oh really?"

"Yes really."

"So, when did you start wearing a size small?" Harry quickly perched himself up on his elbows hitting his head on the hardwood above him in the process until he could grab the demon jacket and place it flat on the floor. Harry quickly opened the panels of the jacket revealing the tag inside, which indeed did say ' Size SM'.

"Oh my god..."

"I told you."

"How did you see that?"

"When it fell on your knee the tag was visible. Also didn't you see how big Louis's jacket was tonight?"

"Wh-when I saw him, he wasn't wearing a jacket?"

"Wait, you saw him before he helped us?"

"Um, yeah?"

"Harold!"

"Hey, still no nicknames!"

"Sorry. when did you see him?"

"I ran into him in the kitchen when I made myself a sandwich."

"Why would you make yourself a sandwich if they had food out?"

"I didn't want that food!"

"Geez okay calm down. Didn't you call him to your window before we left the party?"

"Aren't you supposed to be drunk?"

"Stress sobers you up pretty well."

"Right, I'm sorry."

"Quit saying sorry! But I know for a fact you saw Louis when he had your jacket on! How didn't you notice?"

"I don't know Cas all I noticed was that he looked really cozy!"

"Oh my god, Cassie, do you think he knows I have his jacket?"

Harry was now a hint ball of stress; this truly was the worst thing in the world to him. He completely collapsed down onto the ground shoving his face down into the warm fleece. Even with the extra padding, Harry's nose was uncomfortably squashed. His arms laid flat beside him, his fingers pointing downwards towards his feet.

"Harry..."

Harry let out a low muffled groan.

"What am I supposed to do?"

"Well, first I would take your face out of the ground."

Cassie got on her knees and grabbed Harry's shoulders, helping him to get on his elbows.

"But it smells good."

A soft pout was on Harry's lips. Harry and Cassie both knew at that moment he was such a goner. Cassie rolled her eyes and was just about to speak when they heard a soft ding come from across the room. Both Harry and Cassie started to crawl out from under the desk back into the depths of Harry's room.

A bright light was illuminating from Harry's bed. Another ding went off and Harry ran over to his bed picking up his phone. His heart nearly exploded out of his chest when he read the black letters on his screen.

From Louis: Hey it's Louis I was just checking in to make sure you got home safe.

Cas, it's Louis. What do I do? Cassie immediately ran up to meet Harry and took his phone out of his hand to read the message herself.

"How often do you text him?"

"Not often, usually only to remind him about his curfew or if it's an emergency."

"Has he ever asked you anything like his before?"

"No, never."

"Okay. Well given his past I would say it definitely makes sense since he would ask you if you're safe, I'm sure he hates this night as much as you, but he definitely cares about you. Now if it's a friend or more I don't know yet."

"Well, what do I say!"

“Okay okay. Tell him the truth, well leave out the part about our little crying session but tell him you're safe and ask if he got home safe too."

"Okay."

To Louis: I did thank you for checking. Did you get home alright?

Harry pressed send and almost immediately he saw three little bubbles pop up under Louis's name. Harry could feel his heartbeat in his ears it was so intense. Why was it that once he told Cassie how he felt it all became so much more real? So much more intense?

Harry didn't have any more time to think about his suddenly more intense emotions because Louis had already responded.

From Louis: I did as well, thank you for asking :)

To Louis: Of course!

From Louis: Goodnight Styles.

To Louis: Goodnight Tomlinson.

It wasn't until Harry had lowered his phone down and he looked up that he noticed that Cassie had left the room. With his phone still in his hand, he walked towards his door opening it and walking to his staircase. Once Harry had reached the ground level, he walked over into the living room to see Niall passed out on the couch with a gray blanket wrapped over him. On the other end of the

room, he saw Cassie curled up on the large chair with her hand leaning over the edge reaching for Nialls.
Harry just smiled and spoke with a very soft whisper.

"And you two say I'm the one in love."

When Harry made it back to his room, he closed his door and walked over to his desk and picked up Louis's jacket before walking over to his bed. Harry plopped down and climbed under his warm covers. With a smile on his lips, Harry fell asleep while he kept a hold of the lovely smelling jacket close to his chest.

Chapter Twenty-four:

New Year's Day was very uneventful in the Styles household. Due to the extremely late night, Harry slept in until almost four in the afternoon. When he finally woke up Harry walked down his stairs to see both Niall and Cassie laying down the couch cuddled up with bottles of water and food wrappers littering the end tables.

Noticing that the two were sleeping Harry went into the kitchen as his stomach grumbled. Harry tried his best to keep his motions small and quiet to not disturb his sleeping friends knowing that they were suffering from a wild hangover. Carefully Harry pulled out an old faded blue bowl as well as a box of honey crunch flake cereal. The crinkles of the plastic and cardboard caused Harry to continuously swift his eyes out into the living room until his bowl was filled to the brim with cereal. Once Harry had put the box of cereal back into his kitchen cupboard he went over to the fridge and pulled out his carton of oat milk. Harry unscrewed the plastic cap and let the sweet liquid fall over his cereal. Harry set the carton down and picked up his spoon spooning the crunchy food into his mouth.

After finishing his breakfast, well is it still breakfast at four pm? Harry decided it was best to at least try and wake up Cassie and Niall, even though their families knew where they were Harry was sure they would be made if they hadn't heard from them yet.

Harry gently tugged on the edge of the blanket that the two were sharing and watched as Niall and Cassie stirred awake. Knowing they would already hate him enough for just waking them up Harry was nice and closed all the blinds and drew the curtains so there was only a fraction of the amount of light in the room.

"Hey, have you both texted your parents?"

A few hums and a head nod from Niall were the only response Harry got. Harry knew they were still exhausted, but it was four pm on New Year's Day and he didn't want to be alone. After all, it was his house they were at, so he did have some more control. With that, Harry grabbed a chunk of the fuzzy blanket in his hands and pulled the blanket off of Niall and Cassie in one giant swoop.

"Hey! what are you doing!"

"Give it back! Harry!"

"Ah ah no. I refuse to be alone today, so you are going to get up, take some medicine if you need it, and we are going to have a movie marathon. Am I clear?"

Niall proper himself up on his elbows which in turn caused Cassie to move upwards as well. In a slight protest, she just let the entire of her body fall on Niall who let out a small grunt at the extra force pushing him back down.

"Can we go to the store and get food?"

"Seriously Niall that's what you're going to ask?"

"Hey food helps with a hangover. Besides I'm absolutely starving and if I am going to be forced against my will to watch a movie I might as well be full while doing it."

"Harry, why are you doing this?"

Cassie was so desperate for at least another hour of sleep she still had her eyes closed and her words were mixed with yawns. Harry grabbed Cassie's shoulders and lifted her off of Niall, sitting her up fully while he wedged himself in the new small space he had just created.

"Because. I am a needy person."

"I hate you."

"I love you more."

"ughhh"

Cassie fell over onto the opposite side of the couch leaning her head against the arm of the couch. Harry let out a giggle at the dramatic gesture before turning to his attention to Niall.

"You wanna go with me mate?"

"Sure, anything for food! Just let me go brush my teeth really quick."

"Okay."

Niall headed off towards the guest bathroom Leaving Harry and Cassie on the couch. Once hearing the running water Harry decided to get up and give Cassie back the blanket he ripped from her earlier.

"I'll let you sleep while we're gone but don't you think you're getting out of this."

Cassie just gave Harry a soft smile before pulling the blanket all the way up to her chin and burying herself into the couch falling back to sleep almost instantaneously. Harry ran up the stairs back to his room and grabbed his phone off of his nightstand table and a sweatshirt from his closet and ran back downstairs where Niall was leaning on the kitchen counter.

"Ready?"

"Yup."

"Okay then let's go."

Harry grabbed his keys as the two headed towards the garage door. As soon as they got into the car Harry blasted the heat throughout the car, for some ungodly reason it felt as if they were sitting inside of an ice cube. The thought made Harry's brain flashback to the time his car really was an ice cube, causing him to drive off with a smile.

Once arriving at the grocery store Harry parked his car among the eight other cars before hopping out and sprinting inside to avoid the cold. Niall grabbed a shopping cart for the two of them and they began to head down the aisles.

The store was almost deserted besides the single cashier and the occasional other shoppers. Only having gone through the frozen section there were bags of french fries, pizzas, chicken nuggets, ice cream, and mozzarella sticks already pilling up. In order to keep the frozen still frozen, Niall and Harry decided to split up to get the rest of the food.

Niall went to go get some chips, crackers, and candy while Harry went to get some fruit, caramel dip, and some pastries. Both boys moved swiftly down the aisles, Niall, however, kept the cart which might have been a mistake because the next time Harry saw him the cart was nearly overflowing. However, Harry wasn't about to help the situation by adding a fruit platter along with nearly a gallon of caramel paired with a box of bakery cookies and two cakes.

As soon as Harry put the last of the food in the cart, he and Niall burst into a fit of laughter right in the middle of the grocery store. Niall must have been feeling a lot better because now he was running up and down the aisles with the cart acting like a leprechaun gone wild. Harry began to chase Niall up the aisles like a hooligan, calling after him in the process. Niall's giggles suddenly stopped when he turned down the bread aisle and nearly ran into Louis standing with a loaf of bread, a jar of peanut butter, and a bottle of honey.

"Oh, hey sorry, I didn't see you there!"

"No worries, I'm glad to see you're up and moving today."

"Yeah, thanks for your help last night."

"Don't worry about it."

Just then Harry came running up behind Niall to catch him and ran into him causing Niall to push their cart into Louis. As soon as Harry began to catch his breath he looked up and he was horrified.

"Louis! Oh my god, I am so sorry! Are you okay?" Harry's cheeks became flushed with embarrassment while Niall and Louis were laughing their heads off. Harry was so thankful that Louis hadn't dropped anything, or that anything he was holding would be ruined if it did.

"I guess it's my dad to get ran into with shopping charts!"

Louis said it jokingly adding a laugh at the end, Niall joined him while Harry just raised his eyebrows still filled with alarm.

"I'm fine don't worry. A shopping cart won't kill me, although now that I think about it that would be a cool way to go!"

Harry joined in the laughter by adding a soft smile with a faint chuckle

"Of course, you of all people would say that!"

"Hey, when it's my time to go it better be interesting! Speaking of which, interesting food choices. Are you throwing a party?"

All three boys began to walk towards the single cashier working. Once arriving in line Harry gestured for Louis to go in front with a simple wave of his arm and Louis thankfully followed suit.

Louis cocked an eyebrow as he moved his body in between the shopping cart and the small shelf lining the checkout area.

"Oh right. Harry is being super needy and forcing Cassie and I to have a movie marathon and I only agreed if we could get snacks."

"Niall!"

"What it's true!"

"You make it sound like I'm holding you against your will or something."

"Well, I am very happy I didn't end up kidnapped last night."

Louis's heartbeat quickened as Niall spoke l. He thought that everyone had gotten home safe last night. Without any trouble. If Harry got into trouble, he would call Louis, right?

"for the love of God, I still don't know why you thought we were kidnapping you!"

"We?"

"oh yeah sorry! I took the back roads going back to my place because they are usually safer and when I turned onto the first one Niall here got all paranoid thinking that we were kidnapping him and Cassie."

"Wait seriously?"

"Yeah, he thought you were hiding in the trunk!"

It was now Niall's turn to become a red tomato as he sank back into his heels while Harry and Louis laughed so hard the other people in line turned around and gave them a harsh glare. The two just looked at each other and broke out into another fit of laughter, although this time it was quieter.

The line was moving pretty fast and soon enough Louis put his items on the conveyor belt. Slight confusion and excitement clicked in Harry's head when he looked down at the three products.

"Peanut butter and honey huh."

"Oh yeah, I'm watching the girls for a few days, so I thought they deserved to know what a great sandwich tastes like."

"Are you saying that I don't make good sandwiches?"

"Well, you were about to eat a plain sandwich last night if I remember correctly."

"Touché Tomlinson, touché. So is your mom out of town right now?"

"Yeah, she went to visit her friend down in Brighton for a few days, so I said I'd watch the girls. You know sibling bonding time."

"That sounds fun. I'm happy for you."

Harry's vision went back Christmas Eve. His heart was a mixture of breaking and healing. It still hurt so much to know that Louis was going through so much, yet nobody seemed to know but it eased a little knowing that Louis was beginning to help himself. Niall could sense the slight tension hanging in between Harry and Louis and had no idea what was happening, however, the other two knew exactly what was happening.

Both Harry and Louis didn't know if the other remembered that night or if they remembered exactly what was said. There was also embarrassment about the number of tears each boy cried. At this moment Harry was thankful that Louis hadn't been awake when he let his tears slip. Or so he thought.

Louis paid for his groceries and grabbed the single bag. Starting to walk away Louis let his eyes look back to Harry.

"Hey if you need any help with the girls at any point you can always call me any time. I'm not going anywhere."

"Thanks. I'll definitely keep that in mind. Bye Styles."

"Bye Tomlinson."

Harry could feel the rosy tiny bubble up in his cheeks when Niall elbowed him lightly in the ribs.

"Oh, shut up."

"I didn't say anything..."

Harry burned his eyes into Nialls to keep him quiet. Silence passed as the cashier scanned every food item and put them into bags. Niall and Harry split the cost and headed back out to the car. The boys filled the trunk with the bagged groceries and got back into the car to start driving back to Harry's house.

The drive was silent, the only thing happening was the shifting of the eyes especially Niall as he was practically begging for Harry to tell him what was going on between him and Louis only moments earlier, but it was no use. Five minutes of silence later they were pulling back into Harry's garage.

The oven was full and a half dozen bowls were sitting on the living room table filled with candy, chips, and popcorn. In between sat the fruit platter and a tray with cookies and pieces of cake. When Harry and Niall got back with enough food to feed an army Cassie was more than happy to get up and start setting up everything.

Before they began to dig in Cassie snapped a picture of the set up with all three people in the background and posted it to Instagram before the group turned on their first movie, Hot Rod.

The sun had set leaving only the glow of the television as the light in the entire downstairs. Laughter was filling the air as the movie played, jokes were being cracked left and right from one person to another, occasionally a chip or piece of candy was being thrown in the air.

The first movie had ended, and they unanimously decided on playing Ace Ventura. This night was really turning into something perfect; everyone was happy, full, and making memories.

The light of Cassie's phone created a light beam alerting the boys her attention was now no longer on the movie. When Harry looked over, he saw a puzzled look settled on Cassie's face as she continued to scroll.

"Hey is everything okay?"

"Oh yeah it's fine but Louis liked my post about tonight."

"Louis?"

"Yeah, Louis."

"Since when did he follow you?"

"I don't know, I didn't think he did, so it must have been so because I only just put my account on public like a week ago so colleges could look at my online portfolio."

Niall took his turn to intervene in the conversation.

"He probably followed you Cas after his and Harry's little interaction as the grocery store."

"Wait what little interaction!"

"Well, Harry here ran into me which caused me to run into Louis with our shopping cart, and then the two had their own private conversation until Louis left with his groceries."

"Harry what did you talk about?"

"Stop making talking such a big deal. All he said was that he was watching the twins for a few days because Jay went to the beach with a friend, so he was there getting some supplies for some sandwiches."

"Oh, and don't forget that you offered to help him, and he smiled. I think that it was the first time I saw him really smile."

"He smiles all the time!"

"I'm not insulting your boyfriend calm down, just saying."

"He is not my boyfriend."

Harry fell back dramatically on the couch and let out a sigh while Niall and Cassie just laughed.

"Well, whatever he is, he is now interested enough to follow me on Instagram. Niall, I bet you're next."

The rest of the night went one with more laughter, jokes, food, and movies. Harry was truly enjoying himself. He couldn't think of a better way to officially start the new year, well maybe he could think of one way but that would never happen. Even being surrounded by two of the most amazing people in the world Louis was still always somehow in the back of Harry's mind as he wished Louis was sitting here with them, Harry knew that Louis would enjoy something like this. Maybe the next time this happens he'll invite him; you know as friends.

Chapter Twenty-five:

The next morning Harry drove Niall and Cassie back to their respective houses before returning to his own. It was 10:00 am when Harry got back, and he was still full of the previous night's adventures, but he knew he needed to have a little something, so he settled on an apple before heading up to his room.

Harry's mom had to go back into the hospital again after being home for only about seven hours leaving him all alone again. Harry took the time alone to deep clean his room and organize his closet. Grabbing his speaker Harry connected his phone and put on his favorite 2010 throwback playlist. Was it really a throwback playlist if it was only ten years ago? oh well.

Harry couldn't help but dance along to the peppy beats and the lyrics as he put clothes in his hamper and miscellaneous trash and junk he no longer needed and couldn't donate into a trash bag. Pretty soon Harry's room was decluttered and partially organized so he grabbed his now full laundry basket and walked down the hall to the laundry room where he threw in his first load of clothes.

After Harry went downstairs to the kitchen sink and grabbed the necessary cleaning supplies, wall safe cleaner, window cleaner, a duster, and a washrag and headed back upstairs. The music was still blaring so Harry got back to work.

It was an hour of spraying cleaner, whipping it up and repeating the process until it was finally time to do the final touch of dusting off his furniture and vacuuming the floor. Harry took a slight break before so he could swap out his laundry and add another load.

By the time Harry had finished cleaning his room all of his laundry was washed and fired, the only other thing that needed to be done was folding and putting the clothes away. So, Harry dumped the clothes on his newly clean floor and went to his closet and grabbed enough hangers before he plopped down beside the mountain of clothes.

Harry hung all of his shirts and jackets in his closet while he put his jeans, shorts, and pajamas into his dresser. Once Harry was all finished with his deep clean it was nearly two-o-clock, and his stomach began to let out little growls.

Thankful that he was able to keep most of the leftover food Harry popped some leftover pizza and fries into the oven. While his lunch was cooking Harry went on his phone and decided to look through his Instagram feed. Most of his feed was filled with posts from photography accounts capturing the New Years' celebrations, the art was starting to give Harry some inspiration.

As Harry ate his food, he made the decision to go downtown and take some pictures. Harry rinsed off his plate and put in the dishwasher before going upstairs to change. Knowing that it was still freezing outside, literally, Harry decided on a pair of dark washed skinny jeans, a Beatles band t-shirt, and layered a maroon-red surf shop hoodie. Harry laughed that he was wearing a beach hoodie in the dead of winter but who really cares. Harry laced up his white converse and grabbed his camera bag from his desk before heading downstairs. Even with the layers when Harry walked into the garage to put his thing in his car, he still got the chills, so he headed back inside to grab his other jacket for extra protection.

When He got to the coat closet Harry remembered that he didn't have the jacket he was looking for, Louis did. Harry smiled knowing that he had Louis's handing on the back of his chair in his room but damn, he really missed having his jacket. It was his go-to article of clothing.

Having to rethink his plan Harry remembered that he had gotten a new acid-washed denim jacket for Christmas and decided to grab that instead, it was surprisingly comfortable having not been broken in yet. Finally ready to go Harry went back out to his car and began driving around town.

Harry parked his car in the downtown square and sat in his car as he prepared his camera with his go-to lens and daytime settings. Once it was ready Harry organized what was left in his camera bag and slung it over his shoulder and walked out in the sunshine.

Quickly Harry found a bench and sat down taking a few sample photos to see what exact lighting he was working with. Harry did a few tweaks to his settings then viewed the world as he loved it most, through a lens.
People were out running attempting their New Year's resolutions. Harry decided to go to the end of a street behind a bush to sneakily take some shots.
Harry loved photographing on streets because it was super easy to follow his favorite photography rule, leading lines.

The square still had all of its Christmas lights hanging up around trees and on the buildings, some of which were lit desire it still being bright outside, but Harry used it as an advantage to help frame his many subjects.

Harry was also excited to see people not only running towards his direction but as well as away and diagonally from him. For those people Harry used the bush he was hiding behind as a portal, brushing away the frozen leaves and branches and placing his camera inside which made the runner look as if they jumped in and out of a magical forest into the real world.

Out of the corner of his eye, Harry spotted a little boutique with an old-fashioned candy store next to it. The dramatic change of scenery enticed Harry and he walked over staying close to the wall to not be seen. Harry stopped when he got to the edge of the window.

The boutique was first. There wasn't much to work with as Harry knew he had to stay outside because clothing stores never really liked to have outside photographers photographing their inventory, especially a teenage boy. However, Harry was able to use the very reflective window to his advantage.

Because the streets were pretty much vacant Harry crawled down onto the found underneath the window positioning his camera so that the old brick was in the bottom of the frame and the display counter was filling out the rest of it. The window still had some frost and ice crystals clinging around the edges which created a beautiful prism effect on the window in photos. There were a few customers inside the store, one, however, kept catching his eye. A girl maybe in her mid-twenties with jet black hair and pale blue eyes was trying on almost every scarf the boutique had to offer. The setting was to go to miss as Harry crawled back over the edge of the store to stand up, if he didn't, he was sure he would look like he was in a whack-a-mole game. Seeing that the women still had about seven scarfs left to try on, Harry thought he would try to get photos from not only the front but the back as well. Harry made sure to hide himself while he stuck his camera out a little further, so it looked into the store.

The girl was thankfully in the front corner almost sectioned off from the rest of the store, so Harry didn't really have to worry about any workers seeing him, just the black-haired girl. A large body length mirror wrapped with small fairy lights sat in front while the girl stood behind twirling around. Behind her the scarfs were hanging in a color-coded order, most of them neutrals which popped against the lavender walls of the store. Harry began snapping photos left and right. Harry loved to photograph every movement he could when he photographed people, he loved how fast their expression could change or how a slight angle change could create the perfect photo so everything from the girl choosing the scarf, putting it on, modeling and twirling around to taking it off and looking at it is contemplating if it was the right one before hanging git backup was photographed. After a couple of scarf changes, Harry decided to head to the opposite side of the window to catch another angle. Harry adored this angle so much more as he could see the reflection of the mirror rather than its tan backside. Instead of the scarf wall being the focal point of the photo it was reflected in the mirror while the girl and the surrounding decoration pieces were front and center. The glow of the fairy lights added the perfect glow to Harry's photos allowing the girl to look like an angel with a golden glow around her. Harry took the same process of photos, photographing every movement he could, only looking down to see the photos every now and then as the really fun part would come later on.

Eventually, the dark-haired girl finished trying on all of the scarfs and picked two and headed to the checkout which was Harry's signal to get moving. Not wanting to move next door to the candy shop quiet yet Harry walked directly across the street and sat at a bench facing the front of the store.

Looking at his memory card Harry saw he had enough storage to go ahead and take some photos of the front of both stores and still be able to photograph the candy shop. it was a little difficult to separate the two storefronts because they were just so different. One looked like it belonged in Paris with its pale pink waning, fashion posters, and shimmering jewelry while the other looked straight out of the 1920s, it was stunning, but they were definitely two different aesthetics. If worse came to worst Harry could always just photoshop one side out if he really wanted too so he didn't stress it too much.

Harry zoomed his camera in and as the perfect touch, the girl he had been photographing moments earlier came walking out of the door with a white bag in hand. The wind blew her hair back ever so gently and she was now wearing a light gray coat which complimented her hair and skin perfectly. Harry took advantage of this and focused his camera on the girl as he walked down the street in front of the stores' window. Her bag was swaying in front and behind her fading to the depth of the photos, Harry knew at that moment that he would end up loving these photos.

Once the girl was officially gone Harry turned his attention back to the candy shop. In all honesty, he might have loved the decorations more than the boutique, it was just so rare to see something look so authentic and retro yet still brand new. Harry didn't know if it was luck or not, but the candy shop was closed, according to the sign on the window it would be until the next day.

Harry knew he still had to be careful about photographing the store because he knew other store owners and customers could very well see him and the last thing, he needed was for them to call the cops on him for being suspicious.

Because Harry didn't have to stay crouching down underneath the front window like the last store Harry decided he would have most of these photos taken from higher angles so it would look as if someone could reach down into the store.

The sun was just starting to sink lower and lower in the sky which left Harry with only about forty-five minutes until a perfect sunset and because he really wanted to photograph it, he knew he had to work fast at the candy shop.

Taking the emptiness to his advantage Harry stood on the front steps of the shop and peered downwards through his lens as his finger pressed the proper buttons on the side. There were jars, bags, and boxes full of different candies displaying the front window, and almost perfectly the boxes were left open which probably meant that the treats inside were fake and for display only, but they still looked delicious.

Harry put his camera in his right hand and dropped his left-hand down positioning it to look as if he was reaching for the treats on the other side of the glass. Harry moved around a little bit more before walking back to the center of the town square.

Back at the fountain where he had taken the photos of Louis and Ronnie Harry sat down at the top of the steps and looked down remembering the night. Harry could still remember the night perfectly; it was another gift of his that he could remember almost every single photoshoot he did in his life. As Harry remembered the blueness of Louis's eyes and the sharpness of his cheekbones, he couldn't help but think of how perfect Louis would look in front of the lavender and pink sunset at the moment.

Having remembered one of his favorite photos from the previous photoshoot Harry got up and turned around so he was sitting on the edge of the fountain. Once again Harry crawled onto his stomach and kept his camera not much higher. Because the water from the fountain was falling slowly not bubbles or white froth was being sprayed leaving only clear liquid flowing in the air. Harry was pleased that the water reflected the sunset perfectly, in pictures it looked as if the sky above was melting down into a paste blue bath. It was honestly breathtaking. Just as Harry was finishing up his photos his phone kept buzzing in his pocket. At first, he was just going to ignore it but in a matter of a few minutes, his phone had buzzed nearly ten times.

Setting his camera down Harry pulled his phone out of his pocket to see a bombarding of text, all coming from Louis.

From Louis: Hey, I'm so sorry to do this but I need your help with the girls.

From Louis: Like bad!

From Louis: How do you do this every week????

From Louis: If you're busy it's okay I'm sure they'll be tired soon.

From Louis: What are some of the girl's favorite places in the house?

From Louis: Do they tend to split up or stay together when the play pranks on you?

From Louis: What do they play pranks on you or are they just being mean to me????

From Louis: Okay, I lied, I really need your help.

From Louis: This is a disaster.

Harry laughed knowing that twins must have been running around the house refusing to do anything besides run away from whoever was in charge. Harry knew that they weren't in any immediate danger after going through it many times himself. Knowing that Louis is probably losing his mind by himself he sent a quick text before grabbing his camera and jumping back into his car.

To Louis: Don't worry I'm on my way!

Chapter Twenty-six:

It took nearly thirty minutes for Harry to finally arrive at the Tomlinson residence, once he did, he pulled around to the back and parked in the garage. Harry was thankful that Louis had given him a garage opener, especially so he wouldn't completely freeze to death. All Harry grabbed was his phone before he headed inside.

"Louis!"

Harry called out but got no response, eerily the house was nearly silent. However, that really didn't mean much as the house was so big, they could very well be blasting music and jumping down in the dance hall and nobody would even know they were home.

Harry decided to go and walk towards the front of the house, when he arrived at the front door, he placed his phone on the small table that sat right before the staircase. Only seconds later Louis came running up from one of the halls opening every single door as he moved forward.

Louis's head fell back, and his shoulders dropped in relief when he spotted Harry. Quickly he ran to meet him. Harry had to bite his lip to keep from bursting out into laughter as Louis stood next to him panting trying to catch his breath. Louis bent forward placing his hands on his knees as he continued to pant.

"I thought that you're a star soccer player..."

"I-I- shut up."

Both boys laughed as Louis began to stand upright again now placing his hands on his hips.

"I probably should have warned you about this."

"Yeah, you think!"

"But this is so much better!"

"Styles you better stop laughing before I make you go outside."

"Someone's a little feisty."

"I can't find my sisters in our own house!"

"Relax, they do this all the time. it's really the only thing that keeps me in decent shape. This is just their way of retaliating against bedtime."

"Why are they so fast? Every time I grab one of them and turn to get the other, they both have disappeared!"

"Ah, so they're working together tonight?"

"I think so, I don't know."

"Okay then let us get going, they certainly aren't going to surrender."

Louis nodded in agreement and Harry shook his head lightly with a faint giggle and began to run up the large staircase with Louis by his side. Once the stairs ended bringing the boys back to a solid floor, the split up, Louis going left and Harry going right.

"Oh, and I forgot! Whatever you do, do not call their names, it gives them more time to run if they hear you!"

"Could have used that advice an hour ago!" Harry and Louis each jogged down their hallways and throughout the dozens of rooms that lined them. The boys moved every piece of furniture, piles of blankets and clothes, and checked every single little crawlspace littered among the house. Nothing. Neither Harry or Louis found a trace of Phoebe or Daisy.

It took over an hour to conduct a thorough search of the entire upstairs meaning that when Harry and Louis finally met back out it was nearly pitch-black outside. They ran down the stairs to begin checking the downstairs.

In a sense the first floor would be easier to check than the second as it consisted of fewer rooms, however, the room just so happened to be about triple to quadruple the size. Many of the rooms were minimally decorated with very few good hiding places so the pair felt confident that if the girls were still down there, they would easily find them.

Louis took the liberty of searching through the main hallway which leads on the right side of the house of Harry searched through the living, dining, game, and metro room on the left side of the house.

The one or rather multiple upsides to having Harry search the house was that he basically grew up in the house just like everyone else. Harry knew all of the knicks and crannies that the girls could fit into or the secret ways to move around the house because he and Louis had once done the same.

It didn't take long for Harry to realize why Louis had taken the other side of the house to look through. Even being six feet tall Harry found himself having to climb on top of chairs and shelves in almost every location to peer off the edge and make sure the girls weren't hiding somewhere up high.

On the other side of the house, Louis was having to do the opposite, constantly having to crawl on his hands and knees to get low enough to look through all of the cabinets and closets that lined the rooms.

Both boys used the normally annoying echoes of the house to try and hear any little footsteps that may be creating around out of their sight. Little did they know just how quiet Daisy and Phoebe could be.

Louis was all the way down the long hall in the dance hall while Harry was on the complete other side searching through the meter room when Phoebe and Daisy came running out from a crawl space that landed them right in front of the staircase.

The girls stood up silently, in times like these twin telepathy really came in handy. At the exact same time, the girls turned around and saw Harry's phone and keys laying neatly on the nearby table. A simple smile between them and their plan was formed Phoebe grabbed Harry's phone while Daisy grabbed his keys. With each item in hand, the girls quietly walked back up the stairs and entered their room climbing into a crawl space.

It looked more like a dream treehouse rather than a crawl space that led from a bedroom to another spare room. The girls had brought some blankets and laid them down on the floor and placed pillows across one side of the tiny wall. Two single strands of fairy lights hung loosely around the premier as an old lamp sat in the middle on a nightstand. Jay had decorated this little hideaway for the girls' last birthday so the girls could have a private space away from each other if they needed it without really leaving the other.

Sitting down in their respective corners the girls started fiddling with the objects in their hands. Daisy places the keys nicely on the nightstand, so they don't lose or break Harry's keys or lose any of the keychains that were attached. Phoebe unlocked Harry's phone and went straight for the camera roll.

"Dais, the picture is still here!"

"Do you think he has seen it?"

"I don't know but it's still here."

"Well, there's only one way to make sure."

Phoebe held a confused look on her tiny face trying to figure out what Daisy was up too. Daisy made grabby hands for Phoebe to give her the phone. In a few seconds Daisy was swiping away with a petit smile before handing the phone back to her sister.

"What did you do?"

"Just look and you'll see."

"You're a genius!"

Both girls sat up and gave each other a big hug with smiles on their faces as they looked down at the little rectangle of technology. Harry's lock screen and home screen were now set to the cuddly picture of Louis sleeping on his chest.

The girls decided to just stay inside their little hideaway with Harry's phone and keys in an attempt to keep Harry in the house and at least near Louis. They didn't exactly know that when they started running around that Louis would call Harry over to help him look for them, but they saw it as a good sign. A sign that they hoped was only a good thing.

Back downstairs Harry and Louis made their way back to the center of the house standing around the large kitchen island. Both just shook their heads to signal they didn't find the girls. Louis collapsed onto the sparkling white and gray granite countertop letting out a defeated sigh. Harry let out a peal of laughter as he leaned on his hands slightly falling over the edge of the counter towards the center.

Harry reached into his back pocket to grab his phone when he remembered he had placed it on the table at the front door. As Harry walked out of the kitchen, he gave Louis a quick pat on the back allowing Louis to be brought back to reality.

Turning around all Louis saw was the back of Harry as he was walking away. Quickly Louis dragged his feet to follow Harry until they both stood still. Harry stood blankly staring at the now empty gold and glass table while Louis's head was tilted up looking at Harry.

"What's wrong?"

"You saw me put my phone and my keys on this table, right?"

"Yeah, before we went upstairs why?"

"Well look at the table now."

"Oh. Do you think the girls took them?"

"Do you have a ghost haunting this place?"

"What? No."

"Then yes I think the girls took them."

Harry was looking down at Louis now with a trace of a smirk forming on his lips before a laugh escaped from his lips. Louis tried to keep his face stern, but it was no use as the echo of Harry's strong laugh engulfed him and his head tilted back as his laughter began to overtake him as well.

"Okay well, the only thing left to do is just wait until they give up."

"Harry, that will take ages, besides what if they hid your stuff? You kinda need them."

"They'll give up soon and end up asleep in their beds in eh, maybe an hour or two. As for my stuff, it'll either be right back here or in their room with them."

"So, they really do this all the time?"

"pretty much. And so far, I haven't permanently lost anything, so I don't usually mind much."

"Huh."

Harry turned around and began walking to the kitchen immediately heading to the pantry. Louis laughed knowing that Harry certainly didn't need to be told to make himself at home after nearly eighteen years it's almost a given.

Harry started pulling things off of the self and moving them to the kitchen island. A can of carrots, peas, a box of pasta, and a whole bunch of seasonings was laid out in a neat circle. Harry then turned his attention to the fridge pulling out some leftover chicken shreds and garlic butter.

Louis was fascinated by the way Harry was working, it was almost like in a snap of a finger Harry was now a classically trained chef and completely forgot about his phone and keys missing. Louis knew even if it was just his sisters that took his things he would be freaking out and never stop looking until he found them.

"Have you eaten yet?"

"Oh, uh no not yet, just the girls they ran off before I could make my own food."

"Good. You better still not be picky Tomlinson."

"We'll see about that, but I don't know what you could make with *that*."

"Just wait, I'll have you drooling before you know it."

Harry cringed internally following his choice of words, of course Louis wouldn't even think twice about the statement since everybody knows that he's like a dog when it comes to amazing food, drooling, tinge sticking out, superb scent tracker. However, Harry instantly got a flashback of looking back at Louis's dance photos where he was definitely drooling over those perfect blue waves of his ocean eyes.

"Harry?"

"Yeah!"

"You, okay?"

"Yeah, just thinking about something."

"Okay... this better be some good food."

Harry rolled his eyes and turned around grabbing the tub of chicken and headed over to the stove to hide his red cheeks from Louis. Harry started to prepare the chicken by creating a honey lemon marinade and put the mixture in the fridge to keep fresh while he started on the pasta.

The first step was to prepare the vegetables, so Harry drained both of the cans and dumped its contents into the pot. While the veggies were cooking Harry turned on the oven and grabbed another pot filling it with water before placing it over another burner. Just as the water was beginning to boil Harry dumped two handfuls of pasta into the pot before returning back to the refrigerator grabbing the marinated chicken. Harry poured out the contents onto a lined baking sheet and placed it in the oven.

The next fifteen minutes was almost a total blur of motions, string pots, checking the oven, dumping seasonings into everything, grabbing plates, and trying to clean as he went along. A smile was plastered on Harry's face when he finally finished plating his masterpiece, honey lemon pulled chicken with a side of garlic butter pasta with some mixed veggies, and to say it smelt heavenly was an understatement.

Harry grabbed both plates, one in each hand, and started to make his way to the dining table. As soon as he placed the dishes down, he saw Louis walking towards him peering around the wall that connected to the living room. Harry laughed as he saw Louis lick his lips trying to keep himself from actually drooling like a dog.

"I told you so."

"Okay, it smells good, but does it taste good?"

"How could it not?"

"The universe works in mysterious ways Styles."

Harry nodded as he sat down with a fork in hand while Louis walked over and sat down in the chair across from him where his own plate sat. Harry was already scarfing down his food as he hadn't eaten in nearly seven hours. Harry looked up to see Louis looking at him with his perfectly shaped eyebrow cocked up.

"What?"

"So, you can breathe?"

"I'm hungry. just shut up and eat."

"Your bossy."

"And you're sassy."

Both boys now held a stern look in each of their eyes, silently they were competing in a staring contest. Keep the eye contact Harry lifted a fork full of food into his mouth and that was it for the both of them. Harry and Louis were both hunched over laughing more than what they thought was humanly possible. By the end of the commotion, the boys had happy tears rolling out of the corners of their eyes.

Louis's chest felt light for the first time in forever. It had been years since he had gotten that feeling like he was flying while doing anything other than football. Louis closed his eyes and tried to savor every moment. Harry kept quiet when he realized what Louis was doing. Harry felt his heart rise a little knowing that something as simple as a meal and a staring contest could make him so happy.

Harry kept his eyes down at his plate when Louis reopened his. Louis finally lifted his fork into his mouth and instantly he regretted not doing so earlier. The flavors and warmth were exploding in his mouth and pretty soon he was acting just like Harry shoveling as much food as he could into his mouth.

"So, I take it you like it?"

All Louis could do was nod as he tried to finish the food he was chewing on. Harry meanwhile was trying to hold back a smile of fulfillment. Harry would never let anyone know just how important it was to him that Louis had really liked his food. It was something small, but it was something Harry did.

Louis and Harry began talking as the food began to clear from their plates. Harry listened as Louis joyfully talked about his past few days with his sisters. Everything from a pillow fight to a karaoke session. He explained how each of the girls explained their favorite dresses to him and the princess storyline that went along with it. Not one had Louis had any inkling on his face that he regretted any of the work or time he had spent with his sisters, Harry made a mental note to remember this if Louis ever doubted his brotherly duties ever again.

"So where were you out tonight?"

"What makes you think I was out anywhere?"

"Oh, nothing, it just took you thirty minutes to get here, and even on a bad traffic day it only takes what ten, fifteen minutes tops..."

"I was out taking photos downtown."

"I knew you did something! So, what did you take photos of?"

"Odgers and fire breathing dragons, you know the usual."

"Wow was the smart-ass king there too?"

"No, he's sitting across from me."

"Well played Styles, well played but really what did you take photos of aren't most of the stores still closed?"

"A few are a few aren't but some people still like to go outside when it's freezing for some reason so just photographed whatever I felt was right."

"Can I see them?"

"You want to see them?"

"I mean if you have your camera with you yeah, we have the time."

"Okay, I'll get my camera from my car if you'll clean this up."

"No problem."

Harry and Louis got up, grabbed the plates and took them into the kitchen while Harry walked down the hall and opened the garage door to grab his camera.

Chapter Twenty-seven:

Harry stepped through the garage door back into the house with his camera bag in hand. Harry was slightly shocked to see that Louis had indeed cleaned up the little mess that was left over from dinner. Maybe he really was determined to become the old Louis, the real Louis.

"If you have a computer, I can pull up the photos there or you can just look at them on the LCD screen."

"What's an LCD screen?"

"The little screen on the back of the camera."

"I'll just grab my laptop instead."

"Okay."

Louis walked out of the kitchen placing the dishrag he was using to wipe down the counter in the sink before he began jogging up to his room. Louis walked into his room grabbing his MacBook off of his desk. As he turned around to walk out, he caught a glimpse of the photo he printed out of the girls with Harry. Louis's lip moved into a tight-lipped smile; he was happy to be getting closer to his sisters. Louis also couldn't help but notice how nice it was to have Harry back in his life. though it might not have been exactly what it was like when they were younger, he felt more like himself with him then he ever has in the last four years.

Knowing that his computer was most likely nearly dead Louis shuffled through his desk drawer to find the charger before he began his soft jog back downstairs. Harry was standing next to the kitchen table; his fingers were running over the camera nervously. Harry's shoulders were slightly slumped forward, and his head tilted down so his eyes could focus on the wooden table his camera was sitting on.

Not many people ever asked to see Harry's photos unless it was of them, we actually no one really asked except for Cassie sometimes but even then, it was always the finished product she saw. Louis was about to see raw photos and raw photos was liking looking directly into Harry's brain especially when there was no real purpose to the photos. These photos were just a demonstration of what went on in Harry's head, he couldn't tell anyone the reason or thought behind the photos or exactly why he chose what he photographed or how he did it, it was just something he could do.

"I've got the computer!"

"Great."

"Where do you want to sit, it probably needs to be near an outlet. I don't know how much charge is left."

"Wherever is fine."

"how about the window seat?"

"Sure."

Louis took the lead and walked ahead of Harry to the window seat. Louis plugged the charger into the wall outlet then connected it to his electronic. Sitting down each boy grabbed a blanket and dropped it over themselves to help protect them from the cold window he leaned up against.

Harry was honestly thrilled Louis had suggested the window seat begin that it was his absolute favorite place in the entire house; it helped ease his nerves slightly, but unfortunately only slightly. Harry still felt as if he might throw up. It was weird he knew that it was just some photographs, but they just felt so personal as if they were like his babies.

Louis took a good, long look at Harry and saw the small furrow of his eyebrows and the unfocused gaze in his eyes. He noticed the precise movements and stiffness in his hands signaling he was nervous. Louis made a mental note to keep his sassy demeanor at bay for the rest of the night, he knew Harry rarely got nervous so when he did, he knew it took a lot to get him there.

"So how do we pull these up?"

"Here just plug this into a USB port, a small pop-up will appear on the bottom of the screen asking for access to the computer, press accept then another window will pop up and the photos will begin to load. Usually, there is a progress bar at the top to show how many are left."

"Okay. sounds doable."

Louis followed Harry's directions to a t and soon a large window popped up and hundreds upon hundreds of photos began to pop up one after another. Within a few minutes, all the photos were loaded onto Louis's computer and he was beginning to feel slightly overwhelmed at the sheer number of photos he was looking at, nearly two thousand, and all the ones he could see looked amazing.

Like a lost puppy Louis quickly handed Harry the computer because quite frankly he had absolutely no idea what was doing and the last thing he wanted to do was mess up any of the photos or worse accidentally delete them. Harry let out a trace of a laugh at Louis's sudden nervousness, it was funny to him that he was the nervous one he had nothing to be nervous about.

Now holding the computer in his hands Harry felt slightly better as he felt he had a little more control over the situation than before. Clicking on the first photo it now enlarged to take up the entirety of the digital screen. It was a basic photo just to check the lighting and whatnot, but Louis still let out a little "wow" when it enlarged. Maybe this wasn't going to be so bad.

Harry's fingers quickly made their way down to the edge of the keyboard until the sat hovering above the arrow keys. In almost an instant Harry fell back into his normal self, or rather what he called his photographer self, organizing and grouping photos together, deleting some, doing basic edits as if he could do them in his sleep. Which in defense he probably could.

Louis watching in fascination as Harry worked, he could tell just how much Harry loved what he was doing, he could tell how talented he was. Instantly Louis could imagine his father going through the photos with Harry, he would be so proud. Louis held a soft smile on his thin lips as a feeling of happy contentment as his eyes continued to be blown away by the beautiful photos only a foot away.

"I wish I could do something as good as this." Louis's chest fell with a slight sigh escaping his lips. The soft words nudged Harry out of his photographer's work state causing his hands to still and his eyes to blink as he tried to comprehend what Louis had just said.

"You are a junior national football champion."

"That... that is different. This Harry, this is raw talent, beauty, it's amazing."

Harry instantly felt his cheeks burn ablaze and turned his head back towards his, well Louis's computer however he stayed still. Harry knew how much people loved his photos, but it took the words being said by none other than Louis Tomlinson for him to realize it.

"How exactly do you do them, the photos."

"I-I don't really know, I just take them. When I go out and take photos things just feel right, like it's what I'm supposed to do. I can't really explain it."

Both Harry and Louis sat quietly beside each other, Louis was taking in every detail of Harry. The soft curve of his nose, the way his lips pouted softly out from the rest of his face, how his hair held small curls, the shadow his long eyelashes cast underneath his emerald eyes. Harry looked as stunning as his photographs.

"It's your escape from reality, something that helps clear your mind, forget your worries, and just be yourself. It's a safe place."

"Yeah. it is."

"Dad would be so proud of you, you know."
Harry closed his eyes and felt a warm pull around his eyes. Even if he never admitted it to anyone Harry always wished he could show his photos to Richard, he wished he could go on walks through the family's museums with Richard and talk about all the new paintings.

"Thank you."

Harry's voice was barely audible, he took another deep breath and made sure his tears had officially gone away before he opened his eyes once again. The eminence of the tears made Harry's eyes sparkle like stars in the night sky.

"He would be so proud of you. So proud."

Harry knew by the way Louis's bright blue eyes became slightly darker and began to droop ever so slightly that he didn't believe Harry's words.

"He really would be honored to call you his son, you have no idea."

"He would be honored to know you, Harry, to see the way you've grown up and become the person you are. I've done basically nothing besides cause other problems, made too many mistakes for him to be proud or honored."

It became an unspoken rule that when you speak about yourself you looked anywhere except to the person sitting beside you while when you spoke in response you took your time and closely examined the other's actions. Harry took a deep breath as he tried to figure out a way to get the proper words into Louis's brain and make sure he understood what he was about to say."

"Every person makes mistakes. We do things that we regret almost every day of our lives. No person is perfect, no matter what you may see on the outside no one is living a perfect life. We all have our issues. What separates us from one another is what we make off those mistakes. If you try to fix things you've done wrong if you can take a minute and reflect on what you have done and grow from your past. And given everything you've said to me, the actions you have been doing lately you are doing just that. You are doing what so many people are terrified to do. Admit they've done some not so pleasant things, understand their actions, grow from them, and become the person they want to be. So don't you dare say your dad wouldn't be proud of you or honored to be your dad because you are one hell of a person Louis Tomlinson."

A single tear ran down Louis's left cheek as he looked out the window up at the sky. Harry had now closed the laptop and moved it aside and turned to face the window just like Louis.

Harry let out a deep sigh as he pulled his blanket closer to him, for the first time in what seemed like forever Harry felt completely at ease as if he was floating in an ocean paradise. Harry didn't know how long he had sat there wrapped in a warm blanket looking out at the stars when he felt a small head lean against his shoulder.

"How do you know when it's time to let someone go?"

Louis's voice was light and soft, almost elegant, his breath was smooth and warm. Harry tried not to focus on the tiny details that made up Louis. Harry could tell by the way Louis was waiting patiently that he had already been thinking about the question for a long time, he had a pretty good idea about who Louis was talking about but tried to not let it create butterflies in his stomach.

"I think there are many things to think about when you decide to let go of someone, it's different depending on who the person is. How long have you thought about letting go of this person?"

"A while now. I think it was always in the back of my head but now it's just constantly something I think about."

“When you think of this person do, they make you happy? Are you happy when you're with them?"

"I guess sometimes I was happy that they were around but if it was because of them specifically I don't know. Whenever I'm with her–them things are just kinda a blur, it's a little numbing."

"Do you feel like this person is helping you be the person you want to be? Are they helping you grow, or do you feel trapped by them?"

"no, I don't want to be like this person at all. I feel like I can't do anything or be myself with this person but..."

"But?"

"This person has been the only constant thing in my life for a long time even though sh–they aren't even constant. Everything I've done for the past few years they have been there either to support me or to scream at me. Everything I've worked for somehow connects to them even though it shouldn't, all the people I know only connects me with them. If I leave them people just won't understand they'll think I'm crazy. The people I've made my high school memories with will just disappear. It would be like losing everything all over again. I don't want to stay but I don't know if I can do it again."

Harry's heart twisted and shattered just like Louis's. Harry wondered constantly after their Christmas talk why Louis had stayed with Ronnie for so long and now it was crystal clear, and it broke him. Harry had to use all of his strength to not reach out for Louis's shaky hand and take it in his own, instead he let his head fall on top of Louis's.

"High school is hard. It seems like our entire lives. It's kind of crazy especially when your life completely flips into something you never expected. However, it's important to remember that some people just are not meant to be in our life, at least not for a long time. There is no doubt that this person has helped you, but they can only help you so much before they begin to hurt you and right now, I think they're hurting you. You have so many things that are going to happen in your life. You have college coming up soon, you'll get to continue playing football like the champion you are, you'll get to meet new people that will help you be the best person you are capable of being. And until then you still have the most amazing mom and sisters of all time. I know that sounds lame but it's true."

"You'll also have me. And I'm sure Niall and Cassie would be happy if you join our little group."

Silence followed Harry's words. A light splatter of rain began to hit the window in front of Harry and Louis. Harry kept his eyes upon the sky while Louis looked at their reflection in the window as he digested the words he just heard. Louis knew he was an idiot to let go of Harry all those years ago, he didn't understand why after all the things he had done in the past that he was still here, listening to him, telling him the words he needed to hear.

The boys sat at the window until the rain fell harder beginning to sound like bullets hitting the glass. Harry got up first and Louis followed, each of them neatly folded the blankets they had been using. Harry grabbed the laptop from the window set and unplugged his camera putting gits back into his camera bag.

Harry hadn't noticed that Louis had left the room until he stopped moving and looked around to find himself alone. Louis knew that Harry had to get home soon and decided to try and help him by checking to see if his keys and phone had turned up.

Arriving at the small gold and glass table Louis let out a whisper of a chuckle when he saw a set of keys and a phone. Harry always had to be right. Most of the lights were turned off, the only real light in the house was the glow coming from the kitchen and dining room so when Louis picked up Harry's phone illuminated it felt as if he was being blinded.

After adjusting his eyes to the new brightness in his hand Louis was able to get a proper look at the phone. Time froze and Louis's head began to spin in circles. Louis could tell that the photo was taken on Christmas, but he couldn't figure out how it was taken. Both him and Harry were clearly asleep and both pairs of hands were in frame, it made it clear that it was either of them who took it.

The one thing that immediately popped into Louis's head was why was this Harry's screensaver. It didn't make any sense, it just didn't.

Realizing he had been gone for quite a while Louis decided to make his way back to the dining room.

"You were right they magically showed up."

"I told you, they may be a little crazy, but they can be a little predictable."

"That's good to know."

"Uh i-i should get joining, the rain has lightened up a bit."

"Yeah, yeah here you go."

"Thanks."

Louis gave a half lip smile as Harry threw his camera bag over his shoulder and took his keys in one hand and his phone in the other. Harry began walking towards the door and Louis followed behind him.
Harry unlocked his car and got in, buckling his seatbelt before looking up. Louis was standing in the doorway leaning against the wooden doorframe. As Harry turned

on his car the headlights illuminated the garage, once the garage door was full open Louis spoke one last time.

"You better get home safe Styles."

Louis said it just loud enough for Harry to hear the faintest whisper of it. It made him smile. under his breath, Harry whispered a simple "I promise." before he began driving home.

Chapter Twenty-eight:

Louis sat on his bed staring out at the stars in the sky. A simple replay of the past four years was on repeat in his head. A few smiles occurred but they all shared one similar aspect, none of those memoirs included Ronnie. Surprisingly there weren't many memories that consisted of Ronnie, she really only appeared with memories of parties or group hangouts.

It really scared Louis, knowing he had to let go of Ronnie. Even as bad, annoying, and downright mean she had been a constant in his life when he needed it. Louis's eyes kept flickering back to his phone, if he didn't create a plan now it was never going to happen so at 1:00 am Louis unlocked his phone and sent Ronnie a text.

Can we meet downtown tomorrow? I want to talk to you about something.

There was no going back now. Louis knew that he wouldn't get a response until around ten the next morning and they probably wouldn't even meet up until two. All he really needed to do was to make sure he didn't back out of this.

The adrenaline and nerves from Louis finally making up his mind meant he was suddenly not tired at all, instead he felt jumpy. Louis was twiddling with his thumbs and tapping his feet together as he laid on his back. He tried to keep his focus on the small sparkles in the night sky, trying to copy their calmness. It did not work.

Even though Louis had a massive 40-inch TV in his room he preferred to watch things on his computer. He had to do a small roll over to the other side of the bed to grab his computer, pulling all the sheets with him turning him into a warm burrito.

Louis rolled back over and unlocked his computer; it was taking longer than normal to load. It was kind of annoying until Louis realized he literally had nothing better to do. When the screen finally lit up again Harry's pictures were still being displayed, instantly Louis's interest peaked.

Louis hadn't realized that he and Harry never actually finished going through his photos or that he hadn't even remembered the later photos they did both see. It was like he was seeing the photos for the first time all over again. They seemed even more beautiful when he was looking at them all alone.

The more and more photos Louis was looking through the photos he realized they had a calming effect on him. He was no longer fidgeting; his brain was no longer a messy blur and he felt as if he was standing in the middle of a snow globe. Louis felt peaceful.

By the time Louis had gone through all of the nearly two thousand photographs, it was nearly three am and he was struggling to keep his eyes open. If it had been any other person's photographs Louis was sure he would have given up and went to bed an hour ago, but he just couldn't bring himself to not look through everything.

Not knowing much about cameras or their memory card Louis had no idea if what was on his computer was the only copies of the photos. With this Louis decided to save all of the photos, eyes all of the two thousand photographs were being saved into a folder labeled 'Harry :)' .

When Louis woke up on his own terms and not with Phoebe and Daisy jumping on top of him, he concluded that his mom was probably home which meant he could take his time getting ready. Or rather he could procrastinate getting ready.

Louis dragged himself out of his warm bed, kicking his covers off as he went causing them to tangle around his ankles nearly tripping him. With his eyes still closed, Louis grabbed a towel and his robe from his closet before heading into his bathroom and turning on the shower. Once he was released from the grasp of his pajamas Louis climbed in under the steaming water falling down from the ceiling. Although Louis wouldn't really consider himself pampered or into luxury items the one thing, he knew he could and would never give up was his rain shower, it was easily the best part of most of his days. After shampooing and conditioning his hair, using body wash, and shaving his shadow of a beard Louis stood still allowing the rain like water to block out the world that was spinning outside. Sometime later Louis sunk down now sitting on the shower's light gray hexagon tiles. His back was pressed up against the bench that lined the opposite side of the shower, his finger began to trace the lines of the marble that covered the walls of the shower. Louis's fingers had begun to wither into raisins, but he still continued to trace the never-ending lines of marble under the hot water, it must have taken nearly an hour but when he concluded he had traced every inch of the marble encasing him he got up and sat on the bench, collapsing against the wall behind him. This time Louis started to draw on the glass beside him. Nothing spectacular he just let his finger move aimlessly creating circles, lines, squiggles, a really lame attempt at a dog, and much more.

Louis hadn't realized when the hot water ran out but now, he realized his body was covered in goosebumps and his jaw was shivering. Quickly he got up and turned off the water. Hoping out he grabbed his fluffy towel and wrapped himself in it as fast as he could. When he was decently dry, he grabbed his soft navy-blue robe and wrapped it across his body as well.

Louis grabbed his phone off of the counter and looked to see a few texts from Ronnie.

Sure
I'm available at two
I'm bringing Chloe with me as well.

Typical Ronnie. Louis just sighed and put his phone back down after he replied with a simple "okay". Louis decided it would be best to not be late for his meeting with Ronnie, he knew it was going to end badly, there was most certainly going to be screaming and grabbing from Ronnie and Louis really didn't need to add onto the list of things for her to be mad about, so he began to get ready. First was to blow dry his hair. Once his hair was soft and fluffy Louis turned off the hot hair device and grabbed his hair gel from the medicine cabinet. Louis smoothed his overgrown hair over the top of his head and made it swoop over to the right a little. Once it looked decent Louis then headed over to his closet.

Louis reached for a random pair of jeans and a t-shirt. It was simple but it was effective. His feet were already beginning to freeze so Louis grabbed a pair of thick knighted socks along with a pair of slip-resistant boots. It didn't make for the greatest end for an outfit but now he was comfortable.

When Louis was finally all dressed, he headed downstairs. As he got closer to the living room, he could hear the elegant giggles of his mother and sisters. Following the sounds Louis found everyone sitting on the couch watching movies. Quickly Louis gave everyone a kiss on the top of their head, Daisy and Phoebe giggled as Jay stood up and turned around and pulled Louis into a hug.

Everyone talked about the past few days, the girls loved hearing all about the ocean since they have never been before. As Louis started talking about the previous night the twins kept a mysterious smile. Louis couldn't help but notice the tiny glances they kept exchanging; they had definitely been up to something.

Soon Louis caught a glimpse of the clock on the wall and realized he needed to get going. He said a quick goodbye and gave a hug to everyone before heading down the hall to the garage. Already being able to hear the wind howling outside Louis grabbed a jacket from the coat closet.

Louis got in his car and began the thirty-minute drive to downtown. He was twenty minutes early but that didn't stop him from throwing on his jacket and stepping outside into the cold, gusting wind.

Louis set an alarm on his phone for 1:55 pm and began to walk around the plaza without a thought roaming through his head. Louis knew the worst thing he could do was to just sit and wait, sitting and waiting made him anxious, being anxious would lead to doubts, and doubts would lead to him backing out of this. And he really didn't want to back out of this.

Although there were many people walking in and out of almost every shop Louis stayed focused on his every step, putting one foot in front of the other, head always looking at his feet. When his alarm finally went off, he calmly shut it off and just stared at the time. Five minutes. Five more minutes and his life will change once again.

On his way back to the cafe Louis could feel his heartbeat faster and faster by the second, he began to think he might twist his fingers off if he was any more jittery. As soon as the cafe came back into view Louis saw Ronnie pull up into a parking space not far away. At least she wasn't late today.

Louis walked over to the car and waited patiently for Ronnie and Chloe to get out of the car.

"Hey, Chloe. Why don't you go inside and get a table for you and Ronnie, we just need to talk for a quick minute."

"Oh sure."

Chloe walked into the heated building and Louis tilted his head over in the direction of a bench, thankfully Ronnie got the hint and followed Louis. Louis sat down and immediately pulled his sleeves over his hands, maybe he should have done this inside. Ronnie, however, seemed to be unaffected by the roaring wind swirling around them, ever her long hair stayed perfectly in place.

Ronnie was typing away on her phone and Louis was just sitting there watching her, he would have thought that she would at least pay a little attention to him given that they have never just met up and talked. Surely, she would know something was up, right?

"Ronnie?"

"Hmm."

"Ronnie, can you put the phone down please."

"Hold on I'm almost done I just have to find the perfect caption for my post!"

"Ronnie!"

"Fine, what?"

Louis felt frozen when Ronnie's eyes snapped up to his. Louis took a long and deep breath; he was so thankful he had Harry's jacket around him. The simple scent gave him so much strength, it retold him the words he so desperately needed to hear.

"I- I have been thinking a lot about my life, the things that have happened and the things I want to happen in the future, the person I want to be. And i-i think for me to start that journey I need to do it by myself."

"Was this your lame attempt at breaking up with me?"

"Uh... yes?"

"Well, that was your first mistake, Louis, I don't get broken up with, I break up with them."

"Um, okay..."

"I'm going to lunch with Chloe. You are not invited."

Louis just stared on as Ronnie walked towards the cafe and her silhouette slowly blew away with the wind. A deep breath escaped from Louis's lungs as he pulled his knees up close to his chest. Even though he was happy to get it over with it still hurt, the majority of the last four years of his life was officially gone.

After a couple of minutes, Louis got up and walked back to his car, once he arrived, he unlocked the door and turned in the heat allowing him to defrost from the icy winds dancing in the air outside. Not wanting Ronnie to catch him still sitting near the cafe he put the car in drive and just circled around the perimeter until he found a little empty corner of another parking lot and decided to pull in there and just rest.

The longer Louis sat in his car the more familiar the view in front of him kept getting. Something was just gnawing on Louis's brain causing him to shift in his seat to try and look at things just a little bit differently.

It wasn't until Louis's head was lying down on the door of his car and his body was shifted towards the center of the car that things seemed to fall into place. Everything outside stilled as peace wrapped him up like a giant hug. After a few seconds, the view outside seemed to shift into a photograph, it was then that Louis recognized he was parked in front of a small boutique and an old-fashioned candy shop. Just like what was in Harry's photographs.

Chapter Twenty-nine:

Christmas break was unfortunately over, and Harry found himself just wanting to hit snooze on his alarm clock but instead, he climbed out of bed and turned off his alarm. Quickly Harry grabbed his blanket off of his bed and wrapped it around his shivering body, god Harry hated winter mornings more than anything else in the world.

Harry sent a text to both Cassie and Niall to make sure they were up and told them what time he would be over to pick them up for school. Once everything was properly organized Harry went to his closet and picked out his outfit. A pair of acid wash jeans, a rolling stones t-shirt, a red flannel, and a pair of socks were not neatly folded and placed on the bathroom counter as the shower heated up behind him.

Harry let the blazing water erase all the tension his muscles had been holding onto allowing him to relax and melt back into his normal self. When Harry's second alarm went off and hurried to turn off the water and dry himself off with a towel before changing into his school clothes.

Once he was dressed Harry lightly towel-dried his hair enough, so it was no longer dripping water. Not entirely caring about what his hair did he just left it and decided to let it choose its own path. Call it senioritis or good time management. It worked with Harry's routine.

Now downstairs in the kitchen, Harry grabbed a bowl from the cupboard while also pulling out a bag of granola and a container of yogurt from the fridge. Harry dumped the contents into his bowl and grabbed a spoon quickly eating this breakfast. When he was finished, he rinsed his bowl and put in the dishwasher before grabbing his backpack and heading out to his car.

Harry was happy to see that he still had his new jacket laying in his passenger seat. Harry turned on his car and waited for it to heat up before he sent a text to Cassie and Niall that he was on his way.

Louis didn't get much sleep during the night having way too much pent-up anxiety about the new semester. When his clock glowed a bright red, 4:00, Louis completely gave up and got out of bed, grabbing his blanket and heading over to his window.

In the silence of the early morning, the unlocking of Louis's window sounded like the click of a shotgun shooting through the air. A cold blast winter frost instantly blew in Louis's face causing him to bring his blanket up to his face in an extreme rush.

It didn't take long for Louis to adjust to the new, colder, darker weather and soon Louis grabbed his laptop and climbed out of his window crawling until he was sitting comfortably on his roof sitting in a little corner protecting him from any large gust of winds and from falling off.

Louis let the light of his computer shine brightly like it was a star he had plucked from the sky. His fingers sat patiently on the keys not knowing what to do. It wasn't until Louis saw the folder labeled, Harry :), and opened it. Louis scrolled through all the photos until he landed on his favorite photo, the one of the fronts of the two semi-busy storefronts in downtown. There was just something about the photo that eased Louis. Maybe it was the colors, or the angle, or the aesthetic of the photo but all Louis knew was that it was some form of magic.

By five a.m. Louis started to lose feeling in his fingers and toes and decided it was best to not turn into an ice sculpture when he had school. In three hours, he gathered his thing's and started to slowly crawl back towards his bedroom window. As soon as he was back inside sheltered from the harsh elements, he breathed a little harder. The last thing Louis wanted to do right now was anything, he would do anything for winter break to last just a little bit longer.

After contemplating whether to just skip school or fake sick to get out of going to school Louis just sat down and sighed realizing he would only be mad at himself if he skipped. Nothing worth doing was easy and just kept replaying the words in his head.

There was one more thing Louis could do to help make him ready to get through the day, a steaming hot shower. Instantly Louis was up and walking towards the bathroom and turning on the shower before shedding his clothes and hopping in.

As the steam filled the air and the water rolled over his skin Louis crumbled to the floor as if he were an iceberg being melted. Louis tried to let his fears and anxiety wash away and swirl down the drain. Unfortunately for Louis his alarm started to blare loudly, the sound waves visible in the heat waves rising from the shower. Louis cursed himself for not turning off his alarm before he got in before frustratingly turning off the water and turning off the alarm.

Louis sighed in relief when silence washed over his bathroom once again. Slowly Louis grabbed his towel and wrapped it around his waist before sitting on his bathroom bench in front of the wall-length mirror. Louis sat just staring at himself picking out every little detail he saw. The red tone his skin was now harboring from his shower, the winter paleness of his skin, the navy blue and purple bags under his eyes signaling his lack of sleep, the dangle of his wet hair.

Before he could go too in-depth Louis dragged himself away from the mirror and into his closet. Louis grabbed a pair of jeans and a plain white t-shirt and changed into the articles of clothing. Once dressed Louis lightly blow-dried his hair before brushing it back into place. Louis then brushed his teeth, put on his shoes, and packed up his backpack for school.

By the time everything was done it was only 6:45 am, a whole forty-five minutes before Louis had to leave. Louis just belly-flopped onto his bed and let his brain rest once again. Soon enough Louis decided he needed to do something, he knew he needed to have something with him to keep him calm during the day if things got hectic, something that would keep him grounded and he knew exactly what it was.

Louis logged into his computer and was happy to see that everything was already in place. Louis clicked on the photo displayed on his screen and emailed it to himself. When his phone buzzed with an email alert Louis logged in and saved the photo, he had sent himself. Going into the settings on his phone Louis changed the screensaver on his phone to the photo. Hopefully, now the clam energy produced by the photo would be enough to get Louis through the day.

When it was 7:30 Louis helped his mom wake up his sisters and helped them choose their outfits for school. When everybody headed downstairs it was time for Louis to leave and go to his own school so while Jay began to make the girls breakfast Louis grabbed a bagel and an apple along with a water bottle and his lunchbox before he gave each of them a kiss on the cheek and headed to his car.

Harry, Niall, and Cassie were sitting in the cafeteria all with a coffee in their hands waiting for the rest of the day to start. Everyone was sharing their new schedules and trying to figure out a way to stay connected with friends who didn't share a class. The buzz was mainly kept with grades nine and ten who were all still excited by the classic high school infatuation, many grades eleven students already stressed trying to keep their grades up for potential college applications while many grades twelve students looked like they were just hanging out.

All three friends were excited to start their final semester of high school so when the bell rang instead dreading the day to come all jumped up and walked to their respective classes with an extra pep in their step. One thing caught Harry's attention; Ronnie was strutting down the hall with Chloe hooked around her arm very different from the usual Louis. Harry watched as the friends passed by him and tried to see if he could spot Louis across the hall where the girls were headed.

It soon became too cluttered with students to pick out an individual person, so Harry turned around and made his way to his favorite class his school offered. Photography. Stepping into the room Harry was immediately greeted by his favorite teacher Ms. Thomson who imminently gave him a hug and flash drive.

Harry has kept every flash drive Ms. Thomson has given him in the last four years, every photo he has taken for this class was on one of those and he saw them as the perfect memento. Not only was photography his favorite class but it was also held in Harry's favorite spot in the entire school.

A special third-floor loft had been made for some of the art classed at the school and photography sat right in the middle with the front wall of the room made entirely out of crystal-clear windows allowing heaps of natural light to shimmer into the room, much better than the artificial yellow light glowing throughout the rest of the school. a small river ran in front of the windows along with trees and Harry loved how he would get to see space flourish into a beautiful garden like area every day while winter melted into spring and burned into the early days of summer.

The class was small, it always was. fourteen other students joined Harry in the classroom and sat in the wooden desk all facing the smart board in the front of the room. Once the tardy bell rang Ms. Thompson immediately started her first-day presentation. Class expectations and syllabus were shared, and everyone started working on their first assignment, that is when Ms. Thompson called up the only two seniors in the class up to her desk.

With Harry and another girl named Kayla now sitting, Ms. Thompson started going over their senior project for the semester. The project was to create a photo walkthrough of their entire lives up to their graduation. Immediately Harry was intrigued by the project but very quickly started to worry.

"Ms. Thompson, how do we get photos of our past? I didn't start taking photos until sixth grade six. That still leaves twelve years that won't have photos."

"That's the fun part. You can do either of the following, you can use photos taken by your family or friends, but they cannot be professional photos, or you can recreate the photos you find or memories you have. Or you can do both. The main goal for this project is to be able to tell a story through your photos, string them together in a way that makes it feel as if you are watching a movie and find the little details that link each photo to the next."

Just as Ms. Thompson finished the bell rang signaling the end of the class, Harry smiled and grabbed his things before heading out the door and on to his next class. The next few classes went by smoothly and extremely fast partially due to the fact that Harry had no more core classes and just electives.

As soon as the lunch bell rang Harry sprang up from his journalism chair and found himself nearly running towards the cafeteria to meet Niall and Cassie. Almost at the stars aligned on the other side of the world, the trio arrived at the cafeteria doors at the same time, and instantly they moved to claim their new lunch spot, a small table sitting against the far edge of the wall sitting right under a window.

Everyone sat down pulling out their lunches and instantly they began talking out their day so far, the classes, their teachers, the people who were in their classes, and everything in between.

On the other side of the wall, Louis was sitting in his car eating his lunch watching all the commotion happening inside the lively school. He had successfully made it through half of the day and Louis was honestly doing okay but he desperately needed a break from the hundreds of eyes that seemed to be attached to him, thankfully for him senior could go off campus for lunch so nobody questioned when he walked out to his car and sat down.

After forty-five minutes it was time to finish off the rest of the school day. As Louis turned off his car he watched as the students inside threw away their trash and ran around trying to find the best way to their next class. When Louis walked back into the building, he was happy to be hurled into the busy halls without anybody noticing him.

When the final bell rang Harry, Cassie, and Niall all met by the student parking lot before they headed off to Harry's car. All three were thankful that seniors had priority parking and were able to park close to the entrance. The three got in the car and buckled up as Harry started the car and turned on the heating. As much as Harry loves winter he couldn't wait for the sun to heat up his side of the world a little more.

Harry pulled out of his parking spot and decided to drive around the premier of the parking lot to enter the line of cars waiting to exit the parking lot. As the car pulled around the back of the parking lot which seemed to be a ghost town besides one car with somebody going through the trunk.

"Harry isn't that Louis's car?"

"Yeah, I think it is."

"what's he doing in the back here?"

"I don't know, that's a little strange. What is he doing?"

"Take a look yourself."

"Guys I'm driving and I'm not just going to stop randomly when there are cars behind me."

"It looks like he just pulled out a duffle bag."

"Oh, maybe football tryouts start today, isn't the field over there?"

"Oh, that makes sense. I think you're right."

When silence settled in the car Harry couldn't help but begin to giggle softly.

"Wait why are you laughing?"

"When did we become such stalkers?"

"When the idea of double dates became a possibility."

"This is going to be one hell of a semester then."

Chapter Thirty:

The first week of school passed by with a breeze, everyone was getting in the hang of their schedules and classes were still easy with not much of a workload. As Niall started talking about some plans he had with his family, Harry's attention was pulled towards the flock of girls entering the cafeteria, it didn't take long into the week for Harry to notice something was off because everywhere he looked, he saw Ronnie, but never once did he see Louis. Now thinking about it the only time Harry had seen Louis in the past five days was when he left school on Monday.

"Earth to Harry!"

"Hm-What? Sorry, Ni."

"If I didn't know any better, I would have thought you were checking them out!"

Harry's check reddened as both Niall and Cassie erupted with laughter.

"No, but seriously, what were you doing? Did you hear anything I was saying?"

"I was just thinking, and you said something about your family. Right?"

"Wow, such a good multitasker there Haz!"

"Cassie, you better watch it if you don't want pudding in your hair!"

"You wouldn't dare!"

"Want to find out?"

"Not really."

"Good because I don't feel like running right now."

Now it was Harry's turn to join in on the laughter. The group got a couple of judgmental and questionable glances from the other tables around them, but they didn't care and just kept on laughing. It wasn't until Ronnie and her entourage walked by that Harry was pulled back into the reality of high school and once again Harry's eyes followed her every movement.

Niall and Cassie quickly caught what Harry was looking at and instantly turned to each other with a knowing look.

"Louis." They both said in unison, now that got Harry's attention.

"Where?"

The couple high-fived and smiled knowing what they had just done. If Harry thought, they would forget about his *boyfriend* just because school started back up, he had another thing coming.

"Hey! you can't just do that!"

"Actually, I think we can!"

"I hate you both."

"We love you to Harry. So, what were you really thinking about?"

"Ugh, how do you do that?"

"Do what?"

"Make me mad then instantly get me to spill all my thoughts!"

"Magic?"

"At this point, I'll go with that."

"So..."

"So? Fine. Everywhere I look I see Ronnie but she's always with one of her friends and never Louis and I just realized that I haven't seen him since Monday and I haven't talked to him since, since..."

"Since what?!"

"Nothing, it's not important. But really have you guys seen Louis anywhere?"

"I see him after lunch almost every day heading to culinary arts. He comes in from the parking lot."

Harry moved his eyes in between Niall and Cassie and focused his gaze on the rows of cars neatly lined upside by side on the other side of the window. One by one Harry looked at every car trying to find Louis's black Tesla, in all reality it should be pretty easy to spot, not many teenagers have the luxury to drive such an expensive car.

Finally seeing the shiny black reflecting back into his eyes, Harry's eyebrow shot up when he realized that car was occupied, Louis was sitting in the front seat.

Little did Harry know that both of his friends were now following his line of vision once again and all three were staring out the window like lost puppies.

"Maybe he just chooses to eat off-campus, he does have the money to do that."

"Or maybe he left something in his car."

"Or maybe it has something to do with this."

Harry and Cassie instantly turned towards Niall who had his phone out and opened to Instagram. Harry snatched the device from Niall's hands and suddenly it all made sense. When he stopped moving Harry felt Cassie grab the phone out of his hands and felt her eyes switching between himself and Niall.

"They broke up?"

"It's either that or she's cheating and not trying to hide it. at all."

Both thought that Ronnie and Louis breaking up should make Harry over the moon and in reality, it should. Now he wasn't completely unobtainable. However, neither of them knew what that meant for Louis, yet he did, and it scared him.

The echo of the bells bringing through the packed cafeteria brought Harry back into reality. All three friends slowly got up and gathered their things and began to make their way out into the bustling hallways. Just as he was reaching the door Harry saw Louis walking back up towards the building, it wasn't long, but Harry could tell instantly that Louis had put his wall up.

The rest of the school day dragged on as if it was slowly freezing into a video frame. Every chance he got Harry was in the hall weather it was by asking to use the bathroom or running errands for teachers and every time he stalked the hallways looking for Louis.

At the end of the day, Harry nearly ran out of the building leaving Niall and Cassie to chase after him, so they weren't stranded without a ride. Just as Harry was unlocking his car Niall and Cassie came crashing up behind him with panting breaths fogging up the window as they rested their body on the frame of the car. Instantly Harry apologized and tried to catch his own breath.

Harry unlocked the car allowing everybody to get in and escape the freezing rain that began to fall violently in front of the sky crashing down on to the ground. Finally sitting down and only slightly wet and shivering the silence was broken.

"Are we going to have to get a bell for you?"

Laughter. Harry was relieved that it was laughter that filled the small space instead of screaming, or tears, or worse more silence. Once the heat had traveled its way through the car Harry turned it down just a bit before starting to drive.

"I think a tracker may work better!"

"More like a tracker for Louis..."

"What?!?"

Niall leaned his arm backward and Cassie gave him another high five.

"What are you two doing?"

"It was Louis right. The reason you ran out of the building like you were stepping on a hot stone. You wanted to see him, didn't you?"

"What are you guys, mind readers?"

"We. We are the... love detectives!" Niall and Cassie shouted in unison.

"Oh my god and how long didn't take you to come up with that?"

"Not very long but it's good right!"

"Sure Cas, sure. but why?"

"Harry as your best friend-"

"And I as second in command."

"Yes, and with Niall, it's clear to see that whatever you are feeling with Louis is...different, it's surprisingly strong and we are here to help you, so you don't go crazy thinking about all of the little things by yourself."

"That might be the creepiest yet sweetest thing you've ever done."

"So tonight, we need to get a base, we need to get to the bottom of exactly how strong these feelings are."

"I would love to, but I can't tonight, babysitting. What about tomorrow?"

"Oh right, the twins. Yeah, tomorrow works."

With everything set and a plan sort of worked out Harry drove Niall and Cassie to dinner near their houses. Once they were inside Harry started the comforting and familiar drive to the Tomlinson residence.

Due to the tornado-like wind piercing the chilly air Harry decided to use the garage once again, he wondered if the twins would still run up to him like they usually did when he came through the front door. There was only one way to find out.

The door was locked, and Harry prayed they keep an extra key in the garage as they did in the front of the house. The gods must have been listening because laying on the ground near a shelf was a key, Harry picked it up and let out a sigh of relief when he heard the unlocking of the door as he twisted his wrist.

It was all of ten seconds before the wind was rushed out of Harry's lungs and his arms were feeling the presence of Phoebe and Daisy. Harry spun around and sat the girls down on the kitchen table. As soon as he let them go, the girls started rambling on and on about their week.

It was easy to listen too. With everything from schedules to feelings changing drastically in the last two weeks, it was comforting for his time with the girls to be the same as usual. Harry marveled at the excitement of the girls, he can easily remember when he was that excited about school and how fun recess was. Harry also couldn't help but giggle when he realized that he and Louis had done some of the same things the twins described.

As soon as the girls quieted down Daisy instantly asked Harry about his week. Harry took a long second to think back about all he had done, it wasn't much probably really boring after the stories about recess and class games, but he told them anyway and like the angels they where they listened politely.

"What do you think Louis did this week?" Phoebe spoke quietly to Daisy; Harry wasn't sure if he was meant to hear it, but he did. It made Harry's heart hurt thinking back to lunch, wondering just how much Louis was hurting. The twins saw the little crease forming in Harry's eyebrows and questioned him.

"What are you thinking?"

"A lot of things. what do you want to know?"

"Why do you seem sad..."

"Oh, come here."

Harry grabbed both the girls and walked over to the bay window only a few feet away. Phoebe and Daisy looked at each other with slight worry, they have never seen Harry be so serious besides when he plays the prince.

"I want you to promise me to always do what makes you happy, no matter what anybody says about it. If you love it then it shouldn't matter to any other person as long as it is respectful and kind. Have fun whenever you can and create memories that make you want to live forever because one day, one day life seems to become tricky. Love the little moments and don't take anything for granted okay. Promise?"

"Promise." The girls said in unison.

"Harry?"

"Yeah Phebs?"

"Is that why Louis is sad this week?"

"What do you mean by sad?"

"He comes home really late, like after dinner time, and is really quiet."

Harry had to think, he knew that if Louis did break up with Ronnie he certainly was going to hurt for a while, but it wasn't his place to tell the girls. Trying to think logically Harry remembered Monday afternoon when he saw Louis near the football fields.

"Well, I'm not Louis so I don't know for sure but what I do know is that he's been working super-duper hard after school at football tryouts. Those things run super late so that's why he's home so late and I'm sure it's tiring running up and down that field so he's probably really tired."

"What are tryouts?"

Sometimes Harry forgets that the girls are still only four years old and don't know a lot about the world they live in. It even occurred to Harry that they might not even remember going to all of Louis's football matches even though they've been going since the day they were born.

"Tryouts are like practice. If someone wants to play on the school's football team then they all practice really hard for one week. The coaches test their skills and sometimes they even play games against each other. At the end of the week then the coaches take the best players and create two teams for the school. JV is mostly for the younger kids and Varsity is made of the best players who tried out."

"What team is Louis's on?"

"Well for as long I can remember and for as long you two have been alive, he has been on varsity."

"So, Louis is good at football?"

"He's fantastic at it."

"Do you think he'll make the team again Harry?"

"You know what I think? I think he'll be the team captain."

"Like the leader?"

"Exactly."

"Then we must celebrate!"

"Celebrate? Celebrate how?"

"Cookies!"

Daisy and Phoebe jumped off of the window seat and scrambled into the kitchen trying to find their way to the baking ingredients.

"Why can I never say no to sugar..."

Harry quickly followed the girls and grabbed the basket of ingredients from the top shelf of the pantry, setting it down on the granite countertop instead. Before going any further Harry grabbed one of the plethora's of baking books from the cabinets and set it down beginning to flip through the pages until he landed on a cookie recipe for sugar cookies which were conveniently shaped into little footballs. The following page included the icing recipe to decorate, convenient.

Harry lifted each of the girls one by one on the counter, so they were all on the same viewpoint. With Daisy to his left and Phoebe to his right, Harry plopped the book down in the center.

"So, what do you think? Do these look good?"

"Perfect!"

"Delicious!"

The girls chirped one right after the other. Harry slides the book backward and clipped the pages so they recipes didn't disappear when things got hectic. Next, he grabbed the bowls and the measuring cups.

While Harry went over the fridge the girls took turns listing off what ingredients he needed to grab, butter, milk, eggs Harry carried it all over back towards the counter. Once he sat everything down Harry had to turn on the oven to get it preheating.

Finally, the real baking was ready to begin. Everybody took turns taking scoops of flour and dumping git into the bowl, Harry was sure the aim was to create the big puff of flour as with each dump into the bowl Harry was covered with more and more flour. Baking soda and salt were also added but Harry made sure to do that so as not to have either a baking explosion happen in the oven or accidentally creating salt bricks.

As the twins whisked the dry ingredients together Harry threw the butter into the stand mixer and let it fluffy before adding in the sugar, vanilla, eggs, and milk into the concoction. Once the contents of both bowls where properly mixed Harry gave each of the girls a spoon and allowed them to slowly add the dry mixture into the stand mixer.

Apparently slowly has no meaning to four-year-old's because Harry soon found himself fumbling for the off lever of the mixer to try and stop the tornado of flour that was swirling around in the air. The twins just laughed as they stuck their little fingers into the half-mixed batter and decided to take an early taste test.

"I think I'll finish the mixing..."

Sneakily Harry grabbed the two spoons laying on the counter and slowly turned the mixer back on, keeping git on the lowest setting until he was sure flour wouldn't begin to fly again. It didn't take much longer for the batter to form a dough and be ready to be shaped. Learning from his last mistake Harry floured the countertop himself after wiping it clean then placed the ball of dough in the center before cutting it into three equal sections.

Harry handed a mini rolling pin to both Daisy and Phoebe and they all got to working floating the dough. Once ready Harry had found a circle-shaped cookie cutter and proceeded to cut everyone's dough into perfect circles while the girls then placed them on the cookie sheets.

After what seems like an eternity Harry was finally done cutting little circles out of what seemed like the Marry Poppins of cookie dough. Looking up Harry really wished he looked closer at the recipe as he was now staring at four dozen uncooked cookies. Whoops. Placing the first two trays of cookies into the ovens Harry helps the girls off of the counter and sends them to wash up while he reheats what looks like leftover pot roast for dinner. By the time the girls make it back to the table dinner is ready and they begin eating.

Halfway through their meal, the oven dings signaling the first batch was finished, Harry hopped up out of his chair and made sure to grab the oven it's before opening the oven and being attacked by the flash of hot air being released far too close for comfort and pulling out the cookies before adding in the final two trays.

Harry was pleased when he was able to not only finish his meal but also begin to clean up the mess of flour from the counter and the floor before the oven dinged once again. However, with the sweet smell of warm vanilla sugar, it didn't take long for the girls to come rushing back into the kitchen and try to steal a cookie or two.

"uh uh no you don't. No taste test until they are finished!"

"Just one we can split it!"

"Please!"

"Nope, not until they are covered in frosting!"

Phoebe and Daisy lit up at the mention of more sugar and happily obeyed Harry's decision laying the cookie back onto the plate. Thankfully Harry had already separated the eggs whites by himself, so it wasn't a total disaster. Harry allowed the girls to turn on the mixer as he added the vanilla and powdered sugar into the bowl. Fascinated by the icing forming the girls fully allowed Harry to do all the work.

Once the mixture was ready Harry split the icing into two bowls, one he added black food coloring too and allowed the girls to take turns stirring it while he got baking bags from the pantry. With everything ready Harry poured each bowl of icing into three bags recently giving everyone one bag of white royal icing and one bag of black royal icing.

Since it had taken so long to semi-clean and prepare the icing, all the cookies were properly cooled, so Harry brought the entirety of the large plate of cookies over to the workstation they created, and everyone began to frost the cookies.

It didn't take long for the frosting to end up absolutely everywhere, the counter, the cabinets, the floor, on everyone's faces, literally everywhere. Usually, Harry would try to make his cookies look presentable but not even he could make the perfect little black hexagons of a football on the cookie so pretty soon the cookies ended up looking like cows, but it was fine.

Harry was grabbing another cookie when he thought he heard something rattle from within the house. He stopped for a quick second to listen but with the girls laughing next to him he couldn't really hear anything else and just decided to carry on.

A few seconds later Harry heard the same noise, only this time it was slightly louder and followed by slightly shaking of the walls. It wasn't until Harry heard heavy footsteps that he began to panic slightly.

Chapter Thirty-one:

The footsteps kept getting louder each second that ticked away on the clock. Instantly Harry dropped his icing bags and wrapped one hand around Phoebe and the other around Daisy when he heard a large crash coming from the hallway. Thanks to not having the light turned on Harry had no idea what was coming at them, that was until he saw a very tired and sweaty looking Louis basically sleepwalking towards the kitchen.

Harry released the breath his lungs had been gripping onto and let his hands fall back down to the counter. Phoebe and Daisy noticed the extra presence and install looked up with excitement in their eyes.

"Louis!"

"AHH!"

Louis nearly fell backward from freight and held his hand to his chest, heavy breathing followed as he tried to calm down. Phoebe and Daisy didn't even wait for Harry to safely lift them off of the counter, instead, they jumped down and began running over to Louis.

A large Grunt escaped Louis as his sisters jumped into his arms. Once in a secured grip Daisy started questioning Louis.

"How were tryouts? Are you a team captain? Ew, you're all sweaty!"

The words were a shock to Louis. The girls have never asked Louis about football besides at Christmas, he couldn't help but feel his heart swell a little in appreciation. As Daisy began to squirm away from Louis, he couldn't help but pull a classic bother moment and pulled her closer making sure to rub the leftover sweat on her before finally setting her down while keeping Phoebe in his other arm.

"There, now we are all sweaty! And tryouts were great, how'd you know about them?"

Both girls silently looked over to Harry signaling he was the one that told them before turning back to look at their brother.

"Ahh, Harry tried to bore you to death with my boring schedule."

"It wasn't boring, he made it fun!"

"That's his special charm."

Daisy nodded excitedly before promptly standing up and grabbing Louis's hand leading him into the kitchen stopping once they arrived in front of the pile of cookies. Daisy held her arms up and Harry lifted her onto the edge of the counter trying to stay clear of the mess.

"We made cookies!"

"I can see that they look yummy!"

"They are celebration cookies! You want one?"

"What are we celebrating? And of course, I want one!"

Daisy picked up a cookie and handed it to Louis before grabbing one for herself, Harry then gave one to Phoebe who looked like she was about to fall asleep in Louis's arms. It was the cutest thing Harry has seen since photographing the little twin boys nearly a month ago.

"These are delicious, you all are some amazing bakers!"

"Harry, do you want one?" Phoebe's voice was light and soft with a trace of a smile.

"I think he might be wearing his cookie!"

All three siblings laughed while Louis ruffled Harry's hair causing flour to cascade down and fall to the floor. Harry instantly grabbed a small washcloth and began to hit Louis trying to keep Phoebe out of it.

"Okay okay, I'm sorry!"

Harry eventually stopped hitting Louis and settled on giving him a daring stare as he shoved a cookie into his mouth. Once he pulled his eyes away from the incredible adorable sight of Phoebe and Louis, he was able to the dark shine of the night shining into the house. Looking at the clock on the oven Harry almost let out a gasp at how late it had gotten, nearly 11:00 pm, no wonder Phoebe is basically asleep.

"Okay we need to get you both off to bed, and maybe you too Louis if you continue to act like triplets!"

Harry went to pinch his cheek and the twins let out a laugh while Louis just scrunched his nose and tried to wiggle backward. Harry joined in on the laughter before going to grab Daisy and hoisting her onto his hip before beginning to walk towards the staircase.

Louis followed in the path of Harry's footsteps until they ended up in the twin's bedroom, by the time they actually stepped foot inside Phoebe had actually fallen asleep in Louis arms so Harry decided to let the girls go straight to bed, they could clean up in the morning instead.

While Harry was tucking Daisy into bed Louis stood still by Phoebe's bed not knowing what to do, sensing what was going on Daisy pretended to fall asleep as Harry was talking about what they needed to do the next morning. Harry quickly stopped talking before standing up and turning around.

A soft laugh escaped from Harry's lips when he saw Louis was still standing with Phoebe in his arms while looking at her bed.

"Are you okay Louis?"

"I don't know what I'm supposed to do, I don't want to wake her up."

The words melted Harry's heart instantly, to try and hide the deep blush Harry pulled back the covers of Phoebe's bed slowly until he felt his cheeks return to a normal temperature. Once done Harry walked over and placed his hand over Phoebe's head to see how deep in sleep she really was.

"She's out cold. If you're gentle she won't wake up. Just move her onto your chest, it makes it easier to lay them down."

"Okay."

Louis did as he was told and carefully stepped forward until he was able to place Phoebe in her bed and tuck her in. Louis gave her a quick kiss on the forehead before walking out of the room joining Harry in the hallway.

"How do you do that?"

"Do what?"

"Know when they're sleeping."

"I don't know, maybe it's some long lost mother's instinct."

Louis let out a chuckle but honestly, he could see that being a plausible reason.

"You'll make a great dad one day."

Harry was taken back, had Louis really just said what he thought he said? It shouldn't mean so much to him, but the words made Harry feel as if he was floating on clouds.

"Thanks, I hope so."

For the rest of the walk, Harry and Louis stayed quiet until they walked back into the kitchen. Harry stopped and looked at the disarray of the kitchen, he really needed to stop baking with the twins or at least do it early enough so they could help clean up.

"Don't worry I'll help you out."

"Oh, you don't have too, you didn't make this mess."

"Oh no I meant I'll be the one to eat the cookies."

"Somehow I don't doubt that!"

Louis was now standing at the fridge with the pale light shining down on him as he began rummaging through before pulling out a container of pasta and throwing the entire thing into the microwave.

Two minutes later the microwave dinged, and Louis grabbed a fork and the container and just ate the pasta while standing, leaning on the counter. Harry had gotten a washcloth and started whipping flour and stale icing from the countertop and went to dump the contents into the trash when he saw Louis at the kitchen sink.

"Did you eat that entire thing already?"

"yeah?"

"Geez, your mom wasn't kidding when she said you eat like a horse during football season."

"You try running for three hours and tell me you're not hungry after!"

"Yeah, I think I'm good."

Harry laughed as he made his way back to the counter continuing to try and clean off the counter. Louis soon showed up behind him beginning to sweep up the flour that had called to the floor with a broom and Harry thanked him with a smile.

Once it was clean enough to tell what color the countertops where Louis grabbed another cookie and grabbed one of the bags of icings that was placed on a separate plate.

"I think these cookies need to be finished, what about you?"

"I was just thinking the same thing."

Louis handed the bag of icing to Harry along with a cookie before grabbing the other icing and cookies and they began to decorate the rest of the cookies. It was quiet at first, both of them focusing on trying to make them look good.

Harry glanced over and saw seven perfectly iced cookies that look exactly like the football cookies from the cookbook.

"How do yours look so good?"

"I've spent way too much time looking at real footballs to make bad football cookies, or well in your case cow looking cookies!"

"Hey, I'm trying!"

"I think you better stick to photography!"

"Well thankfully I don't plan on going to school to become a baker."

"Are you going to study photography?"

"That's the plan so far, maybe minor in that a major in business. I've thought about maybe opening my own photography business but I'm not sure yet."

"You would definitely be the best photographer in England, the queen would certainly hire you."

"Ha, thank you but let's not get crazy here. What about you, do you know what you're going to study?"

"I haven't really thought about it much, maybe business. I've thought about a few things I could do with that degree."

"No plans to be a professional footballer then?"

"I don't think so, I absolutely love it don't get me wrong and I'm so excited to play in university but don't think I could travel the way professionals do, I'd miss home too much. It wouldn't be worth it to me."

"I get that, I don't know if I'd be able to handle traveling across the world like that either."

"Yeah, I like having this home base."

"It is a pretty great one."

The boys fell back into silence and continued to work on the cookies trying to finish icing the remaining dozen or so cookies. Near midnight Harry's phone buzzed with a text message from Cassie reading.

Are you still at Louis's?

Ronnie posted another Instagram; I really do think they broke up!

Another small tear in his heart caused Harry to nearly squeeze the rest of his icing bag onto the counter beneath him. Thankfully Harry was able to set down the bag and grab his phone before a mess was made responding with.

Yeah, I am.
We'll talk about it tomorrow, I promise!

"Is that your mom?"

"Oh, ah no just Cassie."

"ah"

Louis went back to working on his pile of cookies silently while Harry's brain was spinning, he didn't know whether or not he should ask Louis about Ronnie or just let it go and let him talk whenever he's ready. However, he knew Louis too well, he would suffer in silence before he talked to anybody.

"Louis?"
"Yeah?"
"Can I ask you something?"
"of course, is everything okay?"

Concern was weighing down Louis's voice and he had set down his baking materials and was leaning on the counter, his entire body facing Harry.

"Did you and Ronnie break up?"

Instantly Harry could see the way Louis tensed up and his head sunk down his eyes focusing on the counter. It was only magnified by the ongoing silence. Shadows danced across Louis's face from the dim lights, it was because of the soft hue Harry was able to see the soft quiver in Louis's lips and the familiar shimmer of water begin to prickle in his eyes.

"Oh Lou, come here."

Harry instantly pulled Louis into a hug wrapping his arms around his waist. Louis slowly melted into the hug as his arms finally gave way and wrapped around Harry as well as letting his head fall onto his shoulder. Louis was thankful to have such a calm heartbeat be so close to him, keeping him steady and holding him together. Louis was able to match his breathing with Harry's and he allowed himself to treasure the safety he felt. He didn't know what triggered it, but a single tear found its way out of his ocean eyes and rolled down his cheek like a soft wave.

"I am so sorry Lou. But I am so proud of you."

All he could do was nod, it wasn't that he missed Ronnie by any means, he was just scared. The unknown had officially come, and Louis didn't want to lose the game anymore.

Harry treasured being so close to Louis again, close enough to feel his heartbeat, his breath, close enough to know they still had a relationship. Even if he wanted it to be more than just friends.

Knowing that they couldn't stay intertwined forever despite the endless wishes of Harry, he rubbed a slow circle in the middle of Louis's back before slowly stepping backward, separating their bodies. Louis's eyes stayed unfocused and gazed on at the floor beside his feet, but Harry just couldn't help but see how absolutely wrecked he was.

It was clear that Louis hadn't been sleeping well and Harry could feel the soreness of his muscles.

"I think you need another cookie."

Harry tried to keep his voice light and mask the concern that was overtaking him. Louis reached out and softly grabbed the cookie in his hand with a limp smile pressed at the corners of his mouth.

"Thanks."

Harry started to place all of the finished cookies on the plate that laid in the center of the counter, setting the few that didn't make it to the icing stage on top. With four people Harry wasn't worried about them not getting eaten. Thankfully the rest of the space was already pretty clean, so Harry didn't have to do much more than do a quick wipe down with a Lysol wipe.

"You should get some sleep, you look exhausted. And maybe take a bath. You also look sore."

"Yes, mom!"

"Hey! You say that now, but you'll thank me later."

"Do I really look that bad?"

"Eh not bad just... just burnt."

"Burnt?"

"Burnt. Used. Walking Zombie. I could keep going if you'd like..."

"Yeah okay, I get the point."

"Okay."

Harry walked over to the kitchen table and began gathering the few teams he brought inside with him. Checking to make sure he had his jacket, phone, and car keys Harry turned back around to see Louis who was leaning up against the door frame looking back.

With everything he needed accounted for, Harry started to make his way down the hall towards the garage door, it didn't take long to notice the footsteps behind him. Louis was walking him to the door. Maybe it didn't mean anything, maybe it was just to turn off the lights after he left, but Harry couldn't help but remember the way Richard used to walk Jay out to the garage or to the front door anytime she had to leave. Maybe all this was just a nice habit installed into him.

Louis was able to grab the door and open it before Harry could even think to open it himself. God, what was happening?

"Thanks."

Timidly Harry turned around and took in his last view of Louis for the night. Even as worn out as he was still the most beautiful person Harry had ever seen. That was it that was the thought that turned reader than a rose petal in Italy on a summer day, he really had to leave before he did anything stupid.

As fast that was still considered to be normal Harry walked over to his car, unlocking it and opening the door. Everything was screaming at him to climb into the car and just breathe but something else was begging him to talk.

"Hey, when do your games start? The twins want to know."

Harry thought it was a safe bet to add the twins into the equation, it would keep him safe from just being creepy. Besides Louis knew the twins would actually want to go to one of his games and if not, well he would force them anyway.

"We start scrimmage next week, but the official season starts in early March."

"Cool."

Finally, Harry got into his car quickly turning the key and putting it in reserves as he clicked the garage door opener to eliminate the possibility of him backing into the large, expensive, metal door. As his headlights flickered in, he could see the door to the house close with a mental push signaling the lock had been turned on. At 12:35 am Harry was heading home with his thoughts racing around his head.

Chapter Thirty-two:

"Cassie, you don't understand, I sounded like a total creep!"

"Oh, come on it couldn't have been that bad, it's just a schedule."

"But why would I creepily ask him at nearly 1:00 am, I could have at least waited until school or I could have just googled it. I'm sure that would have worked."

"It was sweet! I'm sure he appreciated it, knowing someone would be there to support him."

It was late Saturday morning and Harry, Niall, and Cassie were sitting at a window booth at Groundz all lightly sipping on coffee and nibbling on warm pastries. When Harry showed up for his regular weekend meeting with Cassie, and now Niall, he was still replaying everything in his head from the previous night. It was a solid fifteen seconds before Niall and Cassie told him to spill and three hours later words were still seeping out of Harry's coffee burned lips.

Although Niall had only spoken about three words in the entire conversation, he had noted something about the way Harry spoke like he was keeping something on the tip of his tongue but didn't want to say it. Soon Harry got up to go to the bathroom leaving just Niall and Cassie sitting at the window booth.

"Cass this is going to be pointless if he can't get the whole story out of him."

"Okay, so you noticed it too?"

"Yeah, there is something he's not telling us and by the look of it I don't think he will."

"And I don't want to force it out of him if it makes him uncomfortable or if it's something Louis doesn't want us to know."

"Of course, they still do need some privacy and it is their life. It should be their section to share what they want but maybe we can get if it's something like they talk more than Harry lets on or maybe they hangout besides on Friday nights or maybe it's something to do with their old friendship."

"That's a great idea and that would help so much, maybe Harry just needs a little reassurance that they are friends again-"

"What are you talking about?"

"Oh, Harry! Nothing just uh date night plans nothing serious."

"It's been less than twenty-four hours and you're already planning another date night!"

"You'll understand it soon enough don't worry!"

"Yeah, in my dreams."

"Oh, hush you will find a great guy. You've already found us and Louis."

"Cassie was right you do roll your eyes a lot!"

Harry began to laugh and roll his eyes dramatically at Niall to make his point clear. It was then that both Niall and Cassie both knew they had to ask now, or they probably wouldn't get another chance for at least another week, so Cassie went in for the kill.

"Harry, I have a question and if it makes you uncomfortable you don't have to answer and if you do answer you don't have to say everything, but I have to ask. What are you holding back?"

"What do you mean by holding back?"

"It's like you keep wanting to say something but you're holding yourself back. if it makes you uncomfortable to share you don't have to but maybe it would help you."

"Oh that. Yeah, it's just I guess we talk a lot when it's late and sometimes I just forget how much of our lives we shared, and it surprises me I guess how I can still read him, and he can still read me."

"Trust."

"What?"

"Louis trusts you, if he talks to you late at night then he trusts you, so you are clearly doing something right."

"I guess you're right about that, thanks."

"Thanks for sharing. I think it'll help you clear your mind with him."

"I hope you're right. It would be nice to go a day without thinking about him but then again I would rather think about him than other things like school."

"Amen to that, I refuse to think about school on the weekend especially now that I can annoy Niall instead."

"So that's why you keep me around..."

Niall and Cassie started to play fighting across the table, Harry couldn't help but laugh himself as he saw his friends so happy. When Harry's phone buzzed, he was the only one to notice. Reading through the notification he quickly realized it was from the print shop down the street saying his photos were ready.

Harry completely had forgotten that when he got back home the previous night, he decided to print out

almost all of the photos he had taken over the years so he could get a head start on his photography final.
It was while on his phone that Harry realized just how late it had gotten, three-o-clock in the afternoon. Harry nearly jumped out of his seat causing Niall and Cassie to pull apart fast and turn to face him with a questioning look etched in both of their faces.

"You okay their lighting McQueen?"

"Oh yeah I just have to pick up something at the print shop and I just realized how late it is."

"Ah okay well have fun with that Cass and I were gonna catch a movie later, you can join if you want it's at six."

"I'm okay, I'll let you cuddle in peace but thanks for asking."

"Sure. see you later."

"Bye Harry."

"Bye lovebirds."

Harry was already far enough away from the booth that he couldn't suffer any physical harm from his words, but he certainly did hear the snarky remarks they made due to the nickname but after all, it was a perfect match for them.

It was an extremely short drive until Harry found himself in the tiny parking lot. Only one other car inhabited the lot and Harry knew it was the owner Lucy's car. When he walked into the store a tiny bell rang signaling his arrival and instantly Lucy came waddling out from the back room with stacks of white envelopes in her hands.

"Harry! My love, you arrived just in time I just finished all of the photos and they do look lovely!"

"You really are a superwoman are you, Ms. Lucy!"

"I think the printer is the real superwoman but I'm definitely its super cool sidekick!"

"The printer would be nothing without you!"

"I would be nothing without you! I think you're the one keeping me in business with all these photos, are you making another photobook?"

"Close! It's for a project at school. I have to do this photo walk through where I tell my life story through photographs I have taken, or my family has taken so I thought I might as well print all the ones I've taken so I can start going through them."

"Well, you have a big task ahead of you, that stack is higher than Mt. Everest!"

"Yeah, I have a feeling a couple of weekends will be dedicated to it!"

Harry grabbed one of the reusable bags he brought in from his car and began to put the envelopes of photos in so he could carry them to his car easily. It took two bags but eventually, everything was packed and ready to go, the only thing left to do was pay.

Pulling out his debit card Harry knew his bank account was about to be drained but he was lucky he just had a super busy winter season and had the money to do it at all. Harry flinched at the 750 pounds he was about to spend.

"It's a good thing I love photography."

"I'm lucky you love it too."

Harry laughed as he signed the receipt and put his card back in his wallet, his hands grabbing the bags once he was done. Lucy accompanied him out to his car holding the front door open for him as he walked out. Once the bags were in his car Harry gave Lucy a hug and waited until he saw her safely walk back into the store before climbing in his car and driving home.

As soon as he got home Harry took the bags to his living room and started to organize the envelopes by the year they were taken. Harry was really thankful that Lucy was always super diligent with her packaging and wrote the dates in a large black marker on the front of every envelope, it certainly was a huge help to Harry. Anne walked through the garage door placing her purse and keys down on the counter before walking over to the kitchen table placing the takeout, she picked up down and grabbing some silverware from the drawer before walking out into the tiny hallway calling for Harry.

"Harry! Where I have din- What in the world are you doing to my living room?"

"Oh mum, you scared me! It's for my photography final. I'm just trying to organize all the photos."

"Why don't you come enjoy some food then we can figure this out, it's Italian!"

"That sounds so good I'm starving. I'll be right there!"

Anne walked back into the kitchen, Harry not far behind her. As soon as they sat down, they began digging into the plates of pasta sitting in front of them. While enjoying dinner Harry took the time to explain his project to his mother and the reason why her living room now looked like a puzzle piece.

Talking about the photos Anne and Harry started talking about all the little memories they had that he could potentially use in his project. That's when Anne suggested something that Harry hadn't even thought of, going through all of his home photos.

Once all the food was gone Harry cleaned up the trash and threw it away while putting the silverware in the dishwasher. While he was cleaning Anne went into the spare room grabbing as many photo books as she could and piling them up on the table.

When it was all said and done around twenty photo books sat on the table. As Harry sat back down at the table, he grabbed one and began to look through it. Harry was surprised to see some photos that he had never seen before. Photos of Anne during her pregnancy surprised Harry the most, especially the ones where a tall man was included in the frame. Harry knew exactly who he was but didn't want to ask any questions.

Harry kept the photos in the back of his head because he knew that he most likely was going to have to include a picture of his dad in his project because even not being a part of his life, he was still a part of his story. Not wanting to worry about its Harry picked up another book and began flipping through the pages. This time the photos were of baby Harry, there were documents of his first steps, his first solid food, and even the day he said his first words. For all of the photos, Harry wants to include in his project Harry took a photo with his phone so he could quickly print it out to hold its place.

Anne stayed watching Harry go through the photos until she was falling asleep in her chair, knowing how invested her son was with the books in front of him she quietly got up and went to sleep in her room allowing Harry to continue going through all of the photos. Eventually, Harry came to the photos books that told the story of his early childhood in which he could remember, his first day of school, when he learned to swim, the times he and Gemma had made pillow forts. Some of the things Harry saw he had completely forgotten about and he was suddenly beginning to understand why Ms. Thompson assigned this project.

Harry's eyes began to feel heavy, but he couldn't tear himself away from the kitchen table full of photos so instead, he just grabbed another book and flipped through the pages. It only took two pages for Harry to have a smile on his face. Every single photo that had Harry in the frame Louis was right beside him.

The time between each turn of the page began to take longer than the previous and Harry let a buried happiness bubble up from the memories he was looking at. The last thing Harry remembered was a photo of him and Louis in their Halloween costumes then all he was was the blurred image of snow falling from the sky as his eyes closed for the night.

Chapter Thirty-three:

It didn't take Harry long to notice that he didn't have nearly enough room to look at all of his photographs and plan his project within his own house. Harry knew what he needed to do, it was a simple answer really but was the last thing he really wanted to do, but without another choice, he pulled out his phone and texted Jay.

Hi, jay I was wondering if I could use one of your extra rooms for a photography project. I just need a larger space to lay out all of my photos.

Of course, Harry! You know the code so come over whenever you need to!

Thank you so much!!

Harry was relieved to have a place designated to fully dive into his project without any limitations. The only thing that scared him was how close to Louis he would be, Harry knew he would now be spending the majority of his free time over at the Tomlinson's and he would have to stay focused, and Louis did a great job at distracting Harry from just about everything.

Harry's phone dinged alerting him of a photoshoot he had to attend in an hour, so he quickly showered, got dressed, packed his gear, and headed out the door driving to the location he had saved in his phone.

Three photography sessions later Harry finally returned home tired and hungry. Harry appreciated the time it gave him for himself to focus on something he loved doing and not to mention the money he had earned, especially after his larger than life purchase the previous day but that also didn't mean he was happier than ever to be home and be able to stuff his face with whatever food he could find.

Harry's normal school schedule fell right back into place easily as the week started up once again. Every day he woke up, got ready, then picked up Cassie and Niall, and finally attended the grueling seven hours of instruction.

The one thing that was still new to Harry's daily schedule was the constant lookout for Louis. Every time he found himself in the hall, he looked for the Carmel hair and crystal blue eyes, but he could never seem to spot him. The same thing happened during lunch; he always examined the table of footballers but never saw Louis with them.

Harry tried to not let the thoughts and worry of Louis consume his brain and sometimes were easier than others but the less the saw of him the more he began to worry.

By the time Friday rolled around Harry was exhausted, this final semester was not turning out to be as easy as he had thought it would be. Before driving over to the Tomlinson's to do his annual babysitting of Phoebe and Daisy he had to go back to his house and pick up his bags of photos and his camera gear. It didn't add much time to his computer only making him fifteen minutes later than normal.

As soon as Harry walked into the house the girls were ready to greet him as always. Every time he comes over it's always a little shocking to realize just how much he feels at ease in the house, how any member of the family can just make his troubles go away.

Like normal, the girls began talking about their week while they followed Harry up the stairs and into a virtually empty room.

"Harry, what are we doing up here?"

"I'm going to use this room for a school project, and these are the supplies I need for it."

"Are you going to be over more now?"

"I will"

"Yay!"

"But I will have to work so it won't be all fun and games but I'm sure I could work in some breaks."

The girls were dancing around in circles of excitement while Harry quickly threw his bags of photos over in the far corner of the room before he got a text from Jay.

Hey, Harry, there are two special gift bags for the girls in the closet of your room, can you make sure to give it to them before you all leave for the game? Thank you!

Of course!

Opening the only other door in the room Harry quickly found the pink and lavender gift bags and pulled down from the top shelf hiding them behind his back before he walked back to the girls who still stood near the doorway.

"Okay close your eyes! There is a special surprise for each of you"

Phoebe and Daisy instantly listened and became quiet as their little hands cupped their petit eyes. Harry sat the bags down on the floor in front of them before stepping back so he would be able to hear the girl's reactions.

"Okay, you can open them now!"

Instantly the girls began pulling out the tissue paper and sticking their hands inside the bag pulling out the gift. In their hands, each girl held two jersey's, a home and an away, with the number twenty-eight printed large on the back with Tomlinson written across the top in all capital letters.

"Can we wear these tonight, Harry?"

"Of course, you can but you'll have to change fast we need to leave in fifteen minutes!"

"Which one does wear?"

"Where the white one because it's a home game. When you're done changing meet me downstairs in the kitchen okay."

"Okay!"

Both girls ran towards their room to change while Harry went downstairs to begin packing some small snacks for them to enjoy while at the game. Harry packed fruit snacks, crackers, and some chips as well as some water bottles and loaded them into a small rolling cooler just in time.

With everything packed and the girls ready, having already got up to get their shoes and grabbing a jacket, all three of them walked out into the garage where Harry loaded the cooler into the back of his car. Before he could put the girls in the car, he had to grab the extra car seats that were sitting in the garage. Locking the seats into place Harry buckled up Phoebe and Daisy before he got in the driver's seat and began the drive to the football field.

They arrived just in time to see both teams take the field and begin warming up. Harry slung his camera bag over his shoulder and wrapped his hand around the handle of the cooler before he began to walk towards the bleachers with Phoebe and Daisy skipping just ahead of him.

Harry began to take out his camera and play around with the lenses while answering the girls' questions about the game. Harry tried his best to answer everything they asked but there was no way of hiding that he didn't know what he was talking about half the time.

Harry noticed the girls waving every few minutes and quickly realized they were waving at Louis every time he ran in front of the stands. Harry decided to use this as his practice shots so he could finish setting up his camera.

Just before the official start of the game, or rather the scrimmage, Jay joined the trio bringing her girls into a big hug before sitting down between them. With Jay now being able to also keep an eye on the girl's Harry was able to fully immerse himself in his photographer's mind.

Harry really wanted to capture the moment he knew would be one of the most important to Louis, his first time representing his team as their captain. Harry snapped as many photos as he could before the rest of the team took the field taking a break to relax once they did.

Throughout the game, Harry moved around quite a bit to take different photos but also made sure to take some time to actually watch what was happening. He also took his break time to talk with Jay about things going on in his life and his project along with keeping the girls interested in the game by creating little games to help them pay attention.

Sometimes Phoebe and Daisy would follow Harry down the bleachers to the edge of the football field as he took photos. Harry was able to get some amazing shots where both the twins and Louis were in the frame, one of them even being when Louis scored a goal.

After halftime, it was too dark to take photos without a flash and since that was against the rules for player safety Harry packed up his gear and just watched the game like every other person sitting in the stands. Harry actually found himself enjoying the game and paying attention to every little move on the field. Phoebe sat comfortably on Harry's lap watching as well while Daisy sat on Jay's lap and all four of them took turns pointing out Louis whenever they saw him.

Before they knew it the game was over, no official score was kept since it wasn't an official game debut it was clear their team had won with them scoring five goals, Louis scoring three of them! Harry began to take his camera bag and the cooler back to his car while Jay walked with the twins down to Louis on the field.

When Harry made it back and joined the family the rest of the team was beginning to disperse and calling out plans for a team dinner from across the field. Louis who had Daisy in his arms gave Harry a soft smile that held a trace of a dimple as he put Daisy back down on the ground before he got pulled away by one of his teammates.

Harry and Jay made a plan for Harry to take the girls home and for Jay to pick up some dinner on the way home for everyone since Louis got to go out and celebrate. With the plan set, everyone went to the proper car and began to drive.

Harry, Phoebe, and Daisy only had to wait around fifteen minutes once they got home for Jay to arrive with the food allowing them just enough time for the girls to change into some cozy pajamas and for everyone to wash their hands.

Everyone, including Harry instantly began to jump with excitement at the smell of food when Jay walked through the door and put the boxes of food on the table. Instantly hands were flying into the bags and grabbing the food, tossing the lids to the containers in the air. Fried rice, dumplings, orange chicken, and lo-mein were all scattered along the table.

After a couple of minutes of everyone devouring food, they slowly began to talk as their hunger began to die down. The twins were fascinated by Jay's work, they always found it lucky how she got to spend all day looking at various works of art and they loved to learn about all of the new pieces she saw.

Even with their family still owning the art gallery Phoebe and Daisy had never been and have never seen the art they had on display, only the pieces they kept at the house which even to them still seemed to fulfill their artist's brains.

By the time everyone was stuffed to the brim with food Phoebe and Daisy were yawning non-stop and were struggling to keep their eyes open signaling they were ready for bed. Surprisingly for both Harry and Jay they didn't put up a fight when they suggested they head to bed, instead they agreed happily.

Since Jay was home, she decided to put the girls to bed and give Harry a break from it since she knew he would be working late on his project. While Jay and the girls headed upstairs Harry threw all of the empty containers and used napkins into a garbage bag and placed the leftovers in the fridge before making himself a gigantic cup of tea to give himself a little extra caffeine. Once his tea was brewed Harry grabbed his camera bag and headed upstairs to the room that was now dedicated to his project. Before he actually got to work Harry pulled out his camera and began to download the photos from the football scrimmage onto his laptop.

With his photos now backed up on his laptop, Harry pulled up Spotify and played his favorite playlist that always helped him work and began to work.

Harry was happy that he was doing one of the easiest parts first, his only goal for tonight was to hang up a line of fairy lights on the wall and attach the eighteen needed strings so they hung down around a half a meter apart from the others.

It only took an hour and a half to hang everything up and with the amount of caffeine coursing through his veins Harry wanted to continue working so he decided to work on organizing the photos he had brought in the years and placing them under each of the strings where the best would hang.

Another hour passed and Harry had properly put every envelope of photos to its corresponding string. It was only eleven-o-clock and Harry still had some motivation so he concluded that it couldn't hurt to begin going through the countless envelopes and begin picking out the photos he wanted to use.

After about thirty minutes Harry realized exactly what he got himself into and saw his future for what he could only think was the next month or two, just sitting in a room on the floor listening to music sifting through hundreds upon hundreds of photos.

Harry quickly began to lose track of time and just kept pushing himself to get through as many photos as he could. Harry thankfully was able to stay organized and had three bins in which he placed the photos in a definite yes bin, a definite no bin, and a potential use bin. Harry created the goal to go through four of the envelopes for his first year of life or the first string of his project that way he could get through at least a quarter of the photos.

Louis pulled into the garage of his house just at the clock struck one am and he was a ball of excitement and exhaustion. When he first saw Harry's, car parked in the garage he thought nothing of it because on any other Friday night he was would expect to see it, but it was when he also saw his mum's car parked next to it that it hit him that Harry should be at his own home, probably sleeping with how late it was.

One idea kept biting him in the back of the head and for some reason, he couldn't push it away. Had Harry stayed so late just to see him? Louis knew the answer, of course not he was probably just up talking to Jay and lost track of time.

When Louis walked into the house, he was confused to see all the lights had been turned off and silence hung in the air. With people clearly asleep, Louis didn't want to make a ruckus and wake anybody up so he turned on the flashlight on his phone to illuminate the floor so he wouldn't trip over anything as he made his way up to his room.

Once Louis got to the top of the stairs, he heard the faint sound of music humming softly and saw a small stream of light coming from underneath a door frame. Louis made his way towards the door quietly trying to think about what could be on the other side. Upon arrival, the door was unlocked so Louis slowly twisted the handle and let himself into the room.

Walking inside Louis saw Harry asleep on the floor with a stack of photos in his hands. When Louis looked around the room, he was in awe at what was going on. The normally empty room had been transformed into whatever was insides Harry's head. Louis took a second to look around and saw the other piles of photos laying around Harry and couldn't help but notice all of the adorable little baby photos.

Louis started looking through all of these photos, he never realized that he had never seen Harry's baby photos before even when they were best friends. He guessed it was normal for young boys to not be interested in each other's baby photos, but he sure was interested now.

Soft snores began to fill the room and Louis quickly remembered Harry was asleep on the floor next to him. Not wanting to wake Harry up Louis put down the photos he was looking at and went to the linen closet across the hall and grabbed a couple of pillows along with some blankets.

Louis laid a pillow down and carefully moved Harry's head to the fluffy surface. Louis also laid pillows down by each of his sides in case he turned in his sleep then laid the two blankets on top of Harry to keep him warm during the night.

With Harry now properly asleep Louis got up and walked back into his own room making sure to shut off the lights of the room before walking out and getting ready for bed himself.

Chapter Thirty-four:

It had been two weeks and Harry couldn't tell what was left or right anymore. Three to four days a week Harry found himself at the Tomlinson's house locked inside his project room just going through the endless photos. Every school day Harry stayed for three to four hours and more often than not stay for dinner before heading back to his own house to finish any other homework or just to relax.

On Friday nights Harry always found himself working until he fell asleep, always forgetting to stop in time to walk down to the guest room and sleep in an actual bed but somehow every Saturday morning he woke up wrapped in blankets and a pillow underneath his head.

It was late Friday night and Harry's birthday was the following morning and to everyone's knowledge nothing had been planned yet, Harry had been way too busy to agree to do anything and every time somebody asked him what he wanted to do all he said was "rest" and Louis could understand the reason for the answer seeing how hard harry worked himself over his project, but he had something planned.

Louis had learned threw his mum what Harry was doing in the spare room and he made sure to try and not to bother Harry and keep Phoebe and Daisy busy as well, so they didn't disrupt him either. The whole thing was actually a blessing in disguise allowing Louis to spend so much time with sisters.

Over time Louis couldn't help but feel things were going back to the way they were when he and Harry were little, even without seeing him as often as he did back then Louis still felt his life was returning back into its happiest time, all because he was closer to Harry then he had been in years.

At eleven-o-clock, sharp Louis burst through the door of Harry's project room as quietly as he could while being dramatic.

"Okay we are leaving, come on Harry."

"Wait what are talking about its late and have to continue going through these photos."

"Nope you are only seventeen for one more hour and you aren't going to turn into an adult sitting alone in this room, that's not a very Harry Styles thing to do."

"Louis..."

"Nope, you have no choice. Come on."

Louis extended his hand down towards Harry and eventually, Harry put down the photos in his hands, rolled his eyes, and grabbed Louis's hand.

"Fine, I better not regret this."

Louis tugged Harry up while Harry also jumped up from the floor causing him to nearly stumble into Louis when he finally got on his feet. Both Louis and Harry's breath hitched in the back of their throats and the air ran stale between them as their eyes mixed together looking deep inside the others.

"Don't worry you won't"

Still holding Harry's hand Louis turned around and led him down the stairs and into the garage. When they finally arrived at Louis's car, he found himself not wanting to let go of Harry's hand, but he knew the longer he continued to stand there the more tension would begin to rise between the two and now was not the time to be selfish, it was time to celebrate Harry.

"Okay get in the car."

Louis let go of Harry's hand and grabbed the door handle allowing for him to climb into the driver's seat. It wasn't until he was already buckled that Harry opened the passenger door and got in as well.

It didn't take long for Louis to enter an address into his car's GPS system and began driving, following the directions as they appeared. Since it was so late there were almost no cars on the road anymore, it was too late for people coming back from dinner and too early for people to be leaving the bars. After a flexible silence, Harry finally spoke, asking a question that burned in the back of his head for years.

"Louis?"

"Yeah?"

"All those nights that you came back drunk who did you get home? Where are you driving?"

Harry whispered the last few words, but it was obvious Louis had heard them by the way he flinched after they were said.

"There were a few different ways, one was someone sober would drive me then get an uber back to the party to get their car. When no was sober, I would use the self-driving feature on the car to drive. It's not always perfect but it's still much better than drunk driving. I never once drove after I drank; I don't think I could live with myself if I did."

"I'm glad you were safe; I wish more people were."

"I do too, I do too."

Harry let his eyes drift out his window and looked up at the stars as Louis continued driving. Music was playing in the car allowing Harry to let his mind clear from all of the crazy, hectic thoughts that had been bundling up over the last month.

Soon Harry began to notice familiar street signs and roads, but he couldn't quite place it until they turned into an empty parking lot.

"What are we doing here Louis?"

"We are going to go through the exhibits and appreciate the art."

"Are you sure?"

"I've never been so sure, come on."

Harry and Louis got out of the car and walked up towards the back entrance of a large building. Only one dim light was lit causing an eerie feeling to radiate through the air cause Louis and Harry to stay close together the entire walk.

Upon arriving at the door Louis pulled out a set of keys and unlocked the large door opening it and quickly suffering inside. Louis quickly turned on the lights and stood as he watched as the hallways of his family's gallery illuminated back to life.

"Ready Haz?"

"Yeah. Ready Lou?"

"Yeah. here we go."

Instinctively Louis grabbed Harry's hand as they began to walk into the first exhibit, ancient European pottery, and sculptures. Louis allowed Harry to lead and just followed him as he looked around at the beautiful works of art.

Each exhibit leads flawlessly into the next, something Harry was trying to take note of for his own project. It didn't take long for Harry and Louis to end up in the resistance painting exhibit which had always been Harry's favorite exhibit.

Louis was able to sneak his phone out of his back pocket and open his camera app. Because Louis was behind Harry and because Harry was so intrigued at the painting in front of him, Oath of Love by Hanz Zatzka, that he didn't notice the phone out of the corner of his eye.

It was perfect timing; Louis was able to catch the exact moment midnight stuck and he whispered a happy birthday before stopping the recording and putting the phone back in his pocket.

Harry and Louis continued walking through the different rooms for another hour before they ended up at the last exhibit where a large gray plaque stood at the entrance. The plaque was dedicated to Richard and his life and the endless amounts of hard work he put into the gallery for people everywhere to enjoy the beauty of art.

Harry gave Louis's hand a quick squeeze before they walked inside, looking at the final exhibit Richard had designed before he passed away. Once arriving at a painting called Mother and Child painted by Gustav Klimt which depicted a mother and her twin girls Louis stopped and just stared examining the painting. Louis and Harry both had a gut feeling that the painting would have ended up hanging on one of the walls of the Tomlinson residence if Richard was still physically with them.

When they got to the end of the exhibit Louis guided Harry back towards the back door where they had entered two hours previously. Louis shut the lights off and locked the door before walking back to his car with Harry still close to his side.

"Thank you, Louis, I really needed that."

"You're welcome, I'm glad you enjoyed it. Now it's time to go home and stuff our faces with ice cream."

"Classic Tomlinson!"

"You know you want a big bowl of ice cream to celebrate being an adult."

"Ah don't say that it's weird!"

"Trust me I know!"

Both boys just laughed as Louis started the drive home. The drive went by much quicker as Harry and Louis talked about their favorite pieces through all of the exhibits. Harry began to talk about all of the photos he wanted to recreate and even created an order for the ones he wanted to get done first.

When the garage door opened Harry and Louis had to sit in Louis's car to let out the remaining fits of laughter before heading inside so they didn't create loud echoes and wake up Jay and the twins.

Harry and Louis turned on the hallway and kitchen lights and nearly ran to the freezer. Harry grabbed two bowls, spoons, and an ice cream scoop while Louis pulled out two containers of Ice cream one being mint chocolate chip and the other being Christmas pudding.

"Oh my god, Lou how did you get this it's only sold in December!"

"Clearly you don't know my ice cream connections! Also, a freezer keeps things good for a long time."

"I learn something new every day, now give me the ice cream!"

Louis slid the container across the counter and Harry immediately began to scoop as much ice cream into his bowl as he could manage before handing the ice cream scoop to Louis so he could school his dessert in his bowl.

The boys ate their ice cream as if they were starving, causing them to have milk mustaches and brain freezes. The whole thing remained them of their old tradition where they would always sneak a bowl of ice cream to kick off their birthday before anyone else had awoken. Each of the boys started talking about old memories of them playing in the backyard or school pranks each new topic being louder than the last.

Soon Harry and Louis were in a shhing war trying to tell each other to be quiet but it didn't work, and they ended up laughing much louder.

When the boys finally caught their breath, they began to gather their dishes and placed them in the sink, Harry and Louis both letting out heavy yawns as they did so. Glancing at the clock Harry saw it was almost three in the morning and suddenly all he could think about was laying down in a cozy bed with a warm blanket. Just like when they were kids Louis seemed to read his mind.

"And you're not gonna sleep on the floor tonight, adults get to sleep on a bed."

"I won't argue to that."

Louis turned off all of the lights as Harry started walking towards the staircase, causing him to jog to catch up with him.

Harry and Louis were careful to keep quiet causing them to tip toe lightly all the way up the staircase and all the way down the hall before stopping at the linen closet were Louis grabbed an extra fluffy gray blanket and handed it to Harry

"Mums been keeping the window in their open for the fresh air so it's probably freezing."

"Sounds like her. Thanks."

"Course."

"Hey, I have one birthday favor to ask your"

"Okay, good ahead..."

"Don't eat lunch alone anymore please. You don't have to eat with Niall, Cassie, and I maybe with the rest of the football team or maybe a classmate just not alone."

"How did- sure. Good night Styles"

"You too Tomlinson."

Harry turned around and began the longer than normal walk to the guest room at the end of the hallway while turned around to walk the rest of the way to his room.

Louis stood in the middle of his doorframe watching until Harry's shadow faded into the midnight darkness before closing his door and climbing into his own bed.

"What is happening"

Chapter Thirty-five:

The whole weekend was filled with tons of celebrations, Saturday morning Harry had a huge birthday breakfast with the Tomlinson's and his mum. For lunch, Harry headed to Groundz with Cassie and Niall staying until closing time. By Monday morning Harry was refreshed and felt like a whole new person, the time off from his project and the proper meals completely rejuvenated Harry and he was thankful for it.

Monday started just like every other day of the school year Harry woke up, got dressed, ate breakfast, brushed his teeth, picked up Cassie and Niall, then drove to school. Traffic was usually heavy causing Harry and many other students to be stuck in their cars instead of first period. Thirty minutes after the first bell rang students were shuffling into the building, thankfully with nearly half of the student body being late nobody was given a tardy and instead they all just headed to class.

Quickly the day went back to normal sitting in class and taking notes, listening to boring lectures, writing pointless papers. When the lunch bell rang Harry was excited to leave his journalism class and hang out with Niall and Cassie.

It wasn't long after the three sat down and began eating that near silences fell upon the cafeteria. Niall and Cassie quickly stopped talking and shifted higher in their seats to see what was happening, Harry had to turn around like an owl be able to see the door of the cafeteria.

As soon as Harry looked dup, he was the crystal ball eyes of none other than Louis Tomlinson. A flash flood of memories from early Saturday morning came and drowned out every other thought in Harry's brain. Soft shuffles of footsteps and faint whispers began to creep into the air.

Louis kept walking forward completely ignoring a hundred pairs of eyes staring him down. The closer Louis got to Harry and his small table the more whispers could be heard and the faster Harry's heartbeat.

When Louis finally sat down a couple of gaps escaped from lips all across the cafeteria, Louis rolled his eyes and forced a small smile. When did his personal life become everyone's live television show?

"How long do you think until they begin to talk again?"

Louis chuckled and began to unpack his lunch and lay the items out on the table, Harry, Cassie, and Niall did the same trying to act like every other group of teenagers in a high school cafeteria.

"We could start a food fight?"

"I like the way you think Niall!"

Niall and Louis looked at each other with a mischievous grin on their lips and a suspicious cock of the eyebrow. Cassie slowly opened up her pudding cup and slide it over to Niall.

"Okay nope, not today!"

Harry shot up and grabbed the pudding cup along with the bottles of water and a container of applesauce moving it to the edge of the table beside him, out of reach from everyone else.

"Oh, come on!"

"I think team captains need to not get suspended and you two I can't drive home by myself so no detentions."

"Always so needy Harry."

"Was he this bad when you were younger?"

"Unbelievably mate!"

"so, when did *my* life becomes people's personal entertainment?"

"Hey, you forced me to be here so I'm going to talk about whatever, even a needy Harry."

Harry let out a little yelp as Cassie's shows rammed into his shin. Louis' confused eyes darted between the two before finding Niall again.

"Does this happen often?"

"All the time. you better get used to it."

"Could be worse, I guess I could always become a mind reader, so I know what's happening."

"Oh no, you don't want to do that-"

"Cassie!"

Niall and Cassie couldn't help but laugh, it didn't take long for Louis to join in with them.

"How did I get myself into this..."

"Because you love me!"

Louis playfully threw his arm around Harry's broad shoulders and laughed even harder meanwhile Harry instantly froze into a statue, caution lights flashing in his brain. Harry frantically looked over to Cassie and Niall pleading for help with his eyes. Harry began to laugh at default to try and keep the situation moving.

"Well, Harry loves everybody so don't feel too special!"

Harry mouthed a thank you to Cassie for saving the day. As Louis pulled his arm off of Harry, he had to fight his inner thoughts to tell Louis to stay but he was also happy to breathe again and relax.

"I guess I'll just have to work my way up to the top then."

Louis said it so matter of fact that Harry just wanted to scream *You already are at the top, you don't need to work for me I'm right here* but instead, Harry's cheeks turned into warm roses.

The bell rang and relief flooded through Harry's veins and he mentally thanks to the electricity for not letting him down and giving him an escape. It only took a few minutes before the group of now four to enter the hallway, while Cassie went to the left, Niall went straight forwards, Harry went left but now he wasn't walking alone.

"Do people always look at you this much?"

"Usually but normally I'm with more people so it's less..."

"Creepy?"

"Yeah."

Harry chuckled and tried to keep his eyes forwards and not look at all the people lining the halls, but Louis couldn't care less what those people thought and just took in the golden light of Harry laughing.

"What class do you have?"

"Entrepreneurship then business economics. What about you?"

"Photography and creative writing."

"I would say you're lucky with easy classes, but I've seen your photography project, so I don't know!"

"Yeah, easy semester my arse! but I'm not going to complain, I mean business economics I'd actually be in a grave."

"Welcome back dramatic Harry it's nice to see you again!"

"And would you looky their sassy Louis is back too!"

"Uh oh did I bring out defensive Harry?"

Just as Harry was about to speak again, he found himself at the base of the staircase, only a small number of students still filled the halls due to the few classrooms. Louis stood outside a wooden door peering inside before giving a quick smirk to Harry and walking inside taking a seat in the middle of the room.

Harry began to slowly walk up the staircase turning around once he reached the landing in the middle to see Louis doing the same thing, looking at him. Harry made a silly face, one he usually reserved for the twins, and Louis shook his head a laughed quietly to himself. Anybody who saw the interaction probably thought Harry lost whatever game the two were playing but in reality, he got to see Louis smile, so he considered it a win his book.

The rest of the school day passed, and Harry found himself waiting by the school doors waiting for

Cassie and Niall. When all three got back together they made their way to Harry's car surprisingly silent until the doors shut beside them.

"Would you like to explain what happened at lunch or am I going to have to use my detective skills?"

"Geez, Cas can I at least turn the car on before you start your interaction!"

"Right okay. So, spill, what was that?"

"I already regret this. Niall are you writing this down?"

"This is valuable information mate!"

"You two are so lucky you're usually such good friends."

"Yeah, yeah we're great but Louis!"

"We hung out late Friday night and celebrated my birthday and it was really late when we got back, and I vaguely remember asking him to eat lunch in the cafeteria and be around people instead of being alone."

"Uh-huh, and did you invite him to sit with us?"

"Cassie, are we just going to skip past the late-night hang sesh?"

"I'll get to that Niall but one thing at a time."

"Wow, you're taking this detective thing super serious huh. Anyway, I said he didn't have to sit with us but said if he didn't feel comfortable with anyone else then he was always welcomed."

"And who did you say he could sit with?"

"His teammates from football or any other friends from his classes."

"Okay, okay, wait did we confirm he and Ronnie are officially done?"

"Yeah, they broke up right before the semester."'

"Great. now Friday night?"

"Uh, that's... a little personal."

"Okay don't worry but he did celebrate with you right?"

"Yeah, he did."

"Awe I hope it was special!"

"It was, it really was."

Harry hadn't noticed the large smile plastered across his face, but Niall sure did and made a quick note before clicking his pen shut and putting his small notebook back into his bag. The slight rustle brought Harry back to his senses and he pulled his lips closed. Harry turned up the radio and the three jammed out as he drove his friend's home.

Once Niall and Cassie were each dropped off at their respective houses Harry began his drive to the Tomlinson residence again, the more and more weeks that passed the more and more it felt as if he was driving home rather than to a friend's house or a place to work on his project.

Every single day Louis would walk into the cafeteria and sit down next to Harry spending his lunch hour talking to Niall and Cassie just like they had been friends for years. Sometimes Harry and Louis would get sidetracked into their own conversations for the entire period and Niall would secretly write down the topics they talked about and Cassie would try to decipher Louis's facial expressions.

By the time Friday rolled around Louis had been officially initiated into the friend group and pretty much everybody in the school knew. Instead of driving back to the Tomlinson residence alone like he normally did,

Harry was joined with Cassie in his shotgun seat and Niall sprawled out in the back. Somehow while talking about their weekend plans Louis had invited Niall and Cassie to his football game.

Harry gave a quick rerun of the rules for Niall and Cassie before they all headed inside. Just like normal Phoebe and Daisy ran into Harry's arms and gave him a big hug, and just like normal Harry twirled the girls around and hugged them back. Unlike normal Cassie was secretly recording the interaction on her cell phone.

"Niall and Cassie are going to join us at Louis's game today!"

"Yay!"

The girls then ran to give each of them a hug.

"Okay, you two need to go get ready, make sure you grab a jacket or a blanket, it's still super chilly outside! I've got to make our snacks!"

"Cassie, can you come with us?"

Harry gave Cassie a knowing smirk and Niall gave her a small nod urging her to go with the girls. Cassie lovingly rolled her eyes and let out a soft giggle before reaching out to grab Phoebe and Daisy's outstretched hands. As soon as their hands interlocked the girls were running towards the stairs dragging Cassie along as they giggled.

"Girls am I right."

Niall's laugh roared through the halls as he followed Harry into the kitchen. Harry pulled out a big cooler and began to pack waters and snacks.

Upstairs the girls brought Cassie into their room and shut the door before ushering her to their secret room.

"Wow what is this?"

"It's a secret so don't tell Harry or Louis they don't know about it!"

"Don't worry Daisy my lips are sealed. But why did you bring me here?"

"Are Harry and Louis dating?"

"What?"

"Are they trying to date like you and Niall?"

"Why? what do you know?"

Cassie's eyes glared questioningly at the twins as they stared innocently back at her.

"They hang out all the time, even after they put us to bed and when Louis is playing football he always looks towards Harry and Harry is always taking pictures of him. And..."

"And?"

"And Louis is always happy after Harry's here."

"You have noticed that too?"

Phoebe and Daisy looked at each other confused and it was then that Cassie remembered she was talking to four-year-old and not Niall.

"Are you two good at keeping a secret?"

" yes!" Both girls yelped in unison

"Okay well they aren't dating, at least not yet Niall and I are working on that, but Harry definitely likes Louis and from what I know about your brother so far I think he might like Harry too."

Daisy and Phoebe both lit up like Christmas trees and squealed in excitement and Cassie couldn't help herself and joined in.

"Is there anything else you've noticed about how your brother acts when Harry is around?"

"Well, he's been getting nicer and nicer and sometimes he looks at Harry a lot and they talk really late at night and on Christmas they had a sleepover!"

"A sleepover?"

"Yeah, they slept on the bay window in Louis' room, we took a picture of it."

"Wait there's a picture!"

"Uh huh it's in Harry's phone we set it as his screensaver a few weeks ago."

"Holy sh- shoot y'all are good at this!"

The twins giggled at Cassie's near slip up of words and smiled at her sudden appreciation for their work.

"How long have you been doing this?"

"The last time you and Niall came over, when Harry said he wanted a prince."

"What would you say about helping me and Niall help get them together?"

"We say yes! But just so you know you're helping US get them together."

"Sassy, I like it. Okay we better get y'all ready for the game before the boys start looking for us."

"Okay."

Phoebe, Daisy, and Cassie all crawled out of the secret hideaway and entered the main area of the twin's room. Daisy and Phoebe headed straight to their bed to grab their jerseys that had been placed on top by Jay earlier in the day and began changing while Cassie went over to their closet to grab them each a jacket.

All dressed and ready to go everyone stood at the door, Cassie holding the doorknob in her hand to keep it in place.

"When we go downstairs you two distract Harry so I can talk to Niall and tell him we're working together okay?"

"Okay!"

" do you always speak in unison?"

"Sometimes!"

"Okay I'm gonna go with a yes then."

Cassie opened the door, and they all made their way downstairs, as soon as their feet were placed on the floor the twins started running towards the kitchen knowing exactly where to find Harry.

Harry and Niall were standing around the kitchen island with a cooler in between them, instantly the twins ran up to Harry and started pulling at his hands.

"Is it time to go yet!"

"We can't be late!"

"We need to get good seats!"

"We can get a good parking spot!"

"Wow wow you are suddenly very excited."

"Harry come on!"

"Okay okay let's go to the garage and get your car seats ready then."

The girls darted towards the garage door giggling and giving a thumbs up to Cassie who just entered the kitchen. Harry began to jog after them before turning around to grab his keys he left on the counter.

"Oh! Niall can you bring out the cooler? And Cassie there are a few blankets on the couch too."

"Yeah."

"Sure thing."

The garage door shut, and little shuffles could be heard, when Cassie knew it was age, she instantly grabbed the spare blankets and ran up to Niall who was now halfway down the hallway leading towards the garage.

"Niall!"

"Wow, excited just like the girls I see."

"Well, there's a good reason! They are in on the plan to get Harry and Louis together."

"Wait what? Did you tell them?"

"No. Well. Kinda? Anyways they asked me if they were dating, I said no then they talked about how Louis was happier after being with Harry and blah blah blah but then, get this they have been trying to eat then together or least spend time together, apparently they even took a picture of Harry and Louis after they had a 'sleepover' on Christmas and they then stole his phone and made it his lock screen."

"Oh my god there smart."

"Yeah, no kidding, anyway I told them you and I were trying to see if Louis liked Harry and they agreed to help us. They could be a big help Niall, inside info on Louis."

"So, when it's just us we can talk about them?"

"Yeah. We should also see if we can find a time-"

"Are you guys on the way, the twins are already buckled up!"

"Oh yeah, coming!"

Harry walked back out and towards the car and Cassie and Niall followed behind staying close to each other so they could still whisper."

"What I was saying was we should try to see if we can hang out with them just the four of us so they can tell us more about Louis and any other things they may have done."

"That's a good idea."

The pair had arrived at the trunk of Harry's car and put the supplies into it before shutting it closed and getting into their seats, Niall in shotgun and Cassie in the back with the girls. Cassie gave the girls each a high five before smiling at Niall in the rear-view mirror.

"You know I feel like I'm missing out on something..."

"Nope!" All four of them said at the same time, only solidifying he was definitely missing out on something but instead of questioning it Harry just started his drive towards the football fields

Chapter Thirty-six:

Arriving at the field was now a normal event and Harry was able to get both girls out of the car and the cooler all before Cassie and Niall even unbuckled. Niall took a hold of the cooler insisting he was best to guard the food while the twins quickly went over to Cassie. Now with free hands Harry was able to grab his camera bag before locking the doors and walking up to the bleachers with everyone else.

By now everyone except Niall and Cassie knew the normal schedule for football games, Jay day with the twins while Harry took photos until it got too dark to do so. Today however was going to be different, everyone except Harry knew that.

The foremost important thing that had to be done first was introducing Jay to the couple tagging along with them, thankfully she seemed to love them just as much as Harry and the twins. Cassie sat next to Jay with Phoebe in her lap while Daisy sat on her mums. Niall was busy sitting at the edge of the bleacher, which the entire group took up, and digging through the cooler and handing out snacks to everyone.

"See he's not looking at us he's looking at Harry."

Cassie nodded as Phoebe whispered into her ear and pointed towards her brother as he ran up and down the field. It didn't take long to notice that every chance Louis got his eyes scanned the crowd looking for Harry, whenever he did a soft smile lifted his cheeks high but when he couldn't he'd simply nod at his mum or sisters before returning his focus back to the game.

"We need to get Harry off of that camera, here go over to his camera bag and in the side pocket there is a little plastic case. I need you to grab it and bring it over."

"Will Harry get mad?"

"No, he'll love it. Trust me."

Phoebe nodded and climbed off of Cassie's lap walking over to the black bag sitting on the floor, she moved quickly and quietly trying to stay close to the floor so as not to be seen by Harry. Niall gave her a questioning glance before he saw Cassie shaking her head from his peripheral view, a few moments later Phoebe found the small gray container and held it close to her chest underneath the unzipped portion of her jacket hiding it from anyone point of view.

"Perfect."

"What are we going to do?"

"We are going to take some pictures."

"How?"

"You'll see, don't worry, just go along with what I say okay?"

"Okay."

Daisy who was still sitting on her mum's lap gave her sister a thumbs-up silently saying she knew of the plan.

"Harry! would you come over here and sit down with us and enjoy the game already?"

"Cassie, I'm taking photos!"

Harry put his camera back up to his face and began focusing his next shot, clearly dismissing the request.

"Well, are you going to let me see them?"

"Fine."

Harry shrugged taking the strap around his neck off and messing with the settings on his camera before turning around and walking over to the bleachers in between his friends. Once sitting he handed the camera to Cassie to happily take it and shifted sideways so her back was now facing Harry.

"What are-"

"Harry you wouldn't believe how good these are! Here try them!"

"Ni-"

Niall had shoved handfuls of chips into Harry's mouth completely distracting him from his camera and photos allowing Cassie to take out the current SD card, put it in her pocket, and place a new one inside in its place. With the camera now ready Cassie whispered the plan into Phoebe's ear who then whispered it to Daisy, they nodded and began their job.

"Let's go to the fence!"

"Please!"

The twins danced over to Harry who was still being fed by Niall and started jumping up and down pleading for Harry to take them down closer to the field. Harry began chewing faster so he could respond but the twins kept their pleading going not going quiet until he cleared his throat.

"How about a little later I was going to show Cassie some of the photos, you can see them too if you want. Besides, there is still lots of time left."

"Okay don't worry about it, I've worked on this before. It's not really rocket science."

Deliberation was clear in Harry's eyes as they shifted between the black electronics in Cassie's hands, the twins still bouncing up and down in front of him, and the busy football field. As his head moved softly from side-to-side Niall gestured to the field indicating his favorite option.

"Okay, let's go then."

"Yay!"

The girls instantly grabbed his hands and began trying to pull Harry's forward and up off the bleachers.

"Cassie don't ruin my camera!"

"Have I ever before! Wait don't answer that."

With a single roll of his eyes Harry, Phoebe, and Daisy disappeared into the small crowd of people and made their way towards the fence lining the edge of the football field. As soon as they were out of sight Niall slid down the metal bench right beside his girlfriend.

Cassie turned on Harry's camera and held it up to her field of vision, even after years of being around Harry and learning the basics about photography she still

had no idea how to choose the best settings for the time of day or even how to properly focus the camera.
Jay gave the two friends a questioning look when she noticed them messing with Harry's camera, thankfully both were quick thinkers.

"It's to help with his photography project."

"He needs more photos of himself."

Jay nodded and the pair went back to trying to set up the camera not knowing what they just set up for the future. Soon Cassie gave up and just pulled the camera's viewfinder up to her eye and looked and looked until she spotted Harry within the little square.

As the clicks rang through the air Niall kept a running commentary of the game, providing a play by play of almost every action but especially ones made by Louis. It didn't take long for everyone to come into frame. The clicks became faster and faster, and the camera moved up and down and from side to side trying to capture the perfect moment.

Cassie brought the camera down and began to look through the photos she took on the LCD screen, Niall leaning over her shoulder to see them as well. Most of the photos were blurry or had streaks of light covering the faces but every once and a while a decent one would appear.

Cassie's thumbs quickly stopped moving over the forwards button when a near perfect picture of Harry leaning lightly over the fence with Phoebe and Daisy on each side of him and Louis down on the field with the football between his feet while he looked up into the stands right at Harry and his sisters with the biggest smile and brightest eyes the two had ever seen.

"that's it, that the one."

"Clearly the universe is in on this mission too because I don't think I could ever take a photo like this again even if my life depended on it."

The couple laughed and Cassie began to turn off the camera making sure to not to damage the SD card before popping it out and placing it in a little plastic bag then inside of her wallet before putting back the original SD card Harry had been using earlier. Seeing how most of the light was now from the light post set up around the field and not from the sun Cassie packed up the camera placing it in its case and inside Harry's carrying bag for it before placing it next to the cooler and it was perfect timing too as the twins along with Harry were now walking back their way.

For the rest of the game everybody sat and watched as football players ran up and down the field chasing the black and white ball around. Everyone cheered when goals were scored, occasionally everybody would go up towards the fence and cheer everyone on. When the game was over, and the stands began to clear out everyone began to gather their things and head towards the line of cars. While Niall and Cassie were putting the coolers and blankets in the car Harry was talking with Jay about the plan for the night.

"Why don't I take the girls and grab some dinner to go so you can take your friends home."

"That works, they don't live that far from here so it shouldn't take too long."

"Great well you know the code and stuff to get in if you beat us to the house. Oh, and I think Louis will be joining us-girls get back here- for dinner tonight. Alright I better get going before these to run off to god knows where."

"Okay I'll see you all soon!"

Jay wrangled up the twins and strapped them into their car seats before pulling out of the parking lot and onto the motorway. Niall climbed into the backseat of Harry's car while Cassie took shotgun up in the front. As Harry followed Jay's actions and also found himself on the motorway but heading in the opposite direction towards his friend's house.

Niall was the first to be dropped off, as he got out of the car, he told his friends he wouldn't be able to make it to their annual weekend meetup at Groundz the following morning due to some family excursion. Harry didn't think it was such a big deal until Cassie told him the same thing when he dropped her off except, she had a vet appointment for her cat, a nonexistent cat.

the two wanted to have a date they could have just told Harry; he would have completely understood. Afterall he kinda stole their normal date night so he couldn't blame them. With Saturday now completely free thoughts of what Harry should do with his free time came and went until he found himself pulling up the winding driveway of the Tomlinson estate.

Just as he was pulling into the garage Harry saw two more sets of headlights behind him each moving towards the right to park in the garage as well. It was mayhem trying to get everyone inside. Harry was trying to not only unload the twin's car seats out of car but also the cooler and in blankets, Louis was unloading his football gear and school bag, Jay was trying to carry in the bag of food and manage the Phoebe and Daisy who were grumpy due to the mix of hunger and tiredness.

Somehow each person made it inside and to the kitchen table in once solid piece. Two buckets of fried chicken along with mashed potatoes and mac and cheese were being passed around and scooped onto the plates that lined the table.

Having Louis at dinner made it livelier than the normal Friday night dinners, the twins asked him every question they could think of about the game. Who his teammates were, what position he played, what the position meant, if he hated running, who had the best shoes on the team, literally everything they thought of they asked? And Louis always had an answer.

Harry hadn't noticed when his plate was cleared of food as he was too wrapped up watching Louis and the twins. It wasn't until Jay had told Phoebe and Daisy to head upstairs and start getting ready for bed that Harry jerked back into reality. Trying to cover up any noticeable tracks he began reaching for the empty containers and plate beginning to clean.

"Uh uh Harry no what have I told you, you are not our maid! Louis you clean up the rubbish bin should be empty for you."

Harry sheepishly pulled his hands away and watched as Louis's now reached for the same teams. It was always hard to not help clean up so to distract himself Harry went into the kitchen and pulled out the kettle, filling it with water before putting it onto the stove burner.

Quietness filled the room, both boys were thankfully it wasn't silent thanks to their footsteps, rustle of rubbish, and the sound of the flame burning underneath the metal kettle. Already a pro at making tea, especially at 10:30 on a Friday night in the Tomlinson family's kitchen, Harry pulled out a giant mug from the cupboard just as the kettle let out a refreshing whistle. Quickly a tea bag was put inside, string dangling over the edge of the ceramic effortlessly, and the boiling water was poured on top.

"Hey, are you just going to skip me?"

"How did you move so quickly? and quietly?"

"It's a secret Styles, but hey the tea."

"Oh sorry!"

Harry filled Louis's equally large mug nearly to the brim using the last of the water before returning the kettle to the stove to cool off.

"So, no team dinner tonight huh."

"Well, knowing how I just ate fried chicken next to you all of ten minutes ago I would say yeah. No team dinner. Coach had to go out of town to celebrate his mum's birthday and he didn't want, and I quote ' a bunch of rowdies, stuck up, teenage boys' stirring up trouble right before the season officially starts."

"Wow can tell he really trusts you there."

"But hey he's not wrong half of those guys would probably end up in jail if we went out. Not great people but great footballers so I don't blame him."

"I'm glad I don't have to deal with them. I'd turn into a pancake really quick."

"Eh you're stronger than you think, it's not all about physical strength. You could easily outsmart them in a heartbeat all you'd have to say is ' I could edit you into a world cup star is you stand far away so I can get a photo' and poof they'll do anything."

The boys both roared with laughter because even deep-down Harry knew Louis was right, he could easily outsmart a lot of people especially people who cared more about what others thought about them. Another part of him laughed to hide the blush at the thought that Louis was thinking of him even though it really wasn't much, they were friends and it, in thought, was a normal thing to say.

"Speaking of which I have to uh get-go-work uh on my project."

"Oh, yeah, right. Don't let me be the one to hold you back."

Harry grabbed his mug in his hands and began walking towards the spiral staircase, stopping at the rubbish bin to throw away his tea bag, and heading up to his project room. All while thinking, *please be the one to hold me back.*

Opening the door and turning on the lights all motivation to work was lost. Everything was a mess and Harry hadn't gotten nearly as far as he wanted with how long he's already worked, and two months had already passed leaving him just one more until he needed to have a rough draft of the project ready.

Sitting down on the floor and taking in everything, trying to plan out the next month of work Harry simply decided choosing the photos that the wanted to use was the last thing of importance he needed to get done, instead Harry grabbed a notebook along with a pen and began creating a list of all the important and memorable events in his life he wanted to showcase.

The ending credits were rolling on the projector screen while Louis finished sipping on his now cold tea. It was just past midnight and Louis had already taken a shower and decided to kill some time by watching a movie, 21 Jump Street to be exact, and hopefully make him feel a little more tired so he could head to bed easily.

Walking back out into the downstairs hallway most of the lights were still on, unusual when everyone else in the house should be asleep-or working. The more steps he took Louis began to hear what sounded like pages of a book being turned in one of the spare rooms.

"Mum?"

“Oh, hey honey, I didn't know you were still up."

"I was just heading to bed; I didn't think you'd be up either. What are you doing?"

"I'm just going through some of the photos we have of Harry for his project, Cassie said he needed some more of himself."

"Oh. any good ones?"

"Why don't you come and look at yourself."

"You know it's times like this I remember where I get my sass from."

Jay playfully swatted a small photobook at Louis as he sat down in front of her, picking up one of his own to look through.

"I wouldn't want my sass to come from anybody else."

"That's the correct answer son."

A couple photos of Harry were placed in a neat pile on the floor, somewhere of him taking photos of others while others were when their families had taken vacations together and somewhere just random ones from school events.

Jay had continued to pull out some good photos of Harry and place them into the pile but also couldn't help but notice the way her son was looking down at the photos and the slow way he turned from page to page.

"Which photos are in that one?"

"A bunch of random ones, a lot of us running around the house and the park, even a couple of our pranks."

"I remember those days, I thought I would never get you two to separate from each other."

"Yeah, I never thought we would either."

"I'm happy you are becoming friends again; I really do think Harry's good for you."

"Me too mum, me too."

"You know I always thought you two would become something more when you were younger."

"What?"

"You know like, end up together. Your dad and I would actually talk about it all the time guessing when it would be."

"Ha of course you did!"

Louis got a little quieter, thinking over the words his mum had just said. There was no doubt in his mind that Harry was someone special to him, that he always wanted to have in his life, but he hadn't really thought about the deeper reason as to why.

"I'm not trying to push anything on you honey or seem like I'm trying to change you, but I am saying that I think you two have something really special, I see it in both of your eyes when you look at each other. And if you did end up with Harry-or someone like him- that wouldn't change anything. We would still love you beyond what you could ever imagine."

"Thanks mum."

"Alright baby I think it's time we both get to bed."

Mother and son stood up, Jay embracing Louis in a hug and giving him a soft kiss on his forehead before grabbing the photos of Harry and walking out of the room and into the hallway, towards the stairs, and up to her room.

Louis followed slightly behind his mother watching as she dropped off the stack of photos at the door of Harry's unofficial official room. Seeing how it was 1:30am and knowing it was the time he normally got home after a game Louis walked straight towards the linen closet, grabbing a few pillows and blankets before returning at the illuminated door.

Slowly opening the door, it was clear Harry was indeed asleep, so Louis did his normal thing of creating a makeshift bed for his-uh friend- asleep on the floor. After he laid the blankets on top of Harry, he noticed the multiple sheets of paper sprawled out across the floor, Louis knew he probably shouldn't read them, but he couldn't help himself.

After reading the first two bullet points Louis knew exactly what he was reading, the more and more he read the more he found himself knowing what was going to come next. The more he read the more Louis learned about what Harry viewed as important in his life, however he stopped once he reached the head titled "fourteen" not feeling comfortable enough to look through Harry's inner thoughts that he didn't already know or was part of.

Louis organized the pieces of paper and placed them on the little shelf near the door before turning off the lights and closing the door before walking across the hallway into his own bedroom, but he didn't go to sleep quite yet.

Chapter Thirty-seven:

Sitting in his large, black leather office chair in front of his desk Louis pulled out a sheet of paper and a pen before he pulled on a little metal linked chain turning on the small lamp sitting at the edge of the dark stained mahogany wood. A single click rang through the air and suddenly words began to stain the page one after the other.

It didn't take long, only around ten minutes, and suddenly all of Louis' favorite memories of Harry were listed. Some included him but many were just of Harry, little things that he had observed or things he remembered Harry talking about.

Louis put his pen back inside his desk drawer and picked up the piece of paper and walked back out into the hallway and stopped once he reached the door separating him from Harry. Trying to stay quiet the doorknob slowly turned until it began to creak open. Due to the loud and streaky noises Louis only opened the door far enough from him to squeeze through the opening to enter the other side.

Due to the lack of light in the room Louis was sneakily tip toeing around the room to not step on any photos laying across the floor or Harry sleeping beside them. After almost a minute the familiar he found the familiar stack of papers Harry had written earlier and placed his own underneath them before exiting once again.

Waking up the next morning Harry was surprised and delighted to find himself once again wrapped up in warm blankets and that it no longer looked as if a hurricane had swept through the room. Sitting up Harry looked up to the wall beside him and back towards the photographs in stacks of the floor, even though he really didn't want Harry to decide to use his extra day to continue working.

In the kitchen the kettle was already on the stove and Jay was standing in front of the island and was preparing cinnamon rolls.

"Good morning Harry."

"Good morning Jay."

Harry gave the women a soft hug and a smile as he walked over towards the cupboard containing the mugs and pulled one down while also grabbing a tea bag. With the kettle already whistling loudly Harry quickly made his cup of tea before turning off the heat.

"What time will you be off this morning, should I save you a cinnamon roll?"

"No Groundz meeting for me today, Ni and Cass is having a date day. Normally it's Friday but I kinda stole that last night. I was just going to work on my project today, hopefully get close to finishing it-if that's okay with you."

"Of course, darling you could stay here every day single day if you wanted! So, I'm going to say it's a yes for a cinnamon roll?"

"Oh, it's definitely a yes!"

"Okay, I'll bring it up to you when it's ready dear."

"Thank you."

Harry grabbed his mug of tea and started walking back upstairs while Jay finished cooking breakfast. No one else in the house was up yet so instead of walking straight back into his workroom Harry instead decided to walk down the hallway and appreciate the pieces of art hanging on the wall.

Due to the frequency of time spent within the same walls it didn't take long until the wall ended, and Harry found himself standing in between his door and Louis' bedroom door. As he walked past, he couldn't help but notice something sitting on one of the shelves on Louis's wall. Curiosity got the best of Harry and he stepped one foot inside and walked towards the shelves.

Most of the items where the same as the last time Harry had seen the shelves a little over two months prior, however a few new items laid still. A picture frame containing an early photo of him and Louis when they were seven and playing out in the old treehouse, it was that day that Harry knew he wanted to be a photographer and he never even knew that photo existed. Not wanting to just steal the photo from the shelf he made a mental note to ask Louis if he could borrow it later.

Attempting to not feel like the weird creep he was, Harry began to leave but as he turned around, he caught another glance of another photo, this time he remembered the photo. Memories of Christmas came flooding back into his head, walking in the same room and seeing his friend crying, learning of how much he had been hurting by himself, holding Louis as he cried in his arm, falling asleep with him in his arms and waking up the next morning and spotting that same photo sitting in the exact same place. On Louis' bedroom nightstand.

Harry smiled and couldn't help but walk up towards the picture frame placing his mug down on the nightstand and picking up the frame, rubbing his thumb over the cold glass. As he set the photo back down, he realized Louis was asleep just a few feet away hugging his pillow and looking peaceful. A soft smile spread across his lips knowing that Louis wasn't hurting in that moment, he was safe from whatever tore him apart when he was awake.

Eventually Harry really did leave Louis' room and walked back over to his own and began working on his project. Sitting down on the floor Harry noticed the new stack of photos and smiled as he was working his way through them. With the new stack of photos organized he began to get back to work on his timeline picking up the papers he had been writing the night before.

Harry was quickly confused when he got to a page that contained scribbles of writing that described some of his favorite memories, some he had even forgotten about. Just then a light knock echoed off the door and Jay appeared holding a plate in her hand containing a cinnamon roll.

"I see you got the photos, I thought you could have a few of you when you were younger."

"Thank you I really did, also this smell like heaven!"

"Let's hope it taste like it too!"

"I'm sure it will, how could anything made by you not be amazing!"

"Aw I need to send your mum flowers for raising such a gentleman."

"I'm sure she'd love it."

"Oh, and before I forget the girls are starting a dance class today, so we'll be out of the house for a bit, use whatever you need and if you end up leaving before, we get back just lock up normally."

"of course and thank you."

"You are very welcome Harry."

Jay left the room and closed the door allowing Harry to get back to work while she went and woke up the rest of the sleeping kids. A quick round of fast footsteps caused a commotion and Harry just laughed because he could hear the excitement traveling through the halls.

Nearly an hour later Harry had finished choosing enough baby photos of himself and his family and had started hanging the photos to the string of fairy lights running down the wall, attaching them with clothespins. With only a few photos left the door nearly flies open causing Harry to jump back and let out a high-pitched squeal.

"Hey it's just me!"

"Louis. Oh my god. Geez. Okay. Hi."

"Hi."

Louis was leaning against the doorframe and laughing as he watched Harry trying to catch his breath.

"Okay that was not funny."

"Oh, please it was hilarious!"

"I thought you all left already?"

"Uh the girls did, about half an hour ago but I'm just now heading out."

"oh, I thought you went with them?"

"No, I have to uh work today actually."

"Work? Since when you got a job?"

"Not too long ago actually, I thought it would help when I go off to university."

"Being responsible, I see, I like it."

"Thanks, oh and here you go."

"tha-wait how di-"

"Next time you snoop in my room don't leave your tea mug on my nightstand!"

Louis was already at the bottom of the staircase by the time Harry had looked through the two photos in his hands and ran out after him. As soon as the reality of the situation sunk in Harry felt as if he was on fire, embarrassment raging deep within his body as he walked back into the hallway and to his project room.

Turning around the photos a small yellow sticky notes with the words *Keep them if you want :)* scribbled across. The longer Harry was looking at the note the more and more the handwriting began to look familiar. Instantly he reached for the stack of papers sitting on the floor beside him and shuffled through them until he found the mysteriously written one and as soon as he looked at it Harry knew, Louis had written it.

Harry had no idea what to think, everything though was swirling around his brain like waves in the middle of a hurricane, the notes meant that Louis knew him better then he knew himself, the photos meant the moments had to be special to him as well, the things Louis told him meant he trusted him. One thing kept drowning out every other thought as if they were attached to an anchor, if Louis was the one to write the notes, then he had to have been in Harry's room the night prior. Was it Louis who had been tucking him in every Friday night? No, that was crazy. Only somebody who loved you with every ounce of their heart would go through that much trouble. Louis didn't love him, not like that. There had to be another explanation.

In order to keep his sanity Harry tried to drown out his thoughts by blaring his music on his laptop and working on his project once again. Oh, course today would be the day he couldn't be around Cassie and Niall.

"Ms. Lucy! Hi, I've heard so much about you."

"Ah you must be Harry's friend; I recognize you from his photos. Cassie, right?"

"Yes, oh and this is Niall he's new I don't think Harry has photos of him yet!"

"Nice to meet you both, Niall I hope you know what you're getting yourself into!"

"Nice to meet you as well, let's hope I haven't underestimated him!"

All three began laughing as if they had known each other forever, maybe it was the fact that Ms. Lucy was nearly seventy and acted like their grandmother.

"So, what can I do for you today?"

"Well, we need to get a photo printed off of a SD card."

"Okay great, you have it on you?"

"Oh yes, uh here it is."

"Thank you dear."

Ms. Lucy took the SD card and inserted it into a little device that was connected to the computer sitting on the counter. Niall gently wrapped his arms around Cassie and placed his head on top of hers while they waited.

"Here there are a couple photos you can look at all of them and then just double click the one you would like to print."

"Okay, thanks."

Ms. Lucy turned the computer around and gave Cassie the mouse. While the couple looked through the ten photos that were displayed, they whispered about the little details they saw until they came across the photo, they both had been waiting for.

"This is the one we want to get printed."

"Alrigthy let's take a look then."

Ms. Lucy reached for her glasses that hung loosely around her neck and put them back on as she turned the computer back to face her.

"Huh!"

"Is everything okay?"

"You two better warn Harry that he has a whole lot of explaining to do on why he hasn't talked my ear off about this handsome boyfriend of his!"

Niall and Cassie both laughed and looked at each other with a knowing gaze entangled with their eyes.

"Oh, there not dating, yet."

"Were working on it, us and the twins. It's why we need this photo printed."

"Ah I knew I liked you two for a reason. Well let me tell you I've never seen so much love in a photograph before."

"So, we aren't just creating this whole elaborate thing up."

"Oh no Dear, I've printed many many wedding photos and I rarely see two people look at each other like that."

"Perfect, we'll take twenty."

"Twenty, should I even ask what you two are planning on doing?"

"Um? I'm sure you'll hear about it soon."

Ms. Lucy went into the back room to grab the newly printed photos and packaged them in a little cardboard folder and placed its sticker receipt on top before heading back to the front counter and handing it over to Cassie who had already placed twenty pounds on the counter for the purchase.

"Thank you so much, oh and keep the change. Oh, also don't tell Harry we were here if he comes by!"

"Of course, darlings, have a wonderful day."

Walking down the street Niall and Cassie soon spotted Phoebe and Daisy sitting outside Groundz at a little metal table. As soon as they saw the girls the couple quickly jogged over to meet them each giving them a hug.

While waiting outside the four began talking about Harry and Louis, Cassie even opening the photo package and showing the girls the photo, they had just got.

"What are you going to do with it?"

"I don't know yet maybe sneak it into Harry's project while he's not looking, or you can give Louis a copy and just see what happens."

"Maybe we could do both?"

"Now that's what I'm talking about. hey, you said that there is a photo of them on Harry's phone, right?"

"Yeah, it's from Christmas."

"Great I'm gonna try and get that photo too."

Jay came walking out the door holding a tray of hot tea along with a few cookies and croissants for her and the girls, Niall quickly jogged up to her and helped bring the items to the table. While the girls began eating their snacks Jay, Niall, and Cassie began talking about small things like how the twins seemed to love them already and thanking them for accepting Louis as their friend. A few minutes later the couple separated from the Tomlinson family and made their way to a nearby park to have a picnic.

The last customers had just walked out of the exhibit allowing Louis to begin cleaning and closing up. After finally conquering his fear of coming back to his families exhibit with Harry just over one-month prior Louis had determined that he definitely wanted to take over the business one day and asked his mum if he could work during the weekends to see how the place worked.

By ten pm the floors were swept, counters wiped, safes locked, the security system turned on, and Louis was turning off the lights and locking the back door as he headed towards his car. Being exhausted by the day's work Louis drove straight home, when the garage door opened a strange feeling of emptiness began to fill his chest as he realized Harry's car was no longer parked inside. Shaking his head Louis tried to shake the feeling, of course Harry wouldn't be there. He had his own home, his own family, his own life but a part of him just wanted Harry to never leave. Not again.

With everybody else in the house asleep Louis quietly went into the kitchen and made himself a sandwich for dinner and placed it on a napkin so he could take it upstairs. Just outside of his room Louis couldn't help but notice the door across from his being slightly open and found himself walking inside.

Flipping on the lights Louis was in awe at what he saw. Nearly all the photos that had been laying on the floor earlier that day now hung on the diary lights. Once noticing the plug hanging near an outlet, he decided to plug it in, instantly small shimmers of light cascaded downward from photo to photo.

Louis stood in awe as he stared at the photos. Next to every photo was a sticky note saying, move, stay, replace. A few however said, perfect, Louis couldn't help but smile when the two photos he had given Harry earlier in the day had the special note. After a few minutes he unplugged the fairy lights and went back into his room.

After changing into some sweatpants and a t-shirt Louis grabbed a blanket and sat down at his bay window looking out into the night sky. A while later when he could barely keep his eyes open Louis couldn't help it, he pulled out his phone and went straight to Harry's contact.
Your project is amazing, you should be really proud!
A few seconds later his phone dinged next to him.

Who's snooping around now?
But seriously, thank you. It means a lot.

Louis couldn't help but snicker softly, Harry did have a point. I guess they are both good at snooping around. Not knowing exactly what to say he did what he knew would put a smile on both of their faces.

GOODNIGHT HAZ, SLEEP SAFE
HOW AM I SUPPOSED TO SLEEP WHEN YOU'RE YELLING?

good night Lou, sleep tight.

Louis smiled and wrapped the blanket around him and laid down at he looked out into the stars, as he drifted off to sleep, he couldn't help but remember the way he fell asleep in Harry's arms a few months prior, even though he would never admit it out loud he had purposely slept on the bay window to feel that same safeness again.

It was then that he knew, without a doubt what he had to do next.

Chapter Thirty-eight:

Sunday morning Harry had called Cassie and told her absolutely everything from the day before, the photos, the snooping, the (potential) flirting, the text messages, and needless to say Cassie immediately knew what it meant and after they hung up, she called Niall and they decided to speed up their plan which meant they needed to find a way to see Daisy and Phoebe Friday, they also needed to get that photo off of Harry's phone.

The school week had been an absolute whirlwind, guest speakers and assemblies filled the week and caused chaos for everyone's schedules. By the time Friday rolled around all four friends only saw each other three times and even then, it was only for sparing seconds. Niall, Cassie, and Harry however still kept their daily rides to and from school allowing them to sneakily make sure they were invited over to Louis's Friday before the football game.

Thursday afternoon on their way home from school Cassie had made the perfect plan to get into Harry's phone, because they had to get Harry and Louis together this weekend. It was starting to get sickening how the two would look at each other longingly and lovingly but never acted, plus the timing couldn't possibly be better.

"Harry, could I use your phone to text my sister really quick, my phone died, and I need to ask her to stop at the store when she comes home."

"Sure, you know the password."

Cassie smiled and unlocked Harry's phone. Thankfully she was the last person he had texted so sending herself the photo wouldn't be a problem. Niall sat in the backseat with his book bag in his lap covering the fact that he had Cassie's phone in his hands. Cassie sent the photo to herself and tried to keep her eyes on the rear-view mirror waiting for Niall to give her the signal that he screenshotted the photo, when the signal finally came, she deleted the message so Harry wouldn't see then actually texted her sister, who unlike Harry thought was not coming home from college for the weekend. To keep from her ruining the plan Cassie had texted her earlier in the morning explaining her plan and she happily agreed to help out.

"Thanks Harry."

"Of course, it's nothing."

Harry dropped his friends off and went home to finish writing his paper for his photography project. Cassie however didn't stay home, thirty minutes after she walked inside her door, she called a cab and went downtown to see Ms. Lucy at the print shop.

"Cassie my dear your back!"

"I am and I have a photo I think you'll love."

"OH, I'm intrigued."

"Okay well it's on my phone so can I email it to you then print it off?"

"Sure thing, the email is the first one on this sheet."

"Thanks!"

Instantly Ms. Lucy got the photo and squealed out of excitement causing Cassie to smile.

"Did you take this?"

"No, Louis's little sisters Daisy and Phoebe did, around Christmas, I think.

"Wow I guess he's taught them well."

"He really did, and luckily for us they seemed to see the spark before the rest of us."

"No kidding, this makes my heart skip a beat and it's not even me!"

"Well get ready for more heart skipping photos because this weekend we're officially going to get them together!"

"Awe, I better be invited to their wedding!"

"If I have anything to do with it you definitely will."

"Thanks darling, I'll hold you to it. I'm going to package these up for you then you better tell me all about this plan of yours."

"Sounds lovely."

Right as Ms. Lucy went into the back print room the little bell chimed and none other than Harry Styles walked inside.

"Cassie? What are you doing here?"

"Oh um, Annie wanted some photos printed for her boyfriend's birthday present and I told him I could do it."

"Aww that's cute, how long have they been dating now, a year?"

"Yeah, something along those lines."

"Alright darling, I want to know all of the cute detail- Oh Harry! Hi"

Ms. Lucy stopped dead in her tracks and handed Cassie the small package of photos. Silently Cassie pulled out a twenty and gave it to Ms. Lucy before thanking her and saying bye to both her and Harry. After standing confused for nearly a minute Harry finally spoke.

"Uh I just need to print two copies of this on some off-white card stock."

"Easy enough, should only take a few minutes."

Ms. Lucy plugged in the flash drive Harry had into her computer and went to prepare the printer by putting in the requested card stock and changing it to the proper settings. Five minutes later she came back out with two separate envelopes each containing a copy of Harry's essay. Harry paid then left, still being confused because in the last four years he had never seen Ms. Lucy so quiet or nervous.

--

3:30 pm Friday afternoon Cassie ran up the marble staircase hand in hand with the twins as they made their way back to their secret hideout.

"Okay we are fast passing our plan, we've got to get them together tomorrow."

"Doesn't Harry have to move his project tomorrow?"

"Yes, he does which is why it's perfect, so I need you both to listen carefully because you two might have the most important job besides the boys themselves!"

"oh yay!"

"Fun!"

"Okay, so this envelope contains two photos, one is the photo you took on Christmas the other is the one I took from Louis' game a few weeks ago. One of you needs to put it in Louis' room, somewhere where he can see it when he gets home."

"Okay we can put it in now, we won't have time when we get back."

"Great, and one more thing. When Louis opens it, I want one of you to try and take a photo of his reaction with this camera, a little photo will print from the bottom. Then if you can try to talk to him about it, see how he feels. Just ask whatever feels right you know him better than I do so I trust you. And if you get the chance, I want you to put the photo from this camera either in the envelope or next to something Louis always takes with him like his keys or something."

"How does this thing work?"

"Here, it's called a Polaroid it works just like old cameras from the 1900's! You press this button to turn it on and this lens will pop out, then you just lift it to your eye and look through this little square, whatever you see is what will be in the photo. When you're ready you press the little button over here and it will take a photo, when you take it, a small flash will happen but make sure you don't move until after it happens. Then over here where this slit is a photo will begin to come out, you won't be able to see anything at first but after a minute or so the color w appears and look normal."

"Okay I think we got it."

"Great."

"Will we get to see them get together?"

"We'll ask your mom if you can come with Niall and I to the art show so you'll be there when it happens, Harry will have to drive alone so he doesn't ruin his project and I'm going to guess by his track record Louis will be a little late to the whole thing."

"it's a good thing we know how to beg!"

"Alright then let's get things moving!"

The girls all laughed and gave high-fives before opening the small door and walking back into the twin's bedroom. While Cassie found their jersey's Phoebe and Daisy ran down the hall to their brother's room and searched for the perfect place to leave the envelope of photos. After a few minutes of debating, they ultimately decided to put on one of the shelves that lined the small hallway entrance of his room.

Running back quickly the girls changed and ran over the plan one more time before rejoining the boys back downstairs. Harry was already out in the garage packing and preparing his car while Niall stayed inside and waited for the girls. Since it took so long to explain the plan to the twins, they all had to rush out to the car and sit through Harry complaining about how they were going to all be late.

Instantly after pulling into the parking lot Harry jumped out of his car and grabbed his camera bag before tossing his keys to Niall sitting beside him. All four of them still left in the car just sat and watched as Harry ran towards the field already setting up his camera.

"Wow he's got it bad."

"Let's get you out of here."

As Cassie started unbuckling Phoebe Niall got out of the car and started getting Daisy out of her car seat before grabbing the cooler from the back. With everyone out Niall was able to lock the car and they all headed up to the stands and began watching the game.

The next two hours went by as normal, watching, eating, talking, photo taking, that by the time the game had ended things felt normal, well as normal as they had been for the last month. While Harry was packing up his camera Daisy and Phoebe were begging their mum to let them go with Niall and Cassie to Harry's project showing the following morning. It took nearly five minutes but eventually Jay gave in and everything was falling into place.

Back at the Tomlinson's everyone had eaten dinner together and afterwards Harry rushed upstairs to begin dismantling and organizing his project, so it was easy to transport in the morning. Each string of photos had its own envelope, and a sticky note labeled the order of them so they could be rehung in minutes.

Once all the photos where down Harry had to get the fairy lights down from the wall and rolled them up into a circle and placed the item in a box. Next, he placed each envelope in year order along with an envelope containing his printed essay.

Being nervous about the next morning Harry grabbed his computer and began to run through the instructions his teacher had sent him earlier in the week, the address, time, date, along with a schedule for the next day. Still being restless Harry began to practice his presentation portion of his project, talking about his process of choosing the photos and how he got into photography and his favorite photos. He also began memorizing parts of his essay and thinking of answers to every single possible question he could potentially be asked.

11:35 pm Louis walked into his house tired and sweaty. It took everything in him to walk up the stairs and make it to his bedroom, his footsteps dragging loudly against the wooden floors. The steady thumps signaled to Phoebe and Daisy, who had stayed up in their room sitting near their door waiting for Louis to get home, that it was officially time to do their job. Phoebe grabbed the small Polaroid camera and the two carefully opened their door and snuck down the hall.

Quickly the twins realized Louis hadn't opened the envelope and they began to worry, that was until the sound of falling water filled the room signaling the shower was running. Instead of going back to their room and waiting Phoebe and Daisy quietly sat outside their brother's room waiting for him to walk back out into his room.

Just as their eyes began to flutter shut small vibrations emitted from the floorboards and they immediately jumped up and peaked around the doorframe into Louis' room. Louis was dressed in flannel pajamas pants and a gray t-shirt; it was as he was going to turn off his lights that he noticed the orange folder sitting next to an empty picture frame. Hesitantly he picked it up and undid the tiny metal clasp, reaching inside once he has successfully opened it.

Phoebe waited until Louis held both photos in his hand and smiled so big a dimpled appeared in his cheek until she clicked the small button on the camera and took a picture. While they waited for the photo to develop Daisy ran the camera back into their room. Once Daisy was back the girls sneakily made their way into Louis' room.

"Are you his prince?"

Still infatuated by the photos Louis didn't flinch when the soft voice broke through the air.

"Maybe. I hope so."

"I think you are"

"I think Harry wants you to be his prince too."

"Oh, you do now?"

"We do."

"Well let's hope you're right. Come on let's get you two to bed before mum notices we're all up."

Louis set down the photos on his desk and grabbed each of the girls' hands, but not before Daisy was able to place the polaroid picture in between the photos and the envelope. It didn't take long for the twins to fall asleep, only a few minutes after being tucked in. On the short walk back to his room Louis noticed the light was still on in Harry's room, interested he opened the door and just like every other Friday night Harry laid passed out on the floor next to his work.

A soft smile later Louis was back at the door with pillows and blankets and yet again made a makeshift bed for Harry. This time after he had finished Louis found himself sitting next to Harry for a few minutes just admiring everything about him, not only his stunning beauty but his golden heart and precious memories. Knowing he needed his own sleep Louis reluctantly got up but not before pressing his soft lips to Harry's forehead.

"Please be my prince."

Chapter Thirty-nine:

At 6:30 am Harry's phone blared its alarm waking him up instantly, he quickly jumped up and saw a text message from Niall.

"Hey Cass and I are on our way; we'll be their soon make sure to let us in alright!"

"Of course, I'll be waiting!"

Harry sent off the text and grabbed the box of lights and bag of photos and ran downstairs. Setting his things down on the counter Harry quickly filled the tea kettle with water and put it on the stove. As soon as that was done the security system alerted letting everyone know somebody was at the front gate, quickly Harry unlocked it allowing his friends inside and ran to open the garage door.

Niall and Cassie walked inside three minutes later each with a cup of coffee in their hands along with some banana bread.

"One of you watch the kettle for me and the other help me take these out to my car."

Harry had already picked up the bag of photos from the counter and was basically running to his car.

"Well good morning to you to Harry."

"Give him a break he's about to get the love of his life."

The couple smiled and followed their friends' directions, Niall picking up the remaining box and Cassie heading over to the stove. A to-go mug and bag of tea was already sitting out on the counter so when the kettle began to whistle no time was wasted in preparing the tea. Harry texted Jay saying Niall and Cassie where over and also sent Cassie's number in case she needed anything and the next thing everyone knew Harry picked up his mug and ran back towards the garage.

"Wait Harry! We got you banana bread!"

"Oh, my good you are life savers!"

"Go kill 'em Harry!"

Harry smiled and then the shutting of the garage door was the last thing audible.

"Wait, was he still wearing his clothes from yesterday?"

"Oh no, he was. Wait no don't text him he'll freak out we'll just have to leave early. I'm sure he has clothes here that we could bring him."

"Your right. Okay so we'll have to leave in forty-five minutes then, we better get the girls up."

"Let's go then."

The couple tried to stay quiet as the ran through the house and up the stairs. They entered the twin's room quietly and each was tasked with awakening one of the girls.

"We have to get up and ready for Harry's photo show."

"There's not much time left we need to hurry!"

"We'll grab donuts if he has time."

Sure, enough that sentence had both girls up in mere seconds and Niall and Cassie both laughed.

"Alright. Ni can I trust you with picking out some outfits?"

"Of course, you can, I am the epitome of styles."

"Just make sure they match please!"

"I got it, I got it!"

"You two come with me you need to brush your teeth and hair."

The twins followed Cassie into the gigantic bathroom and step onto their little step stools so they could reach the sink and began brushing their teeth. Cassie set the two-minute timer then began looking for a hairbrush, some elastics, and ribbon. With the brush found she began brushing Phoebe's hair while she was still brushing her teeth. Once she finished, she sent her to get her outfit from Niall while she began brushing Daisy's hair.

Once both girls where dressed, Niall had chosen blue and white striped flowy pants paired with a blush pink ribbed top, Cassie began to Dutch braid their hair intertwining silver sparkly ribbon with their hair. With their hair now done the next step was to grab the girls some shoes, arriving at the closet Cassie immediately picked two pairs of tan wicker sandals and handed them to the twins to put them on. As she was closing the doors Cassie spotted two hats that matched the shoes.

"Oh, these are perfect, you'll look so cute!"
Niall gave his girlfriend a wandering glance.
"What just because I don't put this much effort into my own look doesn't mean I can't make them look adorable!"

"Whatever you say my dear."

Cassie rolled her eyes and placed the hats on each of the girls.

"Okay we're ready."

Phoebe grabbed onto Cassie's hand while Daisy grabbed onto Niall's and they nearly ran out the door towards the staircase.

"Wait we need to go to the laundry room; can you take us there?"

"Why the laundry room?"

"Harry forgot to change into fancy clothes."

"This way!"

The girls ran back down the hall giggling until they reached a small door.

"In here."

Niall went inside and flipped on the light switch and began looking through the dozens of shirts hanging on a laundry rack while Cassie followed behind him looking at the pants folded on shelves behind him. It took seven minutes but eventually the pair was able to find clothes that were most defiantly Harry's and grabbed a linen bag to protect the items during transportation.

"Okay now we're officially ready to go."

The group of four ran downstairs still hand and hand. When they arrived in the kitchen Jay was sitting at the kitchen table with a cup of tea in hand while reading a book.

"Good morning girls, you look so pretty this morning."

"Thank you, Niall picked out the clothes and Cassie chose the shoes and hat!"

"She also did our hair!"

"They did an amazing job, I'm quite impressed!"

"And guess what!"

"Harry forgot his clothes so we have to bring them!"

"You better get going then we don't want Harry to be poorly dressed do we!"

"Mrs. Tomlinson would you mind helping us out the car seats in the car, we just want to make sure they're in properly."

"Absolutely"

Everyone went out to the garage, Niall grabbed both car seats and brought them over to his car. Well technically it was his parents' dark green minivan, but he was borrowing it for the day. Jay went step by step on how to make sure the car seat was properly installed and how to detach it for whenever they got back.

"Okay hug your mum before we go."

Both girls gave Jay a giant bear hug and thanked her for allowing them to go with Niall and Cassie. She gave them a quick rerun on her behavioral expectations before sending them off to the car where Cassie began buckling them in.

"General admission starts at 9:00 am right?"

"That's right, but if you need to see Harry before I'm pretty sure you and Louis are on his early entrance list as well."

"Perfect, thank you."

"No problem, I'll have Cass text you when we arrive."

"Sounds good."

Jay waved off the car as Niall backed out of the garage and drove down the twirling driveway. Harry was set to present his project at the art fair being held in Doncaster's small convention center in downtown which allowed the group to stop at Groundz for donuts like they had promised the twins.

When they pulled into the parking lot the coffee shop was just opening as it was barely 7:30 in the morning. Quickly Niall and Cassie got the twins out of the car and they all ran into the sweet-smelling shop. Since it was so early there was no line and the donuts and pastries where fresh, Daisy and Phoebe each picked out a donut, a vanilla frosted sprinkled and a chocolate sprinkled sprinkled, and because it just smelt so good Niall and Cassie each got donut as well there's being an old fashions and cinnamon sugar donut. Niall pulled out a ten-pound bill and paid for the food while Cassie grabbed the little box from the server working before, they all ran backout to the car.

When Niall was back on the road Cassie passed out the donuts to the girls and began eating her own. It was only ten minutes until they found themselves in the parking lot of the convention center. Everyone waited wile Niall scarfed down his donut still sitting in the driver's seat.

"Okay people what are we waiting for, its go time!" Everyone cheered and they quickly exited the car, Cassie holding hands with the twins and Niall holding the bag of clothes for Harry as they walked towards the entrance.

"Hi, we're early entrance for Harry Styles."

"Alright who is all here?"

"I'm Cassie Jennings, this is Niall Horan, then these are Daisy and Phoebe Tomlinson."

"Ok great do you and Mr. Horan have IDs on you?"

"Yes of course one second."

The two both rummaged through their wallets until they found their identifications and handed them over to the booth clerk. After the man had checked the cards, he handed them back along with four red paper bracelets required for entry.

"Mr. Styles is located in ballroom number 2 towards the stage."

"Great thank you so much."

The couple moved off to the side and put their bracelets on before putting the smaller bracelets on the twins and entering the building. It was decided that Niall would run to Harry and give him his clothes while Cassie would walk with the twins to the booth hopefully still allowing enough time to set their plan into motion.

The sun was blinding causing Louis to awaken prematurely from his deep slumber, he tried to cover his face with pillows and blankets, but it was no use he was to awake to fall back asleep. Not having his phone on his nightstand Louis got up to grab it from off of his desk. Picking up the electronic the time 7:54 am flashed upon his screen, that's when he saw the photos laying on his desk.

"Shit!"

Louis ran to his closet and grabbed the first things he saw, a pair of black jeans and a green hoodie and some white Adidas sneakers. Once dressed he rushed into his bathroom where he quickly styled his hair with some paste, brushed his teeth, and put on deodorant. In a flash Louis put the photos back into the orange envelope, grabbed his phone and jogged downstairs nearly running into his mum in the process.

"Wow their Louis."

"Sorry mum, it's late. I'm late. I'm on my way to Harry project presentation."

"Oh, okay. You have early entrance but I'm guessing you know that by your running. Go get him baby"

Louis kissed him mum's forehead and finished his run to his car. Jay stood laughing as she went to get ready herself.

Louis quickly droves to the venue trying to stay at the speed limit but definitely cursing out the slow morning drivers as he passed them. It took him fifteen minutes to get to the venue, many parking spots where already filled with cars of other family members and other town citizens who wanted to arrive early to beat the line. Because of this Louis had to park towards the end of the car park and run for what felt like an eternity until he found himself at the entrance booth.

"Early access for Harry Styles."

"Name sir?"

"Louis, Louis tomlinson."

"I need to see your ID please."

"here."

"Thank you. Here you go, Mr. Styles booth in in Ballroom number two towards the stage."

"Great thank you!"

Quicker than lightning Louis but the bright red wristband around his wrist and began running through the unexpectedly large amount of people who were, just like him, running around looking for last minuet supplies and their family members booth.

"Louis better hurry up, we should have woken him up. Harrys gonna be here any second."

"Don't worry Cass Jay texted saying he left twenty minutes ago which means he's most likely in the building."

"Wait how do you know that?"

"I stole your phone."

"Niall!"

"Hey, I had to text Jay that we got here!"

"Fine you're forgiven."

Once Niall had given Harry his change of clothes he had instantly ran to the nearest bathroom, which for some odd reason happened to be on the other side of the convention center, to change. While he was gone Niall and Cassie each took one photo off of Harry's display, one of him at a football game and one taken of Cassie at Groundz. Both of the photos where on the 18th strand of lights, the one in which Harry had labeled *Understanding Love in Different Form.*

It was a shot in the dark, so much was riding on this and it was truly up to the universe to allow this plan to work, and well everybody was about to find out because Harry was now running back them in his tan polo shirt tucked into navy blue dress pants.

The first thing Harry noticed was Daisy and Phoebe and he swept them both up in a hug.

"You look fancy today!"

"Like a real prince!"

"Why thank you, you both look like beautiful princesses."

The girls hugged Harry back before he set them down on the ground, once he stood back up his face fell flush and his heart sunk to the bottom of his chest.

"You guys why are two of my photos missing? I thought you could watch this while I was gone!"

"Harry relax i's sure they just fell here let's take a look."

"How would they fall they are clipped onto the light!"

"Breath just breath."

Niall got on the floor along with Harry and pretended to help look for any traces of the photos. The longer neither of them came up with photos the faster Harry's breathing got and the more panicked he felt. He was almost on the verge of tears when Cassie finally spoke.

"Harry come here. calm down. Go get a drink of water and breath, Niall you watch after him. I have some photos in the car that were left out on the kitchen table I'll get them and replace them for you."

"Okay, okay. thank you"

Niall ran off with Harry and only a minute later Louis came running through the booths with an envelope in hand. Cassie felt relief flood through her body whispering a simple, *thank you universe.*

"Cassie where's Harry I need to talk to him."

"Are those the photos from last night?"

"What? How do you know? Did the twins tell you?"

"Who do you think printed them?"

"Oh my god you guys are on a team aren't you!"

"Congratulations brainiac you've figured it out."

"Okay well I'm still confused but where's Harry, seriously."

"He's calming down."

"Calming down! Is he okay?"

"He's fine, we'll he'll be fine if you hang these photos up for him."

"What do you mean?"

"Oh, dear lord. The photos you brought we need to hand them in his project on the last string."

"What happened to the other photos?"

"That's not important, what's important is that you did the right thing."

"What?"

"Wow you're dumber than I thought. You and Harry. Your heart chose the right thing."

"It did?"

"It did. Now work he's almost here. Girls you come with me."

Louis began hanging the photos up, the first one of him asleep on Harry's chest was near the top of the string on lights causing him to get on his tippy toes to be able to hang it properly, the second one of him playing football while Harry and the twins watched was the last photo of the entire project.

"Louis?"

"Harry, hi"

"Wait di you find my photos?"

"I uh-"

"And this is Harry Styles, he's my best student by far. Has been taking photos since he was a child and has taken my course every year of high school. I can guarantee you his talent won't disappoint."

"Hi Mr. Styles mind if we get an early look of your work?"

Ms. Thompson was leading a group of men and women who all held clipboards and hand badges hanging around their necks stating they were from London's School of Arts. Harry swallowed the lump in his throat and answered.

"Of course, go right ahead, feel free to ask anything."

"Thank you."

Harry stepped back to view his project while the group moved to the beginning of the presentation. As they all moved the began making marks on sheets of paper with a pen and pointing out certain photos. Some of the people smiled, some held a stern face, some laughed, some turned around and gave Harry a nod.

"Hey, it's okay your project is amazing, there is no way they won't love it."

"Thanks Lou."

Harry passed a tight lip smile to Louis as he continued watching.

"Harry, how did you come up with the titles?"

"Well, I took a look at the most important lessons I learned during each year, lessons that shaped me into the person I am today. I then looked at the photos I had for each year and looked at how they all tied into each other and when I did this, they all shared a similar quality. Some had the same people, some where nearly all in the same place or depicted the same activity. I then looked at how each of those moments tied into the lessons I learned that year and I choose what my heart felt was right."

"how did you come up with this concept of changing the filters of the photos from light to dark then back to light?"

"I decided to change the filter to show the overall feeling I felt during that time. Life isn't always happy, it isn't always sad, life is always changing but you can't help when or how it changes which is why the first color change under An Angle for A Reason is so abrupt. My life changed forever in a matter of one phone call. The colors slowly get lighter over the years as I grew up. Good things slowly began to happen again, the pain was no longer at the forefront of my life, it was still there just it no longer controlled me. For me the light represents, happiness, love, warmth, the good things in life so I wanted to depict that in my life story."

"Your last strand, Understanding Love in Different Forms, why did you choose that to be your last imprint?"

Harry's heart leaped in his chest, out of every question he thought he would be asked this certainly didn't make the rehearsal list. Before speaking he couldn't help but look down at Louis, the next words were going to change things forever weather they were ready or not.

"I choose this to be last string in this presentation is because to me, love has been something I thought I knew. I thought love only came in tow forms, the type of love you have for your family and the type of love you have for your significant other. It took me eighteen years to realize love has no limits or boundaries, love has no set way of happening. During the last year I was able to understand that loving somebody isn't just being with them forever, it's putting them before yourself, it's wanting everything for them, it's willingness to hurt if it makes them happy. For me the strongest love has always been in my life, I didn't know it for a long time though. He was in and out of my life, over the years my loved turned from one kind to another, from just feeling like he was my twin to wanting to glue every piece of his broken heart back together. I lost the person I loved the most for a long time and it was only this year I got it back, but it was also only this year that I understood the love I have for him. But I also know love is ever changing just like life. As life goes on you love more people, you may stop loving people, love will create challenges, but it will also create the best moments of your life. You can't live a life without love. To me this project isn't over at just eighteen strands it will continue until my life has been lived and well, my life isn't over, it's just getting started and so is my love."

"Thank you, Mr. Styles. I look forward to seeing more of your work."

"Thank you."

As the group of people began to dissipate into the multiple booths around him one man gave him an envelope sealed shut with a gold sticker.

"I hope to see you in the fall, I haven't seen your type of talent before."

All Harry could do was smile as the man walked off.

"What's in it?"

Louis voice was shaky, he felt like crying and jumping into Harry's arms and holding onto him forever, but he also needed to know what was inside. Harry's hands were shaking as he broke the seal, slowly pulling out a large stack of papers.

"It's a scholarship, to the London School of Arts. They want me to study in their royal photography program."

"Harry! That's amazing?"

Louis couldn't help it he wrapped his arms around Harry's waist and hugged him like his life depended on it, honestly it really felt like it did.

"I'm so proud of you."

"Thank you."

Harry felt every inch of him melt into Louis' touch, when Louis then slipped away it scared him. Had he just understood what he told the art scouts? Louis went up to Harry's project and pulled off the two photos he brought. He stood still in his place and just absorbed every inch of the photos; all he saw was love. Louis wondered how he had been so blind for so long. But he was done, see could see crystal clear now.

"Haz, what's this?"

"It's just a photo."

"I would think after that speech you would have a better answer."

Harry was trying but he couldn't allow himself to look Louis in the eyes, his nerves where to strong and forbid him.

"Hey look at me Haz"

Louis walked back over to Harry, standing right in front on his he reached up to grab Harry's face and move it, so they were now face to face.

"This. This photo was taken the day my heart finally returned home. You showed me how to love someone, you were there to stitch my heart back together after it had been broken for years. I didn't know it then but you, you are the reason why I'm me again. I'm the person I want to be when I'm with you. This photo is what's been on replay in my head ever since I first saw it, it's where I feel safe. I feel safe with you. I want it be to you, I want everything in my life to be you."

"Lou, it's always been you. No matter what I did it's always been you."

Harry's hand has now made its way to Louis' neck and cradled his head, and he could feel himself and Louis both leaning in. A moment later he felt cloud like lips laying in top of his own and time stopped. All he could feel was the warmth of the lips on his and the taste of honey infiltrated his mouth. Harry couldn't help it, as their lips moved in sync he began to smile. Kissing Louis Tomlinson was like having heaven on earth.

"That was definitely worth the wait."

"I can't argue their Styles."

Just as another kiss was coming, Daisy, Phoebe, Niall, Cassie, Jay, and Anne all came running towards them. Each of the mums picked up one of the twins trying to get them before they ran into the boys.

"I think you might want this."

Cassie handed over a Polaroid of Harry and Louis kissing, their first kiss. Harry took it and he and Louis both melted into each other with embarrassment, Louis diggings his head into Harry's chest while he hid his own head behind Louis'. It was so easy to forget the rest of the world existed when you were with the person you loved, it also was a perfect recipe for PDA.

"Haz, I want that."

"It's just a photo Lou."

"No, it's our photo."

Catch the rest of the story with

"Through The Lens" on wattpad!

Printed in Great Britain
by Amazon

65064626R00231